INCENSE RISING

A novel by
N. J. Schrock

INCENSE RISING

A novel by
N. J. Schrock

*Best wishes &
Peace,

Nancy Schrock*

Incense Rising

Copyright © 2018 by N. J. Schrock

Editors: Earl Tillinghast, Regina Cornell

Cover Design: 3SIXTY Marketing
Interior Design: SGR-P Formatting Services

Indigo River Publishing
3 West Garden Street, Ste. 352
Pensacola, FL 32502
www.indigoriverpublishing.com

Ordering Information:
Quantity sales: Special discounts are available on quantity purchases by corporations, associations, and others. For details, contact the publisher at the address above.

Orders by U.S. trade bookstores and wholesalers: Please contact the publisher at the address above.

Printed in the United States of America

Library of Congress Control Number: 2018932691
ISBN: 978-1-948080-10-1

First Edition

*With Indigo River Publishing, you can always expect great books, strong voices, and meaningful messages. Most importantly, you'll always find…*words worth reading.

TABLE OF CONTENTS

Névé	1
Incense	11
Claret	15
Névé's Windfall	21
Incense Interviewed	33
Claret's New Project	41
Incense Goes Rogue	49
Névé Makes Some Changes	55
Claret Talks to Rigel	65
Névé Plans Her Trip	69
Incense on the Road	75
A Censer of Incense	81
Claret Attends a Meeting	87
Three to Chicago	97
Névé Mugged	107
Jury Selection	111
Incense Gets a Job	115
The CBI Visits Jahn's Office	121
Earthquake	127
The Censure of Incense	133
Up in Smoke	137
A Reading	141
Helicopter Visit	147
Vanity Lyons	151
Southward Bound	157
Merry-Time Marina, New Orleans	163
Bing Schwein	167
Entertaining Strangers	171
Incense and the Brewing Storm, New Orleans	183
Mensa Trial, Round One	191
Weathering the Storm	197
An Unlikely Courier	205
Will Potter	209
Trip to Austin	213
Horseback Rider	217
Mensa Trial, Round Two	221
Virtual Memorial	227

Mensa Blackmon Trial, Round Three   229
Phantom Lady   237
Rigel's Business in Seattle   247
Introductions   255
Project Java, Desiree Yen   263
Jeremi's Letter to Chicago   267
The Cleanup   269
Trip Shortened   273
A Censor of Incense   277
Vineyard Stroll   285
Mensa Trial, Round Four   289
A Person of Interest   295
Arrival in Dakota   301
Dr. Avarita Banks   307
Going It Alone   311
Jeremi's Hearing   313
The Work of Art   319
Alone   323
Ever's Guest   331
Reginald Umbrage   335
Zain Sultana   341
Into the Hills   345
Another CBI Visit   351
The Conch Truth   355

Memorial Services for Orion Rising

Memorial services for Professor Orion Rising will be held tomorrow, August 24, at 9:00 a.m. on the Greenscape University Commons. Professor Rising was killed last week in a fall from a subway platform. He served as a faculty member in the Department of Physics and was well known for proposing theories that challenge conventional wisdom. Tributes may be posted on his memorial page: @MyLog-Memorials-DrOrionRising.

Incense Rising, Journal entry
August 23, 6:00 a.m.

I'm so unsettled this morning. My fingers can't seem to find the right keys. I had a rough night. Couldn't get much sleep.

I woke up thinking about a place back home in Dakota, a place called the Valley of Dancing Cedars. Two rock faces come together to create a deep V through which runs a seasonal stream. This morning, I imagined it dry and the cedars dancing with an erratic wind. I remembered how I used to go there when I was old enough to ride my horse alone. I'd lay down a blanket and read a book in the shade of the cedars because they smelled good. But my favorite thing in that place was a maple tree. The trunk came out of a crack in the rock face and took a sharp turn upward. Gradually, over the years, it grew—but stunted like a bonsai because of the conditions. Every spring, it launched double samaras, its helicopter-like seeds, and I watched them spiral downward. I could make a whistle by placing a seed between my two thumbs. In the fall, the tree would turn bright orange and look like a flame burning in the rock.

I wonder why I woke thinking about a stunted maple tree. I think it's because it reminds me of Uncle Orion, whose life was cut short. His ideas are like seeds. And now I'm riding one downward, feeling dizzy, and desperately steering to a place where it can germinate before the strong prevailing winds hide it from the sunlight.

Crowd-Source News
Notable Quotes of the Week

Since the War for Peace, people live in unprecedented tranquility—if you don't consider, of course, the wars that rage in the human mind.
Shì Nán Xī, philosopher

We have done more to improve the human condition than any company in history.
Harmony Lei, President, YouForia! Drugs

"Grace under fire" is what we experience every day.
Jeremi Duende

Incense has a number of meanings, and I confess that when I named my daughter, I meant every one.
Cadence Rising

NÉ VÉ

On Névé's eighteenth birthday, she stood in the shade of a cottonwood tree along the edge of a beet field that had just been harvested, and she wondered how a two-story gold cow could suddenly die. She tapped the PersonALink, or PAL, on her wrist and started to read the story behind the Blazing News! headline: "Jerzeybell's Sudden Death by Lightning." But she was interrupted by its vibration with a weather advisory: "Severe Storm Warning—damaging wind... lightning...rain...seek shelter within fifteen minutes." The same line of storms that had struck down Jerzeybell in Chicago was now marauding through southern Michigan. Sweat trickled down her spine and dampened the waistband of her jeans. The Jerzeybell news would have to wait.

The first Sugar Queen farm truck of the morning rolled by, loaded high with sugar beets. Its driver waved a mud-encrusted hand and gave her his usual greeting. "Hey, hey, Nay-VAY!" The truck ejected a beet when the left-rear tire hit a rut. The white beet, which was actually more of a latte color, rolled toward her and stopped short of her feet, spraying dust on her pants and canvas shoes. She picked it up and tossed it back on the slow-moving truck, which caused two more beets to fall off and Névé to sigh. Instead of leaving them to rot in the sun, their lives wasted rather than being turned into sugar, she collected the two that had fallen, stuffed them in her tote bag, and then logged the truckload into her PAL.

She watched the pile lose another beet as the truck pulled onto the highway, heading for the processing plant. She walked over and added it to the others in her bag.

After the hum of the farm truck faded, the air became dead still and silent—a ringing silence—like after a snowfall when countless ice crystals capture and hold fast the slightest sound. Wondering if the birds had already taken shelter, Névé took off her straw hat and ran her fingers through her short white hair, lifting it from her damp scalp. No breeze cooled it, so she fanned herself with the hat and wiped her forehead on her long shirtsleeves. They protected her pale skin from the sun but made her sweat. Even though the day was hot and dry for Michigan, she lingered in the wide-open spaces until she reminded herself that she had inventory work to do in the nearby field office.

Only one employee was needed in the office per shift. Usually, she didn't mind working alone, but today she would rather not be left with her thoughts. She found the silence followed her into the office, where she grabbed a cold soda from the fridge and woke up the NetLink—her connection to WorldNet, the global communications network. The calendar showed that her workday ended at noon because today was her birthday. Headlines and alerts scrolled along the bottom of the screen. She went back to the Blazing News! story and was shocked to read how Wise Consumer's Jerzeybell had met her death. Jerzeybell's image as the company's mascot was one of the most recognized and beloved icons of the past thirty years. She read the Crowd-Source text summary, which always had the latest information because it monitored the most recent postings—such as Zings, MyLogs, and MeBooks—from people across the globe and compiled them using sophisticated software into real-time news items.

> Street people on the east side of Chicago received a windfall early this morning from the sudden demise of the Wise Consumer mascot. At 0400, a violent thunderstorm rolled through the city. Lightning strikes

caused power outages, but the most spectacular hit occurred at the Plaza de Tributo.

One witness reported a sudden burst of light surging from the cow to the sky, followed by an earsplitting bang when Jerzeybell exploded. Fragments of gold rained down over streets within two blocks of the plaza. Emergency crews arrived on the scene in minutes. They believe that street people picked up the pieces of Jerzeybell. At sunrise, the only remnants of Jerzeybell were the head and hooves within the plaza gates. Wise Consumer will make a statement about its detonated mascot later today. The plaza reopens at noon for tourists.

Nearly Dairy, a division of Wise Consumer Foods, brought you this Crowd-Source News Now!

One of Névé's earliest memories was seeing Jerzeybell every morning on the side of her milk carton. And Jerzeybell's Golden Spread butter topped her toast and pancakes. When she was six, she'd asked to visit Chicago so she could rub Jerzeybell's sides for good luck, as thousands of tourists did every year. Her mother took Névé and her older brother, Jona. The trip was one of Névé's favorite memories. They visited museums, the waterfront, and Plaza de Tributo. She realized now that they must have had more money back then to go on such a vacation. For a birthday present, Jona had bought her a stuffed Jerzeybell. She had slept with that cow for years until the fur and material had worn so thin that it could no longer be repaired. Jona always bought her a birthday present—until this year, which was the first that she would not receive a present from him. Jona. She had been trying not to think of him. She missed him badly. They would have talked today at lunchtime.

If she hadn't called him on the day of the disaster, maybe he would have survived. Even though she should have been working on the morning's inventory of sugar beets, she pulled up their last conversation.

She had always saved their Vid-chats for at least a few days, but this one she would never delete. It was all she had left of him.

The Vid-chat from last March began to play on her NetLink screen. A small inset showed her face on the lower left while the rest of the screen showed the corporate logo, Sugar Queen, in silver text, across a white crown of sugar crystals. Although painful to relive now, a conversation with him had always been better than a You-Foria! upper. He answered immediately as if he had been waiting to connect. Her screen was a large one for reading spreadsheets, so when his face appeared, it was nearly life-size, and the familiar stab came somewhere around her heart. He greeted her with a smile as always and asked her how she was doing.

Névé watched her five-month-ago self say, "Down. And bored. I'm tired of Biz Ed and don't want more in the fall. I want to do something else, something fun."

Jona ran his fingers through his auburn curls—an old habit—and rested his chin on his hand. "A lot of people would love to have your work contract with Sugar Queen. And think about how much effort you've already put into accounting classes. It seems a shame to bail so close to having a vocation."

She agreed that she was fortunate to have a job but admitted that she'd never wanted the sugar beet business as a career, like their mother, who had worked for Sugar Queen until her death in a processing accident at the plant. Then Névé said what was really on her mind. "I want out of here. Can I come to Austin?" Her eyes pleaded far more than her words could have.

Jona didn't say anything for a few seconds. She could tell he was thinking about it. "I'd be happy for you to come down. But it's a long way from Michigan to Austin. In case you've forgotten, on my way down, I was caught in a blizzard, robbed, and arrested for a crime I didn't commit." He laughed at the memory.

Her camera feed in the inset showed her twisting her spiked white hair.

Then he asked her what her guardians—their cousins Leo and Zeta— would do without her income from Sugar Queen and whether they were treating her OK.

Before she could answer, he turned in his chair to one side and leaned back, considering something off camera to his right, which she knew to be a view into the downtown plaza.

"What are the symbols on your WritingWall, Jona?"

He twisted toward the wall that had been behind him and blocked from view but was now visible. With a wave of his hand, he erased a circle with a roof over it, a number, possibly a dagger, and a couple of other symbols. "Maybe someday I'll explain if we can get you down to Austin —safely." But then he added an odd comment that she had been worrying about in the months since the conversation.

"I'm not sure if now is the best time. My friends and I are…uh…" He turned his head left and right and then faced the camera again, leaning forward. His green eyes locked on hers. "Rogues." The smile returned, and his voice dropped a little lower. "I met a woman named Luisa, and I'm having more fun than I've ever had because I realize now that we *can* change things. I feel it strongly here in Austin."

"What do you want to change?" Névé asked.

"I can't explain now." He leaned back and glanced to his right. "Wait a sec." He moved from view for a few seconds and then returned. "Sorry, Névé, but I'll have to call you back. There's shouting in the plaza. I need to see what's up. See you in a few." His last words to her were "Love you!"

"I want to talk about it some more because I'm not going to change my mind," she said. "And I love you, too." But he probably never heard her. Jona didn't connect back. He would never Vid-chat again. She had saved the texts of the *News Feeds* for times when she couldn't believe that it wasn't all a nightmare, for times when she was sure he would call—and for times when she wanted to punish herself for keeping him on the phone and delaying his escape.

The North American United States today witnessed one of the worst disasters in its history when thousands drowned in downtown Austin, Texas, after a series of dam failures.

Jona wasn't alone in his death. Thousands had died. The Colorado River and lakes around Austin had been swollen because of heavy rains from a hurricane moving inland through Texas. Dams upstream of Austin broke, and torrents of water surged downhill. Levees built to conserve water in the drought-prone area had held the water in and given it no ready outlet. Segments from the *News Feeds* replayed in her head, sometimes when she least expected them.

Uptown residents were swept away while those higher in the hills witnessed a horrific scene. The death toll is unknown at this time.

The NAUS president had responded quickly by asking citizens for donations to help handle the disaster site, and the Southwest Board of Directors had appointed a commission to investigate the cause of the dam failures. Southwest Water, the owner of the dams, was on record as having financial problems, but it said its systems were hacked in a cyber attack, but the *hattack* had not yet been verified.

She found the *News Feeds* in the following weeks hard to accept. She would read them and get physically sick. Her anxiety and feeling of being trapped in a situation she couldn't change caused her to lose ten pounds, weight that she couldn't afford to lose. So many times had she wanted to leave for Austin, but she had little money for such a long trip, and her guardians would legally have her returned so they could maintain her income. Sometimes the *News Feeds* became bizarre.

News Feed, April 1. From the makers of Virtual Vacations—Surface Body Recovery Ends. A team appointed by the Southwest Board announced that all

bodies on the surface were collected, but it did not have the funds for underwater recoveries. Extensive diving efforts are needed to comb the many underground spaces and bring bodies to the surface. Outrage from friends and relatives led the board to have Virtual Vacations help in locating missing persons by using its popular underwater drones. For a limited time, you can rent a drone and assist in locating victims. Enjoy a Virtual Vacation Today at VVToday-NAUS-1WorldNet. Visit the site of the flood disaster and help recover victims. Feel the pain of surviving. Don't miss this one-of-a-kind opportunity! **Apply now!**

Until Jona's death, she had not really thought about whether there should be limits on how money was earned. Anything could be made into a business. But every time she read about the Austin disaster, she thought that profiteering from thousands of deaths was surely a perversion, which then made her feel doubly guilty.

News Feed**, June 1. Provided to you by Senator Diamond, ensuring our businesses stay healthy. Vote for the Job Providers. Vote for a Diamond.—Austin Memorial Lake Honors Dead.** The team appointed to help Austin recover has published a statement (@Zing-AustinComesBack!) naming the new body of water Austin Memorial Lake and setting up fees for recreational use to recover costs. Friends and relatives of the missing posted concerns about swimming or fishing in water containing the remains of loved ones. The team answered the concern by noting that Fisherman's Supply had already stocked the lake with fish and plants, and it was rapidly becoming a thriving ecosystem. Rather than spending time determining whether the dam failure was from a foreign or domestic hattack, the NAUS Board recommends diverting the funds to improving WorldNet security. President Sultana praised the performance of the Austin recovery team and the Southwest Board under difficult circumstances, and he urged voters to keep politicians employed—**especially Senator Diamond**—**a man who works to provide jobs. Choose a Diamond.**

Jona's body was never found. The signal from his ID chip confirmed his location in the downtown plaza. The signal had stayed in one spot until the lake was stocked with fish, and then it disappeared. Névé didn't want to think about what that meant. Her self-inflicted punishment was interrupted by a PAL text from her closest friend, Jemma.

Jemma: happy bday Névé!!! What'll we do?

Névé didn't respond. She didn't know what she wanted to do other than to get out. Ever since Jona's drowning, being indoors made her claustrophobic. She lived in part of the downtown that was just below the surface of the city. For areas not prone to flooding, construction just below the surface or in the side of hills was cheaper and not susceptible to windstorms and other weather assaults. Opti-fiber SunLights and Infi-Scene windows gave the illusion of being above ground.

Jemma persisted.

Jemma: hey girl what's up?
Névé: nada! meet me at cafe B at 2

The Sugar Queen office was suddenly stifling. Névé couldn't concentrate on the inventory list, so she grabbed her hat and went outside. Her PAL vibrated again with another weather advisory: "Severe Weather...shelter immediately." She scanned the horizon, lowering her sunglasses to reveal white lashes and honey-colored eyes. They would have been pink without iris tints. Her albino traits were a bane and a boon. Her cousin Leo's favorite nickname for her was Freak. Yet he didn't mind taking her income from Sugar Queen.

She was paid well to have a prominent Sugarstik tattoo on her right forearm. She wished, as she always did at the end of a workday, that she could bleach her tattoo and end her connection to Sugar Queen, but she had no alternative income. Ever since her mother's death a few years ago, she lived with and helped support her guardians. They needed her income. But she was irritated by their laziness. Her view was that if they'd get off their fat butts, they could hustle more work. As soon as she could find a way, she would leave Michigan, head to Austin, and follow her brother's trail. Maybe she would meet his friends and find out what he had been doing and what he was excited about before he died.

Without the sunglasses, she could tell that the distant bank of clouds ten minutes ago was now a brown-veiled sky to the west. Dust from the harvested fields rose up under the low pressure of the storm and covered the afternoon sun. The air that was dead still moments ago began to stir. She realized that she would have to go back inside soon.

As she turned toward the north, her eye caught movement on the far edge of the field. A small brown animal bobbed up and down over clods of overturned dirt. She couldn't make out what the animal was, but she stayed to watch it slowly make its way in her direction. The legs were too long and it was too thin to be any of the usual wild animals. She figured that it was likely someone's dog or cat. She glanced back to the west and then toward the bobbing brown spot. A curtain of dust and rain now blocked the horizon line, and the towers of the processing plant were no longer visible. She guessed that she might not make it back to the office in time if she headed out over the field, but she went anyway.

Clods of overturned dirt where beets had been removed made her progress slow. The animal stopped. Névé expected it to run away, but instead it sat down and let her come to it. A few meters away, she could tell that it was a small dog, brown except for a white patch on the chest and the tip of its tail, which slowly waved like a flag as she moved closer. It wore no collar, so she approached slowly to avoid scaring it off. The wind picked up, and dust swirled around them along with scattered raindrops.

"Hi there, little one. Can I take you inside?" She carefully picked it up and noticed that *it* was a *he*. His heart pounded in her hand, but he didn't try to escape. He had a scratch on his side, and his paws were bloody. Névé tucked him under her arm and turned toward the office, but it was now no longer visible, so she headed to a lean-to shelter that the workers used on lunch breaks. With one of its sides open, she thought it wouldn't be much protection, but it would be better than nothing, and at least the open face was leeward. She crouched down in a corner and shoved the dog's face inside her shirt, hoping he didn't bite her in the breast.

Dust moved in and chased out the clean air. She, too, stuck her nose down in her shirt and closed her eyes. She smelled a definite doggy odor, but the little guy wasn't restless or shaking. His fur was warm against her hand. His heart rate slowed, and she could feel his warm breath on her chest. Wind rattled the shelter while bits of dust stung her exposed neck and ankles, as if trying to claim her skin as its own. Then the lightning and rain moved in. She stroked his head and told him everything would be OK, even though she wasn't sure herself, and thought about what she was going to do with him. He would need to see a vet, which would cost her money that she had hoped to save from her next paycheck. She would post a notice on the community Net-board. If she found the owner, maybe she could be reimbursed or even rewarded. Leo and Zeta would throw a fit if she came home with a dog, which seemed now to be exactly what she would like to do.

INCENSE

I was taken from my mother's womb in her eighth month. She had an aggressive form of cancer and refused treatments that would have ended her pregnancy sooner. My father, Cadence, named me as my mother lay dying. He is a songwriter and lyricist who plays with words. He told her that "Incense"—a substance that perfumes the air when burned—combined with our surname, Rising, would be a lovely name for a girl. She smiled and quoted a psalm. "May my prayer be counted as incense before you," and she passed away within hours. I imagine she recognized the irony of the double entendre, so common in his lyrics. *Incense. To set on fire, to make angry, to enrage.* My mother's death angered him. He admits now that he intended the double meaning in multiple ways. Incense Rising also captures a zeitgeist: our people's mounting rage with the slow killing of our planet. I'm glad he didn't name me Hostility or Insurrection. I'm willing to be Incense Rising.

I grew up on the plains of Dakota and am part Lakota Sioux on my father's side. I traded wide-open spaces for urban isolation when I moved to the East Coast to attend graduate school. After earning a PhD in physics, I planned to go back to Dakota to set up in a remote valley an array of small radio telescopes, which universities could rent for astronomy education. Funding for the project was delayed when the North American economy went into a recession, and the sponsor of the project shelved it for at least a year. The Lakota didn't know whether to mourn or celebrate. The community would have been paid well for use of the land, but no one wanted the valley littered with high-tech devices. With my first postdoctoral job on hold, an uncle—Orion Rising— offered me a one-year appointment to work with him at Greenscape University in New Jersey. He said I should consider it a type of résumé building, although he warned me of a couple of downsides.

Downside number one was that I'd have to teach freshman math and physics classes. I said that I wouldn't mind teaching because what I'd really like is an academic position back in Dakota, but those rarely come open. Then he informed me about downside number two. He explained that he needed help on his research and the math-modeling aspects. I said that would be fine and asked why that was a problem. He said that people were out to get him, as in silence him, for what he was doing. He was also an environmentalist and political activist with Marxist leanings. So I suggested maybe he should shut Karl up in a closet for a while. He laughed and said that the hegemonic powers weren't threatened by his politics. They didn't like his science—his proposed route to a theory of everything. Sometimes I had trouble following his thinking. His intelligence was quick and radical in intuitive leaps. But this time, I wondered if he had gone past the edge of sanity—until he was killed in a subway fall en route to see a colleague.

Now I think they're after me.

***

Today I have three things I must do. The first is to liberate Uncle Orion's ashes. I thrust my hand trowel into the dirt again and again, digging a hole large enough for the roots of a Seven Sisters rose. This vining flower was his favorite because it reminded him of his mother— my grandmother—Prairie Rose. She always had at least one trained along a fence. And like her other son, my father, words carried multiple meanings for her. Seven Sisters is the common name for the Pleiades, which rise ahead of Orion, the hunter, in the winter sky. Wearing leather gloves, I pull the base of the rose from its container and fit it into the hole so that the main stalks parallel a latticed archway.

As I begin filling dirt around the roots, I think about this morning's *Blazing News!* item about how the Wise Consumer cow—an iconic gold statue and the corporate mascot—met her death by lightning strike in Chicago. Uncle Orion would have had a good time commenting on Jerzeybell's demise. Then I turn over my grief and find humor in imagining his spirit had something to do with the lightning bolt. How like him that would be. Tears of laughter and pain water the base of the rose. I am finally having the good cry that I need, so I hold on to an image of Uncle Orion looking down from the clouds and sending a charge that Wise Consumer won't soon forget. I can see him exacting his revenge in one final act. I'll give him credit for it anyway. No harm in that.

I feel my legs start to cramp, so I stand and retrieve his ashes from the back porch. Earlier, I had found a favorite clay bowl. It was made by a cousin of the Risings and is adorned with pictures of plants and animals that have sacred meaning to the Sioux. I pour the ashes from the urn into the bowl, which I then nestle in a recess at the top of the latticework frame. At first nothing happens—not that I'd expected anything to happen. But then the whisper of a breeze stirs the air, followed by a gust from the sunny side of the house. From the top of the bowl rises a trail of ash, ascending into the air on a nebulous trajectory that carries it into the trees. The moving leaves screen the sunlight, making them resemble green-and-gold glass in a kaleidoscope.

I remove the leather gloves and sit down in a rocker on the back porch to watch Uncle Orion take flight. And I avoid thinking about the second thing that I have to do today.

CLARET

Morning sunlight filtered through the petals of a single orange rose in a glass. The flower appeared to be real but was made from tissue paper. The pipe-cleaner stem showed signs of having been bent many times. Ember had made it in his first-grade art class, and Claret was glad that it was paper. She would tuck it away and keep it unchanged through the years while her son grows into a man. He said that he had picked orange paper because it matched her hair. She had laughed at how honest kids could be and kissed him and thanked him. She hadn't had a real rose in ages. They were too expensive to buy for herself, and she didn't want anyone to get close enough to want to buy one for her—except for Ember or Claret's half-sister, Jade. Ember's favorite cereal box, milk, and spoon waited for him on the table. Claret read weather and news on her NetLink while she waited for Ember and Jade to show up for breakfast.

She noted that Ember would not need boots or an umbrella today. The weather forecast promised one of those glorious Seattle days when Mount Rainier surveys its relatives to the north and south and watches over the cities climbing their slopes ahead of rising sea levels. She was considering a walk to the market later when she noticed the *Blazing News!* item: "Wise Consumer's Jerzeybell Struck Down by Lightning!"

The headline was like finding the obituary of a relative both favored and flawed. She worked for Wise Consumer under a yearly contract that had just been renewed, and this salary paid the bills. She thought of it as her cash cow, and she milked the contract for all she could. Still, she barely made ends meet. As a communication specialist, she read with interest the Crowd-Source summary and then the original sources that were mined to produce the text. The original posts were usually more colorful.

Eyewitness streaming log:

0354 Chickago60: bad storm here. lightning close.

0355 Nightmaid$: power out at lakefront

0356 NurseHalley: South Hospital on generator

0359 ItinerMan20: lightning just struck Jerzeybell. No joke—saw it blow! Bolt from cow to sky, then bang! Nearly broke my ears

0400 Transi5: Holy Cow! Gold rain

0405 NoCasa&Happy: Hombre! Mi día de suerte!

0406 WhoaMan: Windfall! Cha-ching! filet tonite

Claret wished that she had been outside the gates to collect that golden rain. It would have helped pay the bills coming due next week.

0428 Chickago60: streets swept & never so clean. Shocking

0430 EMT63: when we arrived—no Jerzeybell left. only hooves and a head inside gate. Security guard on way to hospital. Where's the gold?

0431 ItinerMan20: What gold? Check the clouds. She blew up!

A visual of the Plaza de Tributo, provided by Wise Consumer, showed the raised platform where the cow had stood. All that remained on the platform were four gold hooves. Another view—taken by a bystander—showed the head lying at the base of the dais. The neck was a gaping hole, and the head was hollow. She had always thought that Jerzeybell was solid gold. Had the company ever claimed it was solid? Or was it something she had assumed? She found herself shocked and transfixed for a few seconds by the hollow neck and had to switch back to the text to shake a feeling of unease. So the cow was just a shell.

She thought about how Jerzeybell would certainly be a topic of conversation at the Vid-chat later. In the news summary, Wise Consumer stated that it would make a statement later in the day. Claret pictured the communication specialists scrambling to craft a precisely spun message—one worded to create the right kind of public pathos from the golden shell. She envied their jobs and yet preferred to stay outside the gates looking in rather than be a part of the hollow interior. From the company posts, she concluded that it was not squandering the opportunity to drum up sympathy.

> 0900 WiseConsumer: After additional cleaning, the plaza will reopen at noon for visitors who would like to climb Jerzeybell's platform and pay their respects by rubbing the hooves. Admission prices still apply. Zing postings may be found on WorldNet at Jerzeybell-demise-zing-NAUS.

There were twenty thousand comments.

Jade came into the kitchen. She and Claret looked nothing alike. Claret resembled the mother they had in common, but Jade resembled her father, a Chinese diplomat. Claret's father had sent baby Claret and her mother to live with an aunt in Quebec while he stayed in Israel to fight in the War for Peace. He had predicted an ugly conflict and didn't live to see his prophecy fulfilled. Several years after the war, her mother tried to move on with her life. She met a Chinese diplomat, whose child she decided to have without consulting him. In a quid pro quo move, he returned to China without consulting her, as relations between the NAUS government and Asia soured. Jade's eyes appeared Asian, and she tried to enhance that look with cosmetics and hair dye. She claimed that it helped her career as a professional juror.

Jade poured herself a bowl of cereal and put it on a tray along with a cup of coffee and her PAL. Claret wondered if Jade was running late. "Do you have a jury post in a few minutes?"

Jade said she did and then read her half-sister's mind or her facial expression and added, "The trial should end soon, so I'll get paid in a few days."

Claret nodded. Sometimes she wished Jade would get a more reliable job that paid weekly, but Jade liked the excitement of being a juror.

Jade tried to raise Claret's mood. "I have a big trial I want to apply for if I can get free of this one. They're recruiting for the Mensa Blackmon murder trial. I'd get a lot of hours and probably incentives, considering who's involved."

"That'd be wonderful, Jade." They chatted for a few minutes about Claret's new Wise Consumer contract and how she was hoping to book a lot of hours. The new team had its first Vid-chat later in the morning. She had worked with two of the team members before—the team leader and an artist. She didn't know the others.

Jade checked the time on her PAL and got up. "See you later. Au revoir."

On her way out, Jade gave Ember's head a pat as he came into the kitchen. He hopped onto a chair at the table. Claret had already helped him dress and comb his hair. He resembled his father, with brown hair and large brown eyes. Claret hadn't seen his father since he left, right after Ember was born, yet she saw him every time she looked at Ember's face. She poured some cereal and milk into a bowl for him. "Good morning, Ember. Would you like juice or milk to drink?"

"Milk, thanks." Ember reached down and pulled off a sneaker. He showed her where the sole had separated from the upper. "I need new shoes. Can we get some after school?"

Claret studied the shoe. "I'm sorry, honey. Not today. I'll have to glue this one. Wear your boots and pretend it's raining."

Even at seven, Ember was astute enough not to ask why.

NÉVÉ'S WINDFALL

With dust covering her hair and clothing and her clothes still damp, Névé wrapped up her morning work at lunchtime and took the dog to a downtown vet, who wrote on a temporary collar "UD," which he said meant Unknown Dog. He also said that UD was a Chihuahua and needed to stay overnight. UD had cut his paws, and the vet's assistant would have to clean them and give him antibiotics. Névé admitted to the vet that she didn't have the money to pay the bill for a couple of days. In that case, he said, she would have to pick up UD at Romano's Used Pets, where he would be held for a couple of weeks awaiting either adoption or "termination," as he called it. Névé fought back the tears at the thought of UD's pounding heart being deliberately stopped. After leaving the vet's, she immediately posted a Found Dog! notice on the Community Net-board and then went home to clean up. One of the first things she did after showering was to check the notice. No one had yet admitted to losing a Chihuahua. But then, the notice had been posted for only thirty minutes.

Névé put on white jeans and her white Sugarstik T-shirt. She turned on her Infi-Scene window and tapped the pane to select her favorite simulated scene: clouds gathering beyond an expanse of water. A French voyageur in a dugout canoe paddled into view, leaving a wake that would take half an hour to decay. Moistened air carried the scent of pine on a breeze generated by the window frame. In this Sim-view of the Straits of Mackinac, Névé could imagine taking a canoe throughout the Great Lakes at a time when the only people around were the First People. She sat on her bed watching it for a few minutes before turning her thoughts back to the present and her eighteenth birthday.

She had no plans beyond meeting Jemma at two o'clock. She checked the local weather conditions by touching the pane of the window again, and the view changed to an uptown monitor. Dust and debris blew along a street lined by low-lying buildings and no pedestrians. Although the thunderstorm was gone, wind continued to blow. Visibility was so poor that the coffee shop two blocks away was a silhouette. Along the windowsill, advertisements alternated between weather conditions and the uptown forecast: "August 23…1330 wind advisory until 1700…Late-evening thunderstorms…High 37°C, low 25°C…Feel fantastic, You-Foria! uppers."

Watching the swirling dust made Névé feel as if she couldn't breathe, and her chest tightened. She switched back to the cliff on Mackinac Island and focused on the horizon, wishing once again that she could enter the Infi-Scene window and canoe away on the blue water. Pent-up frustration made her cheeks hot, and the images in the window became watery, shrinking away as the white walls squeezed in around her, and once again she was suffocating. She closed her eyes and lay back on the bed, willing the feeling to pass.

She was eighteen and had no idea what she wanted to do with her life. She knew what she didn't want to do. But abandoning something didn't give her direction. She condemned herself every time she wanted to talk to Jona. His drowned face floated in her mind again, and she couldn't breathe. The walls closed in like the water must have closed in on Jona. She stood up to get out—go uptown and breathe real air, have some fun with Jemma.

Three sharp raps on the door preceded Leo entering the room before being invited. His scent, like his presence, crowded into every corner. He held a scarlet envelope, and his fat arm, completely covered in tattoo ads, swung toward Névé, flinging the envelope on the bed. "Hey, Freak. How's it going?"

"My name's *Névé.*"

"Well, aren't you special on your birthday, Naay-*Vaay*? Got a Real Carrier delivery. Last paper mail was a package from Jona. Oh, but I guess I'm not supposed to mention him, am I?" He waited, studying her as if she were a work of art with an aura that insisted, "Do not touch."

Névé took the envelope and sat down without making eye contact.

"You're flushed. Been waiting for me?" He tried to touch her hair, and she swatted his hand away.

"Leave me alone."

"Someday, Névé, I'll have my coffee sweetened." He winked and left.

She locked the door behind him. Mail from Real Carrier? She opened the gold seal without tearing the envelope and removed a card in purple and blue:

Madam Angeline, Oracle of the Ancients, requests a visit with Névé Sweet at 1500 hours. Please come to 107 Burro Street, uptown.

Névé knew where the shop was—down an alley off Main Street uptown—but she had not been in it. When she and Jona were kids and they were allowed to go uptown to play, they would sometimes run down the alley, pretending to hide because it was narrow and dark. Jona had said he remembered going there with their grandmother, who would say to him, "Come, let us go to the seer." And they went to see Madam Angeline, who gave him candy. Névé had no memory of their mother's mother and knew nothing about Madam Angeline, so she didn't know what to make of the invitation, but Jemma would.

***

Névé's ascent quickened with each step up the fifteen stairs from downtown. As she emerged among the buildings of uptown, she was relieved to be outdoors, even under an overcast sky and amid swirling dust and debris. The invitation from Madam Angeline had dropped out of nowhere. Névé still had a couple of hours before the appointment time and could spend it with friends, especially Jemma, at Café de Bebidas. She had known Jemma since grade one, and ever since Névé's mother's death, they always found something to do on Névé's birthday. Jemma had found her on that first birthday after her mother died and knew that she would need a friend. They had gone to a soccer game and gambled their combined pocket money—and won. They doubled their money and took their winning as a sign that together they would come out ahead.

A dust devil met Névé at the top of the stairs, but she moved through it, scattering the leaves that circled around her legs. She walked two blocks past several low brick buildings and made a left turn at a sign painted on the sidewalk with black-and-gold lettering: Café de Bebidas. A sign also hung above the door and flapped, creaking in the wind. Café de Bebidas had been through many signs. She entered a small foyer, and then the outer door closed before an inner door slid open to the café. She hesitated, allowing her eyes to adjust and take in the interior of black-and-gold decor and cushioned chairs around Amber-Glass tables.

Brightly colored drinks in glassware with stems lit from the base made them look like gems in settings. Conversations around the tables were stoked by stimulants or depressants, depending on the drink of choice. Screens with various games in progress lined the walls. Betting could be entered from each table by tapping on icons beneath the surface glass. One screen showed the news, which also could be wagered on. The current question flashed at the bottom of the screen: "Will the defendant in the shooting death of a One Bank Corporation executive be found innocent or guilty?" The jury's decision would be released in ten minutes. Betting closed in five.

Névé found the group of friends she was looking for, the one with Jemma. But Casey was the one who greeted her first.

"Sugarstik, happy birthday! You finally gonna let me give you my present?"

"No, Casey. It's not *your* birthday." Névé's face showed no expression.

His comment wasn't a surprise. She went over to the bar, so Casey turned to a plump, large-busted girl wearing a sheer orange blouse and skirt. She was draped in her chair like a colorful throw. Many of her features had been color enhanced. "Come on, Honey. How about you?"

Honey gave Casey a look as languid as her body. "Maybe I don't like being second pick."

"Well, maybe I can find someone else in here who came for more than a drink."

She rolled her eyes and told him to wait a few minutes while her drink, an Orange Climax, kicked in.

Névé returned to the group with a cup of black coffee and a Sugarstik. She lowered the end with the ball of sharp white crystals into the coffee. As it dissolved, the stick disappeared until nothing remained but sweetened coffee.

"So, Névé, what would you like to do today?" Jemma's dark dreadlocks bounced, and her white teeth lit up her face.

"I wish I could do a lot of things. I'd like to quit my job and have my tattoo removed." She rubbed her right forearm, where the tattoo had been from infancy.

Everyone commented at once. "Really? But you're Sugarstik! It's so you." Casey raised a Sugarstik, crystalline ball at the top, and held it next to Névé. The resemblance was undeniable: slender, white, and spiked at the top.

Henri pointed to his ad tattoos. "I'd have to work full time if I didn't have these. What would you do without Sugar Queen?"

Névé had only the one tattoo, and she was a Sugarstik incarnate. The company paid her more for having it exclusively.

"I'd like to leave and get a fun job, but I can't even afford a vet bill." The vet-bill comment had everyone puzzled. "I picked up a stray dog out in the field before the storm and couldn't afford to pay the vet, so the dog will be sitting at Romano's soon." Névé slouched back in her chair, absently watching news on a video screen across the room. "I don't know what I want to do. I guess I'm just down."

Henri told her that she didn't know how lucky she was, before he stood up and wandered over to the bar to chat with a young girl who looked about fifteen.

Honey tried to be helpful and placed a packet of pills on the table. "Here, take some You-Foria! Or maybe you need to see Mom's doc. He works wonders with new uppers."

"They're a fake out, another trap. I want"—she hesitated—"I want out. I want free. I want open sky. I feel like if I stay here, I'll suffocate. I want something I can't name."

"Too heavy for me. Let's go, Casey. We know what'll satisfy." Honey picked up the packet of pills, swallowed the rest of her drink, and led Casey away, leaving Névé with Jemma.

Névé sat up and pointed to the video screen showing the face of a young man. She touched their tabletop to activate sound. The headline for the news item read, "Austin, Southwest Province."

The young man spoke. "Jeremi Duende has been accused of inciting sedition. If indicted and found guilty, he could serve up to twenty years in prison. Duende's followers are outside Southwest Province Detention in Austin, where he is being held. They are demanding his release and claim they are peaceful and have no intentions of committing violence. More on *News Feed* later."

Névé stared at the picture of Duende on the *News Feed*. He was a nice-looking man, probably around Jona's age, midtwenties. He had curly brown hair, a short-cropped beard, and dark, shining eyes. "Who *is* he?"

"I don't know. Some radical stirring up trouble, I think. Saw it on the news this morning. Why does he matter?"

Névé turned toward Jemma and lowered her voice to almost a whisper. "He's in Austin, where Jona was." And this Duende reminded her of a dark man in a dream she had. She'd seen his face only vaguely. He led her through a dark crevasse toward an opening. There were strings on them from above as if they were marionettes. Yet the strings were not controlling them but kept them from falling. She and the man came to an opening and would have to cross a cavern. Some people had gone ahead, and others were following behind. Then she awoke. She'd had similar dreams before, but this one was so real. "What exactly has he done?"

"I don't know, sugar. There are a lot of people in Austin still stirring up trouble. Let's do something to cheer you up, whatever you want."

Névé pulled the scarlet envelope from a back pocket and handed it to Jemma, telling her how it had arrived from Real Carrier. "Why would Madam Angeline send me this?"

Jemma studied the envelope and its contents. "She's a fortune teller, isn't she? Might be a promotion." Jemma turned the card over a couple of times as though some other message might appear. "Maybe she can tell you what you should do. You know, read your future. Sounds like fun. Come on, let's go see her."

***

Madam Angeline felt like the relic she was today. Drugs could push back the pain only so long. She suspected that no one wanted to find a cure for old age and arthritis because there was more money to be made on decades of treating symptoms. Entering life was easy; exiting, not so easy. But she had this one more thing to do. She smoothed the pages of her book. The text was marked and annotated in many places, but phrases were underlined in red: "A Pilgrim Song 134—Come…all you servants…posted to the night watch…"

The room brightened as the WatchfulDoor showed the exterior of the shop and two young women approaching. Madam Angeline's bony fingers closed the leather cover of the book, worn shiny with use, and stowed it in her drawer. She flipped on an Infi-Scene window that covered most of the back wall. The Sim-view showed a portico with large stone columns, matching the imitation-stone walls of the shop. Robed people lounged around a large pool within the portico. A dry breeze from the frame carried suggestions of balsam and cedar.

Madam Angeline watched the women eye the front of the shop for a few seconds, reading her sign and commenting to each other. The sign predated the Peace and Prosperity Era and proclaimed her as a prophetess. Customer reviews on her Community Net-board claimed that she was wise and insightful. In truth, she mostly quoted from a text that no one read anymore. One of the two women—a petite ebony girl—pushed the door open and entered first. Madam Angeline recognized the other girl easily. The old woman's heart skipped a beat, and her pulse went up. A dull ache set into her chest. She had waited years for these few minutes, and she prayed to get through them.

Coughing and clearing her throat, she adjusted her purple head scarf and the folds of her linen robe. She spoke in a crackling voice. "Hello, young ladies. I'm Madam Angeline. Please come in and have a seat. I don't get up easily." They sat down in rattan chairs facing Madam Angeline's desk, where she had a censer of incense and three lit candles floating in a clay bowl of water. The eyes of both visitors scanned the shop. She gave them a moment to look around.

The first one to enter was also the first to speak. "Hi, I'm Jemma, and this is Névé." The candlelight flickered in Jemma's dark eyes, but it sank into the amber of Névé's. Madam Angeline remembered how striking the pink of Névé's newborn eyes had been before the iris tints.

Névé's gaze was steady. She pulled out the invitation. "We came to see why I received this."

"I have something to give you—something important, I imagine. I met your grandma, Lydia, when she was a young teacher. We taught together and became close friends over the years."

Névé's cheeks colored, and Madam Angeline considered how much the girl's complexion resembled her own grandmother's antique china doll.

"You knew my grandma?"

"Yes, very well, and she entrusted me with something to give to you when you came of legal age. So, today, I hand it over to you." Madam

Angeline produced an ivory-colored envelope from her desk. In silver ink on the front was written, "Névé, c/o Angeline Violette." "She didn't trust your mother with it. She wanted *you* to have this."

Névé stared at the envelope. Jemma was not short of words and squirmed in her chair. "Névé, that's so exciting! A birthday present! Let's see what's in it."

Madam Angeline held up her hands, palms toward them, fingers bent with arthritis. "Not here. You must take it somewhere private to open it. I suspect it contains something of value." Madam Angeline wasn't done. She then pulled from her desk the worn leather book, set it in front of Névé, and pushed it toward her. "I'm giving you this, too. Your grandmother had one just like it. We were in a class together. I don't know what happened to hers, but I would like you to have this one. I won't need it soon. I hope that you take the time to read it."

Both girls stared at the book as if it were a crystal ball or a Ouija board. Névé picked it up and held it with the envelope. "Thank you, Madam Angeline. I will. Can I come back and talk to you about Grandma?"

"Certainly, Névé. But don't wait too long. I'm not getting any younger. Take care." She smiled and nodded. The throbbing pain in her chest would force her to lie down as soon as they left. She slipped a pill into her mouth to help the pain.

***

The girls took the envelope to Jemma's apartment and the seclusion of her bedroom. Névé set the book with the envelope on top of the bed. Neither of the girls could imagine what would be so important in a simple white envelope, so they stared at it for a few seconds. Jemma sat down next to Névé on the opposite side of the bed and told her to hurry up and open it. "Do you remember your grandma?"

"No. She died when I was probably about one or two. I remember Mom saying that her mother never adjusted to the Peace and Prosperity Era. I don't think they got along, but I never understood why." Névé carefully broke open a silver wax seal, similar to the one that had been on Madam Angeline's invitation, and wished that what she was about to read would change her life. She wondered if this moment was one of those pivotal times in life that she would always look back on as a turning point or if it would simply be another letdown. She hesitated, not wanting to be disappointed, and held on to the moment of anticipation before opening a completely unknown present.

Jemma bounced with excitement. "Come on! What is it?"

Névé pulled from the envelope a page of writing. Other pages looked like certificates and were labeled "United States Treasury Bond." She read the letter while Jemma squinted at the bonds.

August 30, Year 2 of the Peace and Prosperity Era
Dear Névé,

As I write this letter, you are only a year old, and I am dying. I'll never know you, but I want to leave you something of value. I think that your physical appearance will shape your personality and make you different from my daughter—I hope. By the time you are eighteen, these US Treasury bonds should have significant value and be honored according to the NAUS treaty. I believe a woman should have financial independence. So I bequeath to you— and only to you—these bonds. I didn't trust your mother with them. She would have invented a reason why she would be justified in spending them.

Many people think I'm odd, and I'm sure I am in this so-called Peace and Prosperity Era, but I think this new society will not last. It is already digging its own grave. I hope that you can put the money to good use and that you don't have to spend it just buying food and paying rent to survive.

I wish you much love and many blessings!
—Grandma Lydia

For once, Jemma was speechless. The ventilation system made the only sound as they sat on the bed, considering the letter. Névé's eyes watered. She was so touched that her grandmother, whom she never knew, would care enough to leave her something. Lydia's love surrounded her as though her grandma were in the room. Névé wiped her eyes and said, "I wish I'd known her."

Jemma queried her PAL for the current value of US government bonds. "'US government bonds are now rare,'" she said, reading. "'Most have been redeemed since the formation of the NAUS. Under the treaty, the bonds will be honored at any money clearinghouse. To determine the value of a bond, enter the serial number here.' Névé, these could be worth a lot of money." Jemma entered the serial number of the first one, and a calculated value appeared: 10,000D. "Can that be right?" She entered the other serial numbers. "If these calculations are correct, summing the others could give a value of nearly fifty thousand dólares! No wonder she left this with Madam Angeline."

Névé smiled through more tears, and her face lit up in a way that Jemma hadn't seen for months. "Thank you, Grandma! You've given me my way out." Névé put the US bonds carefully back into the envelope and tucked the letter into the book. A title was embossed in the leather along the book's spine. It said, "*The Message*." She'd have to look at it later and see why Madam Angeline thought it was worth reading. The girls sat and stared at each other. Névé said she wanted to get the bonds into an account in her name before her cousins discovered she had them. She suggested that she and Jemma meet the following morning for a makeover. She could now afford to remove the Sugarstik tattoo and travel to Austin. And then she remembered UD and how she could rescue him from Romano's if no one claimed him.

Jemma was the quiet one for a change. "Névé, you could do more than just go to Austin. You could afford the drugs to be really smart—a Mensa. And then you'd be on your way to becoming one of the really wealthy."

The last thing Névé wanted at this point was more schooling and studying. "I don't want to be a Mensa. And what if I wasn't successful in building wealth? I couldn't sustain the drugs, and I'd go back to being dumber than I am now."

"You're not dumb now. You're the smartest person I know. But I think you should think about it."

"Jemma, thanks for everything." Névé gave her a hug.

Jemma didn't say anything for a few seconds. They both knew the money would take Névé away.

As much as Névé wanted to leave Michigan, she hated the thought of not seeing Jemma again. "Maybe you could join me when you turn eighteen in a few months."

"Maybe."

INCENSE INTERVEWED

A starling lands on the power line. Five starlings sit in a row, facing into the breeze and toward the back of the house. One flies down and lands on the bowl containing the remainder of Uncle Orion's ashes. It studies the contents for a second, picks up a fragment, and flies into the trees. I rest in a rocking chair on the back porch and shift my gaze to the upper branches of an oak tree at the center of the backyard. The leaves make white noise in the breeze and speak of how the summer has been dry and why some have yellowed early. Sunlight filters through, green and gold. Another starling lands on the wire.

"Incee! I've been calling you. There's a man here who wants to interview you." Vikki's voice sounds far off because in my mind, strains of music emerge from a void like threads of remembering. I have to listen carefully and with the right ears to be a receiver. Threads connect everything—ordering and disordering an unseen world. I imagine my cornrow braids as antennas, tuning in, tapping in. Another measure. What a wonderful strain this one is, riding on my melancholy like wind over the North Plains.

"Girl, wake up!" My roommate, Vikki, shakes my arm, interrupting the melody and forcing me to face the second thing I have to do today. Vikki is an elementary school teacher with light-brown hair and hazel eyes, and she's in my face, using her teacher's voice. "Incense! You must come in. The man is waiting."

I take my time getting up from the rocker, thinking about what to tell this man who has come to ask me questions that I don't want to answer. I notice beyond the backyard that something is different. Movement catches my eye on the second floor of the house behind the alley. The breeze moves a red curtain in a window that is never open because no one lives there. The house is scheduled to be demolished. The dreamlike state I was just in vanishes as I sense a feeling of being watched.

I go into the kitchen and close the back door to block the view inside. Vikki asks me if I need anything. In a whisper, I explain that I'd like her to have our neighbor Clarisse come over dressed for work. I put a finger to my lips so Vikki won't ask why. Then I ask her in a normal voice if she could bring in some coffee when it's done brewing, and I mime, "Sorry."

Vikki nods; mouths, "Whatever"; and heads next door. She knows I've had a bad week.

In the dining room, I find a slender fortysomething man in a white shirt and khakis. He stands when I enter the room. Only his mouth smiles. His handshake is moist.

"Hello, Ms. Rising. I'm Jerry Blanco, a writer with *All Things Science*. May I have a few minutes of your time?"

"Hello, Jerry. I'm *Dr.* Rising." I don't mind making him feel uncomfortable.

"Oh yes, of course, Dr. Rising."

"Dean Hall asked me to do this interview today. Why the urgency?"

"Your work with your uncle is quite interesting, so I convinced the dean that I needed to talk with you. You weren't answering my calls or Net-mails, and I'm offering you an opportunity to gain publicity, which as you know attracts funding."

I smirk at his clumsy introduction and his avoidance of my question, and I say that I'm not seeking publicity yet.

His mouth continues smiling. We sit down at the dining room table. I face him and the front window and feel trapped. I notice a woman sitting in a brown WorldNet van in front of the house across the street. Jerry tries to divert what is probably a hostile stare from me by complimenting me on how the gold threads in my braids nicely match— his words, not mine—my honey-colored eyes and gold flannel shirt. I wonder if he notices the dirt on my jeans. I'm sure he does and that he knows exactly what I've been doing for the past hour, for someone has almost certainly been spying on me from the building across the alley.

I don't respond, so he clears his throat and gets to the point of the interview. "In each issue of *All Things Science*, we run a short article on the latest breakthroughs. This week, we want to feature Dr. Orion Rising's work and untimely death. I appreciate your giving me an interview under these tragic circumstances."

"Why couldn't this wait until next week?" I fold my hands on the table, linking my fingers.

"Because it's this week's news, and now in the unfortunate absence of your uncle, you may be the only one able to shed light on his work. I would like to ask you a few questions about the research. You were Dr. Rising's niece and coworker, correct?"

I answer yes and ask him why he believes that we might have something to report. Vikki brings in a tray of coffee with two cups, sugar, and cream. Jerry takes his coffee black. I add milk to mine and stir it.

"He claimed to a colleague recently, before his accident, that he had made a breakthrough toward a unified theory, or theory of everything. At least, that's what we heard. Is that correct?"

"Maybe. Who told you?" I try to stall him until Clarisse arrives.

"I don't recall the name. What does it matter? Can you explain Dr. Rising's new theory to me?"

"I won't say anything more than what he presented at the last conference until I've had a chance to discuss our recent progress with a colleague."

"Then explain what you can in layman's terms. We write our articles for the educated public. Can you summarize what your uncle was going to discuss with Professor Tan?"

I open my mouth to answer and then hesitate, wondering how Jerry knew that Uncle Orion was going to see Tan. As far as I know, I was the only one who knew where he was going that morning. It was Tan's birthday, and he was going to surprise him. I work to keep my voice calm and steady. "I'll describe what I can—because Dean Hall asked me to—but nothing specific until *I've* talked with Professor Tan."

"Agreed. Then let's start with how Dr. Rising arrived at his theory. How is it that after many decades of intensive work by the leading physicists at top universities, progress toward a theory of everything should elude them only to be identified now by two Sioux Indians working at a small university, and you a woman less than thirty years old?"

I feel my stomach tighten and my face begin to flush. "Are you suggesting that the right race and gender are necessary to formulating a unified theory?"

"Uh, well…" Jerry struggles to make a reply. I'm sure my cheeks must now be glowing pink.

"Good, because they're not. In fact, a different perspective is what allowed him to think outside the Gordian knot box that the so-called experts had worked themselves into."

Jerry takes a breath, hesitates, but then presses on. "I know that Dr. Rising received his PhD from Princeton and studied with experts in the field. I'm not questioning his credentials. But I'm suggesting that his stumbling on a new route to a unified theory is rather incredible, and I'd like to know how it happened."

"Uncle Orion didn't *stumble* into anything, which makes his fall from a subway platform rather incredible." I hold eye contact, hoping to make him more uncomfortable, and I wonder if he's a reporter at all. "I'll tell you how he arrived at the theory. He told me last week that the answer circled the previous researchers like the Lakotas fighting a circle of wagons, going around in two rings moving in opposite directions, making it hard to focus on one target. Physicists were searching in the wrong places, such as splitting subatomic particles, looking at smaller and smaller fragments, and searching for one or more particles that would tie everything together. He realized that the subatomic horizon is as infinite as our universe and that there is no limit to how many particles could be found if we had the ability to detect them."

"And so he searched somewhere else?"

"Yes, and in a different way. He was not afraid to enter physics from the 'What if?' questions of metaphysics, and he included another novel approach that he used in his PhD thesis, which was in the area of classical thermodynamics. His arguments wind pathways between the classical and the relative."

"What do you mean by classical thermodynamics?"

"Newtonian physics and the laws of thermodynamics."

"Versus those of, say, Einstein and his theories of relativity?"

"Yes." I hesitate, wondering what is keeping Clarisse. I study the view across the street as if I'm thinking, and then I describe how my uncle did not begin deriving his theory by playing with the math. "At first, he put aside the mathematics and formulated a hypothesis that accounted for many of the experimental observations and then considered what was not there, much like recognizing the design that lies within a stencil. Einstein's theories of relativity, quantum mechanics, and thermodynamics were a framework around which lay the starting point, particularly as they relate to chaos and order." I have to swallow hard and blink to force down rising grief.

"Why had Dr. Rising not shared his recent work in Net-mail or Vid-chat conversations with Tan and other colleagues before his accident?"

"How do you know he didn't?"

"Dr. Tan said that he did not know new details, and he had no explicit mail."

"So you've been to see Dr. Tan?"

I begin to feel a tightness that starts at the base of my skull and works its way to my stomach. He has just confirmed what I suspected: this is no simple interview. Jerry knows what Uncle Orion had or hadn't shared in Net-mail. As he leans forward to ask the next question, I notice again the WorldNet van across the street and realize what is out of place. The elderly couple who live at that house are neo-Luddites and don't have or want a WorldNet connection.

I think that Jerry notices I'm looking out the window because he straightens and blocks my view again. "I understand from many of his colleagues that they were skeptical anything would result from his investigations. He was considered at the fringe of the scientific community with his unconventional views. And then his threat not to share results with the NAUS chief technical officer was not well received by the board. So why was Dr. Rising being secretive?"

I knew that he had been dismissing inquiries, but until now I hadn't realized from whom and how high the sources were. "He wasn't being secretive. He wanted corroboration from colleagues in the field. And he also wanted his results to be globally available and not given first to political or corporate interests."

"Why is that?"

"He didn't want the current political system to have a head start on reaping any benefits from what he believed to be a scientific breakthrough with far-reaching implications."

"And what are the implications of this new theory that would have such value?"

I lean to my left and notice that the woman in the van is checking her PAL or some device on her wrist. I continue to stall, hoping that Clarisse shows up soon.

"As he said at the last physics conference, it could lead to a new energy source, one that taps into the power of atoms but without radioactivity." Uncle Orion suspected after his presentation at the last physics conference—where he postulated new, unlimited energy without radioactivity or carbon dioxide emission—that the NAUS government, which is led by corporate CEOs, had a few scientists publish skeptical reviews as a smoke screen while their scientists began completing the unified theory from our work. He strongly believed that the NAUS government would monopolize scientific advances for commercial benefit first and not share them globally. In Uncle Orion's political language, the leaders of the country would make the whole planet their proletariat if they could.

The woman in the brown van begins talking on a cell phone.

Jerry's cheeks have flushed. I notice his fingers are leaving damp spots on the glossy table. "Why hasn't someone come up with this theory before? Why now?"

I finish my coffee. "Maybe someone did, and he or she never lived to tell about it, just as Uncle Orion didn't live to tell about it." In truth, Uncle Orion believed that the Enlightenment had created a form of blindness.

Jerry tries to act surprised by raising his eyebrows. "Are you suggesting a conspiracy theory?"

"I'm just stating the situation as I see it."

Jerry rubs his chin and leans forward on his elbows. "What are your plans from here, Ms.—Dr. Rising?"

I try to keep my eyes steady and unblinking while I lie. "Tomorrow, I'll attend the memorial service. Then I plan to complete the written explanation of his approach to a unified theory, which I will then publish after peer review."

The woman in the van gets out and stretches her legs. Jerry's forehead is sweating. The room is not warm. "Tragic, his dying just when he was on the brink of being famous—or infamous. However it turns out."

"Yes, and I lost a favorite uncle. We were close."

"On a personal side, I understand that you and your family are musicians."

I explain that my father is a composer and performer. My mother was a singer when she was living, and I compose when I have time.

Vikki comes in to let me know that Clarisse is here. I turn to Jerry. "Give me a minute, Jerry, to talk to a friend, and I'll bring you one of Uncle Orion's diagrams that you'll find interesting." I go back into the kitchen, allowing the door to swing closed behind me. Vikki and Clarisse are standing in the kitchen, with Clarisse in her clown suit. I motion for her to say nothing and take off the suit so I can accomplish the third thing that I need to do today.

CLARET'S NEW PROJECT

Claret held a green umbrella over Ember and herself. A fine mist fell. Most of the people on the sidewalk had no umbrella, but she didn't want Ember cold and damp while riding on the bus. Sometimes the bus was on time; sometimes it wasn't. Today, she thought it must be running late. She pressed his shoulder into her hip. "So maybe you'll get another Sim-holiday today, like a farm or a beach. That would be fun, wouldn't it?"

Ember nodded and looked up. Claret bent down and gave him a kiss on the forehead, wondering if a sudden rumbling noise was thunder. As she straightened, she wobbled with dizziness and took a couple of steps to keep from falling. The pavement suddenly wasn't solid. Ember fell away from her and onto the sidewalk. Claret almost toppled onto him but managed to move her feet again, quickly enough to stay upright. A woman screamed. For a few seconds, Claret teetered as if she were standing on a moving bus, and then the motion stopped. She bent to help Ember up and then noticed down the street why the woman had screamed. A car had jumped the curb, and the woman came close to being hit. In the other direction, a bicyclist sat on the sidewalk, assessing damages. Cars that had stopped cautiously began to move again.

"Wow! That was a big one, wasn't it, Mom?"

"No, I don't think so. It wasn't a very big one, just a strong tremor, stronger than we've been getting lately."

"Will it do it again? I want it to do it again."

"I don't. People can get hurt if it shakes hard enough to break buildings." As soon as her words were out, she regretted saying them. But Ember didn't miss much.

"Would our building break?"

"I don't think so. You don't need to worry about it. It's a big, strong building. Hey, look! Here comes the bus! Give me another kiss."

The bus rolled up to the stop, and the driver, whose first name Claret knew to be Opal, opened the door and nodded for Ember to get in. Opal spoke as Claret lifted Ember over the gap from the curb and onto the first step. "That was some shake we just had, wasn't it? I'm glad I was stopped when it hit. They say one of these volcanoes is waking up and in a grumpy mood."

Claret pointed to the back of Ember and shook her head with a finger to her lips. Opal added in a louder voice, "But I'm sure we'll all be fine. A lot of people don't know what they're talking about. Good morning, Ember."

Ember sat in the seat directly behind Opal and waved goodbye to Claret as the door closed.

"I didn't mean to scare you, Ember. I'm sure we won't have a volcano."

"It's OK, Ms. Opal. My mom's always telling me not to worry. That's how I know when there's something to worry about. Did you know that we *are* really going to have a volcano?"

"What? Who told you that?"

"The museum. At the museum, it said we live on a ring of fire. It said we're going to have a volcano. But nobody knows when."

***

Claret connected into the Wise Consumer WorldNet site for a Vid-chat with the new project team. She watched the scrolling of Wise Consumer product ads and the company's version of the *News Feed* item that she'd seen earlier—Jerzeybell's tragic accident—which read like a eulogy. The text said that a new consumer ad would begin running soon showing a container of Nearly Dairy, which featured a picture of Jerzeybell and a young boy holding up a glass of milk. The caption said, "Drink and Remember Me!" The company assured its workers that a reincarnated version of Jerzeybell would be built bigger and better and lightning proof. Claret was brought back to the matter at hand by beeps announcing the arrival of team members as they connected into the Vid-chat. A gap of several seconds preceded the final beep, which must have been Bull Greene connecting.

"Good morning, team! How is everyone this morning? Ready to go to work for Wise Consumer?" Bull Greene was a morning person, and Claret's experience with him had been that the earlier the hour, the more full of it he was.

Variations on "Yes," "Yep," "Yeah," and "I guess so" streamed in.

Bull expected corporate enthusiasm. "Who had the 'I guess so'? Rigel, was that you?"

Claret thought that Rigel looked like a handsome version of hell: pale complexion, hasty ponytail, and unshaven face. She suspected the camera was doing him favors by not revealing bloodshot eyes and the smell of sweat.

"Guilty. Rough night."

"Not as rough as Jerzeybell's! Must have been some party!"

"No party. Family issues."

"Well, I don't envy you. My family is the Wise Consumer team, and I have to say that we've had a rough morning. I ask that we take a moment of silence to remember Jerzeybell." No one said anything for about three seconds, and then Bull forged ahead. "I hope your java's extra black, because we have an important topic to cover today. But first, I have to ask, Rigel, where's your Wise pin? I don't see yours either, Claret. Come on, guys. You know how the Uppers want our loyalty front and center." Claret reached in her drawer and pulled out her silver-plated Wise Consumer pin, which was an owl with large eyes. She attached it to her sweater.

Rigel rubbed his eyes and had no luck finding his pin. "Isn't our work an adequate show of loyalty?"

"I don't set the policy. Wear it if you want your contract renewed for next year. There are many artists who would be happy to wear the pin and collect the pay." Bull paused for a moment of silence so that members of the team could extrapolate the threat to themselves.

Claret texted to Rigel.

> Claret: What happened?
> Rigel: Can't say now.

Bull continued. "Since you all should have introduced yourselves off-line before the meeting, let's get down to business. Today's agenda includes a briefing from Virgil on the tissue project, planning for Idea Gestation, and finally, organizational changes. Any questions before we start?"

Claret ventured a question by asking if they could start with the organizational changes because they might affect the project decisions.

Bull popped the tab of a cola and poured it over ice in a glass. The sound of thousands of bubbles bursting was transmitted clearly by his Vid-chat mic. He took a sip while he considered the question and leaned back in his chair, causing it to groan. Claret wanted to suggest he switch to diet cola. "No, Claret. I don't like people issues distracting us from our business goals. We'll get to the topic, what it means to the organization, and how you should communicate it. If there are no more questions, Virgil, will you give us an update on where you stand with the new tissue project?"

Virgil cleared his throat and leaned forward. His blond hair was close cropped, and Claret thought she could almost smell his aftershave. His Wise pin was positioned high on the collar of his white shirt. "In collaboration with the Personal Products Division, Ursala and I have succeeded in getting an exciting new product idea through stage one, Conception. It's a product that guarantees improved profit margin, which makes it ultra-attractive to the business Uppers. The revenue potential is so large that it's difficult to assess."

"Explain, Ursala." Bull took another drink of cola, causing the sound of bursting bubbles to rise and fall again.

Ursala started by clearing her throat. "I've run the numbers and can assess the immediate return. It's above our threshold return on investment and could have a sizeable potential for second- and third-generation products." She fingered her corporate pin hanging on a chain around her neck. Claret thought the gold contrasted nicely with Ursala's brown skin and dark eyes. Claret would prefer to have a gold pin, but gold plating had to be earned.

Virgil continued. "For this project, we will sell ads to be printed on rolls of bathroom tissue in a new and distinct product line. The hook to get the customer to buy the new toilet tissue will be a lower price. Even though the income from the product itself will be less, the additional income from the ads will more than make up for the lower price."

Rigel rubbed his temples and then unmuted his mic to ask a question. "Ads on toilet paper? Are you serious? What retailer wants consumers wiping their derrieres on its logos or pictures of its products?"

Virgil had his hands up with palms open in a motion for Rigel to stop. "Of course we've thought it through. The idea went through the rigorous process of Conception."

"Too bad we missed that part."

"And the term is *bath tissue* or *hygiene tissue*. The word *paper* sounds…harsh. We want to call it *hygiene tissue*."

Rigel stroked his two-day beard. Bull said he liked the idea and wished he'd thought of it himself. Ursala nodded and asked what the next steps would be in moving the project forward.

Virgil pressed on. "Rigel, we want you to design graphics to show potential advertisers. We're thinking that the images should suggest the product but not be too graphic. We have to print the image cheaply."

Rigel appeared to be chuckling with his mic muted.

"Seriously, Rigel. We need designs that will help us hook a couple of big fish. If we land them, we're golden. This project could be the biggest innovation to come along in years."

Rigel couldn't imagine what designs were needed. "So, Virgil, what product ads are you aiming to get?"

"We'd like to go to the Foods Division of Wise Consumer and run a trial. They sell meats, fruits, and vegetables, both frozen and fresh. They're a big pond to fish in."

Rigel rubbed his chin stubble again. "I don't know, Virgil. Their Sunshine Cakes would end up with brown icing. Now what would those look like? And in use, cucumbers could be juxtaposed with doughnuts. Or pickles next to ice cream."

Virgil was stoic. "Well, Rigel, you just revealed yourself to be a scruncher."

"A scruncher? What the hell?"

"This is an important point but one that you don't necessarily have to worry about as you design each image for a toilet—I mean, *hygiene tissue* ad. There are three types of tissue consumers: scrunchers, folders, and rollers. Obviously, you must be a scruncher, or a cucumber would not be in direct visual contact with a doughnut. In a folding or rolling process, it might overlay it but not be in front-side contact—if we control the sequencing of the images. *Comprende?*"

That comment set Rigel back a few seconds as he considered it. "Scrunchers, folders, and rollers? Would you like to demonstrate those?"

Virgil reached for a roll of toilet tissue that he had been using as a demo. It had crude ink markings that resembled cartoons hand drawn in each square. He demonstrated to the team what was meant by scrunching, folding, and rolling. "So you see, Rigel, if a consumer is a folder or a roller, they're not going to juxtapose two images in an unsavory way, even though one may overlay another. We'll control the repeat length so that we know what products are likely to fall within several squares of one another for the scrunchers. No problem. We just need you to do some design concepts for several squares. We'll worry about the sequencing of printing the squares."

Rigel stared into the monitor, motionless. "Uh, OK."

Claret unmuted her mic. "Virgil, are you sure there are inks that are safe to use and will give the image quality needed for advertising?"

"We're thinking food dyes will work. Since no one's doing this type of printing, there are no regulations for anal-contact imaging ink."

"Wouldn't those dyes"—she hesitated for the right wording—"uh, stain?"

"Who would know?"

Rigel didn't keep quiet. "Ass-kissers?"

Bull snorted. "OK, team, let's not degenerate the discussion. Kudos to Virgil and Ursala for getting through Conception. Now let's all work to get it through stage two, Gestation. Rigel will draft image designs. Claret, craft a solicitation for customer ads and a communication about our new product concept to other departments. Ursala will continue with iterations on the financials as Virgil gets more accurate cost forecasts. This project is so attractive that it's been fast-tracked. You'll be under a tight timeline, so these actions will be due at the next team meeting, which I will not be attending, and which brings me to the organizational announcement if there are no questions about the tissue project."

No one had a question.

"You all know how I've coveted a job within corporate planning for some time. As of Monday, I will report to the corporate planning team and will be in the thick of helping steer our corporate future—including how to replace Jerzeybell. Your new team leader will be Dr. Vanity Lyons. I envy her getting to see this project to completion because it has such promise. It'll be a feather in any team leader's hat. Any questions?"

INCENSE GOES ROGUE

After giving Jerry the excuse of needing to talk with a friend and the promise that I could show him something of interest, I make a quick change into Clarisse's clown suit. I know that today is her day off, which is what gave me the idea of borrowing it. I hope the huge orange wig and red nose will keep whoever is watching thinking that Clarisse is leaving shortly after entering. I whisper to Clarisse that she can pick it up later at Pépe's, and I give her and Vikki a hug and a kiss. They have become my social friends in the few months since I moved here. Vikki and I split the rent on this old twentieth-century retro-Victorian, and Clarisse lives with her current partner next door. Given my recent circumstances with Uncle Orion's death, they're willing to do whatever they can to help. I see the concern in their eyes, tell them to stop worrying, and then promise to be in touch. I wish I believed they could stop worrying. But now I'm thinking that by the end of the day, I'll either succeed in disappearing or be dead.

I grab my backpack that I loaded up with my PortAble computer and traveling supplies early this morning and then stashed in a cabinet. Ever since Uncle Orion's so-called accident, I've been formulating how to make myself scarce on short notice. I wish I could channel my dead ancestors who could vanish among trees or grasses within seconds. They knew how to blend in and become inconspicuous. Disappearing

49

nowadays with all the surveillance cameras will be tricky, so I've given it some thought.

I take a second to breathe in and compose myself before opening the door and stepping out in Clarisse's style—cheerful clown. I head down the street and try to act casual, as if I'm striding off to work at Bozo's Dream. In half a block, I round the corner to the right and mingle with other pedestrians, avoiding eye contact. I don't want anyone to think I'm one of the Bozos and then realize I'm not. A couple of blocks down, I enter Pépe's and ask to see Manny, Clarisse's partner. The waitress nods toward the back. I can tell that she knows I'm not Clarisse. I head into the kitchen. Manny looks up, smiles, and then sees I'm not Clarisse. His change in expression reminds me of a dog who eagerly snaps a food morsel out of the air, only to find out it's a carrot and not cheese. I pull him aside because there are two other cooks in the kitchen, and I get right to the point.

"Manny, I don't have time to explain, but I need to borrow a Pépe's shirt, a takeout box, and a delivery bicycle. Clarisse can explain later."

He raises his eyebrows. "Sure."

We head back to a storage room. He finds the items I've requested and then leaves to let me change. I shed the clown suit and put on a Pépe's shirt that is at least one size too large. I stuff my hair into a Pépe's hat and fold a delivery box. Back in the kitchen, Manny gives me a code to remove one of the locked bikes in the back alley. I thank him, tell him I owe him one, and head out the back door.

I ride the bike across town to my hairstylist, Thelma. I buzz her back door and check whether there are surveillance cameras in the back. I don't see any. I wish I were trying to disappear fifty years ago.

Thelma comes to the door with a blow-dryer in her hand. I roll in with the bicycle and a Pépe's box.

"Lordy, girl! Has that teacher's salary got you making deliveries?"

I ask to see her for a second, and she sets down the dryer. Her expression tells me that she can see something is wrong. I ask if she can squeeze me in for a haircut ASAP. Thelma has been in the beauty business for twenty years and can read body language like a novel.

"Sure, Incee. I'm about done with this customer, and the next one isn't due for a few minutes."

I stay out of the way in the back of the shop and wait for her customer to leave. Then I go over to the front windows and pull on the cord for the blinds, blocking the view to the plaza. Thelma sweeps the hair off the floor and asks me what's up. I sit in the salon chair while Thelma stands riveted in place with her arms crossed, waiting for an answer. She isn't speechless often.

"I want you to shear my hair down to about a quarter inch all around," I say.

"If you tell me why we're doing it." Thelma takes out her shears and attaches the right blade. She hesitates. "Are you sure about this?"

"Positive."

As the braids fall away, I give her a story about how Orion's death led me to realize I want a change, and I'm going to California to find myself. Thelma knows it's a lie, so she furrows her eyebrows as she cuts my hair. After the shearing, we both stare at our reflections in the mirror for a second. I resemble a teenage boy sitting in front of a woman who could be my mother. I take a deep breath. "I like it. Feels light and cool. I should have done this sooner. If anyone asks, you gave me a chin-length bob. OK?" I pay her and head to her restroom to change. A wig and a dress later, I'm a different woman. While I'm repacking my backpack, I remember one other thing and turn to Thelma and ask her to call Pépe's and tell them where the bicycle is. Then I leave out the front of her shop and stride the few blocks to the train station.

At the Unitrek station, I enter and pause at the doorway. I want to be seen. Like all train stations, it smells of metal, stale food, and sweat. A station worker wearing a name tag, Hazel, stands nearby, glaring at a woman and her kids and leaning on her broom. The woman is reading *Murder on the Orient Express* while her kids fight over a bag of Oat

Wheels. The cereal rolls around on the floor, becoming powder underfoot. A small dog belonging to another family pulls at his leash to clean up the Oat Wheels.

Hazel points to the cereal. "Ma'am, your kids are making a mess."

The woman motions toward the floor. "Well, you're the one with the broom." Then she goes back to reading her book. Hazel looks as though she'd like to commit murder in the Unitrek station.

I make eye contact with Hazel and nod my sympathies. I tell her that I'm going to California and ask her which rail the train will arrive on. She points me to the other side of the terminal. On my way, I stop in the restroom and go into a stall. I open my PortAble to pull Orion's master document from the cloud and send it to Dr. Tan while my trail is likely traceable. Orion's PortAble was destroyed in the subway accident. Another backup was at his office, which would now be searched and taken. I have a partial version—the part with my calculations and some of his diagrams, but it's not the whole explanation of the theory. When the cloud folder won't open, a feeling of pressure in the back of my head returns. Then I realize that the folder isn't locked; it's empty. The pressure extends down my spine and lodges as a knot in my stomach. Now I'm angry at myself that I was in such shock and disbelief that I didn't take action immediately after the accident. Well then, I will have to reconstruct it over the next few weeks. The steps in the argument with the logic and proofs will have to be laid out for the hypothesis to be understood. I'm going rogue, but now I wonder for how long. I may need weeks to do justice to the argument. I'll need a job, room, and board—with no ID. After I consider my options, I send a version of the music I've been working on to my father, with a note telling him I'll be OK. He won't understand at first.

I make sure Hazel sees me come out of the restroom, stop in a pose, and strut over to the ticketing kiosk. Surely other people will also notice a twentysomething tanned woman in a white sleeveless dress, dark-haired wig in a bob, red lipstick, heels, and large flowered tote bag. I purchase twenty ticketags for unlimited ground transportation within North America for one month. The tag reader at the gate will show all twenty tags getting on at this station, but I'll make sure the tags get off at many stations. I go to the gate for the train heading west. I make eye contact with Hazel again, and she wishes me a bon voyage, so I wave and smile.

I board the train with a crowd of other passengers and find opportunities to slip tags into bags or pockets, particularly where the passenger appears to be headed on a long trip. I find an aisle seat near the back and stow my bag in the rack above, finding an opportunity to tag another bag. I notice the location of the security cameras.

About five minutes before the train approaches the third stop, I rise from my seat, take my bag, and drift back two cars. Passengers nearby are asleep or busy on their PortAbles. I slip into a restroom behind a camera. A couple of minutes later, I emerge as a youth in a baseball cap, sneakers, and baggy clothes and carrying a backpack. I take the first empty seat. When the train stops, I pull the cap low over my eyes, put in some earbuds, and disembark in front of a security officer, who is eyeing the passengers getting off. The weather has turned misty, which will help obscure images from surveillance cameras—a lucky break for me. Other security officers are all along the exits of the train, so I suspect they are closing in on me. None of them look in my direction, however, because they are not searching for a young man in a baseball cap.

I wander over to the bus station and onto the next bus headed south. I slip my final tag into the bag of a passenger who gets off at the first stop. With my PAL off, no ID chip, and no remaining ticketags, I am now off the grid. I'll see how far I can get on this bus and then begin getting rides however I can. I have one more change of clothing, which I'll wait to use when I'm sure there are no cameras around, and I have about three days' worth of food. I wonder how far I can get.

NÉVÉ MAKES SOME CHANGES

Near the central downtown plaza, Névé entered the office of PPE Capital for the first time. She couldn't remember ever dealing with hard currency. The entrance consisted of a marble foyer lit by Opti-fiber SunLight and two palm trees in large jade urns on either side of a green glass door leading to a couple of personnel in glass offices. One of the employees looked up and raised her eyebrows, apparently surprised to have a young visitor. She immediately stood up, came to the foyer, and asked Névé if she needed help. Névé said that she had something to deposit, and the woman looked even more surprised but invited her into the office. Névé sat in a seat opposite a glass desk that displayed changing rows of numbers and graphs. The woman's suit nearly matched the light-green glass.

"My name is Zenith. And you are?"

"Névé Sweet."

"How may I help you, Névé?"

Névé pulled one of the US government bonds from inside her white vest. "I would like to open a new account and deposit this bond. Can you tell me what it's worth?"

Zenith's eyes held the bond for a couple of seconds before she reached out her hand to take it. She studied it, turned it over a few times, and bounced glances from Névé to the bond. "I see that it was reassigned to you. Who is Lydia March?"

"My grandmother. She left me the bond for my eighteenth birthday."

"Does your parent or guardian know you have this?"

"No. My mother is dead, and I never knew my father. I live with my mother's cousins, who've been my guardians, but I turned eighteen today. What's it worth?"

Zenith tapped the surface of the glass for a minute and glanced a couple of times at Névé, who Zenith thought had the complexion of Venus de Milo. How appropriate her Sugarstik tattoo was. "Incredibly, this bond is worth nine thousand dólares. Isn't that nice? You're a lucky young lady!"

"Really? I thought it was worth a bit more than that. I think I'll take it over to Wealth Dealer and see what they think it's worth."

Zenith cleared her throat. "Well then, just a minute. Let me check other sources." She spent another minute playing the glass on her desk like an instrument. Névé wondered what her next number would be. "Well, yes, it is worth up to ten thousand dólares. Isn't that nice? After our charge for changing it, I can give you nine thousand five hundred dólares!"

"Five hundred dólares to deposit it in a new account? I'd still like to see what Wealth Dealer has to say. Thank you for your time, Zenith." Névé got up to go.

"Well, you do drive a hard bargain. OK, for you, since you're just opening a new account of your own and depositing the money with us, I'll give you nine thousand nine hundred. No one will do better than that, I can assure you. There are always handling charges with hard currency."

Névé sat back down. "Fine. I accept those terms, and I'd like you to do the same with these other bonds."

Zenith stared for a few seconds at four more bonds. Her palms were sweating as she played the glass desk. Névé's were, too. Her life was about to change.

***

At breakfast the next morning, Leo and Zeta sat studying their HotCola drinks. Each selected a pastry from the box of rolls. In a whining voice, Zeta started nagging Leo. "You gotta get another work contract before rent's due next month."

Leo took a sip of cola. "What'd you calculate income to be in September?"

"Had Névé do it. Incomes from Zeta Rolls, Sugarstik, and HotCola come to less than the rent. Névé's salary makes up the difference. You need to find work. Anything."

Leo didn't bother to look up. "And you? You can work, too."

"I have a household to run with a teenager who ain't yours or mine."

Névé entered the kitchen and squeezed past them to the cabinet for a glass. "I'm leaving soon, so you won't have me to support anymore." She had spent a sleepless night planning how to make her break from her cousins and her job and had no reason to delay the inevitable.

Zeta took another large bite of cherry danish. "Oh really? When'd you make that decision?"

"Yesterday. I'm going south like Jona. I'm going to Austin to see if I can find any of his friends who might have survived. Then I want to live in an uptown until I decide what to do for a living."

Zeta's eyes narrowed in her round face, and she took another sip of cola. "Well, ain't that nice. And who do you think will finance this vacation? We can barely pay rent and food. I'm not giving you money for a holiday, 'specially not all the way down there. Look where it got Jona. If something happened to you, we'd lose your Sugar Queen income."

Névé smiled at the comment. Any small burden of guilt that she may have had about leaving them with less income was just lightened by Zeta and her pointing out that what she would miss most was the income and not Névé. Névé turned and faced them. "I'm not asking you for any money. I'll pay for it myself. Oh, and by the way, I'm having the Sugarstik tattoo removed today and taking back March as my last name, so plan on picking up income from somewhere else."

Leo kept his voice level and spoke as if tired. "You can't do that, Névé. We need that money."

Zeta was more animated. "You can't work a job *and* travel. How can you afford to pay for this holiday? You been holding out?" Zeta's face looked like the cherry danish.

"For my eighteenth birthday, Grandma left me a US bond that I cashed. I'll use the money to go south."

"I didn't know about no bond. How'd you get a bond from *her*? She's been dead since you was a baby." Zeta never could chew with her mouth closed.

"An old friend of Grandma's gave it to me."

"A *US* bond?" Her eyes narrowed again. "So how much is it worth, sugar?"

"Enough to get me to the Southwest and find a job."

Leo looked paler, but Zeta's face grew redder. "After caring for you since your mama died, that money should be ours. I had the job of raising a teenager."

"Since my mother died, I've brought in more than I cost, and I haven't caused problems. Now I'm leaving. You no longer have legal obligations."

"Seems to me you owe us something for the care we gave you the last five years."

Zeta had hit on an angle Leo could agree with. "That's true. We could've sent you to a charity workhouse after your ma was gone."

"And miss out on Sugarstik income? I find that unlikely." What Névé wanted the most was a clean break, and she considered how to ease her leaving. She knew that she had far more money than they would guess, so she decided to let them name a fair sum. "OK, since you'd miss my income for a while, how much is fair?"

Zeta floated an outrageous sum. "Two thousand dólares."

"If I give you two thousand, are we even?"

"You got that much?"

"I can get it. Are you happy then?"

Both Zeta and Leo were nodding and letting the sum sink in as Névé fixed her cereal.

"I'll transfer you the two thousand, and then I'm leaving before the end of the week." Névé left the kitchen with a glass of Nearly Dairy and a bowl of Oat Wheels.

Zeta and Leo sat frozen for a few seconds. Zeta had to voice what they were both thinking. "I wonder how much she actually got if she can pay us off with two grand and not blink."

"The money may be rightfully hers, Zeta. She's not been any problem and more than pulled her weight. Leave her alone until we talk to an attorney."

"You're still sweet on her dead mother."

"Maybe I am."

***

By early afternoon, Névé came out of the NewU salon looking different than when she went in. Her arm still tingled from tattoo bleaching and glowed bright pink where the Sugarstik logo had been. But in a few days, the pink would peel like a sunburn, and the logo would be gone. Blue iris tints now made her pink eyes a light shade of violet. Her short white hair was not cooperating and staying flat, but it would grow out. She had considered dyeing it brown or black but knew that any new growth would always be clearly white, so she decided on a silvery form of platinum blond. And on her left wrist was a small incision, glued closed, where her ID chip had been removed. There was yet no law that they couldn't be removed, although a tax was levied for removal. She didn't want to be located, particularly not by her cousins or, more likely, an attorney. She guessed they might hire one if they thought they could extract more money. She wasn't naive enough to think that the two grand would satisfy them if they learned she had much more.

When she reached the apartment that she shared with her cousins, she took a deep breath and went in. Before she could get to her room, Zeta's son, Harper, came out of his room and turned in her direction. A lopsided smile gave him a sneering look below hair dyed blue-black. He wore low jeans and a half shirt that revealed a You-Foria! tattoo below his navel. Névé stepped aside to let him pass, but he tried to grab a breast on his way by. She swatted his hand away before it found its target, but he grabbed her free wrist with his other hand and twisted it behind her back, bringing his face close enough to hers for a kiss. She drew her knee up hard, but he moved before it could hit its target. She freed her hand with a downward chop to his neck and ran toward her room.

"I'm catching up to your brown belt, you know, Névé," he called after her. "Someday I'll take what I want." He laughed as she slammed her door closed and locked it.

The need to plan her trip gave her purpose and made her forget about the claustrophobia of her room. She turned on her Infi-Scene window and set it to show a view of Jungfrau in the Swiss Alps, before the glaciers melted. Her mother had told her that this view had given her the idea for her name, *Névé*—"glacial snow before becoming compacted into solid ice." On the mountainside, the snow glistened a brilliant white above the aqua color of the glacier. The money Névé had inherited would free her from becoming glacial ice. It would enable her to blow with the wind. Money was the key to any problem, as far as she could tell. How fortunate she was to live in the North American United States. The downside was that it was a big country.

She thought about how to get to Austin. Even though she could now afford to fly, she couldn't imagine getting into a plane, spending hours in flight, and missing the adventure and scenery along the way. She could buy a car, but she'd never driven a real car, only a virtual one when she and Jemma got licenses just for fun. She had heard that outside of urban areas, road conditions were highly variable ever since the privatization of highways. People were unwilling to pay the tolls to drive when they could NetLink and Vid-chat. Bicycling or walking would leave her too vulnerable to the weather and marauding bands of itinerants, who were increasingly common outside gated communities. The best option, she decided, would be to take aboveground trains whenever the weather permitted them to run. Jona had warned her months ago about the dangers of traveling, and he hadn't been talking about only the weather. Jemma had warned her again today and urged her to buy a gun. Névé could now afford weapons for self-protection, but she didn't know how to use a gun and didn't want to learn. She knew what she needed—a big dog, like a German shepherd.

She checked her Community Net-board posting. No one had yet claimed to have lost a Chihuahua. UD would be worthless protection. She could see what else Romano had when she went to pay UD's bill. She could use not only protection but also a traveling companion. And she was pretty sure Romano's Used Pets would have something.

***

A rounded adobe structure with windows and metal shutters sat perched on a hill at the edge of uptown. The shutters on the front, the windward side, were closed. With the dark door between them, from the front, the structure resembled a skull in low visibility. Above the door hung a painted—but not recently—sign: Romano's Used Pets. Névé pulled the heavy wooden door open and stepped in. The smells of animals, disinfectant, and chili powder made her pause. No one occupied the front desk. A sign read, "Un momento, por favor. Back pronto." The walls were bare and had the burnt-sienna color of adobe. Everything looked like clay. The floor needed sweeping, and the windows and skylights were dingy. Névé stood near the front desk, considering whether to come back later or go through a door leading to the rear when a boy around twelve backed through the rear door with a broom and dustpan.

When he became aware of Névé's presence, he said, "*Perdón*, senorita. I not know you *está aquí. Me llamo* Pedro. *Mi papá* be back pronto. You want dog or cat?"

Névé explained that she had paid the vet bill for a Chihuahua labeled

UD and that she wanted to pay his boarding so he wouldn't be euthanized. She said that she might also be looking for a big dog for herself.

"*Qué* kind?"

"I won't know until I see it. Can you show me what you have?"

"*Sí.* You wait for Papá. Not many left now. We end many this morning. *Muchos* dogs *y no casas.* More coming *mañana* from track. You pick color you want *mañana* if you pay Papá more than racetrack does to kill."

Névé walked through the door, and the smell of animals grew stronger. The cages toward the front were empty. A hose and broom were inside the first one. Three dogs were in cages toward the back. She didn't see UD and had a sudden sinking feeling that maybe they had euthanized him by mistake. As she walked between the cages, a dog on the right surprised her with violent barking. He was a small brown fur ball baring his teeth. The cage across from it held a sickly, lethargic-looking beagle mix that growled at the barker. In the last cage on the left was a greyhound the color of ashes. The dog leaned against the side of the cage and looked at her. Then, to her relief, there was UD, tucked behind the greyhound, peering past the big dog's hip.

"When Papá come back with drugs, these three go, too. *Terminado.* More come *mañana.*"

"Why are UD and the greyhound in the same cage?"

"No empty cage when he come. Greyhound from racetrack es good dog. *Se llama* María del Verano, but summer *es terminado* for María." He chuckled as if he'd made a joke. "El Chihuahua stay by big dog for warm or protect. Grandmamá call him Jesús when she see him with María. They now María y Bebé Jesús, so Papá wait to kill María last today." He smiled, but Névé didn't understand what was funny and didn't respond. He added again that María was a good dog, but as he'd said before, there were too many dogs and not enough homes. UD—that is, Jesús— shivered. He had his left-front paw bandaged and tucked under his chest.

He shifted farther behind María, exposing a brand on her hip—an *M* in the logo of Masterkind dog food.

The kennel gave Névé the creeps, and she didn't trust them not to get overzealous with the euthanizing. "I'll take UD now—I mean, Jesús—and I'll also take María. How much?"

"Cost is for Papá. He takes *todos los* dólares."

A side door opened with a bang, and in blew a middle-aged man who looked like a bigger version of the son in a hooded canvas working jacket and jeans.

"Papá, Senorita…uh…"

"Névé."

"Névé *quiere* María y Jesús."

The man considered Névé. "*Hola, me llamo* Romano. Good dogs. A hundred dólares."

"A hundred? How much was Jesús's boarding for two days? And you'll have the cost of disposing of María if I don't buy her today."

Romano chuckled and shook his head. He motioned his son to get back to cleaning. "No, senorita. The racetrack pays for me to get rid of dogs, but free dogs are no business. Have to keep Pedro in school, so he no has to sell dogs. I save purebreds for senoritas like you."

"Unless you have a registration, she's not worth much."

"*Tengo* registration from dog track on María del Verano. You know, Jesús no have records, but I get you some for a price. Maybe you no want Jesús—bad leg y no bark."

"What do you mean 'no bark'?"

"We not know. Maybe born like so or voice cut by old owner. No bark. But maybe that good in Chihuahua."

"I found him in the sugar beet field, brought him in, and paid the vet bill or you wouldn't have him. Twenty dólares for María is fair. Surely the racetrack isn't paying more than that."

"What they pay is my business. I make you deal. I sell you greyhound for fifty and throw in el Chihuahua for nada." He smiled, showing a set of teeth in need of dental work. Névé couldn't fault him for trying to improve his income, but she hated to be taken advantage of.

"OK." She pulled out her PAL, and he pulled out his to make the transaction.

"You need *dos* leashes, y leashes are ten dólares." The smile returned.

"I'll take one for María, and I'll carry Jesús." She pictured herself two days ago throwing one beet on the truck and two falling off.

He pulled a chain from the wall and showed her how to use it as a choke chain on the greyhound, who was now standing in anticipation of something happening. The Chihuahua was limping around, uncertain what to do and where to hide. Névé entered the cage, slowly picked him up, and tucked him under her arm, avoiding his injured leg. Jesús's face was eyes and ears stuck on a nose. She could feel his ribs and hammering heart. She took off the band that said UD, now that he had a name.

"Senorita, you are like José. No—you are Josephina!" Romano bent over in laughter slapping his knee, but Névé gave him a blank look. The three headed out into the blowing wind while he was still laughing and wiping his eyes.

Névé led María and carried Jesús down a stairway to the downtown plaza. A few blocks in, she entered Pet Vet and Groomer. Four hours later, she emerged with a sleek, silvery greyhound wearing a lavender collar on a silver leash. Around Névé's left shoulder was a purple sling like the ones used to hold infants, but this one held the Chihuahua, who had a newly bandaged front leg hanging out. Other pedestrians avoided them or cast preoccupied glances, not seeking to know the story behind the three or where they were going.

CLARET TALKS TO RIGEL

The demons of doubt hovered around Claret on their silent wings. She wanted to see what was going on with Rigel, but she knew her interest was more than why he looked bad on the Vid-chat. They had worked together briefly on another project, and every time she saw his face over the NetLink, a jolt went from her heart to her limbs. Should she show more than passing interest and perhaps start…what? He lived somewhere in Dakota, and she was in Seattle. If she were to start a romantic relationship—which was a big "if"—she needed more than virtual contact. She needed a physical presence. And any man brought into her life would have to be a positive influence on Ember. Claret had no reason to think Rigel wouldn't be. He had an unusual combination of quick intellect, calm demeanor, and artistic intuition. But those ghosts from possible futures and necromancers of dead emotions appeared to her whenever she arrived at a fork in the road. They met her and stalled progress by making her lose her sense of direction and second-guess her intentions. Wasn't this attitude why she had not seen anyone since Ember's father left?

The idle image on her NetLink screen was a representation of the labyrinth at Chartres Cathedral before it was destroyed in the War for Peace. She traced with her finger the path toward the center. Her finger twisted and turned, doubling back sometimes and sometimes moving forward, working its way to the center. Damn. He was more than nice looking. She initiated the Vid-chat call. He answered nearly immediately.

"Claret. This is a pleasant surprise."

"Hi, Rigel. I know we don't know each other very well, but I wanted to see if you're OK. You didn't look well yesterday."

"I wasn't well yesterday. I'm glad you called, and I'm glad we're on a team together again."

His words emboldened Claret to press on and figure out what was behind his appearance and learn more about him. She noted that he was looking much better today.

He opened his mouth as though he were going to add something, but he didn't.

She hesitated, not wanting to come out and ask him directly what had been wrong. What if it were something personal? But then, she would like to know what it might be, so she worked the conversation in that direction. "I hope whatever was bothering you is better."

He rubbed his temples in thought and then unloaded a surprise she never would have guessed. "Not really. My uncle was killed a few days ago, and now my sister's gone missing. I don't know if you saw the *News Feed* about a scientist who allegedly fell from an NYC subway platform and was killed."

"No, I don't think I did." Claret wished she did more than a cursory look at the news, but reading the news was usually not conducive to her feeling of well-being.

"Dr. Orion Rising was his name, and he was an environmental activist and physicist. To make a long story short, my sister, Incense, worked with him at a small university in New Jersey, and now she's missing."

Claret didn't know what to say other than a lame "I'm so sorry." She asked if the authorities were looking for her.

He said that they assumed so because the New Jersey police had been the ones to notify them that she was missing. Her PAL had been off for a couple of days, and she hadn't answered Net-mails or calls, so his family had no way to contact her, and neither did the authorities.

"What about her ID chip?"

"As First People, most of us don't have one or want one."

"Oh, that's interesting. I didn't know you were First People."

"There are a lot of things you don't know about me. Maybe we should Vid-chat more often."

He smiled, and Claret tried to keep her voice casual. "I'd like that. And let me know if there's anything that I can do to help."

"Thanks, Claret. I appreciate the call. You've been a help already."

"No problem. Adieu."

"Ciao."

NÉVÉ PLANS HER TRIP

Zeta sat at the kitchen table, wondering what to microwave for supper. The Infi-Scene window near the table showed a scene from a café with a view down an avenue toward the Eiffel Tower. A subtle breeze hinted at espresso, fresh pastries, and cigar smoke. Someone not in the immediate vicinity played an acoustic guitar and sang French lyrics amid the civilized clink of metal spoons and ceramic cups on saucers. Zeta heard the door to the apartment open and then what was likely Névé's footsteps coming down the hall. She always wore rubber soles that were nearly silent. Zeta suspected Névé was trying to avoid being heard by Harper before she reached her room and locked herself in. Harper was a normal, healthy boy, and Névé was a prude. Zeta wondered how Névé turned out so introverted. Névé's mother certainly hadn't been. That woman could party 24-7 and with either sex. As Névé's footsteps came closer to the kitchen entry, another sound mingled in—a shuffling and clicking on the tiles. Zeta turned around and looked into the hallway just in time to see a gray tail.

Névé didn't make it to her room before Zeta exploded from the kitchen.

"What the *hell* do you think you're doing bringing a dog home?"

Névé turned only her head toward Zeta and opened the door to her room. "I saved her from being euthanized. She'll be here a day or two, and then I'll be gone."

Névé started to enter her room, but Zeta was on her in two strides and grabbed Névé's shoulder, pulling her out of the doorway and into the hallway to face her. The sight of a Chihuahua in a baby sling was completely unexpected, and she jumped back. "Double hell."

Névé pointed to her two unwelcome guests. "This is Jesús, and that's María. We'll be gone in a couple of days."

"You'll pay me one hundred dólares a night to kennel animals in here."

"OK, then we'll be gone in a couple of hours."

Zeta's eyes darted into Névé's room. Névé had already been removing items and preparing to leave. Zeta suddenly relaxed the muscles in her face and shoulders and took on a tired look. She had been an aspiring actress in homemade movies, called Myvies, before gaining weight and having to find more lucrative employment. "Look, Névé, you can keep the dogs if you'll pay for us to live in a better place that allows dogs. Then you can stay as long as you like."

Névé had found freedom and power in not having to acquiesce to Zeta's tactics of manipulating those around her. "I'm not staying, Zeta. But I could use another day to prepare for the trip."

"Then I need one hundred dólares for the risk we're taking."

Névé knew that the risk was small because the rule was that tenants could not *own* dogs, but occasionally dogs visited. She had seen their neighbors with dogs for a few days when visitors came or friends needed help looking after pets. What occurred to Névé in that moment was the radically different view she had as a result of her change in positional power. Now that Grandma Lydia's money had freed her from having to work to avoid becoming a penniless itinerant, she was free to become an itinerant by choice, and one with financial means—a big difference.

So now when she thought of Zeta, she pitied her, Leo, and Harper because she realized that they didn't recognize their prison; they just wanted a nicer cell. They wanted more material possessions: unlimited food and drugs, a bigger apartment, or one of the new Reality-Windows instead of the simulated views. Névé believed she was getting closer to defining what she wanted, and what she wanted had something to do with experiencing other people in other places and all the nonmaterial aspects of life, and it was not a simulated existence in a niche neighborhood. Névé then did something she didn't ever remember doing previously. She shifted Jesús and gave Zeta a one-armed hug; then she said she would come to say goodbye before she left.

Névé's show of affection left Zeta speechless and convicted of her own neglect in never having given Névé a hug. With her cheeks pink and her mouth a thin line, she turned around and went back to the Paris café.

***

The dogs napped on Névé's bed while she planned her trip. She had just about assembled the small number of items she thought they might need. At an antique store, she had found a collapsible walking stick with a handle that detached and became a knife. She bought a Super-Lite tent for two that folded to the size and weight of a loaf of bread, including its two expandable rods. She hoped she and the dogs didn't find themselves out in the elements, but she wanted to be prepared. Other items included dog food, the book Madam Angeline had given her, a lighter, snack bars, a featherlight thermal blanket, a water-repellent jacket with hood, a couple of changes of clothes, her PortAble, body wash, and a towel. All of these fit into a backpack, which could be rolled on wheels if she got tired of carrying it. With the essential items assembled, she began to think about longer-range problems.

She wanted to find the place that Jona had called home and understand why it appealed to him. For those reasons, maybe it would appeal to her also. But Austin wasn't a small place, and how would she find any of his surviving friends? She didn't know what group he had been a part of. She knew only that he considered himself a rogue. She looked up the definitions of *rogue* and didn't like any of them. He wasn't a dishonest person, a scoundrel, or a tramp. The definition that he probably intended was *a renegade*: someone who was no longer controlled or obedient. He had said that he didn't belong in Michigan, which was why he'd left at eighteen. Zeta and Leo didn't try to stop him even though they missed his income. For a couple of years, he had come back to see Névé every few months, but once he went to Texas, he never returned. That was three years ago. Névé wondered what he had found there and gotten himself into.

She ran searches for "rogues" or subversives in Austin, especially anything linking activity with those killed in the flood. One of the top results was the recent report on Jeremi Duende and his followers, the one she had seen on the news a couple of days ago while in Café Bebidas. Something about his face and her curiosity led her to research him further. He led a group whose members called themselves the Pedestrian Way. He had once been charged with sedition and violating the Freedom from Religion Law. His followers were accused of proselytizing.

In a statement in court, he admitted to leading a group known as the Pedestrian Way but said that it was a way of life and not a church like those before the Peace and Prosperity Era. The judge accused him of evasive wording. Jeremi explained that "the Way" was everywhere yet nowhere. It had no hierarchy, no physical buildings, no creeds, and no finances. In short, it didn't exist except in the minds, words, and deeds of its followers. Therefore, it was not a church by the definition of the Freedom from Religion Law, which stated that no citizen may erect a structure—physical, organizational, or financial—that promoted a religion, the definition of which was interpreted differently by different judges. Névé wondered what the attraction of such a group would be and who would become involved in such a crazy organization, one that existed yet did not exist. When she searched for Jona's name, the results stunned her. She found him in the list of flood victims and those for whom memorial services were held.

A Crowd-Source news item summarized the Zing and MyLogs postings from memorial service attendees. One of those was by Jeremi

Duende, who had lost followers in the Austin flood. In fact, he had narrowly escaped because he had left downtown Austin to attend to problems that the heavy rains had caused his business—a vineyard and winery in Bee Cave. Duende commented on the loss of several good friends and listed them. One was Jona March. For a few seconds, Névé stopped seeing the NetLink screen in disbelief, as if she hadn't known her brother at all. Who was he, really—an adherent of some subversive belief system and friend to its leader? She had found what she had been looking for, one of his surviving friends, but at what cost? She had lost Jona all over again.

Light from the Opti-fiber SunLight faded while she considered the news items again and chewed on a thumbnail. She began questioning whether going down to Texas was a good idea. On the other hand, where else was she going to go? She had to get out. That part was clear. But to where if not Texas? She had no other relatives who would even know who she was. If she did go to Texas and find Jeremi Duende, she might piece together what Jona had been doing. A search on the symbols she had seen on his WritingWall showed that some of these subversive groups used these symbols. None of the sources tied a particular one to Jeremi, but maybe she hadn't searched enough.

Névé turned away from the NetLink screen, not wanting to learn more now because the walls were starting to close in. The dogs needed a walk, and she wanted to take them uptown again before the sun set.

INCENSE ON THE ROAD

The latest bus station is nearly deserted. I lie on a bench and pull my cap low over my forehead. I'm using my backpack as a pillow, and I have the straps wound around my right arm. It is the one thing—besides my life—that I can't afford to lose. The next bus should arrive around 0700 and will take me to New Orleans, where I hope I can lie low. I'll need a job and a new identity. With my PAL left behind, I'll have to barter for an old-fashioned watch to know the time. I keep looking at my wrist out of habit. One of the items I packed is a bag of old coins. Without a PAL, I can't make the normal money transactions, so I can't buy anything. I swapped another passenger one of my rare coins for his transit pass. I'm thinking that a pawnshop will exchange the old currency for other items in the shop that I may need. I don't know how I'll get food when what I have in my bag runs out.

Before deciding to disappear, I never thought about how to become invisible in a society where electronic eyes are everywhere. The crime rate has dropped, but each of us leaves enormous footprints with communications and financial transactions. One of Uncle Orion's favorite books was *1984*. He tried to get me to read it, but I never did. It sounds dark and dated and so mid-twentieth century. One evening a few months ago, around the time that he began to think he was being watched, he explained to me the concept of Big Brother. He began laughing and couldn't talk for a minute. I wondered if we were losing him mentally. Then he said something that left me cold. Capitalism had created a more perfect Big Brother; we wore him on our wrists every day, and we would wear him to our graves. He began turning his PAL off for long periods.

At 0630, a monitor at the opposite end of the bus terminal comes on and displays a *News Feed* summary. At this early hour, most of the NAUS news is from yesterday or from time zones across the globe. I listen to kill time.

News Feed, August 24. Jerzeybell to Reincarnate. The president of Wise Consumer assured mourners at a press conference yesterday that Jerzeybell will be back—bigger and better than ever. The thousands of tourists who visit Plaza de Tributo every year to circle the dais and touch the cow will soon be able to plan their annual pilgrimages to Jerzeybell. The company's president, Julius Baha, has appointed a special committee to oversee the cow's reconstruction, and he hinted that Jerzeybell may get a makeover. The remnants of the golden hooves will be included in the corporate museum, located on the first floor of its headquarters just off Plaza de Tributo. The head, however, will be melted down and added to the undisclosed quantity of new gold required to reincarnate the beloved icon. When asked why the head would not be put on display in the museum, President Baha stated that the Board of Directors felt that Jerzeybell's head mounted on a platter would be sacrilege and that the old Jerzeybell would want to be recycled into a new cow. President Baha vowed to keep the public informed of developments during the gestation period of Jerzeybell Two.

One reporter asked about the Zing posting that went viral. In an anonymous cartoon, Jerzeybell was depicted as a victim of a hand from the sky throwing a lightning bolt. President Baha said that he had no comment on such a ridiculous suggestion and that he suspected the cartoon came from an anarchist group. He stated that he has petitioned Zing to remove the posting. He joked that if anyone had a desire to get rid of Jerzeybell, it would be the Everyday Fresh Corporation, Wise Consumer's chief rival in food. **This** News Feed **is brought to you by 24K Butter, the golden spread.**

I consider how the company execs are doing a good job of keeping her in the news because they know they're getting sympathy from consumers. In fact, they've gotten so much attention from it that I'm sure we'll continue to get updates during the whole reconstruction. They couldn't have planned a better marketing campaign for public support. The next news item is brought to me by Medicina Suprema advertising their Coffless Drops, and I learn that NAUS president, Zain Sultana, is meeting today with Eurobloc leaders in preparation for a One-World Forum in December. He wants agreement from the Eurobloc Council that it will support NAUS efforts to secure vital resources and to protect the Alaska Province from Northeast Asian aggression. In return, he promises NAUS help in securing food and energy sources for the Eurobloc. I think he's grabbing a snake by the tail. If Europe falls to Muslim leadership, as some people predict, it would be an odd bedfellow for the NAUS government. Sultana and his board are driven by financial considerations, but Europe would be operating under a different type of ideology. The next news item that comes on is one that Uncle Orion would have liked.

News Feed**, August 24. Unrest in Texas.** The Texas District Council will make an announcement sometime this morning at the Alamo in San Antonio. Sources close to council members predict that the council will move to begin secession proceedings to create a new nation state, and it points to Key West as precedence. Unrest has grown particularly around Austin and San Antonio in the aftermath of the Austin flood. Residents claim they received no support from the NAUS Board, and they would have been better off without its oversight. They further claim that the Board inappropriately funneled off funds that were collected to restore Austin and used the money to cover overhead like board member salaries.

An NAUS Board member stated that the Texas District cannot legally secede and that the Texas situation is not the same as Key West. The island nation seceded five years ago to become the Conch Republic after the NAUS Board refused to repair the bridge to the mainland when it was destroyed by Hurricane 45-7. Leave your comments on Texas secession at Texas-exit?-Zing-NAUS. **This update was brought to you by MegaPorn. Some things can become nearly the size of Texas.**

Uncle Orion would have predicted the Texas secession, if it succeeds, as the beginning of the end for the North American United States, but I think that would be wishful thinking. This government model is not going away anytime soon unless the money flow is disrupted. As *News Feed* alternates serious news with lighter items, I check the clock on the wall again and see that I have only a few minutes before the bus arrives. Other people gradually show up, so the *News Feed* is not as easily heard, but it's showing how exposure to harsh weather has caused the stone inscriptions at the Jefferson Memorial to crumble and become nearly illegible.

The Historic Charitable Foundation raised the funds to reinforce weakened parts of the structure and to update the inscriptions. The Jefferson quote in the northwest portico was completed yesterday and is again clearly legible, as the video feed shows. A commentator reads it with dramatic flair, and it has to do with religious freedom. The news item surprisingly goes on to admit that the original wording was unclear and that the renovators had to guess at the exact wording. No one present questioned whether it had been changed, as happened when the previous portico had been restored, and it was reported that a fistfight had broken out, started by a history enthusiast, about whether the renovators had the right to modify the wording. Today, the tourists who were interviewed said that they liked the current wording and suggested that if it has been updated, it was only in minor ways to fit contemporary English and civil liberty laws that Jefferson would have been the first to champion.

I recall when the southeast portico was being improved. Mensa Blackmon quoted Jefferson's words in justifying the new voting rights amendment, and they were something akin to "laws and constitutions must go hand in hand with the progress of the human mind. As minds become more developed...institutions must advance also to keep pace with the times." Mensa Blackmon held the view that one-person-one-vote was appropriate when all voters were individuals and considered equals, but that times change—as, he said, Jefferson so clearly noted. Now people are selling their votes to special interests in what Uncle Orion called the auctioning of democracy.

The next item sends a shock through me when I see myself on the monitor. It's a recent one, and my hair is long. My height and weight are shown. I sit up and keep my eyes on the floor. I pull my cap down even farther and try to act nonchalant.

News Feed, **August 24. Missing Person Bulletin: Incense Rising**. The Central Bureau of Investigation has issued a missing person bulletin for a woman named Incense Rising. She disappeared unexpectedly, and family and friends are asking anyone who knows her whereabouts to contact the CBI immediately. Locating Ms. Rising is complicated by the fact that she is First People and wears no personal ID chip. A CBI spokesperson, who chose to remain anonymous, stated that this situation is an example of why everyone should be required to have an ID chip. When foul play is suspected, as it is with Ms. Rising, the victim can be located more quickly. Again, anyone having knowledge of Incense Rising's whereabouts should contact the CBI at an office near you or through the WorldNet, CBI-NAUS–gov.

I stand up, pace away from the monitor, and only half listen to other news items until the 0700 bus finally arrives. I board it for New Orleans.

A CENSER OF INCENSE

Rigel put the finishing touches on a watercolor painting of a pair of buns surrounding a narrow hamburger patty. He decided not to get too cavalier by adding ketchup; he wanted his employment contract with Wise Consumer renewed. His PAL toned with a text from Violet Waters, the gatekeeper:

Violet: |}→ Two govs on their way to see you.

Her bow-and-arrow symbol spoke volumes.

The drive from the entry of the reserve to the Risings' land would take at least twenty minutes, so Rigel used the time to read over two letters from Incense. The paper was pale green and flecked with dried sage. She made her own writing paper by old methods and incorporated plants that carried meanings beyond the words on the page, if one knew how to interpret them. He tore the pages and envelope into small pieces and burned them in a censer near the hearth. The fireplace burned logs and kept the room warm, but as the censer fire claimed the paper, a chill took his insides—one that would not be driven away by the warmth of the room. Soon the only remains of her words were feathers of ash and rising white smoke and the smell of burning sage. He sat cross-legged on the hearth and took in the aroma, clearing his mind.

***

Able drove and Baker rode without saying anything for the first few minutes. Hills and sky met in an uneven, hazy line in the distance. To the south of the road, the wind lifted a swirl of dust high into the sky, and it dropped back to the earth on the other side of the road, making an arc the size of a ten-story building. Able offered an observation. "Doesn't seem right, the Indians having all this land."

Baker checked her appearance in the mirror. "Nope. But they bought it fair and square. It's not good for much besides wheat and cattle anyway. No civilized person would want to live out here."

Able hoped that the dust devil didn't rain any rocks onto the windshield as they passed under it. "Want to interview them at the same time or separately?" He checked the display map. His guidance system told him to take the right fork of a Y, which he did.

"Why don't we stay together but interview father and son separately to make sure their stories are the same." She didn't trust Able by himself. He liked confrontation and was irritating, even to her.

After the next rise, the road led to a house with outbuildings and fenced areas where three spotted horses watched their approach.

A man and two dogs came out of the barn as the CBI agents pulled into a winding driveway leading toward the house. The man wore brown leather clothing painted with animals and a headband with two feathers. A black horizontal line was painted on each cheek. Baker thought he would be an attractive man without the native wear, but she wasn't sure she wanted to get out of the car. The dogs looked like yellow curs and barked an alarm for the whole ranch. Able stopped the car in front of the barn with Baker's passenger side toward the man and barking dogs, all of which approached her door. Able lowered the passenger window, and Baker found herself inches from the man's face. He smelled of cedar or balsam or something fresh and woody. She cleared her throat to speak, but Able shoved his CBI badge toward the window and beat her to the introduction. "Able and Baker. CBI. We're looking for Cadence and Rigel

Rising."

"I'm Cadence. My son is up at the house. I doubt if either of us has anything you want, though."

Baker slowly opened her door and got out, as did Able, who came around the front to the passenger side, adjusting the holstered gun under his jacket in a way that made it plain for Cadence to see.

"We want the truth."

Cadence nodded and tucked his thumbs into his jean pockets. "Well then, you came to the right place. I can help you with that."

Baker waded in before Able could ask a confrontational question and shut down the Risings. "Mr. Rising, when was the last time you had contact with your daughter?"

Cadence gave the question some thought. "We talked by Vid-chat just after Orion was killed."

Baker wondered how many times they had reviewed the recording of that Vid-chat for clues on Incense's plans. "And you've had no contact since?"

"Not that I recall." He rubbed his chin, studied the dirt, and then looked up. "No, I guess that she did send me a fragment of music by Net-mail. We collaborate on writing songs, but I assume you mean something like a communication." His left eye twitched, and Baker knew they were nearing an edge on the truth.

Able leaned against the car as though he had all day. "A Real Carrier employee said she delivered two letters to this ranch recently. Produce those letters for me, Mr. Rising."

"You'll have to talk to my son about those. I didn't receive a letter recently."

Baker noted that his eye twitched again, but otherwise Cadence seemed relaxed. He was playing it smart. They weren't going to easily divide and conquer these two.

"OK, we will." Able slapped the hood of the car, startling Baker and the dogs and making her want to slap him. Cadence led the reluctant dogs to the barn while the agents got back into the car and drove up toward the house. Its form was unique, with angled rooflines that Baker assumed were designed to handle the wind and snow that they must get in these high plains. A face at the window turned away.

Baker thought she should state the obvious. "Do *not* piss this man off if you want any leads."

"They have to know something," Able said.

"Of course they do, but I want him talking. I want dialogue that will take the experts hours to analyze."

Able pulled the car into the circular drive in front of the house, and they got out. Baker scanned the vista to the south, and it made her feel small. Near the porch was a spot cultivated with a variety of plants, some of them herbs. She recognized rosemary and sage and lavender. Several metal sculptures stood among the lavender. On a post in the middle of the garden was an object made of feathers and string and designed to move in the wind. Able knocked on the door.

Baker recognized the man who opened the door to be Rigel Rising. He was in his early thirties, had shoulder-length dark hair and dark eyes, and wore a blue plaid flannel shirt and jeans. Their file pictures did not do him justice. They failed to capture a masculine grace. Able flashed his badge again in a way that reminded Baker of confronting a vampire with a mirror. "CBI. We have some questions for you, Mr. Rising."

Baker shot Able a dagger from her eyes. "I'm Agent Baker, and he's Agent Able. May we have a few minutes of your time?"

"Come in."

They entered a living space of wood and stone. Baker guessed that the fireplace was the source of a burning odor. Rigel had a table, easel, and tubes of paint in the back corner near a north-facing window.

Able decided that he wasn't going to pussyfoot around the way his partner was prone to do. "What's that smell?"

Rigel took a long, deep breath and thought about it. "Probably burning sage. It's a way of cleansing the air."

"You use those herbs in your Indian cooking?"

"No. I go to a restaurant in town called Bombay Gardens if I feel the need for curry."

"OK then. Ancient People or First People or whatever it is you want to be called."

"We First People use herbs to cook ancient foods like spaghetti and enchiladas." Rigel smiled.

Able wondered if Rigel had mocked him. "When was the last time you had contact with your sister, Mr. Rising?" Without invitation, he walked over to the studio corner and began nosing around through paints and drawings.

"Incense?"

"Incense." Able handed Rigel a sketch he'd found among the drawings: Incense half in shadow, half in strong light.

Rigel stood holding it. "My father and I had a Vid-chat with her right after Uncle Orion was killed."

"We know that you received two pieces of Real Carrier from her, Mr. Rising. I have a warrant to see them."

"I don't have them. They were burned with other kindling in the fireplace."

"What'd they say, Mr. Rising?"

"She was grieving Uncle Orion and would be in touch."

"Really? That took two letters within a couple of days? Why couldn't she say that in calls or Net-mails?"

"How do you know she didn't?" Rigel wondered if they would admit to surveillance. Silence hung in the air like the scent of the sage.

Baker had been studying two of Rigel's paintings that were above a sofa. The one on the left was painted in browns and blacks and showed a tree that had lost its leaves. Below it read, "'Under the tree that never bloomed I stood and cried.'—Black Elk." The one on the right showed a tree that was green with red fruit, birds, people, and animals all around. It read, "'He told them that there was another world coming, just like a cloud.'—Black Elk." She shot glances at Able when she wasn't studying the room. "Your sister is a missing person, and with Dr. Rising's death, she's a person of interest. We order an investigation anytime someone turns up missing. If you went missing, wouldn't you want authorities to find you?"

"That depends on why I went missing. Her letters were sent before she was missing. Look, I don't have any information of value to you. I don't know where she is. There's not much more I can say."

Able lingered a few more moments at the studio table and then turned to go. "Thank you for your time, Mr. Rising. We'll be in touch if we learn of her whereabouts."

***

After they left, Cadence came up to the house. Rigel motioned for him to say nothing. He was underneath his studio table. He came out with an electronic device the size of a pea in his palm, which he crushed, took into the bathroom, and flushed down the toilet.

Cadence rubbed the soot from his face and removed the leather shirt and headband. "They'll be back, I suspect, until she turns up."

"You don't help things with the getup, Dad. They're already suspicious."

A horse rider pulled up to the porch from the west. They went outside, and she motioned for them to come over toward the horse and away from the house. She was a local teenager in jeans, with a ponytail, a girl they'd known since she was born.

"Hey, Rigel. Cade. What's the getup for, Cade?"

"Intimidation."

She then spoke softly. "The CBI agents came to see me earlier today. Somehow they knew that I'd been out here twice to deliver a Real Carrier. I didn't volunteer any information. I wonder if my truck is bugged or tracked." They nodded. She waited a moment and continued. "What should I do if I get another letter?"

CLARET
ATTENDS A
MEETING

Claret finished loading dishes into the dishwasher. Jade's cooking made for interesting meals, but she was learning. Pasta noodles and a prepared sauce were hard to mess up.

Jade came out of her bedroom in a green dress best described as a shade of jade. Neither the dress nor the black canvas shoes were new. This evening, she wore makeup, which Claret thought might have been applied to enhance the Asian look of her dark eyes. Jade put on a black raincoat that did appear to be new and came toward the couch. "Hey. I'm going out this evening. Like my jacket? Found it sixty percent off at Second Wind Clothing. You should go there, too, and see what they have."

Claret had the impression that Jade was trying to avoid being asked where she was going. Claret wasn't her mother. She wanted to know, but she didn't want to ask. "Maybe, if I get a decent check in before the bills are due next week. Your trial end?"

"Finally. And guess what. I have an interview tomorrow for the Mensa Blackmon murder."

"That's great news. They're not wasting any time."

"He was an important man, and the show will get a lot of viewers."

Claret hesitated but then voiced what she had been mulling over. "Aren't you concerned that if you're connected in any way with this group you're involved in, you won't make juries?"

"I'm careful. I use a different name at the meetings, and they're not that bad. Aren't you worried that if *your* sideline work was known by Wise Consumer, they'd cancel your contract?"

"It's not the same kind of subversion."

"It's all the same to the govs."

Claret couldn't disagree. "You're going out tonight?"

"Oui, to a political forum. Come with me, since Ember's at Bennie's tonight."

Claret had imagined what went on at these "political forums" and what kind of people Jade associated with in the evenings, but maybe her imagination was worse than reality. On an impulse, she agreed. "OK, I think I will."

"I thought you'd come. You'd like to see for yourself what I'm up to."

"Maybe. But maybe I'm just interested."

"Well, maybe I have an ulterior motive for asking you."

"Like what?"

"Like you don't get out enough, and there's a guy or two you could meet."

Claret rolled her eyes and went to get her jacket.

They walked along the street rather than taking the underground tunnels because the evening was clear and calm. With no clouds to reflect city lights, the night sky opened to the universe. When Claret considered the blackness, she understood acrophobia, as if she could fall upward and out without a net of clouds to catch her. Confined spaces were safe, and unfathomable depths were a terror. The tiny points of light shone cold and distant, the opposite of inviting, and a couple of lines from an old poem came to her: "Though my soul may set in darkness, it will rise in perfect light; I have loved the stars too fondly to be fearful of the night." The lines had stuck with her, but not because she agreed with them. The black vacuum of space settled on the earth at night, and she wanted protection from it. She wanted walls and light, so under the stars, she focused on her immediate surroundings.

The fine weather had brought to the streets pedestrians, like ants coming from mounds and underground tunnels. A typical twenty-minute walk from the apartment to the waterfront took the women nearly thirty minutes because they had to circumvent the many hawkers along the way —gamblers at hastily set up gaming tables, fortune-tellers, food servers, trinket salesmen, and vendors of real and virtual sex.

Down at the waterfront, the well-lit boardwalk held a cacophony of voices, smells, and chaotic colors. Claret followed Jade as she went into a busy restaurant known for its Mediterranean cuisine. At the reception kiosk, instead of entering the number in her party, Jade entered a code, and the screen showed them where to go. They headed down a dimly lit hall toward the back of the building. Claret didn't see any surveillance cameras but also knew that didn't mean anything. Cameras could be as mobile and small as an insect.

Jade stopped in front of a door with a sign: "The Minoan Café." She entered another code to gain access to a small dining room, where about twenty people milled around. Jade made sure the door closed behind them. Dining tables for two to four people were scattered around the room. Large Infi-Scene windows along two walls showed a view from a balcony located on a rugged coastline. It overlooked a sea the color of turquoise along the shore and sapphire in the distance. The hillsides and offshore islands were dotted with white stone buildings. Simulated sunlight off the water and buildings had a golden glow as though the day waned. A breeze from the balcony carried the smell of salt water and ancient memories. In the white noise of voices and distant surf, Claret could finally ask a question and have it be private. "How did you know what to do?"

"Someone brings you the first few times, and when you're trusted, you get in a chain of information relays that communicates the next meeting time and code."

"You mean in person?"

"Naturally. Or Real Carrier. The group avoids Net-mails or Vid-chats because they're all monitored."

"Why should anyone care?"

"You'll see."

Claret wondered if she wanted to see. Getting labeled as subversive or even anticapital would make getting an employment contract more difficult, but her curiosity made her stay; plus, she didn't want to face walking the street alone at night. She motioned to Jade that she wanted to sit along an edge, away from where she was guessing someone might speak to the group.

They took a seat at a table for two just as a fortysomething man in a navy fisherman's sweater and denim jeans walked to a table with a box labeled "NW Seafood." He appeared to be the leader of the group because he waved his hands downward and asked everyone to find a seat. Claret scanned the room and realized the dominant colors were black, gray, and brown. She had on jeans and a pink T-shirt under a denim jacket. She buttoned the jacket. Some groups still argued assorted points, and the apparent leader had to raise his voice to alert everyone that they needed to start the meeting. Reluctantly, the groups broke up and took seats. Claret guessed the age of participants ranged from twenty to seventy.

Navy Sweater waited for everyone to find a seat. "Good evening. Just as a reminder, you all know me as Dan. I see only one new face. Jasmine, would you like to introduce your friend?"

To Claret's surprise, Jade responded. "Good evening, everybody. This is my sister, Garnet. I hope that you'll trust her as you do me." Everyone turned toward Jasmine and Garnet with acknowledging nods.

When all eyes were back on "Dan," Claret gave Jade a wide-eyed look. "Jasmine? Really? And Garnet?"

"We don't use our *real* names."

Claret's concern could be read in her eyes. Her abundant red curls that had been carefree in the apartment now contributed to an appearance of panic when combined with her facial expression. "But it's so…clandestine."

Jade gave her a tight-lipped smile and directed her attention back at the speaker.

Dan cleared his throat and pulled out a stack of papers. "First, I would like to share with you some copies of mid-twentieth-century paper documents recovered by one of our members present. He found a small library of books in a rural storm cellar near his grandmother's house. What I brought is reading material for our next meeting and not the topic of discussion tonight."

A voice from the middle of the room asked how he knew they were authentic.

A middle-aged man stood and looked over the room as he spoke. His voice was so low, Claret could just make out what he said. "They're authentic. The cellar appears to have been put together in the late 1950s or early 1960s, possibly in response to the nuclear-arms hysteria that was prevalent then. Other artifacts in the cellar, like magazines and small battery-operated appliances such as an AM/FM radio, date from the fifties. Unfortunately, the cellar had water damage. Over time, the walls cracked, and water seeped in. I was able to salvage some texts and parts of others. Many were philosophical anthologies from the early Industrial Age and fiction and poetry from the first and second waves of what was called modernism."

Dan thanked him for the clarification and then gave them more background. "One of our members, who was working on a dissertation in history, was conducting a survey of texts that had faded from the public domain. Whether their disappearance was by design or by random chance, she wasn't sure. In comparing references within existing texts, she came across an alarming finding: a significant number of texts on alternative economic systems, religious beliefs, late twentieth-century poetry, and science fiction were missing or not locatable on WorldNet. She thought they may exist somewhere in hard-copy libraries, but they did not seem to be accessible electronically."

Someone asked why these types of texts should be missing.

A woman with blond hair that was pulled back in a ponytail stood up and spoke clearly. "I'm the one working on the dissertation. Many of you know me as Sara. I've spoken with the curator at the NAUS System Library, and she says that texts can fall out of use and become lost when maintenance costs and storage costs are assessed. Information deemed of no value is deleted. She said some texts simply have not been maintained because they have no apparent use-value. Personally, I think that there is no way all this loss was an accident or happened simply from lack of use. Science fiction is a good example. I had seen references to a couple of books, one called *Fahrenheit 451* and the other *1984*. The first one I suspected had to do with book purging and the second one with truth manipulation. I couldn't locate copies of either, yet they turned up in this cellar."

Murmurs ran through the room, generating an undercurrent of excitement. The room held a passion that could not be transmitted by Vid-chat.

Dan waved the chatter down. "Thank you, Sara. I made copies of each book and would like a couple of volunteers to read them so we can discuss whether to make them available on WorldNet again. We can cover the loss of information and what, if anything, to do about it at the next meeting. Tonight, I want us to discuss the topic that we agreed to at the last meeting: the rewriting of history and where examples might be occurring, such as, for instance, the restoration of the Jefferson Memorial." Murmuring and head nodding gave him license to move on. Claret was clear on only one thing: the man leading the discussion may have appeared to be a dockworker, but he was well educated and articulate.

He read the current version of the inscription now restored on the southeast portico of the Jefferson Memorial and noted a couple of word changes, such as *technology* instead of *circumstances*.

> I am not an advocate for frequent changes in laws and constitutions, but laws and constitutions must go hand in hand with the progress of the human mind. As minds become more developed, more enlightened, as new discoveries are made, new truths discovered and manners and opinions change with changes in technology, institutions must advance also to keep pace with the times. We might as well require a man to wear still the coat which fitted him when a boy as a civilized society to remain ever under the regimen of their barbarous predecessors.

Dan said that he hadn't been bothered by this renovation too much, although he didn't like how it had been used as evidence that the founding fathers would have approved of changes in voting rights so that corporations and special interests could buy individuals' votes. However, the most recent renovation had prompted this topic to be on the agenda. The rewording was bolder and certainly had altered the meaning from freedom *of* thought to supporting freedom *from* some ideas. He read the new wording and then asked a historian in the group to comment.

> Almighty Man hath created the mind free. All attempts to influence it by temporal punishments or burdens...are a departure from the plan of the only author of our region. ...No man shall be compelled to frequent or support religious worship or ministry or shall otherwise suffer on account of any religious opinions or beliefs, but all Men shall be free to profess and by argument maintain their opinions to themselves in this region. I know but one code of morality for Men whether acting singly or

collectively.

An elderly woman with short gray hair rose to her feet with difficulty. She introduced herself as Deb and said she wanted to tell them of her experience. She spoke with a quivering but clear voice. "I used to visit the Jefferson Memorial routinely as a young girl in school. My family lived in Washington, DC, late in the twentieth century. Later, as a middle-aged woman, I visited it again during the War for Peace one mild February day when tourists were scarce."

Deb's eyes gazed at some distant point that was not in the room, and she smiled. Slowly waving, her arms imitated her words as she continued. "The winter breeze wandered through the portico as I did. Around the memorial are several benches, and I alternated which one I sat on as I contemplated each of the four inscriptions while the sun descended in the west and turned the sky from gold to lavender." Here she paused, reliving the experience and allowing the audience to imagine the scene. Then she focused back on the faces around the room, and the combination of her eye contact and words caused her testimony to resonate with her audience. They knew the experience to be genuine.

"I didn't memorize the inscriptions, but I know their content, and the one on the northwest portico, which Dan read, has been radically altered. Things now attributed to man were originally attributed to God. It used to say, 'Almighty God hath created the mind free.' I'm not a religious person, but that hour I spent contemplating Jefferson's eighteenth-century views within the open pillars of a structure resembling a temple is something that I will never forget. His passionate words—including the acknowledgment of a God—the moving air, and the waning sunlight all combined to give me the closest thing to a religious experience that I have ever had." Her hands overlapped her heart in a gesture of sincerity.

"Although some of the intent of the original wording is still there, the underlying attribution of rights, from God to man, is more than a significant philosophical departure." The pitch and volume of her voice rose. "Future generations will be robbed of getting inside the mind of an eighteenth-century man for those few moments in his memorial. It should have remained a memorial to *him* and *not* to our arrogant and ignorant contemporary society, which is what it has turned into. And now I thank you for listening to the ramblings of an old woman." She had tears in her eyes as she collapsed back into her seat. The audience gave her a standing ovation.

Claret was moved by her compelling testimony. It lingered in her mind, and she had a hard time concentrating on the ensuing conversations and watching the occupants of the room. The discussion drifted into how ultimately the wealthy controlled information and how the systems in place, whether intentionally or unintentionally, nullified any threat—like antibodies going after a virus.

Dan addressed the audience. "Is it any wonder that writings like those of Marx and the books that Sara mentioned have become lost? Any ideology counter to the system is considered sedition nowadays and, in the more extreme form, even labeled terrorism or treason or other terms that can mean the death penalty. Have you noticed how the NAUS Board has to keep consolidating its power in order to get enough control to sustain the system? And the reasons are packaged in terms that are palatable for most people, who are too busy making ends meet to worry about the details of politics. Consequently, I think most people don't question something like rewording the Jefferson Memorial." Most heads nodded, but one man, probably older than seventy, gazed out the Infi-Scene window and slightly shook his head.

After a brief silence, the older man stood up and stopped Dan's forward momentum. "Many of you know me as Stephen. At the risk of being the sole voice of dissent, I'd like to turn these rocks over and look under them. Isn't our current system headed back toward a feudal system with these hundreds of walled communities springing up under the protectorates of either corporate umbrellas or private wealth? With virtual mass communications and walled communities, we're becoming less alienated from one another and more like bees in a hive serving the queen. What's been sacrificed are the reasons for labors beyond food and shelter. Aren't we now aimless?"

The resulting hubbub imitated a beehive. Dan had clearly lost control of the meeting, so he signaled by waving that he was finished. He received a round of applause, and vigorous conversations ensued, although in subdued tones.

Claret had heard about enough for one evening. She wasn't carrying a paper copy of anything out and urged Jade not to. It would be like carrying a mouse in her pocket, although the ideas were now like a mouse running around in her brain.

Jade talked with a woman at the next table who claimed to know someone in a neo-Marxist group, implying that Jade might be interested. Some members began leaving at a measured pace. Claret suspected they didn't want to draw attention with an en masse exit. When Jade turned back to Claret, Jade's eyes were lit with excitement. "Wow. What a great meeting. Now you know why I love to come."

Claret wasn't sure that she did. She had been sullied by subterfuge and knew a different type of acrophobia—one on the verge of some bottomless social abyss.

THREE TO CHICAGO

Névé left the apartment before anyone else was awake. The night before, she had told Leo and Zeta that she was leaving early the next morning. Their responses were cool. Side remarks over the past couple of days had suggested that she was an ingrate for not sharing more of her money with them and that she would be back when she found out how bad things were elsewhere. She knew she'd never be back and closed the door to the apartment. Tears formed in her eyes, not because she regretted leaving but because of the significance of the moment. A chapter in her life was closing, and a new one was beginning.

Last night she had lain in bed and thought about the chapters of her life. Jesús slept next to her, snoring. María slept silently, curled up on the floor at the foot of the bed. Chapter 1 was before Névé's mother died. Her mother had always had a steady job, and Névé, Jona, and her mother lived together as a family with various partners of her mother's coming and going throughout the years. Chapter 2 started when Névé and Jona came to live with Leo and Zeta. When Jona left the area, Chapter 3 began. She hoped in the future she would consider those her dark days because things would be getting better now.

Opening the apartment door was like turning a page and finding the words "Chapter 4." The dogs were panting and excited to be doing something, whatever it was. But her excitement was dampened by concern about whether the dogs would be allowed on the train. She had read that service dogs were admitted and sometimes other dogs if they were calm and restrained, although many stations charged a fee for any dog. Her dogs didn't have service-dog diplomas, so their boarding the train was not guaranteed. She was willing to pay whatever fee might be demanded.

Névé led the dogs to the train station as though she were on a mission. All her life, others had read her pale thinness as weakness, so she had learned to act as though she knew what she was doing. If she acted with confidence and was assertive, she usually had fewer problems with harassment, and she tended to get what she wanted. Her martial arts training helped give her the confidence that if she were harassed, she could deal with it. Nowadays, she wasn't bothered much, but still her complexion was flushed as her eyes studied the station.

The station employee, who was there to help anyone who needed assistance in boarding, was a woman whom Névé recognized from the downtown plaza, although she didn't know her name. The woman worked as one of the Peacekeepers in the evenings. Névé had never talked to her, but she had seen her breaking up quarrels or helping old people with their packages or doing any of the miscellaneous jobs these volunteers in their khaki uniforms thought needed done. Névé hoped that getting this woman here today was lucky. She didn't seem like the kind of person to demand an unreasonable fee for letting dogs on a train. Névé made sure that Jesús's bandaged leg hung outside the sling. María wore a harness, but this woman wouldn't be fooled by Névé's claiming to be visually impaired because she had probably seen Névé before, too. Névé held her PAL to the corner of the turnstile and paid for a ticket as though she did this every day.

The woman approached her, and Névé could now see that her name tag said Coral. "Young lady, on this train, only service dogs and dogs under twenty pounds and in a carrier are allowed in the passenger compartment."

Névé pointed first to the Chihuahua and then to the greyhound. "So you're saying that Jesús is OK, but María is a problem?"

"Those are the rules at this station." Coral's mouth turned down as though she were truly sorry to be the bearer of this news. "How did they get names like Jesús and María?"

"I rescued them from Romano's."

"Then you were a Good Samaritan."

Névé had no idea what that meant.

Coral smiled and asked her if she had a pair of sunglasses with her. Névé did, so she pulled them from her backpack.

"I suggest you put those on and claim that you've had recent eye surgery, and they're in training as service dogs in case someone asks."

"Are you saying that you'll let us on the train?"

Coral nearly smiled. "I'm not sure how far you can get with that story, but it'll get you to Chicago at least. A muzzle on María would be even more convincing." Coral reached in her shirt pocket and pulled out a wooden disk the size of a large grape. "Are you familiar with this?"

Névé took the disk and shook her head. On one side was one of the symbols she'd seen on Jona's wall: ◌̂. On the other side was an *X* or a plus, depending on how it was turned.

"I thought not. I'd like to give it to you. If you see this sign, those people will help you."

Névé became aware of a low rumble growing louder. The train neared the station.

"What does it mean?"

Coral waited for the whistle sound to end. "I'd like to tell you, but there's no time." The train pulled in, replacing early-morning voices with hissing hydraulics and the smell of oiled metal. Névé opened her mouth as if to ask something, but Coral motioned for her to keep the disk and get on board. She looked over the rim of the sunglasses and thanked Coral, who moved away to help an elderly man with his luggage.

The train was about half-full, but Névé found two empty seats. She kept María on the floor against the window, and she sat in an aisle seat, hoping that no one would ask to sit in the vacant window seat. She wondered what a visually impaired person would do on a train for hours, and she didn't want to answer questions about the dogs. Two women across the aisle cast glances her way, so she put her backpack in the seat next to her and turned off her PAL. She had ignored several texts from Leo to call him. He wasn't going to change her mind about leaving, and she didn't want to argue the point again. She just wanted a clean break, to turn the page to Chapter 4. Keeping Jesús in his sling, she put her head back and pretended to sleep, but she occasionally couldn't help watching the scenery go by.

***

As the train approached Chicago, tracks multiplied and converged on Union Station. She thought about all the lives and stories those tracks carried and wondered how many people were here on a new journey as she was rather than simply making a daily circuit in a closed loop. When the train stopped, Névé got off and removed the sunglasses, dropping the pretense of visual impairment. A train heading southward didn't leave for four hours, so she decided to see the uptown. She roamed the terminal, searching for an exit. As she did, the city of Chicago rushed past her, arriving and departing. She'd never seen so many people or been so insignificant. The experience was like looking out on the blue waters of Lake Huron. She would have endless places to see and people to meet. She turned her PAL back on because she had promised to send Jemma at least one picture of every place along the way.

What came on the screen were notices of more attempts to call her by both Zeta and Leo, including a voice message from Leo. In the unlikely event that he had something to say, she decided to listen to it, although his whining voice was hard to tolerate. "Névé, like I told you yesterday, you shouldn't have left. I've been trying to talk to you, and you won't listen, so Zeta and I hired an attorney to talk sense into you and get us our fair share of the money, which, as your guardians for the last few years, we should've had to pay for raising you. And so now if you don't respond to the attorney, a warrant will be issued for your arrest. And I'm sorry that it's come to this, but you should've stayed so we could've worked this out. His name's Baits. He'll call tomorrow morning, and you better answer."

Névé's face flushed with anger, and she decided they would have to catch her first. With her ID chip removed, she might be able to elude them until she got to Austin. But if she didn't respond, maybe they could legally take her money away. In the middle of all the rushing people, she was alone in her frustration. But soon, the kinetic energy of all the people jostling past her—going somewhere—fed her a similar energy, and she knew that she would have to deal with Leo and Zeta. She wasn't sure how to get advice. But Chicago was a big city, and it had plenty of attorneys. She had money, so anything was possible. She followed the signs pointing the way to the street level.

Névé and María climbed stairs into the sultry air of uptown Chicago. A breeze ruffled her hair and lifted the ears of the dogs. Their noses worked hard to analyze the smells of this new place. Out on the sidewalk, Névé stopped, surprised by the size of the buildings, even though she'd seen them as a child. The taller ones were at least forty stories high. She arbitrarily chose to go left and walk down the street, keeping her gaze high and becoming again so insignificant that she was free. She resolved to find ways to travel aboveground and avoid being confined underground again.

Around the first corner, a different sight came into view. The skeleton of a tall building reached into the air. In the sunshine and light breeze, construction workers crawled over the structure like ants on a carcass. Névé stood and watched them work for a minute and realized that they were dismantling it, probably so the materials could be used downtown or in a shorter uptown building that was better designed for wind resistance and energy efficiency. A crane removed a metal beam that pointed up like a finger and brought it slowly down to ground level. Then it went back up for another. The mechanics of taking a building apart looked so much simpler than taking relationships apart. But her distance probably just made it seem so. Maybe that's what she needed: distance. She wished she had more time to watch, but she was now on a mission to find someone who would have the distance and experience to see a way out of her problems.

To Névé, the street level was beautiful with colorful signs and sunlight reflecting off glass windows. The extravagance of so much glass was hard to understand. She wondered if the close spacing of the buildings might give them some wind protection, for she didn't see any shutters or shields as she was used to seeing in rural Michigan. Framing the glass windows in bright colors were the names of the stores and offices, painted on building fronts, wooing customers. Every second, Névé and her dogs passed a fellow pedestrian. The uptown was vibrant, alive.

At the next corner, a fat man in a white apron was selling *perros calientes* from a cart under a large multicolored umbrella. He kept trying to shoo away birds between servicing customers. The smell of his food and the sight of the winged pests caught the interest of the dogs. María pulled on her leash, heading toward the stand. Névé hadn't had a hot dog for ages. As they neared the stand, the birds flew off.

The fat man smiled at Névé. "I need to borrow one of your perros. I could tie him to the cart, and then no more birds!"

"Sorry, but she's not looking for a job. Can I have three perros calientes, please?"

"Sí, senorita. Can I put them together in one wrapper?"

"Yes. Thanks." Névé turned her PAL on long enough to pay him, and then she turned it back off. She took the paper tray with the three hot dogs, squirted a generous amount of mustard on one, and left the other two plain. She and her dogs walked a few yards away to a concrete bench built into the wall of a building. The bench faced a grassy lot where another building must have been at one time. Litter swirled in the corners, lifted by the breeze. She put one hot dog on the ground in front of María, who ate it in a few seconds, bun and all. Jesús fidgeted in his sling, so Névé took him out and set him on the bench.

"You'll get one, don't worry—at least part of one. I think a whole hot dog is too much for a little dog who is not used to eating much. What do you say?" She set a chunk of hot dog in front of him, and he began working it over. She gave him about a third of the hot dog and no bun, and María finished the rest while Névé ate the one with the mustard. She let the dogs take a few minutes to investigate the grassy area and conduct dog business.

Back on the street, they walked several blocks before they stopped in front of an old red brick building that had the type of office Névé was looking for. A sign on the front window read, "Boanerges Law Firm." Then she noticed in the left corner, painted on the inside of the glass, a small version of the same symbol that was on the wooden disk in her pocket, the one Coral had given her. The reflection of the three of them in the glass overlaid the face of a woman inside behind a desk. She had short dark hair and wore a green dress. The woman turned from her work, and when her eyes focused on Névé, she smiled and waved.

***

Marta's day had been busy, but she didn't mind when a young pedestrian with two dogs came into the recessed area of the front door and entered the office. Marta expected her to be lost and in need of directions. "Welcome to the Boanerges Law Firm. May I help you?"

Névé hesitated but knew she needed help. "I would like to speak with an attorney about a personal matter. I know we look strange, but I can afford to pay. Are you an attorney?"

"No, I'm just married to one. Jahn is between meetings, and I think he can see you. May I have your name?"

"Névé. *N-e-v-e* with accents on the *e*'s and rhymes with *Mayday*."

Marta smiled, touched some colored areas on her desk, and consulted with Jahn. He said to send them up. "He'll see you now. Take the stairs one floor up. His office is just above this foyer." She continued to smile as they headed up the stairs. Jahn would appreciate the break from prosecuting a corporate case, and she was interested to hear their story.

Jahn took a few seconds to focus out the window and on the street. With the old skyscraper coming down, he was getting a lot more sunlight in the office. He wondered why Marta's voice was so perky when she asked him to see a client. At two in the afternoon, she was usually in a slump and looking for work. He continued to watch the dismantling of the building until he heard human footsteps plus some muffled steps. When Névé came into view, he understood Marta's amusement.

To: JamzBoanerges49-chicagoNAUS

From: JahnBoanerges13-chicagoNAUS

Jamz,

I hope that the trial in Des Moines is going well. I know that you're tied up with it, so I didn't attempt a Vid-chat. Do I have an update for you today! A girl walked off the street and into our office this afternoon. I wish you had been here. Marta said she was sending someone up, and she seemed amused, but I had no idea who would walk into my office. I looked up to find a tall, skinny girl with lavender eyes; short, nearly white-blond hair; and two dogs—one a pewter-colored greyhound and the other a tiny brown Chihuahua with his leg bandaged. She carried the Chihuahua in a baby sling and led the greyhound on a leash.

I know that we agreed to stop taking so many pro bono cases, so calm down. I invited her to come in and sit down, and I introduced myself. I asked her what I could do for her. She didn't seem to know where to start. She kept blinking and gazing out the window. For a while, she just sat there stroking the Chihuahua's head, so I had to pry the information out of her. I tried to break the ice and asked about the dogs. She said the greyhound is

María, and the Chihuahua is named Jesús. I don't know what I expected, but that wasn't it. To try to get conversation rolling, I attempted a joke and said, "So that must make you...uh...Joseph?" I thought it was a pretty good one, so I laughed, but she didn't get it. She had the same expressionless face and said that the guy who sold her the dogs had called her Josephina. I risked explaining to her where it came from, and then she gave me another surprise, which is why this is not the usual update.

She pulled a copy of the book out of her backpack and told me that she had been given it by a prophetess, and then she asked me where she might find that story. So I offered to show her. She looked as if she'd turned to flint for a few seconds with that pale, nearly transparent skin of hers. But maybe because I was clearly interested and friendly, she handed it to me, and then I got the biggest surprise of all. It's The Message, a version we've been searching for—predating the war—and I couldn't contain my excitement. She didn't understand why, so I explained what I could and asked if maybe we could have it for a couple of days to photo the pages. She said she didn't want to risk losing it. I said I could understand and knew I had to gain her trust. I forced myself to set it down and get on to legal matters, so I asked her what she needed an attorney for. She clearly had a wall up, but as we began talking, it came down.

I learned that she just turned eighteen and has no blood relatives left that she knows of other than a couple of cousins, who were her guardians and whom she lived with. Her brother drowned in the Southwest dam disaster, and she's still not over it. I saw pain in her eyes, and she kept looking out the window as if she wanted to leave. Last week on her birthday, she inherited some old US bonds from her grandmother, but the cousins have hired an attorney to get a chunk of the money.

I asked her why she came to Chicago from Michigan. She said that she is heading to the Southwest to find surviving friends of her dead brother. Then, out of nowhere, she asked about Marta and I being married and why we would marry. I explained our desire for a lifetime commitment to each other and our children. At some point, she stopped polishing the Chihuahua's ears and no longer had a white-knuckle grip on the greyhound's leash.

I can't wait to give you more details when we talk in person. I convinced her to stay a few days with Marta and me to allow us to photo the book while I investigate the actions of her cousins. I don't think she's worried about the money as much as maintaining her freedom. She says she's not returning to Michigan, and she doesn't want more schooling or a job until she's ready. I told her that since she's eighteen, I don't think they'd have a claim to the money, but some legal ties can remain to the age of twenty-one. I told her I'd have to study the case law and her options. I have a good feeling about this girl. Marta will work wonders with her, too.

See you next week. Have a safe trip back. We're supposed to have a couple of weeks of decent weather, so everyone is out and about.

—Jahn ô

NÉVÉ MUGGED

Névé tried not to be frustrated by the delay in Chicago. She knew when she opened the door to her room in the apartment and turned the page to Chapter 4 that everything wouldn't go smoothly, though she had hoped to get farther than her first stop. Leo and Zeta's attorney looked like a vampire. He had dark, slicked-back hair and noticeable canine teeth. His eyes had a deep, hollow look. She had found his law firm and picture on a website with the slogan "Make Today Payday." It promised to get clients what they deserve at the bargain cost of undisclosed commission rates. She wondered what his take on Leo and Zeta's potential windfall would be. Her cousins would spend theirs on the worthless lifestyle that they lived. Most of it would go to buying feel-good drugs and gambling until they ran through whatever sum they received, and then they would whine again about not having enough money. Névé's cheeks grew hot every time she thought about it.

Jahn and Marta had been welcoming. Névé at first had wondered if they were just a less obvious form of vampire, hoping to be present when her funds were bled out, but they didn't seem like it. Jahn planned to draw up a contract. He said that if he was successful at protecting her money, then she would pay him for the hours invested and named the rate. If he wasn't successful, then she didn't owe him anything. She had agreed to the arrangement.

What she noticed about Jahn and Marta was that they seemed happy

107

—really happy. Not the kind of temporary happy that was induced by You-Foria! uppers. They always had something that they were doing. The first evening that she was with them, they had a meeting and didn't say what it was about, but they left her and the dogs a dinner and full access to their apartment on the fifth floor of the office building. Névé watched the lights of Chicago come on and realized that maybe she would live in a large city if she had a view like this one. And she loved how the apartment was furnished. Marta had said they'd chosen Scandinavian style with some Quaker mixed in. Névé had to look up what that meant and now understood that the light colors and simplicity were what had struck her as attractive. The apartment was not closed in, dark, or cluttered the way Leo and Zeta's had been.

And somehow—Névé wasn't sure yet how—this interior reflected their lives. They seemed to have a clear purpose in everything they did, but she didn't know what was behind their actions. They didn't waffle and dither and argue about what to do. They just did things. And usually these things were for someone else. Marta was pregnant, and they were happy about it. On Névé's second evening with them, they cooked a dinner and took it to Jamz's wife because Jamz was out of town and she had a full-time job and two kids. Earlier in the day, they had helped repaint the storefront across the street. An elderly man who sold pipes owned the store, and it had been vandalized with spray paint. When Névé asked if Marta and Jahn were friends with the man, Marta had said, "Not really. He's a crotchety old man, but we feel sorry for him." Névé had asked her why she felt the need to help him then, and Marta had replied that he didn't have anyone else to help and it was the right thing to do. So Névé asked how she could be so certain what the right thing to do was. Marta smiled and suggested that she start by reading the book that Névé had brought, and she would suggest where to start.

To: JamzBoanerges49-chicagoNAUS

From JahnBoanerges13-chicagoNAUS

I tell you, Jamz, you'll have some things to catch up on when you get back. This morning, Névé took the dogs out for a walk. I'd warned her where she should and shouldn't go, but she wanted to walk down to the Plaza de Tributo and see Jerzeybell's hooves. I suggested a route for her to take, but she ended up wandering into section six. A couple of gangmembs spotted her and knew she wasn't from six, so they thought they'd snatch what they assumed was a handbag. They ran up from behind and pulled the bag off, but then they realized all they had was a dog, so the one who'd grabbed it punted Jesús down an alley.

Well, they chose the wrong girl to harass. Névé knows martial arts, and María's bred to run down prey. The hot dog man told me he saw the whole thing. One of them was calling for help, with María's jaws around his ankle, and the other was unconscious when the police from section five showed up. Both gangmembs were taken away in an ambulance. Jesús has badly bruised ribs; according to the vet, he shouldn't be carried around for a few days, so I think it's Providence that Névé will have to stay awhile—at least until the little dog heals enough to travel again.

I don't think that I can resolve her legal problems soon. Her age being less than twenty-one isn't the issue now. Sugar Queen is threatening to sue. I'll be glad when you're back and we can consult more easily. When you're free this evening, maybe we could Vid-chat—at your convenience.

See you soon, at any rate.

—Jahn ô

JURY SELECTION

Claret sat in Jade's room, out of view of the desktop camera. Jade had logged on to a legal site for her interview to be a juror in the Mensa Blackmon murder trial and was waiting for the signal that someone would be activating the connection. She had hung a pale-green cloth behind her and applied makeup to look like a cultured woman of Asian ancestry and about thirtysomething, although she was twenty-five. They would have a detailed dossier on her, so Claret wondered how much difference appearance made anyway.

Claret had an idea about Jade's clothing. "I think that your black jacket would make a more striking contrast against the green than the white blouse does."

"Great idea. Can you get it for me?"

Claret brought the jacket from the closet. Jade checked her appearance in the monitor just as the connection signaled that the other end would link to her in five seconds. Beeps counted down the seconds to the live camera feed and Vid-chat connection.

Jade struck a somber pose for the camera. A woman's voice came through. Claret wasn't in a position to see her face, but she pictured a middle-aged blonde with gold jewelry. "Good morning, Jade Le Carre. Are you ready to answer the preliminary round of questions?"

"Yes, I am."

"If you pass this round of screening, then we will move you on to an interview with one or more attorneys. Have you blocked enough time to complete this interview?"

"Yes, I have."

"Do you have an environment free of interruptions where you can participate in Vid-chats without distractions?"

"Yes, I do. I have a private office."

Claret admired her sister's confidence. The private office was her bedroom.

"Many days may not require the jury for the full day, but some may. Will you be able to dedicate an indeterminate number of weeks to this trial from oh eight hundred hours to eighteen hundred hours each day, if required, Monday through Friday, beginning next week?"

"Yes. I just finished the Hammer trial, and I have no other trials running at this time."

"Do you have any health issues that might require your absence or cause you to be unable to perform the duties of a juror during the next few weeks?"

"No. I'm perfectly healthy."

"We obtained your medical records and see that you had a broken ankle a few months ago. Is that condition healed?"

"Yes, perfectly."

"And what were you doing to break an ankle?"

"Ballet. When a trial is ongoing, I don't dance or play a sport. I don't do any activity that might cause injury."

This time, a man's voice asked the question. Claret guessed that he was bordering on elderly and smoked. "Ms. Le Carre, have you obtained any pets since you completed our questionnaire, particularly any dogs, cats, birds, or other animals that may need attention or cause noise?"

"No. None."

The woman's voice came back and told Jade that she would move on to the next round of interviewing with the attorneys, and she was asked to stand by as they may require up to thirty minutes to come back to her. Jade thanked her and then disconnected. She came away from in front of the monitor, did a little dance with Claret, and then got herself put back together in front of the camera to wait for the signal that announced a callback. They had only a five-minute wait before the call came. Jade gave Claret one last excited glance and then composed herself into the somber woman of before.

A man's voice came on this time, and Claret imagined a face with the voice: stocky build, light complexion, blond hair, thinning. "Jade Le Carre. Good morning. I'm Patrician Ursa, the attorney for the prosecution."

"And I'm Zen Nepal, the defense attorney," a woman's voice added after his. "Do you have any questions before we start?"

"No, although I would like to thank you for considering me for this jury."

"And why are you thankful for this opportunity?" Patrician responded.

"Because I need the work."

"We see that you have a female domestic partner, is that correct?" Zen asked.

"Yes, my sister. We share an apartment."

"Is that all you share?"

"Yes."

Patrician spoke next. "Can you verify for me the highest grade that you attained in academic studies?"

"Twelfth grade."

"And you have no vocational training?"

"No."

"Do you identify yourself with any religious groups?"

"No."

"And if you had the money to become a Mensa, would you become one?"

"No."

"Why not?"

"I would buy a dance studio. I'm not interested in intellectual subjects."

The two attorneys said that they wanted to consult with each other and needed a couple of minutes. Claret assumed that the video feed cut to something else. Their mic was muted. She hoped that Jade knew what she was doing. They could use the income, and these big trials were lucrative.

The five-second signal sounded, and Zen's voice came on. "Congratulations, Jade Le Carre. After reviewing your records and juror voting history, we have decided to select you for this jury. One of our staff will be with you shortly to complete the process by having you agree to the contract. I'm sure that you know how this works."

"Yes. Thank you so much."

Claret felt as if she'd been holding her breath the whole time and could now breathe again. She wished that they could afford to go out to dinner to celebrate. She'd have to come up with something special to cook. Jade's face now looked more like her twenty-five years.

INCENSE GETS A JOB

I sit in Paradise Beverages at an anonymous NetLink and read for the umpteenth time the help wanted ads on the Community Net-board, particularly one for a Real Carrier worker. Real Carrier has a reputation for working at the fringe of society because of the lack of electronic traceability. It has been accused of helping subversive groups, which it denies, saying that its employees have no idea what is in the Real Carrier deliveries; they just distribute them. I like the outside-the-system nature of Real Carrier, and I must have a job—or some way of getting room and board. I've pawned off several of the old coins I'd brought in exchange for food, and they won't last long enough for me to finish documenting the theory. The Paradise Beverages manager is eyeing me because I'm occupying a table and haven't purchased anything. I did get some ice water from the condiment stand, and I sip it slowly. I can't draw attention to myself, but from this position, I can survey the Real Carrier office across the street. After looking through the employment ads on the Community Net-board, I decide to try this business first. Its want ad reads as follows:

> help wanted: Real Carrier workers for letter and package delivery within the New French Quarter. Must be willing to work in adverse weather. RC provides transportation. Skill level required: low. Pay scale rating: low.

115

I study the outside of the office from my table in the coffee shop. A light rain starts to fall. The street is quiet at this time of the morning. A plastic bag blows along like an airborne jellyfish between the office and me. At 0755, an olive-green umbrella comes around the corner and stops in front of the shop. A black hand finds the right key and turns the lock. The umbrella folds, and a tall, dark black man wearing the olive-green shirt of Real Carrier enters the office. A second or two after the door closes behind him, the interior lights up and a neon-pink Open sign comes on.

I'm not sure what I expect to witness, but I want to scout the lay of the land, so to speak, before showing up and asking for a job just as the shop opens. At 0801, a car stops in front just long enough to drop off a teenage girl in the Real Carrier uniform. She runs from the car to the shop. At 0802, an overweight man in a similar uniform motors up to the storefront on a moped. He opens an umbrella and sits on the moped for a couple of minutes, finishing a beignet and licking the powdered sugar from his fingers. He surveys the weather, checks his PAL, and goes into the shop. A few minutes later, the teenager comes back out, rolling a bicycle and wearing a rain slicker. She throws a satchel into a basket on the front of the bike and rides off to the north. Within a minute, the heavyset man comes out in a raincoat carrying two pouches large enough that they have to be strapped down on either side of the back of the moped. Soon the sound of his moped recedes as he rounds the corner and heads east.

For fifteen minutes, I watch a lot of nothing happening along the street. Just as I think that I might as well go in and get it over with, the Open sign changes to Back Soon. The man who had unlocked the door now locks it from the inside. A minute later, a small olive-green van pulls out from an alley beside the shop and heads west. Around 0845, the van returns, and the Open sign comes back on.

My feet have grown as cold as my ice water. Thinking of my uncle and his work gives me the courage to leave the coffee shop and cross the street.

***

The tall man I saw enter earlier is sitting at his desk near a NetLink, but he's actually writing on a piece of paper. I wonder what kind of information he would want on paper. And then I wish we had made a paper copy of Orion's theory. It would still be destructible, but not from a distance the way his writing had dissipated on the Net like a cloud on a clear day. Given Orion's paranoia, I consider that he might have a paper copy somewhere outside his office—which would have been searched right after his death, if not before. But I don't know of a copy. I focus my mind and open the door to the Real Carrier office. The man at the desk has skin so dark that I guess he's of recent African descent. He looks up as I blow in with the rain. I've tried to look like a teenage male, just to throw off the scent of the CBI, so I have on baggy denim, a black hat with a wide brim—for less visibility on security cameras—and a backpack with all my possessions. The man says hello and waits to see what I have to say. He's shrewd and calculating. I can see it in his eyes.

I clear my throat and try to speak in a low register. "I saw the help wanted ad. I need a job and like working outside. Are you still hiring?"

"Yes, I am, and I need the help." He motions behind him to a room beyond the front office, where envelopes and boxes of all sizes have been sorted and, I assume, are waiting for delivery. "My delivery time has increased because of all the rain. What's your name, and how old are you?"

"Frank. I'm eighteen."

The man introduces himself as Kit Larson, which quasi-rings of the Old West to me, and I wonder if it's intentional. He studies me for a few seconds. I assume he's trying to decide which one I'm lying about—my age or my gender. "Can you ride a bike?" he asks.

I assure him I can.

"Can you operate a motor vehicle?"

"I can, but I don't have an ID. I was robbed while sleeping, and it was stolen along with my PAL." I'm finding that lying gets easier the more I practice it.

He nods and doesn't seem surprised. He explains that he has several modes of transportation that don't require a driver's license. He turns to the NetLink screen and begins to ask for the usual information. "Full name?"

"Frank Burning." I anticipate the next question. "I don't have an address yet. I just got into town. I'm at a hostel."

He studies me again, perhaps trying to assess character and consider his risk. "I see. So you're off the grid. How would you like to get paid? In goods?"

I nod, surprised at how quickly he assessed my situation, at least in part, and how willing he is to operate "off the grid," as he says. I'm supposedly a young man on his own with no ID, no local accent, and no address other than a transient shelter. I figure he's assuming, and rightly so, that I've just come down from up north, where I probably had some kind of trouble. I could be gone next week, or I might be grateful to have the job and stay awhile. Kit takes what information I can give him and then asks me to follow him to the room where the packages are stacked. On one wall is hung a large paper map of the New French Quarter. I wonder why he would need a paper map and then realize it allows him to look up locations off-line. Only someone standing in this room would know what addresses he looks at. Packages probably come in and go out without any traceability. But somewhere there has to be a traceable money flow. Or not?

He gestures toward the work that needs to be done and turns back to me. "When can you start?"

"Right now."

"Good!" He picks up a bundle from the counter. "I have several letters that need to be delivered within a five-mile radius of here. The bike and moped are in use, so you'll have to walk or use one of these." He opens the door to a coat closet with two hover boards and a stash of food like a small kitchen pantry.

I haven't used a hover board for some time, and then minimally. Where I come from, we prefer to walk and would have been ridiculed for using one. But considering the distance I need to cover in this job, I say that I'll use one.

"Pick out a rain slicker," he says, motioning to a rack. And then he gives me a pouch to keep the mail dry. He reads my mind and suggests that I stow my backpack in the closet and says that I'm welcome to the food.

I choose one of the boards and a rain slicker, and I load mail for parish three in the pouch along with some snack items, trying not to appear ravenous. He shows me where the streets are on the map, knowing that I'm not familiar with the area. The guy is what I had read in his eyes. I wonder how long he will take to connect me with my past.

***

By the time I return to the hostel, my legs feel like cooked noodles. I've been spending too much time on my PortAble for the past few months and not enough time exercising. The hover board was a big help, but I still had to climb a lot of stairs and walk over obstacles. This job is going to firm me up. I have an alcove with a privacy screen and a twin bed. I remove the wet poncho Kit lent me and my cap and hang them on a hook. I put on a dry cap and pull my PortAble from the backpack, set it on the bed, and turn it on. Making sure again that connectivity with the WorldNet is still disabled, I spend a few minutes staring at the screen, and then I begin an outline of notes.

***

At the end of my third day of working for Real Carrier, I receive a surprising proposal from Kit. He asks me if I need a small apartment.

I nod and say that I can't afford much. I hadn't even begun looking in the New French Quarter, figuring that nothing would be cheap enough and within walking distance from the Real Carrier office.

"I'm not sure what your standards are, but I have space upstairs where I used to live," Kit says. "Want to see it?"

I try not to sound too excited. "Yes."

Kit walks toward the shop's back door and then hesitates. "I keep pet pigeons. Ignore them." He opens the back door, which leads to a small grassy courtyard. At the back wall is a lean-to, sheltering perches and colorful houses. Pigeons mill about. A few of the residents are perched on the wall and eye the intruders. "After you." He motions to a metal stairway that leads to the second floor. I climb the stairs ahead of him, self-conscious that my shape and movement doesn't fit that of a young man. Over the past couple of days, I thought that I'd caught his eyes noticing my figure. At the top of the stairs, Kit unlocks the door, and we go in.

The room is more than I expected. The back near the stairway is used for the storage of packaging materials, but the front, which faces the street, is much larger than my space at the hostel. There is a table, a twin bed, a small refrigerator, a stovetop, a closet, and a bathroom. I stop trying to hide my enthusiasm. "I'll take it if I can afford it. How much?"

"You're a good worker, and I'd like to keep you, so how about you work for room and board. I'll keep the pantry stocked."

"When can I move in?"

"As soon as you like."

I don't know why he's being so accommodating to me. I suspect an ulterior motive.

THE CBI VISITS JAHN'S OFFICE

Agent Delta stopped in front of the glass window that read, "Boanerges Law Firm, Attorneys for All Matters Legal." And there in the bottom left corner was the symbol—ô—the source of the complaint. It was inconspicuous unless one were looking for it. Through the glass, he saw a woman working at a desk, so he went in.

The woman had short dark hair and blue eyes and smiled when he came in. She wore a tan dress with a simple elegance to the design. "Good afternoon, sir. May I help you?"

"I hope so. I'm CBI Agent Delta, and your name is?"

"Marta."

"Marta, I'm here to follow up on a complaint. You have the symbol of an *o* with a caret above it on your window."

"Yes?"

"What does it signify?"

"I'm not sure what you mean. What do you want to know?"

"What's the meaning of it?"

"Well, it has various interpretations and can mean different things to different people."

He thought her teeth were like pearls set between the pink clamshell lips of her mouth, drawn back in a frozen smile. "Suppose you give me an example."

"We run a law office. The *o* is like a person's head, and the caret is a roof over the head. We work to protect individuals and specialize in defense trials where the defendant is frequently a victim of circumstance." She still smiled.

"And what else might it mean?"

"Some think of the caret as a hat, also protecting the head."

"Are those the only interpretations?"

"I doubt it, since readers are free to assign an infinite number of meanings to symbols."

Agent Delta decided to take a different tack. "Your sign says, 'Boanerges Law Firm, Attorneys for All Matters Legal.' The attorneys' surnames are not actually Boanerges, are they?"

"No. Jamz and Jahn chose that name because they thought it would be a good one for two attorneys."

"The complainant thinks it's a biblical reference."

"Well, it is a word in ancient Hebrew that means 'sons of thunder.' Jamz and Jahn wanted a unique name because their actual surname is common and could be confused with other attorneys a few blocks away. They also wanted something that started with an *A* or a *B* so it would be near the top of an alphabetical listing."

"I see. So it has no religious connotations?"

"Only if you apply them yourself. Considering so few read a Bible anymore, I don't see why anyone would care even if it were a biblical reference."

"The problem with your explanation of the symbol being a head with a roof or a hat over it is that it doesn't explain why this symbol is showing up all over Chicago."

"It is? Well, isn't that interesting? All over Chicago?"

"Some are suggesting that it actually stands for a flame."

"A flame?"

His throwing out the word *flame* hadn't melted the smile.

"Yes, and we have other intelligence, in written form. It says there is a group planning to set Chicago on fire—suspected arsonists."

Now the smile faded. "Oh my. Well, I can assure you, Agent Delta, that no one in this law firm would ever set fire to a physical structure in Chicago. We work only with individuals and organizations, not buildings."

"I see. I would like to speak to one of the attorneys. Is Jamz or Jahn in the office today?"

"Jamz is out of town. Right now, Jahn is wrapping up a trial, and then he'll return to the office. In fact, if you'd like to take a seat, I can put the trial on the lobby screen, and you can watch what should be the concluding remarks since it's nearing the end of the show." She motioned with her hand toward an area where clients waited for their appointments. Two brown leather couches in an L faced a large monitor. Marta touched a couple of points on her glass desk, and the screen came on.

Agent Delta took a seat to watch. A middle-aged woman with the subtitle "Plaintiff's Attorney" addressed the viewing audience and ended what must have been summary comments. She asked the viewers to see that justice was served. Her manner was matter-of-fact and not passionate. Then a second attorney with the subtitle "Defense Lawyer from the Boanerges Law Firm" faced the viewers and began speaking.

"My client, Mr. Jacob, wanted this forum for his trial because he knows that the viewers of *Trial by Peers* are fair, and he couldn't afford a private trial. The income that Mr. Jacob will receive from his appearance on the show will be donated to the fund for Chicago renovation because that is the kind of man he is—a community asset and a caring individual.

"Let me review the facts. Mr. Jacob was walking down NAUS Avenue, holding hands with his seven-year-old granddaughter, when the plaintiff, a street vendor of juvenile sex photography, stepped into his path and inferred that Mr. Jacob might have a personal interest in the plaintiff's merchandise. Mr. Jacob is not arguing that the plaintiff has no right to sell pictures of whatever he wants. We all know that our NAUS constitution has protected fundamental freedoms, two of which are freedom of expression and freedom of conducting business. But rather, Mr. Jacob feels very strongly that he has at least an equal right to walk down the sidewalks of Chicago on a fair day with his granddaughter and not have his path blocked by street vendors. So this trial is not about—as the prosecution claims—Mr. Jacob being offended by or trying to restrict the plaintiff's right to sell what would have been considered child pornography decades ago. No, Mr. Jacob just wants to be able to stroll the sidewalks of Chicago unencumbered. They were going to be late for a show at the museum, and he did not want to spend time looking at the plaintiff's wares. What if every street vendor jumped in front of you as you were trying to get to a bus stop? Mr. Jacob admits that he didn't need to strike the plaintiff, and he is sorry that he threw the first punch. He admits that perhaps he could have gently pushed him out of the way, but the punch is not what is at the heart of this case—and that is our rights as physical bodies to move through a physical space unencumbered by pushy vendors." Jahn paused to let the audience consider these remarks, and then he continued in a steady, no-nonsense tone.

"The vendors of wares such as the plaintiff's can market twenty-four hours a day on WorldNet. And anyone who has an interest in those wares can purchase them there. But as the audience has no doubt become aware, the search for buyers doesn't stop with their selling only over the Net. To increase their sales, they bring their merchandise into physical spaces like subways, sidewalks, and parks. They have a right to do so, and Mr. Jacob is not arguing with that right. But he also believes strongly that all of us have some fundamental rights to physical space even though these rights are not spelled out in the Constitution. We have the right to enjoy a park—or a sidewalk—without being accosted by the hawkers of wares. Mr. Jacob and I hope that you will agree and clear him of any wrongdoing and set a precedent for our physical rights. We thank you for viewing Mr. Jacob's trial and for your time."

The video switched to the host of the show, Judge Jack, a somber middle-aged man with black hair. He says to the camera, "Now *you* be the jury. If you've been streaming this show for the past hour, you are now able to vote for the acquittal or conviction of Mr. Jacob. The charge is obstructing the plaintiff's rights of free expression and free commerce. You have thirty seconds to cast your vote, beginning now." While the votes were being registered, a chart showed the faces of the plaintiff and the defendant bobbing up and down over a pile of accumulating votes. A shapely blonde woman sang the show's anthem, "The Power Is Yours," while ads appeared on the screen.

At the end of the song, the voice of Judge Jack returned. "Thanks to our viewing audience, we have a clear verdict. Mr. Jacob has been found *innocent* of the charge of obstructing the freedoms of expression and commerce. Does the plaintiff's attorney have a final comment on the verdict?"

The face of the plaintiff's attorney came on again, and this time she spoke with more passion. "This verdict is most disappointing. Mr. Jacob clearly violated the rights of my client, and there is no law that justifies Mr. Jacob's actions. We will be applying to the *Supreme Jury of Peers*, so look for us again with a broader, more representative audience."

Judge Jack thanked the plaintiff and asked the defense for closing remarks. Jahn's face reappeared. "Thank you, viewers, for understanding the right of my client to stroll a sidewalk. And if the plaintiff wants to take this case to a national level, then we say, 'Bring it on.' This issue is one of fundamental individual freedoms, and today, the viewers got it right. Thank you again to all who voted!"

After a few more ads, the judge concluded the program, and the next show came on: a trial related to the theft of a dog.

EARTHQUAKE

The stalls at the outdoor farmers' market displayed piles of late-summer produce. Claret found bargains every time she came, and today she came early because a storm called a Pineapple Express would run the recent fair weather out of town. The forces of such a storm—fierce winds and rain—were something to be avoided, and residents of the city usually could avoid its visit by staying inside and taking underground routes. But on a sunny morning like this one, craft and produce vendors overflowed from the underground market into the city park aboveground.

Claret stood amid a row of booths and studied her options for produce: tomatoes, corn, watermelons (a favorite of Ember's), squash (not a favorite of Ember's), endive (a favorite of Jade's), and apples (a favorite of hers). She considered ways to put meals together for the least amount of money. With her PAL, she took a photo down the row of booths and sent a text to Jade.

> Claret: Request from F-market?

A minute went by, and Claret moved down the aisle between the booths.

> Jade: Salad stuff

Another minute went by.

Jade: & melon
Claret: OK

As she approached the melon stand, she heard a low rumble like distant thunder, but not from the sky. Then she had the dizzy feeling that she'd had at the bus stop and an inability to stand up. Down the aisle of booths, the ground moved in a wave, knocking people off their feet. Just as she landed hard on her left hand and hip, the stand of melons collapsed and dumped its contents into the aisle. Melons broke, and some rolled in her direction, one hitting her stomach and another hitting her leg. Sluggish tomatoes and bouncing apples attacked from the rear. The market became a chaotic concoction of fruit-and-vegetable salad tossed roughly together before serving. Shelves of pottery contributed just that right amount of crunchy texture to the mix. Voices were muffled by the sounds of splats and wood snapping and glass breaking.

And then the rumbling and rolling stopped, turning into a trickle of tardy objects joining the fray. The air was quiet for a full second before erupting into crying and shouting and sirens. A nearby civil defense horn went off, drowning out all other sounds for a few seconds before it was silenced.

Claret sat up and took inventory of her damages. Her left wrist and hip hurt and were probably badly bruised. No one in her immediate vicinity was crying for help. The owners of the booths were getting up, smoothing hair, and dusting themselves off. The aisle had turned into a killing field of produce. Adrenaline lobbed a phrase into her head from some long-ago history lesson on Abraham Lincoln: *We are met on a great battlefield.* Claret went to help the melon woman corral her produce and put the good ones back in a basket. *It is altogether fitting and proper that we do this.* The woman was shaking and starting to cry. She probably couldn't afford to lose any of her stock and the morning's income. Claret tried to calm her by noting that the mess looked worse than it was. Only a few had broken open. *The world will little note nor long remember what we say here.* The woman thanked her and told her to take all the busted melons that she wanted, free. Otherwise, they would go to the garbage. *We here highly resolve that these dead shall not have died in vain.* Other vendors began giving away damaged fruit for assistance in righting their stands. Claret helped pick up fruit for half an hour while trying to get either a call or a text through to Jade, who should be at home, and to the school, where Ember was. When she thought her work had justified the amount of produce stuffed into her two totes, she headed back toward the apartment, wondering what she would find on the floor, even though they didn't have china or anything breakable that was worth much, except their lives.

When she left the park, the magnitude of the damage became more apparent, and she started to get a sick feeling about Ember and Jade. She tried not to translate the chaos and busted melons in the market to what might be occurring at a grade school.

Traffic flowed slowly. Most cars remained on the street, but a few drivers must have panicked and leaped curbs and run into buildings. A cluster of sirens came from around the next corner. When Claret could see around the building, she was shocked at the scene. A gaping hole had opened in the street. She could see that cars, and she assumed people, must have been swallowed by a sinkhole. Her stomach was now feeling as much in chaos as the street, and a headache was settling into the back of her head. If anything had happened to Ember, then life wasn't worth living. Emergency crews worked to rope off the edges meters back from pavement that looked unstable, and it probably was. A neighboring building had sunk directly down at least one story. At that point, she'd seen enough. She walked back out of the street and considered another route. Obstacles and chaos hindered her progress. She still hadn't heard from either Jade or Ember, but PAL service was at least now intermittent.

When she reached the front of her apartment building, she found a large crowd on the street. Her name rose above the hubbub, and Jade came running up with watery eyes. Her face was splotchy pink as if she'd been crying. "They think the building may have structural damage. What'll we do?"

Claret struggled to project a calmness that she didn't feel. "I don't know. Don't worry yet. Have you heard anything about the school?"

"Don't worry? All our stuff is in there! Everything we have in the world!"

"No. It's not. We're not in there. Did you hear anything from Ember?"

"Matty heard from her daughter that the school wasn't damaged, but they're not sure when they can get the buses through to bring them home."

"Oh, thank God!" As soon as the words were out of her mouth, she looked around to see if anyone had heard. But then she immediately thought, "What the hell?" Relief caused the tears that had been held in check for so long to well up. She dabbed them off with the sleeve of her blouse. Her building appeared the same as it did when she'd left it earlier. "Why do they think there could be structural damage?"

Jade explained through tears that a crack had appeared in the basement and along a wall on the first floor. The superintendent was inside waiting for a fireman to investigate the damage. She expected them to be a while before they knew anything.

Time stagnated, as did the atmosphere and their spirits. Neighbors mingled along the street, particularly in shady areas. Claret's blouse clung to the sweat on her back, and she began wondering when the Pineapple Express would roll in. Some air movement would be helpful, but not so much as the storm would bring. They would have to find shelter before it hit. She tried to capture the scene in her mind for a later time—maybe when she was an old lady—when she might be bored and wished life were more exciting. Today marked an event that people in later years would say, "Remember when the big quake hit and..." So she filed the scene away in her memory. Right now, she just wanted Ember and their cozy apartment. She could see the window so close—but who knew what distance separated them from their being back at home. Others had their faces upturned and were probably thinking the same things. Although they'd lived in the apartment for a couple of years, Claret was meeting most of her neighbors for the first time, and she wondered what they'd be doing if the earthquake hadn't struck. In the early afternoon, an emergency-services woman showed up. She went inside with the apartment superintendent, and they didn't come out for an hour.

Eventually, the building super came out and gave them the news. The building would have to be assessed by a structural engineer, and considering other damage all over the area, they weren't sure when they could get one to do an inspection. In the meantime, they could have more tremors, and the building might be unsafe. He didn't want everyone rushing back into a possibly unstable building.

Residents began talking among themselves. "But all our things are in there," said someone near him. "We have to get back in."

He said he understood and explained that the emergency-services chief recommended that residents from two apartments at a time could enter the building and remove items that they'd need for a possible extended stay at a nearby shelter. He said he'd begin with the first-floor front apartments and asked if those residents were present. They were. He gave them ten minutes to get in and get back out. He reiterated that they had a limited amount of time, and out of courtesy for other residents, they shouldn't take more than ten minutes or any longer than they had to. The next apartment resident or residents would go in when the previous ones came out.

Several residents became angry and said that they were not going to wait, and they pushed past him and entered the apartment. The super said that all present were witnesses to their behavior and that he wasn't responsible for their safety. They had been warned.

Claret and Jade groaned and knew that they were in for a long afternoon. Their apartment was on the fifth floor.

THE CENSURE OF INCENSE

Kit sat in the Real Carrier office reviewing topics in the news. He liked to read a few lines and then imagine a rebuttal or a Zing posting that he could make anonymously. In local news, he read that the city board had voted to cut back on the current schedule of garbage pickup and street cleaning, citing insufficient donations to maintain the current service level. In this hot, humid environment, garbage needed to be picked up *more* often, not less. He wondered if the residents had any idea how the wealthier neighborhoods dealt with garbage. He doubted it.

The affluent were safe behind their gated communities, where robots did labor like garbage collection, lawn mowing, and hedge trimming, thereby preventing them from having to release some of the great unwashed masses within their midst. He knew because he had a benefactor within the gates, a cousin from his mother's side. She had caught the eye of a wealthy, but elderly, international trader while he was on a trip to Africa. He'd brought her back to North America as though she were just another find, but he did take care of her. When he passed away, he had included her in his will. She and Kit had been on close terms in Nigeria. She finagled immigration status for Kit, which was not his name in Africa, and he came to North America. She also funded starting up the Real Carrier office so they could conduct off-the-grid trading of information and small goods. She was an independent-minded woman who now had financial independence. He visited her when she invited him, which was nearly every week. He suspected that she missed him after hobnobbing with white men.

He also liked his independence and running the Real Carrier office and other sideline interests, such as the carrier pigeons. He thought again about the garbage pickup. Maybe some garbage buildup would show the locals the garbage in the political rhetoric and turn the current local apathy into discomfort with the status quo. Locals just went about their business and took what the board decided without complaining, in some kind of groupthink. "What can be done anyway?" was what they thought. They needed a political renaissance like the one Africa had undertaken.

The next news item concerned the weather:

> Tropical Storm C2 is predicted to come on shore somewhere along the northern Texas coast within the next few days. Tides will be higher than normal on most of the upper Gulf Coast.

He should check the lines on his sailboat to see if they need adjustment. New Orleans could have gale-force winds. Texas continued to be in the news nearly daily.

> Residents in the Austin area are still trying to recover from the March dam failures. Donations are urgently requested. Working dams are needed to prevent uncontrolled flooding. And without additional pumps and gates, Austin Memorial Lake could overflow its banks, affecting communities downstream in the event of heavy rains. Please send contributions for restoring the Austin area to Austin–HelpNow–WorldNet.

What a mess. If anywhere was likely to kindle the fires of insurrection, it was Austin. Kit had heard some positive thinking coming from there before the flooding. Lately, the population seemed preoccupied with regaining normalcy. When the rains allow them to dry out, they would be like a pile of dry brush ready for a match. Sometimes he envied their situation. But public sentiment would be stirred here also. It would simply take longer for the stage to be set. More guilt shift:

> The NAUS president Sultana is blaming Sino-One for a hattack that disabled air traffic control for several hours in Chicago, one of the busiest airports in the country, with around fifty consumer flights and 1,200 private and corporate flights every day that weather permits.

In addition, the Eurobloc was warning of increased activity and personnel buildup along its border with the West Asian States. The threat of a real, physical war—not these cyber games—might give the Europeans a wake-up call. They still had the ability and time to restrain the bourgeoisie, but there was always the danger of a dictatorship. Fascism could be appealing for keeping order yet allowing personal property and wealth to remain in place, especially when the leader was a puppet of the rich, like Sultana.

A red exclamation point popped up on the NAUS news—"!Missing Person Bulletin!" A picture of the person missing appeared below the title. The eyes held Kit for several seconds while his heart rhythm settled.

> The NAUS Central Bureau of Investigation just issued a missing person of interest alert for Incense Rising. Citizens who know the whereabouts of Rising are required to contact the CBI immediately. The CBI is offering a reward of 500,000D for information leading to her return. No other information has been released regarding why Rising is a missing person of high interest. News Feed has learned that Rising is the niece and colleague of Dr. Orion Rising, who was killed in a recent subway accident in New York City. Some sources are speculating that Dr. Rising's death was not

accidental and that Incense Rising is now a murder suspect. If you have any information on the whereabouts of Incense Rising, contact NAUS–CBI–Info–Rising–WorldNet or call the Civil Peacekeeping Authorities in your area.

Kit switched away from the bulletin to another story and leaned back in his chair. Traffic to the bulletin would no doubt be monitored. He rubbed his chin. He knew exactly where Incense Rising was. So *he* was indeed a *she* and was something of value—high value. 500,000D! What had she done to go from being a citizen commodity to an item with an exchange value of 500,000D? If they were willing to pay so much, they would pay any price and do anything to recover her. Perhaps she had information that was either highly dangerous or highly useful to the NAUS government. Only power—or its precursor, money—could justify such a reward. He wondered again what she had done.

And here she was, his employee. Like one of his carrier pigeons, she flew in and had something of value to convey in one of life's quirky twists. Kit Larson, deliverer of tangible parcels, finally had a package of priceless value, and he'd need to make sure she didn't fly the coop.

He locked the door and changed the sign to Back Soon.

UP IN SMOKE

I have just delivered my last package for the morning when Kit's small olive-green van pulls up alongside my hover board. He rolls down the window. "Hey, Frank," he says. "Can I give you a ride back to the office?"

I figure he's trying to save me time on the return. I put the hover board in the back and climb into the passenger seat. But as he drives, I become uneasy. He is not taking a direct route back to the office. Instead, he pulls into an empty lot and parks under a shade tree. I wonder why. I've found that he doesn't do much randomly. Everything is toward some end. Perhaps our position is not captured by nearby security cameras. He leaves the windows up and the engine running.

"We need to talk, Frank. Will you please hear me out and not bolt before I can explain?"

I feel my chest tighten, and I stare out the windshield. What might he ask for? Insist I get a valid ID or driver's license? Pay for the apartment? He has been considerate and professional over the past few days, and I hope it's not sex. Considering my options, I agree. "OK. Talk about what?"

"When you walked into the office, I knew something was odd. You couldn't provide an ID, you claimed to be an eighteen-year-old male, yet you walk and talk like a female."

He's studying his hands, still gripping the steering wheel. I wait for him to say whatever is on his mind.

"Hear me out. This morning the CBI put out a reward for a missing person—a woman who has your eyes, someone named Incense Rising."

My worst fear is realized. I wish he were demanding one of the other things that I might have expected. I turn toward the side window and put my hand on the door handle, but then he says my name, so I freeze and wait. The only sounds are the running engine and our breathing.

"It didn't say why they are looking for you. I'd like to know why, but I don't want to make you feel threatened. I'm not going to turn you in. If you want, you can walk away from this van right now, but please listen first. I'm not interested in collecting a reward. It would go against what I'm working for behind the front of the Real Carrier office." He turns toward me. "I can help you, at least in concealing your identity. Back out on the street, it's just a matter of time before a security camera makes a positive facial ID, even below your cap."

He waits for me to say something, but I don't. I don't know what to say. He sighs. "Also, I suspect that you can help me. Can we try to build trust in each other?"

I turn toward him and search his face and body language for duplicity but find none. Leave or stay? I wonder what's in it for him to keep me around. "What is the reward for my return?"

"Five hundred thousand dólares."

I don't flinch because I'm not surprised. If they—whoever they are—are willing to commit murder, then money is no object. "How can helping me possibly be worth more than five hundred thousand to you? You could become instantly wealthy."

"But I would be supporting the system and not bringing about the change that we have to have. Plus, I have sufficient financial support. Trust me, please. I'm not one of them. Tell me what you want to when you're ready. In the meantime, I can help keep you off the streets until they forget about this bulletin and reward. Can we do that?"

He needs to know some basics. "Trust *me*, then. They're not going to forget about me until I'm dead. Harboring me will endanger you."

"I can accept that."

"How would you help?"

"I'll make up an excuse to have you doing office work and stockroom work, like sorting. You need to stay away from surveillance cameras and microphones. I can tell the others that you sprained your ankle. You could also help tend my pigeons. You might staff the office while I deliver in the van. If you go out, keep the hat on."

I still don't understand why he would do this for me when he doesn't know anything about me or why they're even searching for me, and I tell him so.

"You will understand when you get to know what drives me. Will you stay?"

I don't answer right away. My mind is going in ten different directions, considering my options. I lean my back against the door, facing him as much as the seat will allow. "Yes, I'll stay. What I would like to have is time to work on a summary that will disclose a truth they want kept quiet. Once it's out, I won't have the same value to them. They may want to silence me out of revenge, but publishing this summary will make me no longer worth five hundred thousand dólares."

"What is it you know that they don't want public?"

"It's complicated. I'm willing to work on trust."

"It's a deal." He offers his hand to shake. It's warm and dry. His palm covers my fingers.

A READING

Marta invited Névé to attend a reading of a letter from someone whom she and Jahn and the other Flames in Chicago respected highly. It had arrived by Real Carrier around lunchtime, and they would share it with their friends this evening. The letter gave them a reason to gather in community.

Over the past few days, Névé had pieced together an understanding that Marta and Jahn were leaders of a community network called the Flames that operated off the Net or hidden from surveillance over the WorldNet. She also knew that they put a high importance on the book that Madam Angeline had given her. Each day, Marta spent some time with her explaining what she called the book's fundamental messages and how to understand them from the written text. They believed the book contained "the Way"—with a capital *W*—that they should live their lives. Névé didn't yet see why she would turn over the way she lived her life to the authors of a book written thousands of years ago. Times had changed. But she was keeping an open mind because Marta and Jahn were kind and helping solve her legal problems, and their organization might have some connection to her brother.

Most of all, she wished that she could ask Jona what he thought about the Flames. Because he'd had the same symbol on his board, he may have had some knowledge of them or a similar organization, but did he like or dislike them? They might warrant the word he'd used to describe his group of friends: *rogues*. In the book's stories that Marta was sharing with her, she was beginning to understand how the message was inherently subversive to the NAUS government. Marta and Jahn—and Névé assumed the rest of the Flames—thought the material world was subordinate to a spiritual realm that had power over death, and they had a cynical view of NAUS motives. Jahn explained to her that although history lessons attributed the War for Peace to religious conflicts, it was really about economics and control of resources. Religion was what he called a scapegoat—which was a term she didn't understand until he explained its origin—and so they were careful to call their beliefs the Way and not use one of the old labels that would fall under the Freedom from Religion Law. From what she could tell, it was a religion without an organizing structure above the local community. They invited her to the meeting but warned there was always some risk. She said she wanted to come and left the dogs sleeping in their beds. Jesús was sore from being treated like a soccer ball. The vet had said that it would be a few days before he could travel in his sling again. Staying in Chicago so long hadn't been part of Névé's plan, but everything seemed to be coming together for her in positive ways, and she would be back on the journey soon.

Névé followed the aromas of coffee and hot chocolate and found the meeting room within Jahn's offices, where the letter would be read. She hadn't been in this room. The door had always been closed, and she was surprised to see what resembled an old-fashioned library with shelves of books. It also had the smell of paper, like Madam Angeline's book. A couch and upholstered chairs surrounded a coffee table offering a tray of sugar cookies. Several people milled around, drinking from china cups and eating cookies.

She'd expected a larger meeting, considering the importance that Marta had implied. But then she thought about the nature of a hidden organization and how having a stream of thirty people show up would attract attention. She didn't know anyone there, and some of them noticed her but did not seem surprised when she came in. To occupy herself and avoid eye contact, she took a cookie and went to get some hot chocolate from Marta, who was pouring it from a thermos. Névé sat next to her when Jahn suggested they start. He said that he'd make the meeting brief. He had a copy of the letter for everyone. As he passed it out, he suggested that they take a minute to read it and then have a short discussion before going back to their own groups. Someone asked him to read the letter aloud, as they would have in the days of Paul. Névé assumed Paul must be someone they all knew. When everyone was settled in seats, Jahn did something that Névé found odd and uncomfortable. No one moved, and the room became quiet as he gave thanks and asked for inspiration to come into their midst. Then he cleared his throat and started to read.

To the Flames in Chicago,

I thank you for your last letter and your concern about me. I know that you've had your own share of perverted justice, and I send this note hoping to lend encouragement.

Before writing this letter, I visited Habakkuk. I like him. He is so sanguine. "Look among the nations! Observe! Be astonished! Wonder! Because I am doing something in your days—you would not believe if you were told." This prophecy is true again today. I'm optimistic, and I'll tell you why. The legacy of our persecution is to bring us back to our original form—individuals in community spreading the good news. And for us today, part of the good news is that the old structural barriers are gone. I came to this conclusion several years ago.

In my late teens, I decided to see another continent, so I crewed on a ship headed to Europe and then hiked all over from the Baltic Sea to the Mediterranean. I walked through many old cathedrals, straining my neck to look at the buttressed ceilings and marveling at the stained glass and empty pews.

But then one day, I visited the remnants of a cathedral—Our Lady of the Carmo Hill, in Lisbon. In the mid-1700s, a devastating earthquake brought

143

down the ceiling and most of the walls. I sat in the ruins of that sanctuary and imagined the violent shaking and what must have happened that morning. A rain of stone and colored glass came down on congregants gathered for All Saints' Day. After the shaking, autumn sunlight filtered through dust settling on a November breeze. Silence was replaced by screaming as fire and water ran through the streets in a perverse Pentecost and baptism. I looked it up and read about it as I sat there.

The sanctuary is now like the rib cage of a giant dead whale where my feet stopped running that day, like Jonah's. The foundation held, and the light now comes in. The nave is open above, and I prefer the ceiling removed. Only stone arches remain and hang on blue sky.

The Portuguese have a legend, called the Barcelos Cockerel, of a man acquitted by a judge when he brings to life a dead rooster. I was a dead rooster before that day. I realized in that sanctuary that I had been condemned but was now acquitted. I also knew where Nineveh was and what I had to do. So I came back home.

For us today, the upheaval of persecution has brought down the stones and weight of centuries of hierarchy. Organizational structures and rules that had to be buttressed with cement and stone are gone—like rubble below sunlight. The dust is still settling, and we should be thankful for the Light and blue sky. But, you may say, we still have so many barriers.

To return to the same prophet, for a while now those who are hostile have surrounded us, as in his day, and justice has been perverted. But this time will not last. "Their justice and authority originate with themselves… They whose strength is their god." But we know to live by faith because at the appointed time, the looters will be looted. Prophecies like these are continually true and repeated throughout history. We can rely on a replay. We know from where our strength originates, and He has made our feet like those of a deer so that we can walk on mountains—as you are doing metaphorically in Chicago.

From what I hear, you are all doing wonderful work. Miracles. I would love to visit sometime when I can legally come. For now, my freedom is restricted. I have to stay here and prove that I'm not plotting a violent *overthrow of the Babylonians. I appreciate your warm wishes, and I encourage you to keep the faith and continue your work.*

You remain in my thoughts,

—JD

Névé asked Marta if JD was Jeremi Duende in Austin—the one who was arrested for sedition. Marta smiled and said that at a later time she would tell her about the man who wrote the letter.

HELICOPTER VISIT

Rigel had just ended a Vid-chat with the project team when he heard the flogging of air by helicopter blades. As the pounding came closer and the chopper descended, dust and the fur of two barking dogs rose to meet the guest. Rigel's kinematic copper sculptures frantically waved it away, but the violence was too much for some, and they appeared to faint from fright. Rigel stepped on the porch as the pilot turned off the engine. Rigel then called the dogs to him and ordered them to settle down. Two men in dark suits jumped out of the helicopter. Each carried a black case.

They came up the steps and onto the porch. Rigel didn't prevent the dogs from conducting a thorough investigation of the intruders. The first agent on the porch flashed a badge showing his name was Juan and that he worked for the CBI. "Señor Rising?"

"*Sí*. Rigel Rising."

"*Y donde está su padre?*"

"In el barno."

The second agent, a man with a blond crew cut, had a similar badge, but his name was Bob. He folded his arms. "Cut the caca, Mr. Rising. Get your father up here, now. What's he doing down there that he didn't come out?"

"He has a music studio. Maybe he had his headphones on." Rigel sent Cadence a text. "What's the problem, anyway?"

"*Tenemos orden de registro.*"

"I'll need that in *Inglés, por favor.*"

The blond man spoke. "We have a search warrant. We'll be searching the property, so we'll need you to stay in the front yard and remain there. Touch nothing."

"Searching for what?"

"Don't play dumb, Mr. Rising."

"I'm not playing anything, especially cops and robbers. I'm ignorant. Enlighten me."

They watched Cadence walk up from the barn, his face in a scowl. Both suits reached in their coat pockets and pulled out identification. They worked for the CBI and were known only as Juan and Bob. Juan nodded to Bob, who did little to enlighten Rigel. "The Risings have a long history of subversive activity. We'll find what we're looking for."

Rigel turned to Cadence as he came up the steps. "Dad, they have a search warrant."

Cadence smiled and extended his hand to each. "Fine. Make yourselves at home, gentlemen. Would you like something to drink? Fine weather we're having, isn't it?"

After thirty minutes of searching the house, Bob and Juan turned up nothing of interest, so they went to the barn. Another thirty minutes yielded nothing to fill their empty black cases. They returned to the front porch and sat on the railing opposite Rigel and Cadence, who were slowly rocking in rocking chairs. Rigel stopped rocking as Juan lit a cigarette. Cadence broke the silence. "Anything else we can help you boys with?"

Bob came to the point. "We know that you received a Real Carrier delivery within days of Incense Rising's disappearance."

Cadence laughed and crossed an ankle onto one knee. "So what? Every day, thousands of people receive Real Carrier mail."

"Thousands of other people aren't related to Dr. Rising. I'm ordering you to turn over anything you received from her since her disappearance."

Rigel had his shoulders hunched and leaned forward. "We don't have anything. As I told Able and Baker, I received two brief letters, which were disposed of already."

"You're lying, Mr. Rising. Failure to turn over evidence immediately will result in a felony offense and a long stay in the slammer. You wouldn't want to leave this fine ranch you have here, would you?"

Cadence rocked slowly and smiled as though visiting with old neighbors and apologizing for not having cookies. "We're sorry to disappoint you boys, but we don't have anything to turn over."

Bob took his time pulling a cigar out of his pocket and lighting it. "We found a journal in Orion's apartment. In it, he states that capitalism was ill equipped to deal with what he termed 'hyperissues,' like stewardship of the environment."

"My brother always was the sharpest knife in the drawer."

"We also found writings by Marx and other leftists. Did you know your brother's a communist?"

"That a felony, too?" Cadence rocked slightly faster.

Rigel studied the distant hills, rubbed his chin, and smiled.

Bob flipped cigar ashes into the herb bed. "It is if you're plotting to overthrow the NAUS government."

Rigel relaxed his shoulders, leaned back, and began rocking at a pace slower than Cadence's. He took a deep breath and let it out slowly.

Bob inhaled to say something else, but Juan cut him off and jerked his head in the direction of the helicopter. "*Vamos.*" Bob closed his mouth and flicked more ashes into the bushes. Both men left the porch with their black cases and returned to the helicopter. With Juan at the helm, they gave the front yard another flogging and were gone.

Cadence leaned forward and put his hands on his knees to get out of the rocker. "Well, hell. Now we have to search for bugs again. I'll ride over and get Violet's detector. What are you smiling at?"

Rigel stood and breathed deeply again. "Bob made a mistake. That's why Juan cut him off and hustled him out."

"What mistake?"

"He said, 'Did you know your brother's a communist?'"

"So? We all knew he was a Marxist. He didn't hide his political views."

"No, he didn't. But Bob used the present tense."

Now Cadence stared into the distance and smiled. "And they said they cremated Orion's body before Incense could see it, claiming it was too mutilated."

"Naturally."

VANITY LYONS

Claret signed on to the Vid-chat, wondering what Dr. Lyons would be like. She'd been too busy to ask around about her. When the camera came on, she selected the view of Dr. Lyons and saw a dark-haired woman with a salon look: big hairstyle, eyes darkened like a raccoon's, and red lipstick. A gold Wise Consumer pin with a small diamond sat on her lapel. Exactly on the hour, she began the Vid-chat.

"Hello, team! I'm Dr. Vanity Lyons. But you can simply call me Dr. Lyons. I'm *very* excited to be joining a team in New Marketing, and I'm so looking forward to hearing about your project. Bull Greene said it's a good one. Let me start by telling you a little bit about myself. I have a BS degree in corporate epistemology from Harvard and a PhD in consumer ontology from Princeton. I'm working on a second PhD in stockholder metaphysics from Berkeley. Aren't we glad we live in an age when we can get degrees and remain in a cozy home somewhere like Martha's Vineyard where I grew up and where I still live?"

Rigel's text to Claret: short timer

Claret: ++. I feel a team-building exercise coming.

Rigel: Hope not. You OK today? You look tired. You said yesterday you were OK after the quake.

Claret: Surviving

"Fortunately, I have prime property on a high point overlooking the harbor, so we're not sinking into the sea like some. Our family have been industrialists since the late 1800s, and I could name a few, but I don't name-drop. Grandma Vanderbilt always said that name-dropping was middle class. Back to business, I haven't worked in New Marketing before, so I'm excited to be able to put this experience on my résumé. I'm sure you know that all our Uppers have at some time worked in New Marketing. I learned from our HR database what your backgrounds are, but I would like for us to get to know each other better since we'll be working together. So I thought we could go around the group and share something about yourself that others may not know. Let's start alphabetically with Claret. Hi, Claret! What can you tell us that we may not know?"

Claret tried to remember what she had said the last time a team leader had dredged up this exercise from the murky depths of management charm school. She didn't have time to think about it further, so she said the first thing that came to her mind. "I survived an earthquake yesterday."

"Super! I'm so glad because we need you on this team. I see that you're located in the Northwest Province and are probably used to earthquakes."

"Not ones that big. We're in a shelter until our building is deemed safe enough to live in."

Ursala leaned back in her chair as Virgil leaned forward. Rigel had his arms crossed. Dr. Lyons held up a finger indicating to give her a second, and she moved to the side, saying something to someone not in the camera field. The team could now see a mirror behind her. It reflected her monitor. The inset of her camera feed was the largest, and the feeds of the team members were smaller. The parallel mirror and monitor reflections created an infinite series of teams and a metaphor to Claret of Rigel's short-timer prediction. Claret wondered what he would say and figured it would be evasive.

Claret's text to Rigel: Your turn. Be honest.

Dr. Lyons was back in front of the camera. "Well, I'll rely on you, Claret, to have a creative way with words so that you can do justice to the team's work. And I hope you bring to the team's attention what the customer might think or feel."

Claret assured her that she'd do her best.

Dr. Lyons asked Rigel what interesting fact he could share with the team.

Rigel leaned forward and said that he lived on the Dakota Plains.

Claret thought he could have been less modest, so she contributed. "Rigel's artwork has helped make a number of Wise Consumer products popular with customers. On the side, he produces beautiful Lakota art."

"You've been doing some homework on me. Here's something personal that no one knows about me. I wish the North Plains were closer to Seattle."

Claret acted surprised to draw attention from her cheeks, which she knew must be turning pink.

Dr. Lyons made the sports time-out sign in front of the camera. "OK, well, let's move on to Ursala. I see that you are in Mexico City and have impressive credentials. We will rely on you for financial analyses that protect the team's efforts."

Ursala waved her hand as if to mean "of course." She said that in her spare time she bred pedigree show cats and had won this year's prize with Lord Wensley Churchill.

"Super! Then you'll be good at grooming this project for show! Thank you, Ursala. Virgil! What don't we know about you?"

"My middle name is Passion, and I bring passion for business development. I love to get new projects started and see them climax into successful businesses. I bring excitement to a team. I'm an energizer, and I want this team flush with profit."

"Wonderful! And what products have you worked on that we may already be buying?"

He admitted that none had gone commercial yet, but some were getting close. Timing was important, and with a little different angle or thrust, success would come.

Dr. Lyons nodded. "I can see that we're going to get along very well, Virgil. And you are located in New York City? Of course, that's just below me. Perhaps we might meet in person—have dinner—one of these evenings."

"I'd like that."

"Thank you all for sharing your talents. Now, Virgil, can you give us an update on Project Wildfire? I haven't had time to read Mr. Greene's notes, but I'm sure it's a project on fire. He named it Wildfire, and it's already igniting the Uppers, even before it's had a project review."

Virgil motioned thumbs-up. "I like it. Wildfire it is! Ursala and I were successful at getting Project Wildfire through the first phase, Conception, in record time because it is so hot. We'll be printing ads on toilet tissue and undercutting the price of competitive products. Our profits will soar because of the revenue from ads. We are now in the next new product phase, Gestation. Rigel has a few ad designs drawn up, and Claret has crafted a short communication soliciting advertisers."

Dr. Lyons appeared to be wrinkling her brow. "Ads on toilet paper? What advertiser would want its ads on toilet paper?"

Virgil started to make the time-out motion and pulled back his hands. "I ask that you review the financial numbers and see the initial designs before you jump to judgment on the merits of the project. I have my aux-camera aimed at the prototype design on a series of five squares of tissue. I hope you can see in these images the vibrancy of color. Don't the ads just jump out at you? They're very colorful and eye-catching. Certain colors can dominate different products so that consumers can color coordinate with their bathrooms."

Ursala smiled and lent Virgil and Rigel support. "Those designs are stunning. They're more than ads. They're design statements. People will want this tissue for its artistry."

Dr. Lyons had leaned back and crossed her arms. The furrow hadn't left the bridge of her nose. "But these food ads are…well, I don't visualize wanting to rub a walnut or a banana on my…wait, aren't these just a bit too—"

Virgil's enthusiasm didn't wane. "We want them to have appeal, and we didn't want to start with hot sauce, tortilla chips, and bean dip just yet. When consumers are used to seeing the ads, then we'll work in a more diverse set. Could we have Claret read her communication for the solicitation of more advertisers? We've bought ad space on the Net site of *Modern Life*."

Claret referred to a screen on her right. "Should I read it now, Dr. Lyons?"

"Yes. I suppose you should."

"'Wise Consumer is excited to announce the opportunity for advertisers to expand into an entirely new ad frontier, one seen and handled by every purchasing consumer every day. How many ad venues will put your product in contact with all consumers daily? Be the first to become intimate with all those consumers! Contact the Wise Consumer rep today at Virgil-WiseC-NewMktg.WorldNet.'"

No one said anything, waiting for Dr. Lyons's response, which took a few seconds. "But the communiqué doesn't tell potential customers what the ad space is."

Claret explained she was confident that Virgil could sell customers on it. She was concerned that if they disclosed too much too soon, the team wouldn't get any inquiries.

Rigel's text to Claret: Good job.

Claret: Nice art.

Dr. Lyons's eyebrows rose. "Yes, I agree."

Virgil loomed large in his camera. "Dr. Lyons, I'm not feeling the commitment and excitement around this opportunity that the financials warrant. Where's the enthusiasm for something that will secure our jobs for the next year?"

Claret leaned into her camera. "Our financials haven't factored in culture."

"We can change culture. You'll see."

Dr. Lyons toyed with the gold chain around her neck. "I suggest we go ahead with the solicitation in *Modern Life* and see what Virgil can sell. I'd like to thank you all for your efforts on Wildfire. I have a meeting with our Wise president in a few minutes, so I'll sign off and let the team take care of any further details. Ciao." Her image winked out.

SOUTHWARD BOUND

The scene in Jahn's office was a teary one on all sides. Jahn and Marta had made clear to Névé that they would like her to stay. They said that they could help her find a job and an apartment. Having her around would be more convenient while Jahn worked to resolve her legal issues. But they also admitted that he didn't need her there to continue working on the case. She promised that she would consider returning after she investigated what her brother had been up to in Austin. When she told them after the reading of the letter that Jona had apparently been a friend of Jeremi's, they were less worried about her going south and connecting with her brother's past. In fact, they encouraged her to find Jeremi Duende and see for herself what he had going on within his network.

Névé's violet eyes were rimmed with pink, matching the color rising in her cheeks. She closed the fasteners on her backpack and blinked repeatedly to stay the pooling tears. The backpack had grown to the size of a suitcase. She left Jahn's office, and Marta walked with her down the stairs to the foyer, giving her one final hug before she left. Marta bent over and put her face in María's and rubbed her ears. "I hope your new harness and muzzle make you convincing." She kissed the dog's head and turned to Névé. "I always feel that anytime I part with someone I love, there's unfinished business. And that's how I feel with you. There are conversations we didn't have and times we haven't shared. I'll miss you."

Névé hadn't heard the word *love* directed at her since her brother's last conversation. No amount of blinking could check the tears that now ran down her cheeks. "Thank you so much, Marta. I love you all, too. I'll come back sometime. We'll be Vid-chatting so much you'll get tired of seeing me. And I do promise to write."

Four-way hugs and kisses on fur and skin sent them toward the door along with a parting comment from Marta. "*Vaya con Dios*, Névé, and may angels protect you."

Before Névé opened the door, she saw the symbol that had brought her there—ô—in the lower corner. It looked the same from the office interior as it did from the exterior because of its symmetry. But in that instant, she realized now how entirely different the symbol was when viewed from the interior of the organization. Her perception had changed. She now had at least a partial insider's view of what it meant.

Yesterday, she had marveled to Marta about the coincidental links that brought her to them: seeing the Flames symbol on Jona's board, receiving the wooden disk with the symbol from Coral at the train station, and finding the Boanerges Law Firm, which ended up with a connection to a friend of Jona's, bringing the link full circle. Marta explained that she didn't view the links as coincidental and that God was at work in their lives, just as he had been in the lives of the thousands of witnesses in the book that Madam Angeline had given Névé. For Névé, the coincidental link to the Flames symbol was an interesting one, but only one—and certainly not enough evidence that she should subscribe to what the Flames believed. She wanted to get on with her trip.

The train that ran directly south out of Chicago was running that afternoon in fair weather, and she planned to be on it. Marta and Jahn would have preferred to see her take a commercial flight to Texas. But not only did Névé not like the idea of being cooped up in an airplane, she also wanted this trip to be a journey where she experienced the greater Midwest landscape until it turned into the South and then the Southwest.

***

Watchman Seven was wondering when to take a break when a thin, visually impaired girl with two dogs came into the train station and proceeded toward platform seven.

"Excuse me, miss, but where are you going?"

"Platform seven. I want the train to Carbondale. Am I in the right place? It sounds like I am." She moved her head back and forth as if she were trying to hear better.

He explained that she was but that only some dogs were allowed in the passenger compartments. Her eye movement behind the sunglasses made him doubt her blindness.

"Yes, I know, Officer, but they're personal-assist dogs. I was told that those are allowed with passengers."

Watchman Seven noticed the sign of a flame hanging around her neck on a silver chain. "Yes, you're right. I'm sure those dogs are a big help. Let me escort you to the right car. There will be another watchman to help you find a seat." He led her to stairs where she could board the train. "Go in peace."

She responded in a way consistent with the Flames. "And peace be with you also, Watchman. Thank you."

He waved to the conductor within the train and pointed to Névé. The conductor nodded and helped her find a seat before leaving the train for the shift change.

Soon the Illinois plains displaced the cityscape of Chicago and southern suburbs. Afternoon sun came in Névé's window and warmed her face. An hour into the ride, open fields turned into a manicured lawn behind a high chain-link fence. Outside the fence, security guards patrolled on foot and in vehicles. The train rolled on, and within the fenced area, horse stables, a small village, a golf course, and flower gardens gave way to a castle. *Castle* was the first word that came to Névé's mind. The structure looked like something from a fairy-tale book and was set off the road at least a kilometer, embedded in extensive manicured hedges equipped with gardeners—many of them robotic—who mowed, pruned, and raked. Heavy shutters flanked all the windows. Some were closed. On the roof perched a shiny gold eagle with his wings spread. Névé wondered how it didn't take flight during windstorms. A running banner below her window described the view.

> Home of Mensa Pierce Hartworth, You-Foria! Drugs president and creator of millions of jobs in North America. At his Chicago South summer home, Mensa Hartworth employs dozens of families who work full- or part-time maintaining the residence. To the west of the estate and not in view lies his militia compound that protects the estate with the latest in defensive weaponry. Mensa Hartworth is one of the ten top executives who provide peacekeeping forces for the NAUS government. He serves on the NAUS Board of Directors...

Minutes passed before the train left the Hartworth estate behind. Névé couldn't imagine that kind of wealth. It was beyond her reckoning. A cemetery occupied the southernmost edge of the fenced enclosure. One mausoleum structure dominated the center. Stone grave markers in many shapes and sizes surrounded it like a theater in the round. Just outside the fence squatted an old, unkempt cemetery on a grassy hill.

After the Hartworth estate slipped away, the countryside became completely flat. Except for the occasional stone dwelling or gathering of trees, the horizon might have been drawn with a ruler. Few notes of interest scrolled below the window, so Névé began exploring the display on the seat in front of her. It offered WorldNet connection, so she could catch up on the news.

***

The quality of passengers was deteriorating every year, the conductor thought. Who did those punks think they were, trying to hide in the cargo hold? How could they have even gotten in there? There must have been a breach in security. Well, not on his watch.

He looked at his PAL. They were an hour and a half out of Chicago as he approached the rear of the final car of his inspection before stopping in Kankakee for more passengers. The car was an older one and noisier without the latest in Noizdead technology. Maybe it would get the overhaul next year, he thought, but he doubted it. The rail system was deteriorating even faster than the clientele. Few wanted to travel anymore. Virtual vacations and meetings were so much easier. Only a handful of passengers occupied the last car. All seemed to be in order until the conductor came to a gray tail draped into the aisle. A platinum-blond head of hair showed over the faded-blue upholstery. Some punk kid must have brought a dog on board, he thought. Well, he'd see about that. As he came level with the aisle, he realized the passenger was a young woman. She was reading the map of the train route displayed on the screen behind the seat in front of her. She glanced up and quickly brought down the sunglasses.

"Well, what have we here?" the conductor asked. "How did these pets get on board?"

"They're not pets. These are service dogs."

***

When the train pulled out of the station in Kankakee, Névé stood on the platform, listening to the receding clickety-clack. The train tracks ran parallel to a highway beyond. A car drove by—the only one in sight. "OK, guys. We did plan for this possibly happening. No Carbondale this evening. I guess we'll have to do it the hard way." She checked a map and a weather report on her PAL. The forecast showed a thunderstorm in the night. She wasn't worried. They had a tent, and she wanted an adventure, so she didn't even try to find a hotel. From her backpack, she pulled out the walking stick and extended its length. Then she pulled two wheels and a handle out of the cover of the backpack and rolled it behind her, heading for the access road beside a nearly deserted highway. They walked south for a couple of hours. She knew from the map that the road paralleled the rail that led to Carbondale.

MERRY-TIME MARINA, NEW ORLEANS

I decide to ride the bicycle because it's available. The young delivery girl who usually uses the bike has the day off. A thick envelope addressed to the owner of Merry-Time Marina came midafternoon for delivery before the end of the workday. I'm not sure when Kit will be back, and I could use a break and some fresh air. Kit has kept me doing mostly office work, out of concern for my safety—or so he claims. I still haven't figured out his agenda. I check the location on the map, don my wide-brimmed hat, put the Back Soon sign in the window, and lock the door.

I roll the bike around to the front of the shop and put the envelope in the basket. The day started out sunny, but bands of clouds have rolled in. The wind is chaotic, yet it feels good and smells of salt water and living things. When I reach the marina, the Merry-Time flag—black with a skull and crossbones—is flying erratically, as if uncertain about which way to blow. I stand on a rise of lawn near the marina office and survey a view much different from the rolling hills of Dakota. Several floating piers with side docks like tree branches reach into the harbor. Sailboats and large motor yachts fill the slips like white ornaments. Movement on the far side of the marina catches my eye. A mast moves among the other masts like a hiker through a pine forest until it enters a gap between two piers, and with the sound of an engine thrown into reverse, it comes to a sudden stop. A couple of crew members work to tie the boat to the dock as the pilot cuts the engine.

I notice the hustling clouds and wonder what the marina will look like in a tropical storm, which is increasingly likely that we'll get—but probably not for two or three days. I picture the boats bucking against their ropes, trying to break free like tethered wild horses. Water around the docks either reflects gray sky or reveals dark-green depths. The pirate flag on the pole near the office now points inland in an onshore breeze. Ropes used to raise and lower the flag slap against the pole, while the rigging on a few sailboats clang against their masts, improvising a complex rhythm in the breeze. A mama duck and ducklings swim between two of the piers, now sheltered from a hawk circling overhead. My thoughts are interrupted by a question, startling me.

"Is that delivery for me?" A tall, suntanned man is heading my way, which draws my attention away from the marina's performance.

"Maybe. What's your name?"

"Sam West."

"Then yes, it's for you."

"You work for Kit, right?"

"Yes, I'm Frank." I hand him the envelope.

He tucks it under one arm and waves his free arm toward the docks. "Let me show you something, and you tell Kit about it. I noticed it this morning."

I follow Sam down one of the piers. I can feel it swaying as we walk along, and I see that it's floating. Then I realize it's one way the marina adapts to the rise and fall of tides and storm surges. Toward the end of the dock, he goes down a finger pier and stops beside a sailboat that I think is medium size for the marina. It's unusual in that it has a black hull and sails the color of iron oxide—rust. The name *Gilead* is written in white on the side and back.

Sam points to the side of the boat where it nears the dock. "I think he needs another bumper for the stern and a couple of spring lines on this side so it'll ride better in the slip. We're going to get a few days of wind and chop. May not amount to much, but I think it'll fare better to pull it out more and cushion the stern." I nod that I'll tell Kit. He says that he can do it if Kit wants to pay him for the rope. He may sense that I don't know anything about spring lines because he adds that a boat this size will take meters of rope for what he's suggesting. He then draws closer and speaks in a lower tone. "Also tell him that Henry the Eighth will be coming home sometime before the storm." He starts walking back toward the office.

I follow. "Henry the Eighth?"

"He knows who I mean."

"Right. I'll tell him."

In the cabin of a large motor yacht near the front of the pier, someone is watching the news. I hear my name: "Still searching for Incense Rising. Anyone with information on her whereabouts…" I glance toward Sam, but he doesn't seem to take notice.

When we reach the walkway to the office, he turns back toward me. "Well, good day, Frank."

I'm not sure what to make of Sam, but I am sure that this wasn't the typical delivery. Why hadn't he just called Kit on his PAL or texted him unless he didn't want an e-trail? And what or who is Henry the Eighth? Pedaling back to the office, I decide to relay the messages to Kit and not ask any questions; I don't want any reciprocal prying on his part. So what if we both have secrets?

BING SCHWEIN

"Hello, team! I'm Bing Schwein. I know you expected Dr. Lyons, but she received another opportunity not long after your last Vid-chat with her. She's moving up so fast, she's a blur. I hope you don't mind my eating a snack while we chat." Bing reached into a bag of pork rinds and began crunching them and talking at the same time. "I've reviewed the personnel files from Dr. Lyons, who didn't have them long enough to make any notes. I see you've had a series of team leaders, but hey, that's our world reality now, isn't it? Virgil, can you give us an update?" Bing bit into something that was probably a chocolate bar.

Rigel's text to Claret: He looks like he's eating a turd.

Claret: He'll fit right in.

"Project Wildfire is accelerating, as we'd expect for something so hot," Virgil said. "The ad we ran in *Modern Life* solicited hundreds of inquiries. Some advertisers opted out when they heard what the ad venue is, but we have a significant number who are excited to jump on board with this project and be one of the first to utilize this revolutionary new ad space."

Rigel leaned forward and unmuted his mic. "Really? I can't wait to hear who they might be, Virgil."

"Ursala and I have grouped them into three arenas: political, legal, and personal ads. The Freedom Party wants to run ads for the Prosperity

Party. They expect a bitter, expensive election, and they're excited about this opportunity."

Bing took a swig of cola and burped. "Is that legal?"

"Of course. There's no law against running ads for your opponents. We think this customer base may be very lucrative, although intermittent, with sales peaking before elections. In the legal arena, trials by mass juries, such as the Net show *Trial by Peers*, which is advertised for months before airing, would like to feature other attorneys, defendants, and witnesses. These ads would be useful for small runs, no pun intended. The personal-product ads may catch fire with things like deodorant, soap, lotions, body oils, hemorrhoid cream—which we think will be a big one—and other miscellaneous products. We're very excited about the response to the ad. So you see, Rigel, your initial skepticism was unfounded."

"Nice job, Virgil." Bing set aside his pork rinds and leaned toward his camera. "And that is a good lead-in for my proposal. We should buy another company for the sole purpose of advertising on our tissue and demonstrating what a boost in business is possible from our tissue ads. We'll create a Cinderella story." Bing smiled as though pleased with his contribution to the team.

Claret considered how group conversations could be like musical scores. Silences, or rests, were as significant as notes, and the current score just had a full-measure rest. After four beats, Ursala spoke first. "What would we buy for a price that wouldn't dig a big hole for financial returns?"

"Oh, we don't have to worry about that. My group won't pay for the acquisition. I'll convince corporate of the plan, and the money will come from an investment fund. But we'll make it successful. And then we can replicate the process and churn out many Cinderellas. Comprende?"

"Sí," said everyone, almost on beat.

"Virgil and Ursala, take an action item to see what we might buy. And keep up the good work, everybody!" Bing popped another rind in his mouth and blinked off.

Rigel's text to Claret: Can I call you @12?

Claret: Sí!

***

Claret wondered what Rigel would want to talk about. She had to admit that she looked forward to seeing his face on the Vid-chats. She freshened up her makeup and hair.

He called a minute before noon. She had underestimated her reaction because seeing his face full size today caused her heart to flutter, followed by a feeling of hopelessness. They were hundreds of miles apart. Maybe that was a good thing, for she didn't want any more complications.

"Hi, Claret. You were quiet again today and look tired."

"I moved back into the apartment because they don't think there's an immediate structural threat. So I've been busy and had a harder time getting everything done."

"Can I come to Seattle?"

She hated her hesitation but wasn't sure what to say. That certainly wasn't what she'd expected him to ask. Maybe he wanted to help postearthquake. "Why? There isn't anything you can do to help. And we're still having tremors. Now there are rumors of volcanic activity from Garibaldi or Baker or one of the many other possible volcanoes in the area, maybe even Rainier."

"All the more reason to see you in person."

"I don't know. My life is…complicated."

"So's mine."

"When are you thinking you'd come?"

"Soon. I'll let you know."

"We're still not feeling settled."

"We?"

"I live with my sister."

Rigel was quiet for a few seconds. "I wish we did. My sister is missing, and we're worried about her."

"I'm so sorry."

"It's a long story, and one I'll have to tell you in person."

ENTERTAINING STRANGERS

Late in the afternoon, Névé crossed under an overpass and headed toward a grove of trees enclosing an old cemetery west of the road. Stray plastic and garbage collected against cracking columns, which were probably the first obstacles the litter met after blowing across open fields —too open for the concealment of one woman and two dogs. Even though they were capable of going farther, Névé wanted the grove of trees to offer cover for the night, concealing their fire from a distance. Also, the weather forecast now included a high-wind advisory, so the trees would help provide a shelter.

They entered the grove. Grave markers sat at random angles and showed varying states of decay. Some were so old that the inscriptions were no longer legible. At first, the setting was creepy, but then the opposite: the markers were like people who had waited for Névé, and now they invited her to join them. With limited options and evening coming on, she got to work. She left her backpack in a flat, clear area where she might set up camp and began exploring the area for firewood.

Toward the back of the cemetery, her footfalls stirred flies into flight. Decaying apples littered the ground under trees with thick trunks. Many had at least one broken limb. Névé wondered if they had been here as long as the cemetery. The nutty smell of fallen leaves mingled with the scent of ripe apples, and she realized how the richness of smell was not something an Infi-Scene window could recreate. When she stepped out from the trees and scanned the flat prairie and the sky turning mauve in the evening light, Névé knew that she never wanted to live in a downtown again. She stood still, taking in the scene until the dogs became restless to do their own exploring.

Because the highway was at least a hundred meters away and no cars were in sight, Névé turned the dogs loose. Both began conducting an investigation of the cemetery while she collected apples. Some good ones were still in the trees but above a level easily reached. She guessed that deer had already grazed at the lower levels. After some climbing and collecting, she had several apples good enough to eat if she cut out the bad spots. She headed back toward where she had left the backpack. Watching where she stepped for other fruit and firewood, she found some small white nuts. Her PAL identified them as hickory nuts. Then she discovered a pecan tree with its nuts all over the ground, once she trained her eyes to see them. She had her hands full of apples, but this windfall was hard to pass up, so she collected a few nuts, wondering how easy they were to shell.

When she decided she had enough, she returned to her backpack, deposited her collection to the side, and began searching for a spot that wasn't directly over a grave. The gravestones nearby were hard to read, but the dates that she could decipher revealed that they predated the Peace and Prosperity Era by as much as two hundred years. Considering their longevity, she reckoned that they'd still be standing after tonight's windstorm. The weather report had said that the storm would come from the northwest because it had arctic air pushing it along. She chose a stone that was low lying with a broad base but high enough to block some of the wind, and she set up the tent on the leeward side of it. From the side of the grove nearest the road, she considered the cemetery and where to build the fire so it would be hidden. Preferably, she wanted it blocked from view and downwind of the tent.

Névé rummaged through the backpack, looking for supplies with the dogs still nearby. Abruptly, María bolted into the open prairie. A rabbit ran for its life, zigzagging and darting, but not fast enough. The dog was a blur and then a killing machine. By the time Névé and Jesús trotted to the scene, María stood over a dead rabbit, stringing drool on the dry brown grass.

A man's voice came to her from the west, followed by his umbra. "Looks like a clean kill."

Névé jumped and spun around. A figure eclipsed the setting sun, creating an annulus around him. He approached and became an old man about her height with a stocky build. "I'm sorry. I didn't mean to startle you. No need to be afraid of old Jubal."

"Where did you come from?" Her heart was pounding.

"Over yonder." He jerked his head toward the west. "I reckon I came out of the sun." He smiled and had the worst set of teeth Névé had ever seen. He wore coarsely woven wool-looking tan pants and an ochre plaid shirt. A small white feather clung to his shoulder. A yellowed felt hat shaded his face. He carried a bag that looked like real leather over his shoulder, and a blue handkerchief was wrapped around his neck.

"Them's good eating." He nodded down at the rabbit. The expression on Névé's face made him laugh and show his stained teeth again. One in the front had a gold filling. "I'll skin it for you and show you how to make rabbit stew. Best eating there is."

Névé froze in place, still recovering from the dual shocks of the kill and his sudden appearance, until she found her voice. "But María sank her teeth in it and slobbered on it."

"Just the neck. You don't eat the head. I'll skin it. You wait and see." Without invitation, he picked up the rabbit and headed toward the cemetery, collecting wood for a fire.

Névé took longer than the dogs to follow him and called out, "I'm armed, so don't try anything."

"Oh, I'm not here to try anything. I like some people's society and want to help them as I can. I don't get much company in these parts anymore. Used to be you couldn't swing a cat without hitting somebody —before people became like moles and bats."

Névé watched him set the firewood several meters away from the tent. He pulled a faded cardboard box from his bag and struck the red tip of a small wooden stick on the side of the box. She figured they were something called matches and asked him where he had bought them.

"Oh, at an old store a long time ago."

"What did you say your name is?"

"Jubal. Keep your dogs from follering me." He walked into the field to the north and dug a hole with a trowel that he pulled from his leather bag. Sunlight through flesh in a flash of red made her turn her head away. She busied herself trying to crack and clean nuts and wondered what his strange accent was.

Jubal returned and pulled a pot and a can of diced tomatoes out of the leather bag. He cut the rabbit into pieces, put them in the pan, and added the canned tomatoes along with a potato and an onion, also pulled from his bag. Névé wouldn't have been surprised if he had pulled out another rabbit. Using two flat rocks for a stand, he set the pan over the coals and put the lid on it. He then pulled up a couple of logs for them to sit on.

"We'll just let that simmer about an hour. I'll help you move your tent to this side of the cemetery."

"Why would I want to do that? I set it up there so the large trees can be a wind block."

"That hickory's coming down in a good windstorm like tonight's. You'll need to be behind that big granite obelisk so it can block the wind and debris, like branches. Come on. Let's get it done."

Névé didn't move at first but then decided she had no reason not to. He'd been around here a long time—long enough to know where to sleep at night. She grabbed her backpack before he could, thinking that, for all she knew, he might be a common thief.

After moving the tent and making some coffee, he sat down on one of the logs. She sat on the other one, but after considering the situation, she got up and put the dogs' jackets on them and then their leashes.

"What do you do, Jubal?"

"Not much. Walk the fields, making use of myself where needed."

The stew had cooked about an hour when he removed the lid with his handkerchief. "Do you have a bowl?"

Névé pulled a bowl and spoon from her backpack. He divided the stew between them. A steady breeze unrolled evening across the prairie and a cover of clouds across the sky from the west.

Névé cautiously tasted the stew and found it savory. "Jubal, this stew is heavenly. I had no idea what rabbit stew would taste like."

"No, rabbits are earthly. Angel stew is the only heavenly thing I've tasted. And that was a long time ago."

Névé asked him what angel stew was and whether it was white like angel food cake. The stew was warming her insides all the way down and restoring her humor, but she still wondered how she was going to get rid of this guy after they ate. She didn't want him around after supper. He was too odd.

He grinned and said, "I'll tell you a story I haven't told many. It happened during the Black Hawk wars."

"You piloted one of those old helicopters during the war?"

"No. I'm talking about an earlier war. We were fighting Indians."

"Oh—the cyber wars before the consolidations."

"Not exactly, but I was traveling on foot hereabouts and came upon a band of ruffians who were putting a stew together. I offered to contribute some vegetables if they'd share with me. They agreed and said they weren't sure how it'd turn out but I was welcome." He chewed another bite. A fleck of gold on his right boot reflected the firelight. Like the satchel, the boot appeared to be real leather.

"That stew had the sweetest, tenderest meat ever eaten—melted in the mouth. Can't describe it proper. Well, I commented on the flavor and tenderness, and that's when they told me where it'd come from. Claimed to have cooked an angel. Killed him by accident. Said he come all of a sudden like out of the woods, startling them and telling them not to be afraid. He warned 'em not to fight the Indians the next day 'cause they'd lose. They'd been drinking, and an argument broke out. A gun went off— so they claimed—and he ended up dead. Said he turned into a white dove on the spot, so they plucked it and put it in the stew. Didn't believe 'em at the time, seeing as how they was a troop of crazies, but that stew surely was good. Headed out as soon as I ate. Never did find out what the stew had in it, but I think of it as angel stew. Next day, there *was* a big battle. Settlers and trappers were massacred, including those men, I heard tell."

"Settlers and trappers? You mean back when Illinois was still a state?"

He finished his stew, threw a thighbone to María and a front-leg bone to Jesús, and then got up to rinse out his bowl and the pan. "Oh no. This was before Illinois was a state."

Névé sat like a statue. The blood drained from her face and then rushed back in. The guy was a crackpot or a jokester-storyteller. Either way, he needed to go.

"I never eat a stew but I don't think about that night." He spoke his words in all seriousness.

She tried to laugh it off. "OK, you had me going there. Do you always wander around the countryside providing entertainment with dinner?"

"Only since that night." He pointed to the largest tree on the west side of the clearing. "You'll be glad we moved your camp away from that hickory. Well, it was nice meeting you, but it's time I moved on. And thank you for the company—for entertaining a stranger."

Her mouth had gone dry, but she managed a reply. "Thank you for the delicious stew."

He doffed his hat. "Good night, Névé." He picked up his leather satchel and headed west across the field. Before rising to finish the cleanup, she sat for a minute, wondering when she had told him her name.

In his absence, she realized how dark the night was under the cloud cover and how vulnerable they were. The wind was already beginning to blow, and it carried the sound of howling and yapping. Névé hoped those were coyotes, which she had read tended to stay away from humans. Wolves, however, did not. She also hoped that the bad weather would hinder the rumored marauding bands from coming around.

With the night came heavy wind. Névé and the dogs huddled in the tent, sharing their warmth and listening to tree limbs cracking around them. An especially loud crash turned out to be the hickory tree coming down. None of them slept well. Névé dreamed of the man she'd seen in the news reports. This time, he led her over a crevasse instead of through one, and as always, they were hanging on ropes. His large brown eyes came so close that she almost tried to kiss him. He smiled. She woke and couldn't sleep the rest of the night.

When the sun came up, Névé considered their situation. She estimated that it would take them a couple of days of walking to reach Champaign, so she inventoried her supplies once more before closing the pack. They had food for today but would need water by this evening. Positioning Jesús in his sling and taking María's leash, she rolled the pack and followed the unpaved access road on the west side of the highway southward.

Around midmorning, she stopped near a bank of poplars that provided shade, and she let Jesús down. She held María's leash as the dogs took a break. Turning around to the north, she noticed a spot of color and dust on the access road behind them. With only the poplars to hide among, she picked up Jesús and moved farther off the road. The vehicle, whatever it was, came on slowly.

***

Hannah lifted the binoculars to her face for the hundredth time.

"Hannah, if you couldn't see them ten seconds ago, how're you going to see them now?" Jesse asked.

"Well, you never know." Hannah scanned the field again. "I thought I saw something move over to the right. They can't be much farther."

"They might have managed to hide, and we passed them."

"Dust blowing off the field isn't helping." She turned her face again toward the east to allow the bonnet to block the wind and her watering eyes to clear. Then she scrutinized the trees again. "There. Did you see that movement over there? Something's waving just above the grass."

"Well, what's it look like?"

"Uh…a dog tail…I think."

"Jubal said there'd be only the young lady."

"He meant no other *people*. It has to be them." Hannah fidgeted. Between the wagon creaking and the horse hooves clomping, they certainly weren't going to sneak up on anyone who didn't want to be found. When they were about even with where Hannah had seen the movement, she told Jesse to stop the wagon. It creaked to a halt and took a few seconds to settle. A light breeze shuffled the poplar leaves and carried away the dust they had stirred up. A truck rumbled by up on the highway. If she wasn't mistaken, a small patch of lavender and gray was visible just beyond one poplar. "Hello?" she called out. "We're here to help you! Névé, can you hear me? We can give you a ride to Champaign. Jubal sent us."

***

The back of the wagon was a faster way to get to Champaign, but the bottom of Névé's pelvic bones pounded against the wooden seat. The rough ride didn't appear to bother Hannah, who had climbed into the back with Névé to keep her company while Jesse drove. Between answering questions from Hannah, she watched the dogs' ears bounce up and down with the movement. She had already given Hannah the short version of her story, including where she was going. To divert any more questions, Névé asked Jesse and Hannah a few of her own. "Why ride in a wagon instead of a car or truck?"

Hannah did the explaining. "We're members of a community that lives a simpler life. We're called Makers. Within our community, we run our own commerce and make nearly everything we need. Jesse is a carpenter, and I'm a seamstress." She smiled as though proud of what they did and how they lived.

Névé nodded, wondering about all the effort that would be required to make her own goods.

"We purchase some of our raw materials, such as fabric and lumber, but we grow our own food, make our own furniture, build our own houses, and generally live as far from the rest of society as possible." Without Névé asking, Hannah added that the community had formed just after the Peace and Prosperity Era because they wanted to be able to survive when society collapsed.

"Do you think society is going to collapse soon? Is that a religious belief?"

Hannah shrugged her shoulders but kept her smile. "We're survivalists. For most of us, the prediction of an apocalypse is an obvious result of recent trends. Some in the community base the prediction on religious beliefs, but the Makers were not formed around a single religious belief. We have many spiritual practices. Mostly, we want freedom from 'consumer slavery.' Similar communities exist all over the country, but since they stay to themselves, you don't hear about them."

Névé wondered how there could be subcultures and economies that she had never heard of. Yet if they were off the grid, they were, in their own way, nonexistent from a WorldNet commerce perspective. Névé asked how they could buy their raw materials without using the system of money transfer.

"Makers are responsible for the Just-Money exchange, based on coins of silver, copper, and gold. We, and similar communities, have distributers who deal in hard currency, although many times we exchange our Maker-made products for other goods. A bartering economy is probably the oldest of human economies. We've chosen to live a simpler and more humane lifestyle."

Névé asked what the Just-Money coins looked like.

Jesse pulled a few silver and copper ones from his pocket and handed them back to Névé. They were square, about two centimeters in width, a couple of millimeters thick, and warm from having been in his pocket. The only markings were the bank, date, and location of production. "What's to keep someone from making fake ones?"

Jesse nodded and turned his head to the side so that his voice would reach back toward where the women were. "Sometimes that happens, but rarely. For one, there just isn't enough of a demand for these. Anyone with a lot of coins would be suspicious. And their value floats with the market price for each metal. Most merchants who take hard currency have a test apparatus that can confirm whether coins are authentic, and it calculates current value based on weight."

Hannah pulled a few coins from a small purse and gave them to Névé. "Any Just-Money bank can make them, according to standards. You should carry a few for emergencies. A lot of people in this area don't deal in electronic money exchange. We can go in a store near the train station where we buy our goods, and you can see for yourself."

Névé nodded and said she would be interested in seeing such a store. She wondered what they might have. Maybe they had matches like Jubal had.

October 8—I'm Névé March, and this is the start of my journal. I was Névé Sweet, but Sweet wasn't the surname I was born with. I was a walking ad for Sugarstik since before I could walk, but I changed all that last month when I turned eighteen. I got rid of my Sugarstik tattoo, changed my name to March—Great-Grandma Lydia's name—and I left Michigan to go to Texas.

I bought this journal at a store that Hannah and Jesse took me to. They picked me up this morning, knowing from Jubal that I needed to catch the train south. The whole story is too long to tell. My fingers are already getting tired. I'm not used to writing. I wish my handwriting were better, but writing isn't easy. Hannah suggested that I add sketches also. Right now, María, Jesús, and I are on a train heading south to Carbondale where it will stop for the night—which is good because the dogs will need a break.

I would have loved to spend more time with Hannah and Jesse and see their home, but it wasn't on the way. Their life sounds interesting to me—being self-sufficient. I don't know what they said to the conductor at the station, but we were allowed to board the train with no questions asked and given first-class seats. María has room to lie down, and Jesús is lying on the seat next to me. They just ate some dog food and are asleep. Hannah had the conductor contact someone to meet us when the train stops in Carbondale late this evening. I think I'll try to get some sleep. We had a wild night last night with the howling wind. This train seat is feeling comfortable, and my writing hand is getting cramped.

October 9—We're finally back on the train again. We had a delay in Carbondale. Trains to the west were canceled for the next two days because of a lack of passengers. I found out that the train to New Orleans was still running though. So now we're headed to New Orleans. At least I'm going south. In New Orleans, I can get a train that goes west. I see on weather radar that a tropical storm may come into New Orleans, but it's not expected to be much. I might have to wait a day in the New French Quarter, where my transfer to a western line should take place. The schedule may be interrupted. I read that even the New French Quarter is now not too far above sea level. I suppose that sometime soon, they'll have to build a New New French Quarter even farther in. I've never seen the sea, only Lake Michigan and Lake Huron, so I'm hoping to see the Gulf, but I don't think you can do that from the train station. I wanted to see the countryside, so I don't mind going a longer way to Texas.

INCENSE AND THE BREWING STORM, NEW ORLEANS

For the past couple of days, I've monitored WeatherNow! and watched a tropical depression turn into a tropical storm in the Gulf. Now Tropical Storm C2 is making its way toward New Orleans, and we're already experiencing the outer bands of the storm. I'm sitting at the desk in the front of the Real Carrier office, wishing Kit and my other two colleagues would return. Wind and rain are creating a transient work of art against the front window to an improvised rhythm of water on glass. Light from the neon-pink Open sign tangles in the raindrops and streaks down the pane against a background of muddy sky. I was planning delivery routes for tomorrow, but our plans will have to change. The wind and rain are predicted to intensify for at least another day. When Kit returns, I can go back upstairs to finish the summary. It's all I've been able to think about lately. I'm close to having it done, and now I'm worrying about how to get it published.

Movement catches my eye through the window's kinetic artwork. Across the street, I see a figure in a hooded raincoat, accompanied by a greyhound dog. Looking closer, I see what appears to be the head of a small dog sticking out the front of the coat about chest high. They turn to stand inside the bus shelter. A gust flings the hood back, showing the wearer to be a young woman with silver-blond hair. The woman replaces the hood and pulls the greyhound beside her into the bus shelter, but it's providing only partial protection from the swirling wind. She appears to be consulting the bus or train schedule and is probably learning that the routes have been suspended for the rest of the day. A notice came up on the city bulletin board earlier.

I watch her for a minute, wondering what they'll do. She must have seen the notice about the schedule because she sits down on the bench and leans forward with her chin resting on the hand holding the leash and the other hand stroking the small dog's head. I put on my raincoat and go out, keeping my back to the wind.

A colorful beach ball bounces down the middle of the street.

As I approach, I can see that her shoulders are slumped. The greyhound shakes rainwater off its back, and the young woman tries to pull it as far into the shelter as possible. I wave and ask if they need help.

The woman's voice has to compete with the pounding rain. She starts to speak and then repeats the first part louder so I can hear her. "We need to find somewhere to stay until I can get the next train west. Is there an itinerant house nearby?" She pauses and then adds as if to explain the circumstances, "Because of the storm, the train didn't make the stop where I'd planned to get off."

I tell her that there's no shelter close. I invite her to come inside until Kit returns with the van and suggest that maybe he can drive her somewhere. She follows me across the street toward the buttery office lights. We both jump a stream of water running along a high curb. I throw back a comment. "I haven't lived here long, but I hear it floods like crazy during a storm. In a few decades, this'll be under water."

"Are you safe here, or will you need to evacuate?"

"It's just a tropical storm. New French Quarter is safe enough—or so I'm told."

We blow into the office and close the door, leaving the wind and rain pounding to get in. I realize that the young woman may still be a teenager. A puddle collects on the floor below her and the dogs, and she apologizes for the mess. I introduce myself. "Hi, I'm Frank."

She glances around the office. "I'm Névé. This is María and Jesús. Thank you for letting us come in here for a while."

"We're not busy today, and you looked lost. I felt sorry for you. No one should be out in this weather."

"I know where I am, just not what I'm going to do until I can catch the train to Texas."

I take Névé's dripping raincoat and hang it on a hook near mine. "Texas. That's a long way."

Névé adjusts Jesús's sling and her blue flannel shirt, which suggests she's from up north, and her next words confirm it. "We're going to Austin from Michigan. My brother used to live in Austin."

I go over to the desk and sit down, wondering what to do next. I offer Névé a chair, and she sits down. "Where is he now?"

"He drowned in the Austin flood." She strokes Jesús's ears while María begins investigating the room, tail down.

I offer my condolences and ask if I can get her some coffee or tea and the dogs something to drink.

"Water would be nice, and water for the dogs?"

Before I make it to the back room for drinks, my heavyset colleague —Mr. Chubbs as I think of him—comes in, bringing more rain. The large surface area of his rain gear creates a pond on the floor. He throws a set of keys on the counter, unconcerned about the water on the floor or Névé. "Hey, Frank! I'm outta here. Moped's in the garage."

He rolls out as our teenage courier sticks her head in, leaving a crack for the wind and rain and her pronouncement. "Gotta get home, Frank. Deliveries done. Bike's in the garage."

When I return with a tray, Névé is mopping. I set down the drinks. "I can do that, Névé. Kit will try to hire you if he thinks you're a worker."

Névé takes Jesús out of his sling and sets him on the floor along with the bowl of water, and the dogs drink as if they're parched. "I hope they remember their indoor manners and don't add more puddles to your floor."

I think in that instant that I'm going to like this girl, who can find humor in a rather desperate situation.

Outside, the stream running along the curb has risen just in the few minutes since we came in. Kit comes into view. He hesitates with his hand on the doorknob when he notices our visitors. But the wind herds him in like the rest of us. I'm mopping the floor, and Névé is tending the two dogs. He shakes off his raincoat and hangs it up. "Sorry, Frank. But I bring more water to mop."

I shrug it off and mop more water.

Saying that he saw the moped and bike in the garage, Kit turns off the Open sign, and we are done with business for today. He motions toward Névé. "Looks like we have guests."

"I'm Névé. Frank rescued us from the bus stop." She explains to Kit how she ended up stranded. "He invited us in until I can figure out what to do."

Kit rubs his hands through his hair and asks her what she would like to do. He can't want to go back out into the weather, but he's such a decent guy that I expect him to offer to take her somewhere.

"I thought I'd go to a house for transients, but Frank says the nearest one isn't within walking distance in this weather."

He wipes his face on his sleeve. "Those places can be a bit rough anyway—no place for a young lady like you."

Névé shrugs and turns her attention to the dogs. He sits at the desk, I suppose, to contemplate the options as I did.

I decide that he needs to hear more of her story. "She came all the way from Michigan and is on her way to Austin to see where her brother was killed in the flood."

Kit's eyebrows go up. "Really? Interesting. Your brother was killed in the Austin flood?"

"Yes. I wanted out of Michigan anyway, and I decided to see if I can find some of his friends who survived."

Kit continues to surprise me. "I have contacts in Austin. I think this calls for a pot of coffee. I have a spare room in the back where you can stay tonight if you like. I would be honored to have the sister of a brother killed in the Austin flood. Will you stay?"

Névé sighs as if in relief and nods. "If my dogs and I won't be too much trouble." She picks up Jesús, who has finally stopped drinking, and introduces them to Kit. "They're usually no problem."

"I can see that. I think Jesús says he doesn't want to go back out tonight. I'll make the coffee. Let me show you to your suite, madam. Then I need to take care of my birds." He shows Névé to a small room that may have been a coat closet at one time. I've always suspected that he uses it for taking naps, but I've not seen him do that. It contains a cot, a nightstand with a lamp, and a chair. "As you can see, it's cozy and cheap."

"It's perfect, Kit. Thanks. I really appreciate this."

He nods and retrieves his raincoat before heading out the back door. I grab my slicker and follow him. The pigeons are hunkered down in their houses. He says that if the weather continues to worsen, we'll have to move them inside. At least they all made it back. Early this morning, Henry the Eighth returned from the front lines—the marina. Sam told Kit that Henry made three circles over the marina as if he was deciding whether he wanted to be flying anywhere.

We make sure that their houses are secure, and then he decides to close the shutters on the lower level of the shop while we're out. He says that the lower level takes more abuse from blowing debris, and we don't need a broken window. We start with the ones in the back and move around toward the street. He tells me to go inside, and he'll finish.

Back in the office, I go to the desk and wake up the NetLink monitor to get the forecast. The storm is cranking up. The radar image swirls green, yellow, and red. A beeping alert causes the dogs to get up and start pacing. Névé reads the forecast with me over my shoulder.

WeatherNow! Forecast is brought to you by Bonita Rain Gear, designs that make you wish for a rainy day. Forecasters just issued hurricane warnings for the upper Gulf Coast. They expect to upgrade Tropical Storm C2 to a hurricane by this evening. Counter to early model predictions, the storm stalled offshore this morning and began building strength. Originally predicted to make landfall around 1900 hours this evening, the current landfall estimate has been pushed back to at least 2200 hours. Residents in and around the central Gulf Coast should seek shelter. If you can safely move to higher ground, please do so. The chairman of New Orleans posted instructions for residents to move to upper levels and shelter in place. Evacuation at this time is too risky. Travel conditions are dangerous. Forecasters will provide updates every fifteen minutes.

Don't forget your Bonita Rain Gear! You'll need it.

I recall a hurricane on the East Coast last year. We evacuated to a friend's house, where the good times rolled until the storm passed. But I've never ridden out one near sea level. Fortunately, Kit will know what to do.

Névé's face reflects the neon green of the radar when she turns to ask me a question. "Frank, may I check the train schedules between here and Austin?"

"Sure." I get out of her way. I need to tell Kit about the worsening forecast, so I go back out to see if he needs help.

Outside, I find Kit has finished closing shutters on the ground floor except for the large front window, which doesn't have one. He's huddled on the leeward side of the brick wall surrounding the patio and looking pensively toward the pigeon cages.

I have to lean in close to give him the news. "Forecasters will upgrade the storm to a hurricane soon, so we're now under a hurricane warning."

Kit closes his eyes and shakes his head.

I go on with the bad news. "It's stalled offshore. They're not sure how long it'll continue to sit there and increase in strength before moving inland. Conflicting prediction models."

He leans toward me and admits that he wishes he'd had a chance to check on his sailboat. I say that at least it's on a floating dock. He nods and points around the courtyard. "I'm sorry, Frank, but we're going to have to move the pigeons inside your apartment. I'll show you how. Let's go."

He closes a small shutter door on the front of one house and reaches below it to pull a pin. The house detaches, and he pulls it up by a handle. He does the same to a second. I start on another and realize I can handle only one at a time. We carry them against the wind up the fire escape stairway and set them in the back of my room. Soon we have all seven pigeon houses upstairs.

When we come back into the office, Névé asks Kit how she can help.

Kit puts his hands on his hips and considers the question for all of us. "Frank told me that we're in for a hurricane. Well, that'll be an experience. I've never been in one. Have either of you?"

Névé looks at me, and I look at her. Then we both look at Kit. "You've never been through a hurricane? We were hoping you'd have this all under control." I smile.

"Nope. Lived here two years, and we've had several good storms but not a direct hit from a hurricane." He clears his throat and straightens his posture. I guess that we've put pressure on him to put up a good front. He's a tall man, and his long fingers grip his hips, indenting his olive-colored Real Carrier shirt. The collar has become wet. Water glistens on his black skin, and in his hair the drops sparkle. He says that he has a good idea what to do. He reminds us that the New French Quarter isn't far above sea level, so a good storm surge will flood the lower level.

Névé considers her dogs and shudders. "I'd better take them outside for a minute."

"Good idea. There's some grass on the back patio. The wall is still a wind block. Frank and I will move the NetLink upstairs." He still has his hands on his hips and looks thoughtful for a few seconds. "Frank, let's start in the garage. I have a couple of jacks and some blocks that we can use to raise the van. Maybe it'll be enough to save it. Also, there is a piece of plywood for the front window. Then we'll move inside for the evening. We'll close the shutters on the second floor last. That can be done from the inside." He rubs his chin, probably considering what he might have forgotten. "Névé, after you take care of the dogs, you'll find some food and supplies in the kitchenette that we should take upstairs, and you could start moving them. Also, fill any empty containers with water. You'll find the stairs out back."

We all go to work.

MEN/A TRIAL, ROUND ONE

Ember shuffled into the kitchen for breakfast. He sat at the table and rubbed his eyes. Claret bent over him and rebuttoned his shirt. He had a hard time lining up each button with the right hole. Seeing the NetLink screen, he asked, "Why's it on already?"

"I was watching the news about a storm brewing in the Gulf of Mexico, and also this morning begins the Mensa Blackmon murder trial that Jade is a juror for. It's a special trial, and she was fortunate to get picked, so we need to leave her alone in her room. OK?"

He nodded. Claret poured Nearly Dairy over the Rainbow Treasure cereal that she'd set out for him. The cereal began sparkling, and Ember stirred it around in the bowl to increase the sparkles. He and Claret listened to the show and ate their cereals.

The Trial Entertainment Network showed a video feed of the studio, with two men and two women ready to act as commentators. All were dressed in shades of gray and black. Claret wondered if they were trying to foster a feeling of solemnity. The wall behind them displayed the courtroom. One of the men introduced the sponsor.

"The Mensa Blackmon murder trial is sponsored this morning by Arctic Cruises. Cruise over the North Pole next summer and celebrate the solstice in style! And we are brought to you by Wise Consumer Foods in fond memory of Jerzeybell, who will be back bigger and better before the end of the year. For those who want to visit Jerzeybell Two, plan your trip now. Tickets may sell out, so book your pilgrimage today."

The video feed focused on one of the women. She was light skinned and had long black hair and bright-blue eyes.

"Good day to our viewers across the globe. For those who are just tuning in, the attorneys have arrived at the courthouse in Houston. The Mensa Blackmon murder trial promises to be one of the entertainment spectacles of the year that you won't want to miss. The uncertain outcome guarantees us hours of suspense and surprise."

The camera feed switched to a handsome blond man in a navy-blue suit. "That's right, Sapphire. The current defendant is Mensa Blackmon's longtime companion, Mensa Carmen Darnelle. But the case against Mensa Darnelle is considered weak. And during the course of this trial, and as testimony is given, a new defendant could be named. Some of the potential suspects can be found on Mensa-trial-NAUS-WorldNet along with their odds. Betting will begin as soon as the judge sounds the gavel. Wagers may be placed on nearly all aspects of the trial. Trial Entertainment Network ensures fair odds, guaranteed by our third-party auditors. All bets placed by the one thousand jurors participating in this trial are available to the public in real time, and more than ninety percent of money wagered is returned to viewers as earnings. Win big, and make your wagers today's wages!"

The camera focused on the second man, who was of Asian ancestry. "Thank you, Sol, and a good morning to everyone. We know that this is an early hour for those of you on the West Coast, but today promises to be an interesting one in a trial that is touted as the trial of the year and maybe the trial of the decade. This case has so many unknowns that we're sure to be in for some surprises."

The second woman began to address the audience. She was the color of dark caramel and had runway-model looks. "That's right, Steel. We can't even be certain that the current defendant will remain the defendant. The outcome might change suddenly and dramatically with any of the witnesses' testimonies."

The first man began speaking again. "Let me recap for our viewers the situation, as the attorneys make preparations for the trial to begin. Six months ago, Mensa Blackmon was found dead from a stab wound in the apartment that he shared with Mensa Darnelle, who found the body and claims to have been in another room and heard nothing. She was named the prime suspect in the murder, primarily because no other suspects were identified. Speculation is that she had no alibi and a probable motive that has yet to be revealed."

The camera shot went back to Sapphire. "And what can you tell us, Sol, about Mensa Blackmon's story?"

Claret admired the network's ability to keep the pace up when nothing was happening. The camera was back on Sol, and he leaned in toward the camera and spoke slowly, as if disclosing the plot of a complicated mystery novel. "Mensa Blackmon came to national attention last year when he led a team of the brightest minds, who were able to demonstrate something unprecedented in human history. The team conducted research on millions of people and concluded decisively, after rigorous statistical analysis, that the alleged benefits of the world's religions were strictly a result of scientifically determinable parameters such as dietary restrictions, stress relief, abstinence from unhealthy habits, and other regimens dictated by devotees—"

Claret turned off the show, stood up, and began to clear off the table, putting the dishes in the sink. "OK, Ember, we don't want to be late. It's time to head to the bus stop. Do you have your jacket and lunch?"

He nodded and jumped out of his chair. They put their jackets on and left the apartment. The forecast and the low-hanging gray sky promised wet weather. Few people were out on the streets. Claret wondered how many were watching the Blackmon trial. TEN had hyped it for weeks.

Claret knew what Ember was going to say before he said it. "I wish I could watch the show with you."

"I'm glad you'll be at school. I don't know what kind of details they'll drag up. You're better off studying."

"Are you going to watch it?"

"Only for a while, and then I have work to do. I can let you know what happens after school. If there's an exciting part, we can play it back, OK?"

He nodded but didn't seem satisfied. "Why can't I study at home like a lot of kids do?"

"I think you're better off getting to know other kids, and I have to work. I spend most of the day at my desk, and Jade will be at hers with the trial. I have a job, and your job is to go to school. It's good for you, and you'll thank me when you're older—maybe." She smiled.

He smiled back as the bus pulled up. "It's OK, Mom. Bye."

Before she returned to the building, rain fell from an ashen sky. The day was so dark that the streetlights came on.

Claret went into her office, which was also her bedroom, and turned on the trial. She half concentrated on a piece that she was writing and half watched the trial, turning toward it when something caught her attention. The courtroom was traditional: wood paneling, a small area of spectator seating behind tables for the attorneys and the defendant, which were across from the judge's bench. Ads ran along the bottom of the screen, as well as betting odds and options. Blackmon's physician was on the witness stand and must have been for a few minutes. Those who bet he would be on the stand for less than five minutes would have no winnings. The payout for others was mounting the longer he stayed on. The prosecutor asked him questions.

"Doctor, can you explain for the court how Mr. Blackmon became Mensa Blackmon?"

The doctor was a middle-aged, overweight white man. "Certainly. Mr. Blackmon made a very large sum of money running an import-export business in exotic meats. He said that he'd always wanted to become a Mensa, and now he could afford it. That was twelve years ago. So after

194

screening him to make sure that he was an appropriate candidate, I prescribed the usual cocktail of drugs that induces the enhanced mental and physical capabilities."

"And did he respond as expected?"

"Yes, very well. His IQ soon exceeded one seventy-five."

"And to your knowledge, was he functioning as he should?"

"Yes, certainly. He was my patient for twelve years, and he was a success story when he turned his intellect to the political arena and social issues."

"OK, thank you, Doctor. That will be all from the prosecution."

The defense attorney rose and approached the witness stand. Odds on testimony time continued to scroll along the bottom of Claret's screen. An inset picture showed the defendant, who appeared to be wiping away tears with a tissue.

"Dr. Fryer, you've stated that you were Mensa Blackmon's doctor for twelve years."

"That's correct."

"Did you know that Mensa Blackmon had been supplementing the drugs you prescribed with other drugs prescribed by a Dr. Lee?"

The prosecution stood. "Objection! No witness named Dr. Lee is scheduled to appear. Where did this Dr. Lee come from?"

The judge banged his gavel to quiet the courtroom audience. "Defense counsel, explain yourself."

"Your Honor, Dr. Lee has left the country and cannot appear in court. We will hear about him from Mensa Darnelle when it is her time to testify. I have the documents that verify Dr. Lee's whereabouts and his prescriptions."

The judge banged the gavel one more time. Claret suspected that it helped keep the viewing audience awake.

"Proceed."

"Dr. Fryer, did you know that Mensa Blackmon had doubled the recommended dosage of the Mensa drugs?"

Dr. Fryer flushed and used a tissue to wipe sweat from his forehead. He took a few seconds to answer. "No. I had no knowledge of his taking more than the medications that I prescribed."

"And is that because you hadn't seen him for several months?"

"I'm not sure when I saw him last. I don't recall."

"Your records show that you hadn't seen him for eight months before his death. Is that typical for your Mensa patients?"

"No. I don't know what happened."

"I do. Your records show that his medications were provided without the requisite visit. So you don't actually know what his mental condition was within eight months of his death, do you, Dr. Fryer?"

"No, I don't."

"Isn't it true, Doctor, that too much Mensa medication can push an individual over an edge into mental instability?"

"Yes, with some. What typically happens, though, is that they begin making intuitive leaps that normal human minds don't follow and that can't be confirmed by data."

"Thank you, Doctor. That will be all."

The four commentators came back on, buzzing about the unexpected development in Mensa Blackmon's medical history. Betting odds and winnings scrolled quickly across the screen while the network broke for commercials as the next witness, Blackmon's housekeeper, was queued up. Claret had work to do, and she turned the trial off, reluctantly. She could catch up on it later because she couldn't seem to multitask this morning.

WEATHERING THE STORM

For three hours, we sit in the upstairs apartment and listen to rain and wind pound against the shutters. The electricity has stayed on, and the weather has gradually worsened. Kit sits in the desk chair. Névé and I are on opposite ends of the bed. María is stretched out on the floor with her eyes open, but Jesús wants to be in Névé's lap. He gives her a lick under the chin.

I consider the pair of them. "Jesús says he loves you," I say to Névé.

"He's my baby." She strokes him nearly constantly, as if he were a talisman. Sometimes she gives him a kiss on the top of his head. The lamp on the table behind Névé lights her hair, and they resemble a comic version of a Madonna painting from the Middle Ages, only in silver instead of gold.

Kit leans back in the desk chair, and it creaks loudly enough to be heard above the wind and rain. He points to Névé's wrist and speaks up to be heard. "Your PAL hasn't been turned on since you've been here. Why?"

Névé strokes Jesús under his neck and takes a few seconds to answer. "I'm avoiding a couple of cousins and their attorney." She explains that they are trying to get a subpoena for her detainment to force her to talk with them. The latest instructions from her attorney, Jahn, are to avoid talking with them until he can get a temporary decision from a judge.

I ask Névé why her cousins want to talk to her so badly, and she gives us more of her story in a faltering way as though she's making a confession.

She repositions Jesús on her lap and rubs his chest. "I lived with them from the time my mother was killed in an accident at a Sugar Queen plant when I was ten, until August, when I turned eighteen. I wore a Sugarstik tattoo ever since I can remember and was an exclusive Sugarstik walking ad. They relied on the royalty income." She moves Jesús again and crosses her legs. "On my eighteenth birthday, I inherited some money that they didn't know about, and it gave me a way to get out of being a Sugarstik."

When she turns to address Kit, her profile with Jesús at her chest makes me want to laugh in one of those moments of inappropriate humor. I manage to keep a straight face.

"I gave them some money and had my tattoo and ID chip removed and the color of my irises changed. Then I left. Now they're demanding more money, and according to Jahn, Sugar Queen is suing me for breach of contract. He's looking into how they'd have any legal claims because I never signed a contract."

Kit raises one eyebrow and leans forward. I wonder why he is so interested in her background, unless he's trying to distract us from the weather outside, which sounds like a massive catfight. "You didn't, but your mother may have. Did you know your father?"

The wind slaps something against the shutters. "No. I have no idea who he is."

Kit interlocks the fingers of his hands on the desk. "And are you albino? Is that why you're so light?"

She nods.

"Well then, if your mother had a gene for albinism, she may have been paid to produce an albino girl from a sperm bank of donors with albinism. She'd have made a good sum of money. Sugarstik probably has an investment in you beyond your understanding." Kit inhales and looks as if he might add something, but then he closes his lips.

Névé turns her head toward the window for a few seconds. Her thoughts may have wandered into the past. I'm wondering if her mother could have been a surrogate mother and not even her biological mother at all. Maybe that's what Kit didn't say. Névé seems even paler than she normally is.

"That would explain some things. I didn't know companies were doing that."

"Not many people do. Part of the contract with the mothers is a secrecy agreement."

"How do you know about such things?"

Kit doesn't say anything at first. "I'm part of a group that makes it our business to know what corporations are up to."

"What group is that?"

"I'd rather not say."

She gets up off the bed and walks around, restless. "I was with a group called the Flames in Chicago."

"Ah, yes. Christians," Kit says.

Névé barely nods. "I think my brother, Jona, had some connection to the Flames before he was killed. I saw their symbol, among others, on his WritingWall."

"Interesting." Kit stands up, goes over to the window, and tries to look through the slats of the shutter and down on the street, but I doubt he can see anything. I think he's considering what exactly he wants to say. "Some friends and I speculate the dam breaks in Austin were not the result of a foreign hattack."

"Then what happened?"

"The publicly available information points to an obvious explanation. The dams broke because they were not maintained, and money wasn't available to keep them safe. But there is another hypothesis, one that I favor." He rolls his chair around to the front of the desk, closer to Névé and me. Névé sits back down, and he sits, bending forward with his elbows on his knees. "Austin has become a hotbed of subversive groups ranging from religious to environmental, like the Seven Sisters, to political, like the neo-Marxists." A rattling of the back door stirs up the pigeons, but they settle down quickly, having little free space in their houses. "They all want to revise the current form of capitalism because they feel either persecuted or enslaved; however, challenges to the system are labeled 'subversion' by the governing boards. Whoever felt the most threatened by these groups might have seen an opportunity to wash Austin clean with a flood. And one way to do that is to have an apparent and *explicable* failure of the dams."

Névé and I are quiet. I expect that Kit isn't finished. "My ancestors came from Africa, where the population still suffers from the vestiges of colonialism. The same type of exploitation is happening to us here. We're colonial citizens for the wealthy."

Névé rubs the shadow of her Sugarstik tattoo. "All of us are?"

"Yes, in various ways. You are because your body was an advertisement for eighteen years." He pauses, maybe allowing her and me to consider how colonialism could be individual.

And then Névé adds an insight that Uncle Orion would have understood. "Marta said that the tattoo was, as she called it, 'yet another violation of the temple because our bodies are temples.'"

I once heard Uncle Orion claim that Earth is a temple and that someone needs to drive out the money-changers. At the time, I let the comment pass, as I did with many of his other rantings. But now I see the connection within the context that Marta comes from. I haven't thought of the exploitation in quite this way before, as personal as what Névé experienced.

Kit raises his hands, gesticulating in his excitement and using them in the conversation like a Lakota medicine man drawing in the unseen. "And this new system of buying votes is a prime example of undermining democracy. When individuals sell their votes to voting blocs, they become colonial citizens, authoring their own subjection. We can't eat freedom, so people sell their votes, and the voting blocs run the political system that sets policies."

Kit adds more volume to his voice to be heard over the rain, which sounds like gravel pelting the shutters. "You've probably seen Jeremi Duende on the news. We think he was one of the people they hoped might disappear in the flood, but he didn't. I suspect he's not really a subversive but happens to have connections in his organization to all these groups. They all have a reason to want change, so they band together in a common cause."

He pulls a cigar from his shirt pocket and asks us if we mind. We say no, so he lights it and takes a draw. He's on a roll, and I want to hear what he's thinking. He's been an enigma to me since I've been here: a native African, running a Real Carrier office, which couriers more than letters. Upon exhale, the smoke lingers around his head and begins to drift toward the back. I hadn't realized we had that much of a draft. He continues his revelations.

"You'll be going to a very interesting community, Névé, or what's left of it, which is quite a bit from what I can tell from the Real Carrier traffic. Their activity was stifled for only a couple of weeks after the flood. Now it's resurging like flowers after a desert rainstorm."

For a few seconds, we listen to the wind and rain. I consider my situation and see an opportunity for Névé to help me. She might. I did rescue her, in a way, earlier today. I ask her, "Névé, do you think that you'll have contact with any of these groups?"

"Maybe, if I find some of Jona's friends. According to a search I did, this guy Duende attended his memorial service. And in our last conversation, Jona did refer to himself and his friends as rogues. I don't know much else."

Kit rubs his chin. "Can you describe the symbols that you saw on Jona's wall?"

She closes her eyes as though she is trying to visualize the images from months ago. "The ones I remember are the flame, which is a circle with a caret over it, then something that may have been a dagger. There was a six-pointed star, a crescent, and a number like three fifteen. I think. I'm not sure what else."

"And do you know which of them he was associating with?"

"No. I've no idea. Only that he was in some way associating with Duende."

"Those are diverse groups. And many don't want to be found."

"I see." Névé then turns to me. "Why did you ask about whether I would have contact with them?"

I'm having trouble forming the words to make the admission. "I have information that subversive groups like the Seven Sisters would be interested in. My uncle and I worked on a scientific theory that the NAUS Board probably doesn't want made public yet."

Both of them—and even Jesús—have their eyes locked on me, waiting for what I'm going to say. I explain that my uncle had a unique approach to a theory that could lead to much cleaner and cheaper energy. He was angry at what was happening to the planet and wanted to see an end to what he called a consumption society. I tell them how he used to say, "The pigs are running the farm," and how he wanted to undermine the NAUS leadership by publishing his work globally so that they wouldn't monopolize it first. Also, I want his work published so he receives his rightful recognition, and I'm willing to risk my life to get it out. I pause, thinking about how to proceed, but I just say what I'm thinking anyway. "I need it out by multiple routes because I may not survive when the CBI finds me."

At first, Névé sits blinking, just staring at me. I assume she's trying to take in what I've just disclosed. "They would kill you for what you know?"

"I don't doubt it. I think they killed my uncle, Dr. Orion Rising." I straighten and wait to see if she recognizes the name, but her expression doesn't change. I speak now with more confidence and more volume. "I want it published, and I could use your help getting it out, but you must know the risk you might be taking. I don't see why they'd deliberately try to harm you because you don't know the science, but they might do whatever they can to eliminate any copies."

Névé stares at the floor in front of her and strokes Jesús's head. She kisses the top of it. "Who would I need to give it to?"

"I'm not sure. That's part of the problem. Uncle Orion was the one who went to conferences and talked with his colleagues. I haven't been able to contact the one I do know without risking revealing my location, and I'm sure he's being closely watched." I explain how not just any physicist can judge the value of the science, so it has to go to someone who is familiar with the area. Also, I'm concerned about whoever gets it selling it to the NAUS Board before it goes global. "What needs to happen is for it to be posted on the WorldNet so that scientists everywhere can evaluate it." I stop to think for a few seconds and then turn to Kit. "Do you have a suggestion?"

Kit blows out another exhale and leans back in the chair, smiling. "Well now, ladies, aren't we three an improbable assembly?"

I notice his calling us ladies and wonder if Névé does. After a few seconds of wind and rain filling the conversation void, she answers. "Improbable, but not impossible. My friend Marta in Chicago would say that Providence is at work. And Frank—is your name really Frank?"

Reading Névé's body language, I can tell that she's not pulling away. "I'm wanted by the CBI because of my uncle's work. Are you sure that you want to be involved?"

She thinks about it for a few seconds. "I'm sure. If I get into the group or groups that Jona was involved in, and if I decide I like them and want to be a part of whatever he was up to, this might be something I can do for them." I sense that she has a need to belong to something, which is not surprising given her background that she's shared with us. She crosses her legs again on the bed. Unfortunately, she doesn't forget about the question of my name. "If you're not a Frank, then who are you?"

If she's willing to take a risk for me, then I'll risk disclosure to her. She needs to know what she's getting herself into. "I'm Incense. Incense Rising." I extend my hand with a smile as if we are meeting for the first time. "I've gained some notoriety lately. You may have seen the CBI wanted bulletins on me."

We all jump when something large slams against one of the shutters, but the window holds. For the first time, I begin to feel a sense of fear that this apartment might not be secure. I don't see how the window will survive a harder blow, and I imagine the water outside rising higher and swirling.

"I'm willing to help," Névé says.

"The CBI may come looking for anyone who had recent contact with me."

She nods. "Maybe. But I'm already avoiding being found. I'll hand it off as soon as I can. Tell me what I can do."

After another object slaps against one of the shutters, Kit says that we may lose power soon. Earlier, we laid candles, a lighter, and a couple of flashlights on his desk. Now each of us scans the room as if we're committing the position of each object to memory so that it can be found in the darkness.

I take one flashlight, set it next to me, and then pull my backpack from under the bed. "My PortAble is fully charged, and so am I." I have our recent work on the theory reproduced, but if a copy is going with Névé, I need to add notes explaining how it might be concluded. I had intended some final work, which I won't get to now. That's OK. I'd rather Névé not hang around here but be gone with most of it and an explanation for its intended conclusion and application.

The thought occurs to me that the noise from the storm now sounds exactly like a crowd pounding to get in. The wind begins a high-pitched howling, and so does María, as the lights go out.

AN UNLIKELY
COURIER

The morning after the storm, wind and rain continue, although not in the raging fit of the previous night. With the shutters closed, we have no idea what the night has brought. We all tried to doze off and on, which wasn't easy with the racket going on outside. When daylight starts seeping through the slats, Kit opens the back door and surveys the damage.

"We're flooded, but not too much. I can see standing water up to the first step." He looks toward the garage. "I think the van should be dry." He closes the door and comes over to the table where Névé and I are collaborating on where to incorporate a couple of memory chips that will contain Uncle Orion's theoretical work. Kit continues. "I'll work on opening the shutters. Not much else we can do right now." He raises an upper window and unlatches the shutter. Opening it wide, he fastens it against the building and then does the same to the rest of the upper-story windows. The room brightens with every shutter that he opens, and so does my mood. Then he puts on a raincoat and heads out the back door.

Névé considers the dogs, who haven't been out all night. "I wonder how long the water will take to drain."

I say I don't know and finish attaching one of the memory chips to an unlikely place for something important.

***

By midmorning, the water recedes, leaving a soggy, muddy mess, and we start to clean up. During the afternoon, a more penitent rain falls and begins washing the mud from the feet of the city. By evening, the pigeon houses are back in the yard and the office floor has been hosed down. Electricity must have evacuated well inland because it hasn't returned by late afternoon. Itinerants and residents wander the street, checking on others or just snooping. I hope that we don't end up fighting off looters. At least we're an office that isn't likely to have much that people want.

We three sit around the desk on the ground floor and drink warm sodas.

I know I have circles under my eyes; I saw them in the bathroom mirror. Kit asks me if I have what I need for Névé's help. I say that I think so. Three different memory chips are squirreled away, one on each of the travelers who will leave here on the next train out.

I'm not the only one looking tired. Kit's eyes are red, and he has bits of dirt in his hair. I've wondered how old he is but have never asked. My guess is thirty-five. He leans forward across the desk. "How else might you be able to get this out?"

I've been thinking about just that question. Nothing says that Névé will get Orion's theory to someone who can publish it. "I've thought about posting through an anonymous WorldNet link, although it can still be traced to a general area. But Uncle Orion believed the government has technology to block or erase something seconds after posting, and certainly they can block Net-mail containing key words or symbols."

Kit shakes his head. "We could take the information and drive somewhere hours away and post it. Or we could deliver memory chips by Real Carrier."

I hold his gaze but tear up. I'm touched by his willingness to help. I tell him that, even with doing that, I can't stay. I've been around too many cameras, and I think that a resident down the street is suspicious because of the way he looks at me. I'm going to have to move on soon or get the theory out.

***

By the following morning, the electricity works its way back to the Real Carrier office. I listen to Névé's brief conversation with her friends in Chicago. She assures Jahn and Marta that she's fine. I imagine their love and relief for Névé, and I realize how much I miss my family. I start thinking that when I leave New Orleans, which I know I need to do soon, I could head in that direction, although there is no way I can show up there unnoticed. I wonder what Rigel and my dad are going through. Have they been questioned? Any further attempts to contact them will certainly be tracked. I'll need multiple disguises to get anywhere. The sooner the information is out, the safer I'll be. I hope that then I won't be worth the hunt anymore and that the CBI will cancel the reward.

Kit has been out in the van and returns with the news that the first train heading west is in the midafternoon. Névé gets herself and the dogs ready to be on it. I don't want to be seen with her, so I say goodbye in the office. I reiterate something that I've told her before. "Névé, please don't take any risks to yourself just to get the theory out. Destroy it if you have to. I'll be trying other ways."

Névé nods. "Even if I was seen coming into the shop, I don't know why anyone would suspect me of being a courier of a scientific theory."

I'm not so naive, and I tell her that I have no doubt they'll make the connection in time and assume the worst—that she may have a copy. I recommend that she keep her location unknown for as long as she can, although I know she has to check in with her attorney.

She doesn't seem worried.

I make one final request. "If I don't survive, can you contact my father and brother and tell them that I was thinking about them and did want to get home? And give them my love?" I tell her where she can find them in Dakota. I have also told her that they have a possible way to help get the theory out if she has any problems.

She nods and says that she is so glad the storm delayed her here.

I suggest that she reserve judgment until she sees how this all works out.

Kit had remained silent but now offers his opinion to Névé. "You're probably not the first trail they'll follow up on." Then he turns to me. "Maybe we should consider how to make other diversions—false trails that they'd want to follow."

I nod and ask what he has in mind, although I'm not sure I'll stay long enough to do much.

"We can discuss it after Névé leaves. Let's keep her as innocent as we can."

Névé gives me a hug. "Which I need to do—leave, or you'll have me for another night." She and the dogs go out the back and down an alley, where Kit says there is no video surveillance—that he knows of.

WILL POTTER

"Morning, team. I'm Potter, Will Potter. I'm on only my second cup of coffee, so pardon my slowness. I was pleased to hear that the price of coffee will be going down with our successful annexation of Central America. It should have been part of the NAUS deal in the first place. Looks like they've learned that freedom isn't free. It has to be bought and paid for by financial security. Speaking of which, it's time to get an update on Project Wildfire. I imagine you were pretty excited when Bing went to corporate acquisitions and your group aligned with Milk Products."

"I think *puzzled* would be a better adjective," said Rigel. "What is the synergy between Milk Products and New Marketing? Milk products are as old as cows."

"And the business is as successful, too. But you make a very good point, Mr...."

"Rising."

"And your first name is?"

"Rigel."

"Well, Rigel Rising, Milk Products is a highly successful, long-established business. We know how to optimize organizational structure, and we have the money to fund the project if we want. We don't have to rush into anything now."

With a rising pitch in her voice, signaling her frustration, Ursala said,

"Wildfire is just getting started. We'll need additional financing and time to make it successful."

"Oh yes, we understand that. And Project Wildfire will be given time to squeeze out profits, so just keep doing what you're doing to make it successful. We'll be making some organizational substitutions, though. We have teams in Milk Products that know how to implement new-product introductions. Just last year, we successfully launched Nearly Dairy, which I'm sure you're familiar with—the dairy product that doesn't require a cow for production. It's a breakthrough in bioengineering. And then last month, we launched Sirius Milk—a tasty drink, genetically engineered from an alternative milk source that is high in nutritional value and flavor. So you see, something like Project Wildfire will be a natural fit for our crew. Did that answer your question, Rigel Rising?"

"I'm not sure that I agree with the logic, but I don't have to."

Claret wondered what the organizational realignment meant specifically for the team, and she asked Will if any of them would be changing jobs.

"I'm glad you asked that question, since it's the main item on my agenda this morning. I'm moving Virgil to work on Sirius Milk and bringing in a veteran who helped launch Nearly Dairy. Her name is Aries Smith."

Virgil hunched his shoulders and leaned toward the camera. "But this project was my idea and has been my baby for the past few weeks. No one will champion it the way I have. I don't want a different project." He had visibly reddened.

Will's face remained expressionless. "As you well know, Virgil, projects have different phases, and we all have to be flexible and accept redeployment for the good of the company. Now that Wildfire is moving into the next phase, we need some adjustments."

Virgil's look of shock had turned into a scowl. "What phase is that, Will Potter? The successful phase? When it begins churning revenue, no one will remember who started it."

"Not at all. Because of your success here, you'll be given important projects. That's how you should view this move—as an opportunity. Now, moving on, I want to tie in Aries to explain how we will get the budget under control and revenues up." A woman's face replaced Virgil's as one of the camera feeds. Aries appeared to be middle-aged and a heavy user of cosmetics. Gold owls dangled from her hoop earrings.

Will kept his momentum going. "Good afternoon, Aries. I just set the stage with the team and told them that you will be explaining our plans to make Wildfire profitable."

"Hi, team! I'm Aries, and I'm delighted to join this team at such a critical phase. We'll be able to turn Wildfire into a profitable product with the following plans to control costs."

No one said anything for several seconds. For Claret, the silence spoke louder than words.

Aries continued. "Well, let's get to it then, shall we? One of the first changes I'd like to propose is a project name change. *Wildfire* sounds a bit too chaotic for Milk Products. I suggest you're the *Cream Team* because we'll consolidate roles and rise to the top with this success. And I know just the organizational changes that we need to make. I have an extensive background in both marketing and finance, so Ursala will be fortunate enough to be moving to Nearly Dairy. I'll manage the marketing and the financials, and we'll leverage other skills from the Milk Products Division, like science and engineering. Also, Claret and Rigel will have additional responsibilities on Sirius Milk, so their time will be only partially on the Cream Team. I'll be working with each of you over the next few days to adjust your responsibilities. Any questions?"

Rigel's text to Claret: Vid-chat in a few?

Claret: :-)

Claret felt so relieved that she would be retaining work and possibly picking up more hours that she gladly accepted the recommendations from Aries regarding her action items.

Rigel called Claret a few minutes later. "Can I come over in a few days? I could use some new scenery."

She knew this question might come at some point, but it still caught her by surprise that he might actually come all the way to Seattle to see her. She hesitated, but not too long. "Yes, although as I've warned you, my life is complicated."

"And like I've said, so is mine. A train is scheduled for Seattle on Thursday. I can be on it."

"I'll meet you at the station."

TRIP TO AUSTIN

The dogs settled down and went to sleep within minutes of the train leaving New Orleans. They'd had a rough couple of days. María sat on the floor in front of the window seat, which Jesús occupied. The train was almost deserted, so Névé had her choice of seats in coach class. She chose one toward the back and watched while flooded swampland around New Orleans turned into rolling hills. Soon she and the dogs were gliding toward Texas.

A couple of hours outside Houston, the number of large estates increased. Some were miles wide. Architecture and landscaping varied, but all were fenced. According to the scrolling description below her window, the estates were the major employers in the area. They all had life's essentials self-contained: shopping, entertainment, health care, agriculture, a court system, and a militia to ensure security. The information included data showing that citizens who lived within an estate were healthier, happier, and employed. All the descriptions included contact information for applications of employment. The minimum requirements usually included being at least eight years of age, having no physical impairments, and being willing to wear emblems of loyalty, including tattoos. Névé wondered what life would be like in such a community and what happened if someone became ill and more of a burden than a producer. Did the system take care of those people? She might have to consider getting a job in one of these communities at some point. But she'd have to find one that didn't require a tattoo. She was done with those, particularly after Kit's explanation of what they really meant.

In Houston, Névé had to change trains. She had a three-hour layover and exited the train station to find a place for the dogs to stretch their legs. The weather was cool and pleasant in the aftermath of the storm. She found a hot dog stand and treated the dogs and herself to what had become one of their favorite meals. They sat on a bench looking toward the east.

The train station was northwest of the downtown but close enough to see the city skyline. She had read that all the buildings had sturdy framing to protect their glass surfaces from wind damage. There were also few spaces underground because of the area's tendency to flood. The city was gradually migrating westward like an urban glacier. After her experience in the hurricane, she'd decided that she couldn't get west fast enough, and if she didn't like Austin, she'd keep on going west.

While she sat in the station waiting for the train to Austin to arrive, the main topic of conversation among the other passengers was the Mensa Blackmon trial, which was going on in Houston. Between the hurricane and her desire to keep her location unknown, Névé hadn't seen a *News Feed* recently, so she eavesdropped on the conversations. One passenger had been in the audience for the first day of testimony. She described the atmosphere as charged with anticipation as though everyone were on a You-Foria! upper. Unfortunately, the woman had made some poor bets and had only enough money to return home to El Paso.

Another passenger said that he had come to sell memorabilia of the trial, and he ran out in two days because business was so brisk. He was going home to Dallas to manufacture more and was hoping for a long, extended trial. Sometimes conversation focused on speculation as to the identity of the murderer. None believed that Mensa Darnelle was the murderer. A Mensa murderer was so unlikely that betting odds would pay well for anyone who ventured to place a bet that she was the murderer and won. The man headed for Dallas thought that Blackmon had committed suicide, but the woman believed another suspect would be identified because Mensas don't commit suicide.

When the train to Austin rolled into the station, Névé acted visually impaired and asked directions to the right car. This time, the train was mostly full, so she held Jesús and put María at her feet. Fortunately, this final leg of the trip was scheduled to take only four hours.

HORSEBACK RIDER

Rigel's PAL vibrated with a text message. It was from a cousin, Ever Runningbrook.

> Ever: Hey, Rigel. I have a nest of owls to show you. Can you meet me at the valley of the dancing cedars at 2?
>
> Rigel: Yes

Rigel wondered what Ever could want. He hadn't seen Ever for several months, and they hadn't ridden together since they were teens. The Valley of the Dancing Cedars was the local name for a deep cleft between two hills. Ever must have chosen that particular location for a reason, possibly because electronic communication was difficult.

Rigel rode up to the valley from the east. A seasonal stream ran from the west, and today the riverbed was dry. Ever stood under the cedars at the bottom of the V between the rocks, through which a thunderstorm was sighted like a target in the notch of a gun. Rigel took a photo of the scene for future reference. An oil painting of it would sell. He dismounted and led his horse between the cedars. "Beautiful day for a ride, but not for long." He motioned toward the west.

Ever took Rigel's extended hand and pulled him into a hug. "I should have let you know before now how we've been thinking of your family—

and Incense. I think what I have will cheer you up. Got a Real Carrier this morning."

Ever handed Rigel an envelope containing a single-page letter and another envelope. Rigel smelled frankincense. The scent gave him a shock of relief. The letter was brief and dated after her disappearance:

Ever,

Please give to Rigel the enclosed envelope—without anyone knowing. It's very important that he gets this. Then forget you got it and where it came from. Love,

Frank

"Before I opened it, I didn't know who it could possibly be from. And nobody sends me scented letters. But the name Frank brought back that Christmas your family spent in town. She remembered my teasing her."

"I can't tell you how much I appreciate this, Ever. We haven't heard from her for weeks. She didn't think Uncle Orion's death was an accident. She might be right. The CBI's been to our house twice, once to search it."

Ever nodded and patted him on the shoulder. "Let me know if I can do anything to help."

Rigel motioned toward a deep recess. "I think I'll stay right here and open the envelope and then decide what to do with it." He nodded toward the storm. "You better hustle home."

"Right. I'll be off." Ever mounted his horse and galloped off in the direction of the storm.

Rigel sat in the shadows of the recess and opened the envelope. He found a short note dated weeks before.

I want you to know that I'm fine, but I don't know for how long. I expect you'll get a visit from the CBI, if you haven't already. I'm traveling and will be working to rebuild my work with the star and then publish it. If I can't do that directly, I'll send it to Dad to encode on strains for interpretation among the star's friends. But the work is still incomplete. I hope to send the completed version in a few weeks. Love.

The sharp rock edges against his back made him feel alive, and the scent of the paper made Incense alive. His dad would be elated and alarmed. Cadence had loved his brother, Orion, and helped him work out a method of putting information in music that defied traditional decoding so that Orion could communicate with his politically subversive friends. He had called it a musical version of a wolf in a deerskin in Lakota—like a Trojan horse device. Cadence had expressed his concern to both Rigel and Incense and advised them to keep some distance from Orion's activities, but Incense had shrugged it off when she went to work for him. Rigel wondered now what she thought and whether she was in over her head.

MENSA TRIAL, ROUND TWO

Claret turned her monitor on for the first time this morning. She wasn't keen on Ember watching the details of the murder trial, so she had seen him off on the school bus before settling down to drink her morning coffee and catch a recap. The sky had cleared overnight, and their walk to the bus stop had been pleasant. She opened a window to invite in a fall breeze and the living sounds of the city street. On the screen, the trial commentators were speaking.

Sol spoke first. "The Mensa Blackmon murder trial made less progress than expected recently. Would you agree, Candi?"

"Yes, Sol. The surprising disclosure by the defense attorney that Mensa Blackmon had a second, unknown physician, who is unavailable for testimony, caught the prosecution off guard. When his request for an adjournment to review the documents was granted, we knew that he might not call any further witnesses for the rest of the day, and he didn't."

"Sapphire, did you have something to add?"

"Sol, I agree with Candi, but we expect that the revelations will continue to surface today as the attorneys try to uncover the secrets behind the death of one of North America's most prominent Mensas. He was highly influential in a number of board-appointed investigations, including Recommendations for Lunar Utilization; Rationale for Unequal Voting Rights; and the most recent committee, which he led,

Exposing the Fallibility of World Religions. Steel, I believe that you have the lineup of witnesses for today. What can you tell us?"

"Well, Sapphire, as yesterday proved, we can never be sure what to expect. The surprise disclosure of a second doctor and Mensa Blackmon's overmedication kept the oddsmakers busy. The first slated witness is expected to be a colleague from the most recent committee. Odds are that her testimony will be predictable. She is expected to tell us what a brilliant job Mensa Blackmon did leading the team. Since the team's meetings were public, the outcome is well documented. The prosecution is trying to reinforce the brilliant state of Mensa Blackmon's mind in order to undermine any claims by the defendant to the contrary—"

"I'm sorry to interrupt you, Steel, but the first witness is approaching the stand. Is she the colleague you were referring to?"

"Yes, Sapphire, she is."

Claret recognized the prosecuting attorney, who approached a thirty-something woman on the stand. She had close-cropped blond hair and a tattoo on her forehead that Claret didn't recognize.

"Mensa Azul, is this your first time testifying in a trial?"

"Yes, it is."

"Then I should remind you to attempt to keep your language at a common-speak level so that the jury and viewers can understand your testimony."

Mensa Azul smiled. "Yes, I'm used to simplifying to communicate with others."

"Good. I don't know why I even reminded you."

Claret was sure that he did know why. Very little would be left to chance.

"You were on the Exposing the Fallibility of World Religions committee, is that correct?"

"Yes."

"And how did you find Mensa Blackmon's state of mind during the committee meetings?"

"I found him brilliant. He was so intuitive. He knew the answers before the data could even be analyzed, and his predictive intuitions were always accurate. And he was intense. His eyes seemed to see right through everyone and down to the heart of any matter. He was clearly one of the most brilliant Mensas whom I have had the privilege to serve with. The North American United States is poorer for his loss."

"Did he confide in you anything about his relationship with Mensa Darnelle?"

"Very little. He hinted that they were having some problems and that she might move out."

"So his personal life was not going as brilliantly as his professional life. Is that correct?"

"I would say so."

"Thank you, Mensa Azul. I have no more questions at this time."

While the defense attorney prepared to come forward, Claret watched the real-life entertainment down on the street. Someone in a pink gorilla suit danced to music for donations, and an itinerant rummaged through a garbage canister. Hawkers of wares and gamers worked at setting up tables—early birds hoping to catch worms. The smell of funnel cakes drifted in. She pulled her attention back to the screen. The defense attorney acted thoughtful and smiled at the witness.

"Mensa Azul, we understand from your testimony just now that Mensa Blackmon was a brilliant individual during the most recent committee investigation. When was the last time that you spoke with him?"

"The day before he was murdered."

"Really? The day before he was murdered?"

"Yes."

"And what was his state of mind on that day?"

"Well, uh, he was agitated and said that he had been for some time."

"Agitated? About what?"

"He seemed dissatisfied with the conclusions of our committee. He wasn't making a lot of sense. He said that we—the committee—had made a serious error in our logic, which had been brought to his attention by someone named Matthew."

"And what was that error?"

"As I've already said, he wasn't making a lot of sense. He said we hadn't taken into account the weather, or in his words, he said the sun shines on the good and the bad and rain falls on the just and the unjust. I told him that was obvious and asked why he was worrying about something like that."

"What was his explanation?"

"He didn't explain other than to say that he'd been reading the texts that the world religions were based on, the religions we'd collected our data on."

"During the committee's work, had he or anyone else on the committee read any of the focal documents for these religions?"

"No. It wasn't necessary. We collected actual data from adherents of the religions. What the texts say was considered irrelevant to the investigation. We were demonstrating the lack of any substantiated divine intervention or impact of prayer on the wealth and success of those who pray after factoring out quantifiable lifestyle effects, such as diet, stress relievers, and other practices that are dictated by most religions."

"Did he say why he began to read the texts?"

"I think the suggestion came from someone with whom he was corresponding. He said he regretted not having studied the texts sooner so that we could have collected the data differently. But other than the cryptic comment on the weather affecting everyone, he seemed as if he wasn't in a mood to talk." She held up her hand with a raised finger. "No, wait. He did make one other non sequitur comment. He said that even today, weeds are left among the wheat until harvest when they're separated out. What that had to do with the weather affecting everyone, I didn't know. As I said before, he could make these intuitive leaps that were hard to follow. On that particular day, I didn't have time for an explanation, so I told him that I'd call another day, and I wished him the best on his next project."

"Thank you, Mensa Azul. I have no more questions at this time."

The neutral colors of the scene in the courtroom were replaced by today's gaudy colors of the panel. Claret wondered why the commentators had put away the black and gray. Perhaps they weren't getting the ratings they had hoped for and were working harder to grab attention.

"Hello, this is Sol, back with our panel of commentators. The courtroom is taking a brief recess, and so will we in a moment to hear from our corporate sponsors. But before we do, what can you tell us, Steel, about the last testimony from Mensa Azul?"

"Mensa Azul's disclosure of the possible mental instability of Mensa Blackmon did not come as a complete surprise to the oddsmakers. Rumors just after the murder were that he may have suffered from a form of depression and committed suicide, but investigating authorities did not find conclusive evidence, such as a suicide note. This revelation of mental questions was not expected to arise, however, until Mensa Darnelle is questioned, so the timing of the disclosure did come as a shock to many. Bookies are adjusting the odds on outcomes as we speak. Once again, this trial is proving to be full of the unexpected."

"Thank you, Steel. Candi, what can you tell us about the lineup of witnesses for the rest of the day?"

"Well, Sol, we don't expect any further surprises, but this trial continues to prove us wrong. The remaining witnesses are also colleagues who worked with Blackmon on investigations, and they're expected to confirm the brilliance of Mensa Blackmon and support his mental stability in contrast to Mensa Azul's testimony. But who knows? As we've seen, we have no shortage of twists and turns with this trial."

"Thank you, Candi. And now, a word from our sponsors."

Claret turned off the monitor. After the day's testimony, the trial was expected to break for a couple of days. She had work to do.

VIRTUAL MEMORIAL

Névé was finally nearing Austin. Weather-related repairs had caused a long delay an hour out of Houston, but now she was closer to her goal. Now that she was in the greater Austin area, she risked turning on her PAL. She owed her attorney a call and figured at some point she would be traceable to Texas. She hadn't read Jona's Net-memorial since she started her trip south. And today, she wanted to leave a message. Today would have been his twenty-fifth birthday. Some of his friends must have put the memorial together. The background was his favorite shade of blue: a deep-ocean, violet blue. Many people had left comments. Most said how they missed him. She couldn't read it for long without crying. She scrolled through the comments. Most were signed with only initials that were usually followed by a variety of symbols. The most common one looked like a dagger pointed down (†). Some had the dagger pointing sideways or up. Others had two wavy lines (≈≈) or the flame (ô). A less common one was a barbed *J*. She kept the note short.

I love you, Jona. Happy birthday. I'll be in Austin soon, even though I know you're not there. I'll feel closer to you if I can find your friends.
Love you always, N.

For a minute, she worried again about having made herself traceable, but then Marta's influence surfaced in her thoughts. She could almost hear her saying that things will work out for Névé's good. Marta had seemed so sure of it.

When the train arrived in Austin, she removed the dark glasses, dropping the pretense of visual impairment, which was a relief. The late afternoon turned into a clear evening. She felt as if she needed a long nap, but the dogs were restless after hours on a train. She walked them around until exhaustion led her to find a pet-friendly hotel near the station. She could have immediately gone to bed but instead spent the evening considering where to go the next day. Austin Memorial Lake was high on the list.

From the hotel window, four floors up, she could see the lake. A windless evening made the water a mirror. It looked to be on fire, reflecting the flaming orange colors of the sunset. The tops of a few buildings protruded through the water and reflected the orange glow as though consumed by fire on a sea of glass. But she imagined the water below the surface as cold and dark and littered with human debris.

MENSA BLACKMON TRIAL, ROUND THREE

Claret already had a sandwich made for Jade and some soda on ice when Jade came out of her bedroom, on break from the trial. She sat down at the table and slumped, propping her chin on her hand and rubbing her eyes. "Thanks. I'm starved."

Claret asked her, "How do you feel about the trial?"

"Exhausted. It's grueling. I could take more breaks, but I like to hear what the commentators are adding and how the wagers are going. You've been watching this morning?"

"Not for long. I had work to do, and it's hard to concentrate on both."

"You have to tune in after lunch."

"Why? Who's testifying?" Claret took a bite of her own sandwich and wished that she could afford a more tender cut of beef.

"Mensa Darnelle."

Claret's eyebrows raised into the orange ringlets that had fallen on her forehead. "I thought they might not put her on the stand because she's the defendant."

"And miss out on her entertainment value? No way. Betting's been heavy on what she'll say. Odds are she wasn't very aware of his mental state. He was keeping to himself, and she was getting ready to move out. She'd signed a new lease. Her new landlord testified this morning she'd told him everything was fine but she just wanted a change of scenery."

"Sounds like they're dragging in everyone they can think of."

"This afternoon may be critical. She's the one person who hasn't testified and might have a clue who killed him—if she didn't." Jade's PAL buzzed. "Gotta go. At least I'm getting a lot of hours out of this one. See you later." She picked up her sandwich and soda and left.

Claret turned on the kitchen monitor. The usual four talking heads exchanged commentary like a ball at a doubles tennis match. Somehow they seemed to know who would speak next, so they never got in each other's way.

Steel spoke first. "At the Mensa Blackmon trial this afternoon, we're anticipating the long-awaited witness, the defendant, Mensa Darnelle. Sapphire, can you tell us what the oddsmakers are expecting in Darnelle's testimony?"

"Certainly, Steel. Expectations are that Mensa Darnelle will point to other explanations for Blackmon's murder. She is expected to name other potential suspects—although authorities have found no other credible leads—and she will probably suggest suicide as a possibility."

"That would be a rather risky move, wouldn't it, Sapphire? After all, Mensas are known to gain a euphoric sense of wellness and unlimited capabilities. None to date has noted depression or attempted suicide."

"Although that's true, some have wondered if Mensa Roja's death might have been a veiled suicide, for a Mensa couldn't be dumb enough to step in front of a truck."

It must have been Sol's turn to volley. "No, Sapphire, I believe the cause of that action was attributed to her being in an argument on her PAL."

"Yes, Sol, that is totally correct. There has never been a verified suicide of a Mensa, and with no other suspects, Mensa Darnelle remains in the hot seat."

Candi raised her palm as if to call the ball hers. "But would they give a Mensa the death penalty?"

Claret wondered if Sapphire was today's designated team captain. "Well, Candi, we're in uncharted waters here. There are no precedents, but they probably would not because Mensas are so valuable to society. Her movements would probably be monitored, and she would continue to work on government investigations under some kind of probation with surveillance. They are truly a special breed of human."

Sol raised his hand for a pause. "I hate to interrupt this interesting discussion, but Mensa Darnelle has just taken the stand. Betting closes in ten seconds. Let's go back to the courtroom."

The prosecutor approached a woman on the stand. She had short black hair and a pale, gaunt appearance.

"Mensa Darnelle, you were a longtime companion of Mensa Blackmon, is that correct?"

"Yes."

"How would you characterize your relationship with Mensa Blackmon before his death?"

"Strained."

"And why was it strained?"

"His behavior had become irrational."

"In what way?"

"The irrational behavior manifested itself in a number of ways. He referred to people who didn't exist, he had wild dreams, and he made crazy claims."

"How and when did this behavior begin?"

"It began with his reading some ancient texts."

"Which texts?"

"I don't know. I didn't care and didn't ask. I do know that they related to the religion-debunking committee that he led because he said he felt they needed to reopen the investigation and reconsider the conclusion."

"We learned from the defense counsel that Mensa Blackmon was, at least on occasion, double-dosing the Mensa drugs. Were you aware of this?"

"Yes."

"Was he double-dosing drugs at the time of his death?"

"He was when he came to the conclusion that they'd made an error."

"Can you please explain for us the other symptoms that you mentioned, especially the ones that led to a strained relationship?"

"He claimed to be having dreams. I knew he was losing his grip on reality when he said an angel visited him in a dream."

The courtroom erupted in laughter. The prosecutor smiled.

"And did he tell you what the angel said?"

"They wrestled, mentally and physically, and the angel won. He said the angel told him how to claim an inheritance to a kingdom. He babbled nonsense, and I cut him off."

"And did this revelation anger you?"

"No. I just told him to stop double-dosing the Mensa drugs, or I was going to leave. I can't stand nonsense."

"Did he stop double-dosing?"

"He stopped the drugs entirely."

An audible gasp went up from the audience in the courtroom. The judge banged his gavel and demanded silence. Claret thought the judge acted a bit too theatrically.

"Did I understand you to say that Mensa Blackmon completely stopped taking the Mensa drugs?"

"That is correct."

"And then what happened?"

"Naturally, he got dumber. He kept reading the texts and spouting more nonsense. I told him that he was talking foolishness, and he said, 'That's what Paul said you'd say.' I didn't even ask who Paul was. He had these imaginary friends with no last names."

"Didn't you feel the need to silence him before he could disgrace the Mensas?"

"Certainly not. I felt the need to get out."

"What precipitated your finding another apartment? Something must have been, as they say, the last straw."

"Yes, he'd started reading poetry. I hate poetry. Most of it is either juvenile or gibberish. Anyway, as a result of some poem, one day he stopped wearing shoes."

A chuckle went up from the courtroom audience. The judge banged the gavel again.

"Why would he stop wearing shoes?"

"I asked him that, and he said something like, 'He who sees takes off his shoes. The rest sit around and pluck blackberries.' Again, it was gibberish."

"So even though this behavior annoyed you, you felt no compulsion to silence him?"

"No."

"If you didn't kill him, then who did?"

"I don't know. There's a door to a fire escape in the hall near the room where I found him. Possibly someone came in through the fire escape."

"But the authorities found it locked and the windows down. How would you explain an illegal entry that leaves no trace?"

"It was a professional job."

"Your fingerprints were on the handle of the knife."

"The knife came from our kitchen. I had used it at breakfast, in fact."

"But who else would have a motive to kill him?"

"I didn't have a motive to kill him, and I don't know who did."

"Before you were named a suspect, you made a statement that you thought suicide was unlikely. Do you think now that he may have committed suicide?"

"As much as I'd like to exonerate myself, I don't think that he committed suicide. He'd been in good humor. Almost giddy."

"So you claim that you didn't kill him. You don't know who would have wanted to kill him, there is no evidence of entry by an intruder, and you don't think he committed suicide. Yet Mensa Blackmon died of a knife wound to the chest. Doesn't that about sum it up?"

Claret thought that Mensa Darnelle was showing increasing signs of irritation. She had leaned back in her seat and was scowling. And if Claret wasn't mistaken, Darnelle's hands were shaking.

"I would summarize by saying that his overdosing Mensa drugs caused an instability in his episteme, which precipitated an ontological crisis and an ineluctable desire to engage in exegesis, which led to a conviction of divine heteronomy. He went from being an iconoclast to exercising what amounts to Mensa apostasy by creating a simulacrum of reality through religion."

"Yes, well, can you put that in common speak for our jurors?"

"The drugs caused him to question what he knew and who he was, so he went from being a critic to a practitioner of mysticism in order to create a reality that he could live within."

The prosecutor hesitated. "I have no further questions for this witness." He took his seat.

The defense attorney came forward. "Mensa Darnelle, you've been adamant from the beginning that you did not stab Mensa Blackmon, causing his death."

"Correct."

"When was the last time you saw Mensa Blackmon?"

"At breakfast."

"And how did he appear?"

"Tired but in good spirits."

"What did you talk about?"

"He said that he had another dream, and he had spent a couple of hours writing it down and researching what it meant. I told him that I didn't want to hear any more and that I would be out by the end of the week. He said he wanted to explain to me what he had come to understand. I said that I was late for a meeting, and I left the room."

"And what did you do after that?"

"I was Vid-chatting most of the day. I didn't go near his room until later when I noticed a pool of blood coming from under his door."

"So that's the first suspicion you had that something was wrong?"

"Yes."

"According to authorities, he'd been dead for hours before you found him. Did you hear anything unusual?"

"No, as I said, I was on a Vid-chat."

"What was his next committee project going to be?"

"It was one that he proposed. He wanted to investigate how the internal hattacks were being conducted and how to prevent them without restricting liberties."

"Did he get agreement from the NAUS Board to pursue this investigation?"

"Yes, after some effort. They said that they knew the answers to fixing the problem and didn't think that his work on a hattack committee was the best use of his abilities."

"But they eventually agreed to let him do it?"

"Yes."

"So he would have been starting a project that the NAUS Board didn't want done?"

"I suppose so."

"Were you aware that Mensa Blackmon had begun a number of Real Carrier correspondences?"

"No."

"You had no knowledge of his receiving Real Carrier mail?"

"No. Once we moved into separate bedrooms, I didn't go in his. He could have been raising rabbits in there, and I wouldn't have known."

"Thank you, Mensa Darnelle. I have no more questions. Your Honor, the defense requests a recess."

"Granted."

PHANTOM LADY

A chilly December wind blew in from the west and agitated the water of Austin Memorial Lake. Cosmo sat on a park bench, hoping the girl would show up. But by late morning, his mood was as gray as the cloud cover. He couldn't look at the lake without thinking of all the friends and relatives he'd lost the day the deluge came down from the north. The tops of the buildings protruded above the water like icebergs but more accurately were mammoth grave markers. The park depressed him, adding psychological pain to his physical, freezing-butt discomfort. What if she took days to show up? He would run out of disguises. The park was under constant surveillance, allegedly to prevent vandalism. But he and his associates knew of alternative explanations.

He sat considering how to pose as a female artist if he had to return tomorrow. The weather was supposed be more moderate. Today he wore a ball cap. He should have gone with the hunter's cap to keep his ears warm. He adjusted the collar of his jacket to cover his neck. In one way, his job was easier today. Because of the weather, few tourists paid the five dólares to enter the park and stand above the levy surrounding what had been the heart of downtown Austin. Today he would have drawn the scene as a charcoal drawing. The wind shifted, and he moved to a different bench blocked from the wind by a blue spruce. The smell of pine triggered childhood holiday memories, but he kept his attention on the few tourists.

Cosmo had a clear view of the Tribute Terminal. It looked like a bus stop shelter, but in it were microphones where tourists could speak and post messages to a Memorial Board the size of one at a sports stadium. Kinetic Sports had donated it and had a slogan emblazoned at the bottom: "Keep Moving. Don't Stop till You're Dead."

Between Cosmo and his view of the Memorial Board, an elderly couple sat on a bench facing the water and the wind. The man held the woman, who had her face buried in her hands. A few minutes ago, they'd posted a memorial to someone named Beth. At the other corner of the park, a middle-aged man held the hand of a small child. Both gazed out across the water, with steel faces. With each visitor who entered, Cosmo's mood dropped.

From the entrance to the park came a slender visitor, who he guessed was female, but the face was blocked from view by a lavender shawl wrapped like a hood. She wore a bulky gray sweater open at the top, revealing the head of a small dog or cat. She led a greyhound by a leash and carried a backpack. After staring out over the water for a few minutes, she went up to the Tribute Terminal. He could now see the side of her face, and his hopes rose. She had pale skin and wore pink lipstick. Her lips spoke into the microphone, and then she touched the Send button. Posted on the Memorial Board in large letters appeared her tribute.

Jona,

Not a day goes by that I don't miss you. Thank you for being the best brother. Love always, Névé.

Névé stood reading the other tributes; for once, she was not crying. The wind would have blown away the tears anyway, she thought. She would have to come back tomorrow when the weather should be much nicer. But at least for today, she was able to make a post for Jona, although she knew it was for herself. From behind her came a man whom she didn't hear approaching. He startled her, and she jumped when he pushed a paper note into her hand. He stood beside her just long enough to speak barely above a whisper. "Read it outside the park." Then he wandered around the park like any other tourist. Névé pushed the note into her pocket and willed her heart rate to slow down. She told herself she must be more observant. He might have robbed her.

Back in her hotel room, she unfolded the note.

At seven tonight, go to El Calderón, a theme bar in Bee Cave. Dress in a hooded cloak that conceals your identity. Tell the bartender with the moustache that you are looking for La Dama Duende. Then take a seat in a secluded booth and wait.

La Dama Duende? She could look up the name and place but didn't want to turn on her PAL. She sat holding the note a long time, wondering if it was from friend or foe. If the CBI wanted her, then why wouldn't they have just detained her? If the note came from a friendly source, how could they know she was here? She had posted the note to Jona on the Memorial Board, but who would recognize her? Yet this note had to have some connection to Jona's friends. She was going to the bar in Bee Cave to find out, but first she had some shopping to do.

***

Névé, with Jesús and María, managed to arrive early at the vicinity of El Calderón. The bar was built into the side of a hill at a secluded end of a side street that was lined with shops, which were all closed for the day. She watched the entrance from half a block away in the shadow of an awning above a shop that sold antique books. The wind had died, and the sky was clear and full of stars. The temperature was predicted to fall below freezing before morning. This end of the street was nearly deserted, and the only sound was music coming from the bar every time the door opened or closed. The three of them were bundled in clothing she'd found rummaging through a secondhand store. Jesús was tucked under her left arm. He shivered even though he wore an infant's hoodie. She kept pulling the hood over his ears, and he'd shake it off. María had on a coat, held against her midsection by a belt. Névé had found for herself a hooded robe in a platinum color. She wished that it didn't have the metallic sparkles, but she didn't see anything else that qualified as a "hooded cloak." As she stepped from the shadow, she kept the hood up.

Cosmo sat on a barstool just inside a covered entryway to El Calderón and watched the girl linger for several minutes in the shadow of a store down the street. Eventually, she and her dogs stepped into the light and made an angle toward the bar. He buzzed the bartender and checked his PAL: 6:59. The girl had done an adequate job on the getup. He couldn't see her face, but the gray cloak wasn't exactly covert. The small dog she carried shook off its hood. The greyhound looked like a skinny friar. It scanned the street and nosed the air.

The girl approached the entrance to the bar slowly and asked if there was a cover charge. "Not for you," Cosmo said. When she hesitated, he pulled from just below his neckline a small gold dagger hanging by a chain around his neck. Then he tucked it back in. He thought it would mean something to her, but she showed no reaction. He pulled open one of two heavy wooden doors and nodded toward the interior of the bar. "The bartender is expecting you." She hesitated again but then stepped through the doorway.

Névé's first thought upon entering El Calderón was that it was nothing like Café de Bebidas. The lighting was lower, and so was the volume of conversation. Drinks were lit only by sconces of real candles hanging from the ceiling. The smells of wax and coffee mingled with the music of stringed instruments that entangled individual voices so none stood out. Patrons and staff wore cloaks with hoods or hats. She would have a difficult time identifying anyone even if she had friends in the place. She made her way to the bar. A bartender came toward her and pushed back his hood enough to show her that he had a moustache. He asked what she would like to drink. "Coffee, thanks. I'm looking for La

Dama Duende."

"Have a seat. A waiter will bring the coffee to your table. I'll let her know you're here."

"Who is she?"

"You'll find out."

Névé found a booth along the wall and had a seat. She put Jesús on top of the table so she could adjust her own cloak. María sat on the floor just outside the booth. A busboy with a wide-brimmed hat and eyes deep in shadows carried a stack of cups as he walked past her table. He hesitated long enough to scold her. "Oye! Get *su perro's* butt off the table!"

The bartender told him to leave her alone.

A sword and a couple of daggers hung on the opposite wall just above the row of booths. What caught Névé's attention was a script that faded in below the sword, lingered for a few seconds, and then faded out: "For the Word is living and active and sharper than any two-edged sword." When it was gone, the absence of its golden glow on the objects in the bar made her wish for its return—or something similar to enlighten the space. It reappeared in a few seconds, but in Spanish: "*La palabra es viva y poderosa, y más cortante que cualquier espada de dos filos.*"

Conversations from other tables blended into a monotonous murmur from which she couldn't recognize more than an occasional phrase: "we'll do more than whisper," "a time to tear down," "come *mañana.*" Then she realized why this bar was unusual. Nowhere did she see an advertisement. The ever-present voices of corporations and the NAUS government had been muted in this space.

A figure in a dark hooded cape emerged from the vague shapes across the room. The person's movements were fluid and deliberate as he or she headed toward Névé's table and then stopped. The figure sat down across from Névé in the booth and pulled back the hood far enough to expose a woman's face with dark hair and large, dark eyes that were familiar to Névé.

"Hello. Can you pull your hood back a bit so I can see your face?"

Névé did as she requested.

The woman smiled and eyed all three of them. "I'm La Dama Duende." She nodded toward Névé's companions. "And whom do we have here?"

"This is María," Névé said, placing her hand on María's head. She scooped the Chihuahua to her side and kissed his head. "And this is Jesús." Jesús rested his head on Névé's chest.

"Jesús loves you. And you are?"

Névé hesitated a second. "Josephina."

La Dama Duende laughed a soft, stifled laugh. "Isn't your name really Névé? I hope that it is because I've wanted to meet you. I'm Luisa."

Névé's eyes widened. "Luisa? Jona's Luisa?"

"Yes, I'm happy to say." And she laughed again.

Névé, on impulse, stood, reached across the table, and gave Luisa a hug. "I'm *so* happy to meet you!" Her emotions, which had been dammed up for months, came pouring out. "There is *so much* I'd like to talk about—so many questions to ask about my brother." She wiped her tears on the hood of Jesús's coat and began searching for a napkin. Her hood fell away.

A cloaked figure, face hidden within a deep hood, brought two cups of coffee. The hood bobbed and motioned toward the back.

Luisa leaned across the table and said to Névé, "Replace your hood and follow me, but leave your coffee as though you plan to return."

Névé slid from the booth and collected the dogs. Moving slowly, Luisa followed the waiter toward the back of the bar, and Névé trailed her. They entered a small, dark storeroom, and Luisa closed the door, locking it behind them. The waiter slid aside a cupboard, revealing a downward staircase. Cool, fresh air met them as they started to descend. Again, Luisa closed and locked the concealed entrance.

At the bottom of the stairs, the waiter unlocked another door, and they entered a room with warm lighting, a high ceiling, and rows and rows of barrels. The smell of wine eliminated the need for Névé to ask what was in the barrels. Each one was numbered. The waiter turned around, and Luisa spoke. "Névé, I have someone for you."

The waiter pulled back his hood. Névé inhaled and blacked out. He caught her fall as she went down. Luisa caught Jesús.

***

Jeremi wondered for the umpteenth time how Luisa was getting on upstairs. Was the young lady really Jona's Névé? He hoped so. He'd had an inexplicable desire to meet this young woman ever since the first time Jona described her. He rubbed his palms on his pants to wipe off the sweat and berated himself for being nervous. To kill time, he read the letter from Jahn again. Real Carrier and its network of handoffs had taken a few days to deliver it. After reading it, he worried that they'd missed her; she may have arrived and left the area already. Travel by train from Chicago should have taken maybe four days. But when they saw her posting on Jona's memorial page, they were thankful and began posting a watch at the Memorial Lake site, thinking she would go there. The watch paid off—if she was indeed Névé.

Greetings JD,

I hope that this letter finds you well and out of harm's way. I wish that you would use a WorldNet with anon access, but I understand your mistrust. The Flames in Chicago send our greetings. We read your last letter at all our meetings. It was much appreciated and well received, so we encourage you to continue sending us your writings and teachings. Perhaps someday we can meet in person. You would be more than welcome in Chicago.

I will take the time to update you on our progress in my next letter. But for now, I wanted to send a brief note letting you know that a very special young lady is headed your way. Her name is Névé. She lost her brother, Jona, in the Austin flood; inherited some money from a grandmother on her eighteenth birthday; and is headed toward Austin to see where her brother died and possibly meet some of his surviving friends. She found our law office because she needed legal advice and recognized our flame in the window.

243

She'd seen a similar symbol on Jona's Writing Wall during a Vid-chat. She also saw something on the Net that connected you to Jona.

She needs the help of your faithful if you can locate her. I warned Névé that I had no address to give her because of how we send and receive letters. I suggested that she start at the new memorial to find and connect with others who lost a loved one.

We have invited her to return to Chicago after visiting Austin, and selfishly, we hope that she does. Mostly, though, we're concerned for her safety in a strange city. She's tall, very pale—looks frail but is as tough as nails—has short silver-blond hair, and travels with two dogs that she rescued from being euthanized, which says something about her personality.

I hope that you have a chance to meet her. Please let me know what we might be able to do for you. Know that you are welcome here at any time.

For you, we are thankful that "the Word is living and active."

—JB ô

***

"Stay with me, Névé. Stay with me!"

Névé opened her eyes and was again stunned by the man's face. Even though it was bearded, flushed, and tearful, she recognized it immediately.

"Jona?"

"Yes, yes. It's really me."

Névé, mouth agape, said nothing for a couple of seconds. "Why? How?"

"Some others and I near my office managed to get out because of the way the water came in. I allowed myself to be listed as dead for reasons I'll explain later. Let's go to our office and catch up."

"Your eyes are brown."

"I changed their color, for now."

"And what about your ID chip?"

"I'd had it removed months before and put on a bracelet, which I lost in the escape. That's what gave me the idea of not letting anyone know that it wasn't me down there."

Luisa's eyes were watering as she spoke to Névé. "You don't look so well. We'll get you something to eat or drink. You've had quite a shock." Luisa still held Jesús, and she took María's leash. Jesús kept his eyes on Névé, but María sniffed the air.

Névé was shaking and as white as a Sugarstik. Jona scooped her up and carried her across the cellar toward the lounge area. She insisted that she could walk, but he shook his head. "Let me take care of you for a while at least."

***

Jeremi heard the SecureAlert signal that the entry door from El Calderón had opened and closed. He hoped they had her. Jona would be so disappointed if the girl was not Névé. They all would be disappointed. The security camera showed three hooded figures entering the cellar. He put away Jahn's letter, tidied his desk out of nervousness, and left the office to meet them.

As he came around a rack of barrels, they were coming toward him. Luisa carried a small dog and led a large one on a leash. Jona held what looked like a snow nymph wrapped in an icicle. When she saw Jeremi, her eyebrows raised and her mouth opened in obvious surprise. She put a hand to her forehead and closed her eyes, as if she was dizzy. Jona carried her through the office door and into a lounge. He set her on a couch and knelt in front of it, taking both of her hands in his.

Jona apologized again for the shock he'd given Névé and gave her a couple of hugs. His face was still flushed, and his eyes were red. He noticed her looking at Jeremi, so he introduced him as Jeremi, Luisa's brother. Jeremi hung back with his hands in his pockets and nodded to Névé.

Névé turned back toward Jona as if for an explanation. "You could have told me you were alive. I don't know whether to punch you or hug you."

"I couldn't get word to you right after the flood. By the time I was able to make indirect contacts, you'd left home. One of your friends told a contact that you were headed down this way." He pointed to Jeremi. "I've gone underground and off the grid. I work for Jeremi's organization and live in a storage-room-turned-apartment in the winery."

Jeremi corrected him in a low voice. "It's not *my* organization, as I keep reminding everyone."

Jona dried his eyes, wondering why Névé seemed to find Jeremi's presence a surprise, but he thought he'd wait to ask. "Jeremi is nothing if not modest."

Névé was still stunned and sat with her mouth partially open, so he continued. "So then I had someone try to contact you directly a few times from an anon site, but your PAL was off, and I wasn't going to leave a message."

She hugged him again for several seconds as if she didn't want to let go. "I almost didn't recognize you with the beard and brown eyes."

"I'm glad to hear that because I have a new identity, and I see that you do, too. You don't have your Sugarstik tattoo, and I like the new eye color." He was thoughtful for a second, then added, "Also, you've changed —grown up a lot. I can tell. How'd you manage to get down here?"

She took Jesús back from Luisa and gave them the first smile they'd seen from her. "It's a long story. We have a lot to catch up on."

RIGEL'S BUSINESS IN SEATTLE

Rigel stepped off the train. A heavy drizzle had settled in for the afternoon. He expected Claret to be easy to spot, but hoods and hats blocked faces. He didn't put his hat on for that reason. Instead, he searched up and down the station. Passengers dispersed, others boarded, and the train pulled away from the platform, disappearing down the tracks. Beyond a group of three men making plans, he spotted a woman in a hooded blue windbreaker looking in his direction. She held the hand of a boy with copper-colored hair, wearing a sailor's cap. She pushed back her hood and walked toward Rigel, leading the boy, who had some difficulty walking. Something was wrong with his legs. She stopped about an arm's length away. "Hello, Rigel. This is my son, Ember. He's seven years old and a real sweetie." She turned to Ember. "I would like you to meet Mr. Rising." Ember was more interested in studying the tracks where the train had disappeared.

Rigel smiled and extended his hand to Ember. "Well, I'm very happy to meet you, Ember."

***

Rigel had a room booked in a nearby hotel, but they decided to walk to Claret's apartment to visit for a while. She pointed out places of interest along the way, leading them in a serpentine route around the hawkers of goods and services. After spending most of his life on the Dakota plains, Rigel felt as if he couldn't process everything. The scene was an assault on the senses. He pictured doing an abstract painting with a gray background and splashes of color, but it would never capture the smell of fish and chips and cologne, the mingling of voices and machinery, and the chill of the Pacific air. They passed several large cracks in the concrete sidewalk. Down one street, Claret pointed to the large sinkhole that had opened up during the quake. The street in front of her building sloped steeply for several blocks down to the water. Rigel was getting a knot in his stomach thinking about them living in this environment, but then he told himself that he shouldn't judge. Maybe it suited them. Her apartment building appeared solid on the outside, but just inside, a foundational crack ran up the wall like ivy. They took an elevator to her apartment on the fifth floor.

Claret made some coffee, and they sat on a sofa, which was nestled in a bay window overlooking the street. She wore an emerald sweater and had her legs tucked underneath a green plaid skirt, which hid her only ad tattoo—a bottle of Zin-Blanco wine on her left calf. Her forearms had the faint blotchy appearance of having had other tattoos removed.

Rigel wanted her to know that he wasn't there to impose but to spend what time he could with them. "I should probably check into my hotel before dinner. Can I take you and Ember out tonight?"

"We'd like a dinner out. We don't go out much." Her tone implied there was more left unsaid. "My sister, Jade, and I moved in together. She'll be home soon. I'm trying to get her to be self-sufficient, but..." She trailed off.

"What does she do?"

"Currently, she's a professional juror. She brings in an income that helps us make ends meet by being on one jury after another. I worry, though, about how reliable it is."

He said that he'd heard it could be lucrative on popular trials. He felt their making small talk was forestalling the real conversation that they needed to have. But now was too soon.

She said those big trials were hard to get on because they picked experienced jurors but that Jade had a recent success by getting on the Mensa Blackmon trial, and Jade actually enjoyed the trials. Claret rolled her eyes when she said that she herself wouldn't have the stomach for them. Then she made a face as if she'd smelled something distasteful and added that one of Jade's last trials was a murder by bludgeoning. The details were gruesome.

Rigel laughed.

She had encouraged Jade to consider writing fiction based on her experiences from being a juror, but Jade didn't have the temperament for sitting by herself for long periods, occupying her own head. She was an extrovert.

As if on cue, the electronic door access beeped and a young woman came in, out of breath. Her hair was black beneath a green beret. She had many tattoos and body piercings with dangling trinkets. Her Asian eyes studied him before she addressed Claret. "Bonjour, Roux. *Il est ici?*"

"English, Jade. Rigel, this is my sister, Jade. Jade, this is Rigel."

Rigel nodded. "Hi, Jade. I was just telling Claret that I would like to take her and Ember to dinner tonight. Would you like to come?"

"I have a meeting this evening. Maybe you two would like to come to it."

Claret tried to give her sister a warning look with a slight hand movement across the throat, but Jade avoided her eye contact. "Claret thinks I should not rock the boat, but I'd rather stand for change than sit through boredom."

Claret smirked. "I'm concerned she won't get selected for juries if she gets arrested or labeled a rabble-rouser. This meeting is all about shaking things up. I tell her we get enough earthquakes here."

Rigel laughed again, appreciating Claret's ability to hone humor on the edge of a painful truth. He read Claret's expression to Jade and declined their attending the meeting.

Jade turned to leave the room. "Have fun, then. Nice to meet you, Rigel."

"Where would *you* like to go, Claret?"

She gave the question some thought. "I like The Luau. It's fun and not too expensive, and I'm sure Ember would like it." Claret nodded in the direction Jade had taken and smiled. "It's a long story that I'll explain tonight."

"She calls you Roux?"

"Unfortunately."

***

At The Luau, guests enjoyed an evening in Hawaii. An Infi-Scene along one wall showed a beach at sunset. Waves broke onshore with gusto, occasionally overriding the luau background music. A rose-colored sky turned a volcanic island across the water dark purple. Lavender clouds lingered around its peak. A planter of fuchsia bougainvillea and a palm tree sat near the window. They swayed in the breeze generated from the Infi-Scene frame. The scents of pineapple and coconut basted the aroma of roasting pork. Ads for virtual vacations and tropical products ran along the top and bottom of the frame.

"I wish I could go play on the beach." Ember took another drink of his Pacific Blue soda.

Claret smiled. "Me too, but those waves would pack a wallop. I'd like to feel the sand between my toes and collect shells. Wouldn't that be fun?"

Ember nodded and ate a banana chip. Rigel smiled at him. Claret liked the way Rigel's hair brushed his shirt this evening. He usually had it pulled back on the Vid-chat meetings. The camera didn't do him justice. His dark eyes shone in the torchlight. She fingered the rough exterior of a pineapple that was carved out to serve as a candleholder. "What are you thinking, Rigel?"

"That I'm so glad I'm here. I needed a break."

A waitress came to the table with drinks in coconuts. She wore a hula skirt and made sure that it swayed from her hips as she moved. Ember stared at the grass and her belly button, which held a large blue gem. She asked if they had any questions about menu items. Rigel pointed to an item at the bottom of the menu under the Exotica Room, which had a cover charge of 500D. "What's HS^2?"

"If you have to ask, you can't afford it. Latest fad from Asia. Brought in fresh every day. Served only in the Exotica Room." She turned and went back toward the kitchen.

Rigel searched on his PAL for HS^2 and found a link for specialty foods. In a list including Homininae Panina, he found "HS^2, *Homo sapiens sapiens*, the ultimate experience in delicacies." He turned it off but not before wondering what the source was. They chose a couple of appetizers to share and entered an order on their table's kiosk.

Claret became distracted by something toward the entrance. She smiled and returned the waves of a middle-aged couple who waited at the e-hostess desk for their table. Their eyes lingered on Rigel. To get to their table, the couple went behind Claret's chair, patting her shoulder and Ember's. "Nice to see you out, CJ."

Claret nodded as they moved past her and over to their table.

"CJ? What's the *J* stand for?" Rigel asked.

"Jael. There's a lot you don't know about me, Rigel."

"That's why I'm here. Can I get a quick sketch?"

She studied the beach scene and turned to answer him, fiddling with the umbrella in her drink. "I've lived in Seattle about a year. I followed my sister out here because I was afraid she'd end up on the streets, and she probably would have. I grew up and went to school in Quebec. Our mother still lives there. My father died in the War for Peace. My sister is from an affair that my mother had with a Chinese diplomat. When he left to return to Asia, he didn't take us with him as my mother thought he would, but we've managed. My sister has a rebel streak and a hard time holding a steady job, so the jury jobs fit her lifestyle. She can work sporadically when she wants to, and sharing an apartment gives her some stability." She gave Ember a hug. "And Ember here is my sweetie pie." She addressed him. "Would you want to go over to the big window for a while?"

He nodded and hobbled over toward the beach scene.

Claret continued. "I was living with a man when I was in my mid-twenties. He said he loved me, but apparently not enough to stay when I delivered a child who would need several surgeries and never walk normally. As soon as I get out of debt from one surgery, I get him the next one that he needs as he grows. He's much better than he was." Rigel's eyes were still shining and bottomless. A curtain hadn't gone down over them as had sometimes happened when she explained her situation to other suitors. "So you see, Mr. Rising, I have financial burdens and family obligations."

"Is there something else? I feel like there's something else on your mind."

She twitched her mouth and rolled her eyes as though she were debating what to say. Then she leaned forward across the corner of the table and spoke just above a whisper. "I'm Jewish."

Rigel suppressed a laugh until his eyes watered. He had to wipe them with the back of his hand.

Her cheeks colored. "You find that funny? I take it very seriously."

"I expected something like 'I'm in love with someone else' or 'I'm just not interested in a relationship with a man' or I don't know what, but I didn't expect that." He tried hard to stifle his chuckling. "I can accept that."

"But I need more than *accept*, and therein, I suspect, will lie the problem."

Rigel smiled with his dark, wet eyes, and Claret thought that he still didn't get it. "I'm committed, Rigel. On the side, I write promotional material and song lyrics for the Jewish Underground. It's part of who I am."

Rigel leaned in toward her. "My mother was Jewish."

INTRODUCTIONS

The next morning, Névé checked out of her hotel and thought about what a difference a day could make. Twenty-four hours earlier, she had believed her brother to be dead and had gone to a miserable Austin Memorial Lake to post a tribute. And here she was today, heading out to meet Jona with the sun warming her skin and the dogs' fur. From the hotel, she went back to Bee Cave and followed Jona's directions to the bottom of a hill. The cellars, where the wine was brewed and stored, were at the base of the hill, with the uptown shops and the entrance to El Calderón at the top. Next to the cellars was the business office. About a hundred meters away sat the ranch house that Jeremi and Luisa called home and where they had invited her to stay. Jona had suggested a picnic in the vineyard. Carrying Jesús and leading María on a leash, Névé found him down a row. He was bent over a vine and armed with a pair of pruning shears.

Jona stood and squinted in the bright sunlight as she approached. The sun reflected red highlights from his curly hair. "We need to get you a hat and sunscreen. You'll burn badly, even in October." They gave each other a long hug. He told her that he'd planned for the lunch with Jeremi and Luisa so she could get to know them, and he would take the afternoon off to spend time with her.

Névé nodded. "Can I let the dogs loose?"

"María will be fine—unless she starts digging up vines—but I'd keep

Jesús close." He pointed up. "Birds of prey. An eagle or a hawk will snatch him away if they can."

She surveyed the sky. Then she pulled a leash from a satchel that she carried, hooked it on the Chihuahua's collar, and set him down. They walked between rows of vines while Jona explained the grape varietal and the wine-making process. "Harvest season is nearly over, and our preparations for winter are underway."

Névé used her PAL to take photos to send to Marta and Jahn when she could. She took a close-up of sunlit leaves, mottled green and gold and crimson, and a long shot of the rows combing the rolling hills. "The vineyard is so beautiful."

Jona agreed. "I'm happy here, and I hope that you will be, too."

They ended up in a small clearing under a sycamore tree not far from the ranch house, which was unpainted and had been left to weather to a warm gray. Névé found it inviting in a rustic, Southwestern way. Jona suggested she set her things down and wait in the shade of the sycamore. He went up to the front porch and brought back a quilt and picnic basket that had been waiting on the step. He spread the quilt on the ground. It had been pieced from red, green, and gold fabrics. They opened the basket to see what was inside as Jeremi and Luisa came out of the ranch house. Both were dressed in jeans and flannel shirts. Luisa's was autumn shades of gold and rust. Jeremi's was a turquoise mix. Luisa brought a hat and sunscreen for Névé, who noted that she must have read Jona's mind.

Luisa gestured toward the food. "I didn't know what you like to eat, Névé, so I've put together some picnic items. I hope you like cheese, bread, and grapes."

Névé smiled. "They sound delicious."

And they were. Névé thought she had never tasted food so good. Jeremi and Jona sampled one of their recent vintages of white wine and discussed its merits and shortcomings. Jesús begged cheese from Névé while María continued her investigation of the immediate area.

Jeremi swirled the wine in his glass before taking a sip. "This will be a good vintage for us."

Névé had been thinking about how much Jeremi resembled the man in her dream. She must have seen him in the news and didn't realize it until she had the dream and then saw another news item about him. The whole thing seemed odd and coincidental, but she was sure there was a reasonable connection. She considered how much the white wine resembled the color of sunshine, and then she brought her attention back to the conversation. "How did you two come to own a vineyard?"

Jeremi explained between sips of wine. "Our mother's side of the family has owned the land for decades but didn't do anything with it. They live in a northern province of Mexico. I decided to make the land fruitful and convinced Luisa to come with me. She has all the business sense anyway, especially marketing. That was several years ago, and finally the vines are producing. The income supports us so that I can carry out my real mission, for which, ironically, the vineyard serves as a metaphor."

Jona turned to Névé. "You asked me what I did for Jeremi. I do whatever is needed to enable our group, which uses the symbol of the sword, to spread what we've started to call the Pedestrian Way because we're all sojourners, one step at a time. Sometimes I go to other groups and cooperate with them and recruit their help. Usually, they're receptive to anti-establishment causes. Jeremi's arrest came when he organized a meeting of leaders from some of these groups. We wanted to discuss how we could become more open."

Jeremi nodded. "We have a lot of members in common."

Névé decided she liked to hear Jeremi talk. While watching his lips form the words, she felt in that instant a strong attraction to him—but one that was like a double-edged sword, with the other edge being fear. A small gold dagger hung on a chain around his neck. Without the shaping of a handle and a point, it would simply be a cross. But it was a double-edged sword. He was driven by a cause, and her fear came from a reluctance to turn over her independence to some intangible purpose. She focused back on the conversation. "Which groups do you mean?"

"They're the marginalized: environmentalists, religious adherents, neo-Marxists, and a few other special interests."

Névé asked about the group using the number 315 and said that she had heard about them in New Orleans. She had suspected that a man named Kit was a member.

Jeremi said that 315s were sometimes called neo-Marxists, but not like Chinese or Soviet Marxists. "They're trying to define a form of capitalism run by workers and not capitalists. And they want to take the influence of money out of the democratic process. I'm not sure about the soundness of their economics, but they're a useful group because standing up for the downtrodden is central to their purpose—and ours. We think a high percentage of them are Christians, Jews, or Muslims. Contacting them and the Seven Sisters, who are environmentalists, is what landed me in jail because they actually do want to overthrow the current system. I just want our religious liberties back, but the authorities don't see the difference, so I'm guilty by association." He held his glass up to the light and noted the pale color that they had hoped to get. "I have an upcoming hearing to determine if charges of sedition will actually be filed."

Névé still wondered about the names of these groups. "Why are they called Three Fifteen, which seems like a random number, and Seven Sisters?"

Luisa said she'd wondered the same thing and had asked one of them. "Three Fifteen comes from March 15, the ides of March, the date Julius Caesar was murdered—so it's a symbol of taking down the empire. The name served them well until recently. Most people didn't make the connection, but their intentions surfaced when a member outed their activities to the regional board. I'm not sure about the origin of Seven Sisters."

Jona nodded. "I think it has to do with the constellation called the Seven Sisters."

Névé inhaled as though she'd just thought of something. "Is it safe to say anything here? Could we be under surveillance?"

Jona moved his head in a motion somewhere between a yes and a no. "Maybe. It depends on where we are. The storage room you passed through is set up with electronics to detect bugs and other devices. We talk in the ranch house, office, and lounge and assume it's safe because we scan for signals. Outside the office and house, security is less certain. In the bar, you should assume that you're being monitored. Out here in the open, there's no guarantee."

Névé considered how to approach the subject. She suggested that they go into the house when finished. Because they were finished eating, but not finished with the wine, they picked up the picnic items and headed in. In contrast to the exterior, which looked like a weather-beaten log cabin, the interior had smooth log walls and contemporary furnishings and electronics. Névé thought that she shouldn't have been surprised. They were a family rooted in the past, yet they were future building. They showed her to the guest room where she could put her belongings. It smelled of cedar and had a window facing the east.

When she joined them again, they sat around a polished wooden table inlaid with turquoise and waited for her story. "I have information from a physicist. She claims that it has far-reaching implications and needs to be published, globally, but it's been suppressed by the NAUS authorities like the CBI."

The other three were quiet for a few seconds. Jona shrugged. "Sometimes subversive groups claim to have critical information that never amounts to much. What kind of information does the CBI want to suppress?"

"She says it's an approach to the 'unified theory' or 'theory of everything,' whatever that means exactly, that's been worked on for so long."

Jona shrugged. "Well, so? That's good news, isn't it?"

"Her uncle, Dr. Orion Rising, believed that NAUS government leaders want the theory suppressed until they have a strategic hold on its use."

Luisa leaned forward. Névé envied her tanned skin, as well as her eyes and hair the color of dark chocolate. A couple of strands had previously blown loose from her ponytail, and they now framed her face. "Do you mean the Dr. Rising who was killed in a subway accident not too long ago?"

"That's the one."

"And your friend is then *Incense Rising*, whom the CBI put out that huge reward for?"

Névé nodded. They all exchanged glances, considering the implications.

Jeremi wrinkled his forehead. Except for his curly hair, the resemblance to his sister was striking, whereas Névé and Jona looked nothing alike. "What else?"

"Incense claimed that Dr. Rising had been a strong supporter of environmental stewardship. He—and Incense—are, by heritage, First People. According to Incense, the theory should lead to a new energy source. Orion had wanted to ensure it was not just in the hands of the NAUS government. He wanted scientists globally to have it. He had hoped to force leaders to recognize the need for drastic changes in environmental regulations, and he did not trust them to share the benefits. Incense and her boss, Kit, took me in when I wasn't sure where to go or what to do, and I want to do what I can to help her." Then Névé paused.

The only sound was the mechanical ticking clock on the fireplace mantle. When no one commented, she continued. "Incense's uncle was convinced that the NAUS Board was maneuvering globally, at the expense of others, to protect its own interests, particularly the interests of its wealthy backers. He wanted to expose the almost dire situation that the human race could be in, but exposure at this time was not in the interest of the NAUS Board. By suppressing the theory, it was buying time."

Jona rubbed his beard. "And so, suddenly, Dr. Rising is killed. How convenient."

"Exactly. Incense didn't believe his death was an accident. He had ties to groups wanting to overthrow the NAUS government because of its environmental policies. That's about all I know, other than she was adamant the information gets out so his life's work won't be wasted. She feared for her own life and wanted to make sure copies of the theory survived her in case the CBI succeeded in silencing her." Névé hesitated and explained the link to her personally. "She gave me a couple of copies."

Névé counted five ticks of the mantle clock. Luisa smiled and nodded. "We can get one of our professors here in town to look at it. He's one of our inner circle. Where are the copies?"

Névé pointed to the dogs, who were investigating their new surroundings. "On their collars, and then I have another."

PROJECT JAVA, DESIREE YEN

Rigel and Claret had a Cream Team Vid-chat on Rigel's third day in Seattle. She showed him the downstairs NetLink ports in isolated, quiet rooms. He booked one for the appointed time, and she took the chat in her room as always. When the Vid-chat showed all the team tying in, one of the members was a new face. A woman with Asian features and multicolored hair sat in front of a red background. She spoke first.

"Hello, team. I'm Desiree Yen, and I'm so glad to add the Cream Team to my responsibilities within Milk Products because I think you'll be successful. How are all of you today?"

Claret was the first to ask the question that everyone was wondering. "I'm fine. What happened to Will Potter?"

"His contract was, unfortunately for him, not renewed for another year. The consolidation of supervisory responsibilities will help reduce overhead for the Cream Team and almost ensure profitability. Since I have only a few minutes to spend with you today, let me get right to the point." She had clasped her palms together in front of her and leaned forward, toward her monitor, in a way that resembled praying.

"Now, as you know, the Uppers have intentionally avoided doing business in the Sino region because financial projections have shown that the return on investment does not warrant product development. The average household income is too low." Her praying hands didn't last long.

She occasionally punched a finger in the air to emphasize a point.

"In addition, the NAUS Board wants to protect against the loss of natural resources. And then, of course, we have hard feelings on both sides as a result of the disasters blamed on hattacks. It's understandable that the Wise Consumer CEO is adamantly opposed to any discussion of growing business in the region. But *I* think"—she pointed to herself —"we need a plan for business in the Sino region. *I* want to be ready with a Sino plan when the NAUS Board strikes a deal for reopening trade and when the Wise Consumer Uppers discover that we can actually make money in this region. Therefore, I desire ideas from each of you for ad campaigns and concept definitions for Cream Team products—and Milk Products in general—in the Sino region. But remember, because the CEO has not sanctioned efforts toward business in the Sino region, these plans do not exist. If I learn that any of you admitted to working on the Sino plan, I'll see that your contract is not renewed. Are we clear on that point?"

Rigel was the first to speak. "If I assent, am I by default actually acknowledging the existence of what does not exist?"

Desiree ignored his comment. "I want to keep this group agile and ready to spring on any opportunity that presents itself." She pointed to herself again. "I want us to rise to the top. I want us to be recognized for having a passion for profit. Let me repeat that. It sounded so good. Passion for profit! Are we all on board? I hope so, because this train is leaving the station! Next stop, Sino Platform! Now let's all get to work!"

Aries managed to get in a few words. "I'll have to have evidence of the Sino plan on my WorldNet portal, as will the rest of us. That's a problem because everything we do is monitored and traceable, right?"

"Hmm, yes. In my passion for profit, I forgot that we need a code name. Something that is nondescript. Something that might be anything."

Claret considered her mug of coffee. "Java. It will sound like one of our advertisers."

Desiree perked up. "Java? I like the sound of that one. It's stimulating, and I do have a passion for coffee. Don't we all? Java it is! Good suggestion, Claret. I can see why you're our communications expert. So for our next meeting, come prepared to discuss action items on Java. Any questions?"

JEREMI'S LETTER TO CHICAGO

To the Second "O'Leary's Cow" of Chicago,

I am forever in your debt. I can't thank you enough for all you've done and are still doing for "Josephina"—and by association, for us. We were indeed able to find her. I think that she has already sent you a message telling of the surprise she found waiting for her here. I love her frail beauty combined with her inner toughness, and I love the effect she's having on my close friend. For the past few months, the thought of her situation was like a black cloud hanging over him, and he'd spend hours trying to figure out how to resolve it. Our (and your) petitions to the One Who Listens paid off.

We hope to keep her with us as long as she wants to stay. I suggested to her that we plan a visit to Chicago when I get my legal issues resolved and can travel. You know the message I teach is that "the Word is living and active." We believe not merely because of ancient texts but also because of what we experience today in our lives. Therefore, I've started writing a modern-day "Acts," and I want your stories. This kind of research is best done in person!

I am so thankful that you are igniting Chicago in a fire that won't be quenched, and I hope that I'm able to feel the heat of your flames in person someday. Thank you again for taking good care of "Josephina." And please keep in touch. We love to receive your letters.—JD

THE CLEANUP

Over the past few days, Kit has been going around the New French Quarter, helping others who had more damage than the Real Carrier office. We are fortunate. He spends much of his time washing mud from floors and repairing windows. I've been staying in the office to keep a low profile and take care of business. The other two Real Carrier workers have had excuses for not coming in: the teenager lost her cat and then claimed to be sick, and "Mr. Chubbs" has his own apartment to fix up.

I've been wondering if Névé and the dogs made it to Austin without incident. They should be there by now. I would love to contact her and stay in touch but won't establish a link. I wonder if I did the right thing by involving her, but now is not the time for second-guessing my actions. I need to focus on my future and what I should do next. Kit says he should drive up to Jackson or Shreveport and attempt to post Uncle Orion's work. I'm not so sure. I suggested that I just take a bus or train up there myself and not make him a target also. He pointed out that the surveillance cameras in the public transportation places would be watching for me. All they would need is probably the lower half of my face to get a positive ID.

I am getting the feeling that I have to move soon. It's the feeling I learned to cultivate on the plains in Dakota—recognition that someone or something is watching. In Dakota, I hunted with a bow and arrow. The sense of finding prey served me well. I'm now getting more of the sense of *being* prey. But maybe it's just my imagination. With the theory to a point where it can be handed off and my being confined to the office and vicinity, I probably have too much time to let my imagination go. I need to separate the real and present dangers from my overactive imagination, which can create predators where there are none.

Around 1:00 p.m., a message from the sector council asks everyone who is able to attend a New French Quarter community meeting to discuss the raising of donations to repair losses not covered by personal insurance. Kit received the message on his PAL, so he returns to the office to clean up before the meeting. I sort mail and otherwise busy myself until he comes out of the bathroom, smelling like soap. I give him an update. "We had only one drop-off for delivery since this morning. It's a package for the east sector."

"I can take it when I go to the community meeting," he says.

"I'll stay here. Again."

I think he senses my low spirits and says that he doesn't like my being here alone, especially when most people will be several blocks away. He asks if I have some way to defend myself if someone wants to cause a problem.

"You mean like this?" I pull out my switchblade. I've carried a knife since I was a kid—at least whenever I'm outside. After leaving Dakota, I've rarely been without one.

He smiles. "Is that a First People requirement?"

I put the knife away and smile. "You bet. And we still bow hunt because the tax on guns doesn't apply—saves a lot of money that way." I haven't actually been hunting for about five years, but I've started to gain some pleasure in appearing unusual to Kit, who never opens up about his background, but it has to be unique.

"I'd like to see you bow hunting," he says. "And I believe you could carve anyone up who got out of line."

"I might be rusty."

He is ready to leave. "Lock the doors and close the shop if there's anything suspicious. I've seen looting and itinerants snooping around. And text me often so that I won't worry." He does appear genuinely concerned—the tone of his voice, the wrinkling of his forehead. I wave him off.

Around ten minutes after he leaves, I'm outside tending the pigeons. A strong odor enters the courtyard. I send Kit a text.

Incense: I smell gas.

TRIP
SHORTENED

The day was forecast to be the last cloudless day of the month, so Claret, Ember, and Rigel packed a picnic lunch and took a light-rail train to a ski resort where hikers still enjoyed the slopes until the first snow. Ember climbed a boulder, and Claret handed him a sandwich to eat on his perch. "If we get a tremor while you're up there, you better hang on." Ember moved one leg so he straddled the rock like a horse.

Rigel read a text that he'd just received from his father. He became quiet and studied his PAL instead of the spectacular view down the green ski slope.

Claret thought his time with them couldn't be going better. "What's wrong? You're scowling."

"I wish I knew. I just got a text from Dad that says, 'Don't forget we have to go deer hunting as soon as you get back. Don't delay, or the grandfathers will not sleep peacefully.' That's crazy."

"What does it mean?"

"I have no idea. We haven't hunted for anything since I was a teen. I don't like hunting." He thought about the text for a few seconds. "I think 'the grandfathers' comment probably implies family obligations."

"Sounds like he needs you at home but doesn't want to say why."

"Exactly. There must be something going on. I've been gone only three days."

"Would it have something to do with why your life is complicated—which you haven't explained yet?"

"I'm sure it does." He chewed on a bread roll before answering. "Claret, I came here to spend time with you. If I need to go back soon, I'd like to invite you to come with me. Dad and I have a ranch with guest rooms and horses and open scenery, but I can't guarantee there's no risk because of something my sister has gotten us into."

"What's that?"

"She's wanted by the CBI for some theoretical work she did with my uncle, Dr. Orion Rising, the scientist who was killed in a subway accident in New York."

"I had no idea. If I saw the news item, I never connected the last names. I'm so sorry."

Her cheeks had a pink flush that Rigel thought made her even more attractive, if that were possible. She looked puzzled, though. "So what does her work have to do with you in Dakota?"

"The CBI thinks we're hiding something—information."

"Are you?"

Rigel shrugged. "Not yet, other than the fact that we've had a couple of communications from her. When we get a copy of the work she did with my uncle, we'll try to post it to the WorldNet, but Incense thinks it will be blocked. Dad can encode it on music, and we'll go that route if we have to. Maybe he's heard something else."

"Sounds intriguing. I'm surprised at myself for saying this, but I'd like to come. I can do my work from anywhere with a WorldNet connection, and staying here isn't low risk."

"No, it's not. I was going to point that out. You're getting too many tremors. I think they're not telling you what's really brewing because of what it'll do to the real estate market. And the apartment you're in scares me."

She didn't try to argue.

He seemed reticent about something and to be considering the Pacific

Ocean, visible on the horizon to the west. "Life on the Dakota Plains is very different from here, and I can't say if that's good or bad for you." He thought for a few moments. "Ember might like horseback riding. The snows will come soon, though." He pictured the slope they were on covered with snow, which gave him a feeling of vertigo. Surely this run was for experienced skiers. "I have no trouble occupying myself with artwork. But the isolation of the location caused my previous partner to leave a couple of years ago."

Claret had wondered how it was that he wasn't attached. "Honestly, I could use isolation for a while, except…" She started to say something and stopped.

"Except what?"

"I feel an obligation to my sister. I'm afraid of how she'll end up if I'm not around."

Rigel interrupted his intent to take a sip of wine and laughed. "I don't know why I keep expecting you to drop a showstopper. Maybe because I feel like I'm already in pretty deep. Bring your sister. I'm serious about wanting to spend time with you and to get to know you. We have plenty of room. I hope you come, although I can see how you have a tough choice deciding between isolation with CBI surveillance and a pyroclastic flow."

Over the past couple of days, Claret had come to realize how much she loved his sense of humor and how much she needed it. "I'll come, but it may take some convincing to get my sister excited about going."

"Tell her we're a hotbed of anti-establishment radicals in Dakota. It's the truth."

"That should do it."

"How soon can we go?"

"Jade has a two-day break starting the day after tomorrow. If she agrees to go, that would be the best timing for her. I can get us ready tomorrow."

"Then I'll tell Dad when to expect the four of us."

She leaned over, kissed him, and hoped that she knew what she was doing, even though she was pretty sure she didn't.

A CENSOR OF INCENSE

Jeremi was watching the Mensa Blackmon trial while catching up on correspondence when a Crowd-Source item on the New French Quarter caught his attention.

Crowd-Source, October 15. New Orleans Explosion. Sources are reporting a major explosion in the New French Quarter. Witnesses say they believe it was caused by a gas leak. The area has struggled to recover from the recent hurricane. Location mapping of the Crowd-Source accounts indicates it may have devastated three blocks in the heart of the New French Quarter and broken windows a kilometer away. The death toll is unknown at this time, but residents believe that it could have been much worse. Many were attending a sector meeting on the storm damage and were not in the vicinity of the blast. Crowd-Source will keep you current on the scene in New Orleans. This update has been brought to you by Wise Consumer. Would you like to own a piece of the original Jerzeybell? For a limited time only, fans of Jerzeybell may purchase a certificate containing a five-millimeter square of gold leaf from the actual remains of Jerzeybell's head. Proceeds will go to constructing a bigger and better Jerzeybell. Help reincarnate Jerzeybell today, and get your luck going.

The video of the New French Quarter showed the type of devastation he would have expected from a bomb blast. Pictures taken by residents did far more than the text in conveying the seriousness of the blast. He muted the sound and sat quietly for a minute, closing his eyes and blocking out the images. A verse came to him from Revelation: "And the smoke of the incense, with the prayers of the saints, went up before God out of the angel's hand." He took a deep breath and let it out slowly in an effort to calm a rising anxiety about how Névé would take this news, and then he sent a text to Jona. Névé had been with them only a short time, and already he couldn't imagine being without her.

Jeremi: Come by ASAP.

And then he prayed for all of them.

Jona was in his office within a minute. They frequently had problems, but when Jona saw the expression on Jeremi's face, he froze.

"Have you seen Névé yet this morning?" Jeremi asked.

"No, why?"

"We have a problem." He played the Crowd-Source news on his WritingWall.

Jona sat down hard on the chair opposite the desk. He then leaned forward, elbows on knees. "Are you thinking what I'm thinking? The explosion was planned to get Incense Rising?"

Jeremi nodded. "Unfortunately. Too coincidental, and it fits the pattern Névé described from Incense. Rather than take her in and deal with the publicity or have an accident befall her as happened with her uncle and have to answer questions about that, why not destroy the whole area and any copies before anyone even knows she's there? No questions to answer about Incense."

"Makes sense. Maybe she wasn't there, though. Névé said she had plans to get out."

"Maybe, but if the explosion was planned to get her, I'd say they got her. How convenient that most of the residents were over at a sector meeting called by the local council. The explosion didn't reach that far. It was a diversion that limited damage. Well planned and executed, I'd say."

"Névé's going to take this hard."

"Yep."

They heard the door to the outer office open. A few seconds later, Névé made an appearance with both dogs trailing behind. "I'm going shopping with Luisa uptown, and I wondered if I could leave the dogs in the office."

Jona stood up. "Névé, we have a news item from Crowd-Source that you need to see."

"Why?" Reading Jona's body language, she went into her marble-statue imitation.

"Maybe you better sit down." Jona motioned to the other chair near the desk.

***

The next day, Névé felt exhausted from the previous day's shock of learning that Incense may have been killed in the New French Quarter blast. She sat on the couch at the ranch house and stroked Jesús's chest. She could visualize Incense's face as if she'd seen her an hour ago. How could someone go from being that alive to dead in an instant? Névé hoped Incense hadn't been near the blast, but her instincts told her that she probably had been. The whole situation was suspicious. She picked up Jesús and went to look for Jona in the vineyard. He was with Jeremi among the grapes, looking at something and conferring. She knew they were wrapping up their busy season and didn't want to interrupt. The day had grown unseasonably warm, so she waited for them on a bench in the shade just outside the office.

Workers in white overalls were bringing in the last of the year's harvest and filling giant tubs with grapes. Sunlight shone crimson through the ones on top of the piles. Névé wanted to remember this moment for the day when it would be shining through a glass of wine.

Watching the activity triggered a memory of her mother reading her the Aesop fable of the ants and the grasshopper, and she realized what she felt like here—the grasshopper. Everyone had a worthwhile job except her. She would have to figure out the long term, but now she had a short-term goal. She just needed to work on how to do it.

She scratched behind Jesús's ears and waited for Jona and Jeremi to finish their conversation. They must have come to a decision on something because they turned and began walking toward her. She thought she saw relief in their eyes, maybe because she was out and about instead of staying in her room. She greeted them with a "Good morning" and asked if they could go into the office, and they did. Each took a chair. They smelled faintly of sweat. Jona wiped his forehead with a red handkerchief, and he asked if she needed anything.

She still hadn't gotten used to his brown eyes. "I'm thinking I want to get the information that Incense gave me out by multiple routes and as soon as possible. We can't let the CBI get away with this. In the past few hours, I've gone from sad to mad."

Jona nodded that he understood. "I'd like to help, but I'd prefer that we keep Jeremi and Luisa out of it. Jeremi has a testimony for another trial and a hearing coming up, and we need him cleared of all charges."

Jeremi's eyes showed his concern as he leaned toward Névé. "I would like to help, but I think Jona's right. I'll soon be tied up with the hearing."

"Jeremi, I understand." Turning to Jona, Névé continued. "Here's my problem. Incense was afraid the CBI wouldn't stop at finding her. They would suspect that anyone who had been in contact with her might have been given a copy of the theory. Therefore, once they identified her, they would eventually come after me, too. I also know that Incense didn't want to implicate any more people than she had to."

Jeremi suggested they take the problem of publishing the theory to a man named Professor Fairday, who was the one Luisa had in mind, or his graduate student, Blake.

Jona ran his fingers through his hair. "I have a confession to make. I knew you'd need to do something soon, and the sooner we get this hot potato off our hands, the better. Anyway, I already contacted that professor. Blake will go shopping in uptown Bee Cave this afternoon and just happen to wander into a typically noisy café called Sammy's Platters. He doesn't know what it's about yet, but I'll give him a note and a copy of the information if you agree." He waited for her response. "I guess we were thinking along the same lines."

Néve's shoulders relaxed, and she kissed the top of Jesús's head. "I agree. Let's make him another copy and leave mine and these on the dogs' collars—for safekeeping, OK?"

***

Later in the afternoon, Jona had tinted his beard darker and donned glasses and a cap. He sat at an open table in the middle of Sammy's Platters. He waited for Blake to come in and wander around until Jona signaled him with a wave. Blake's appearance did not draw attention. He was a medium-height, dark-haired man in his mid to late twenties. He would soon have his PhD in electrical engineering, and he had long been a member of Jeremi's circle, as was his advisor. He took a seat in the booth with Jona, who already had two coffees waiting.

Jona explained that he had obtained a copy of a theory from a Dr. Orion Rising and that Rising's relatives—Jona didn't specify who—wanted the theory published. They suspected foul play in Rising's death, and they didn't want to see his efforts wasted.

Blake raised his eyebrows and leaned toward Jona. He talked rapidly as if he had difficulty masking his level of excitement and keeping his voice down. "I met him at a conference a couple of years ago. His work was incredibly interesting but still in the early stages. It wasn't taken seriously, though, because of his unusual approach. I remember one person in the audience telling him bluntly that he was 'barking up the wrong tree.' I guess, as it turns out, he wasn't."

Jona put his elbows on the table and his hands near his mouth and talked barely loud enough for Blake to hear him. "Are you saying that his theory might be correct?"

"Maybe. It'll be a radically different approach, but that's probably what we've needed. I'll discuss it with Fairday. No doubt, it needs reviewers, and we're not particle physicists. Unfortunately, the university lost a guy who would be knowledgeable about this. He died in the flood."

"So what are you thinking you can do to help?"

"A couple of things. The problem we could run into is that posting it on our community science board could be blocked. If the CBI has any parts of it, which they probably do, they could have a filter to block anything being posted with that content. It would also not go out through Net-mail. The only encryption now that is legal is what the NAUS authorities have software to decode—all in the name of commerce and national security."

"My source for the information predicted as much. When you try to post it, you'll use an anonymous Net address, won't you?"

"They're not anonymous if the CBI wants information."

"Can they *legally* do that? Allow anonymous NetLinks that aren't actually anonymous?"

Blake put his coffee cup near his mouth. "The NAUS authorities have the legal right to block anything they think could threaten commerce or national security. I wonder what other approaches we could try." He sipped his coffee for a few seconds. "If the information could be posted as something else and then translated into the real information, then we might get it distributed." He leaned even closer to Jona as though they might be lovers. "One of the students who was killed in the flood had a WorldNet port that we learned was never inactivated. A couple of us were able to hack into it for use as a type of decoy account. I've posted general information using it."

Jona rubbed his dark beard. The coloring itched and was coming off on his fingers. He covertly rubbed it off on his jeans. "Are you sure they wouldn't be able to trace the source of the information back to you or at least the engineering department?"

"She was an English graduate student, and I didn't know her. That's the beauty of it. We can attempt to post the mathematical derivation, and if it's blocked, it came from a deceased English grad student's NetLink."

Jona suppressed a smile. "Let me know how we can help. We have another route we're pursuing, but it's not as direct."

"What's that?"

"The information can be encoded on music. The music can be posted and disseminated widely, and then independently the method for decoding it can be posted. It's a Trojan horse method."

"I think that'll work. If this other source can post the music with the embedded information, this decoy account could post the decoding, and both would be out and dispersed before whoever is blocking it could act." Blake hesitated. "Can I ask how you got this theory in the first place?"

"I don't want to get you in any deeper than you are. Just don't do anything to implicate yourself, OK?"

"I'm willing to do whatever I can for the organization that Jeremi claims isn't his."

"This isn't for Jeremi's organization. We're involved because we don't think a scientific hypothesis should be silenced because it's inconvenient."

"The enemy of my enemy…is my friend."

VINEYARD STROLL

Névé came out on the porch and went into the vineyard, headed in the direction of the offices. She wore long sleeves and jeans and put on the straw hat that Luisa had given her. She'd found the sun in the Southwest had a lot more punch than it did in the North—and it shone a lot more, as it was doing today. She hooked a leash on Jesús so that he couldn't get too far away. One of the vineyard workers had told her the same thing that Jona had: hawks in the area liked small dogs. María ran through the vineyard looking to harass ground squirrels or rabbits. Névé kept an eye on her because sometimes she started digging. She was a silver bullet in the gold, orange, and green of the vineyard. Today the vines were empty of fruit. Close up, Névé marveled at how each leaf was a work of art.

She approached a utility shed while Jeremi talked to a couple of the workers about preparing the vines for winter. He nodded to her and asked if he could walk with her up to the office.

When Jeremi was around other people, he was lively and witty. Whenever he was alone with her, he was quiet and she needed to ask questions to keep the conversation going. His dark eyes always searched hers, as if trying to read her thoughts, and he usually asked if she needed anything. She would tell him no and that he'd done everything he could to make her feel welcome. Because he was quiet as usual, she asked him

285

more about the extent of the vineyards, mostly to make small talk.

He waved a hand toward the south. "Luisa and I have kept old vines from a former vineyard on the southern edge of the property, and we continue to plant more vines every year. Each new vine takes time to produce the quality of grape needed for a good wine." Névé had not seen Jeremi so talkative with her.

"Luisa was happy to come with me, I think mostly at first to get away from an overardent suitor. I was excited to get a place that I could build up and make something of. I thought that I'd have to start from nothing, and then my parents offered us this property. The irony is that I already knew I would be teaching the Way, and to get an opportunity to run this vineyard was perfect for me."

Névé nodded. "We've both been the recipients of an inheritance that changed our lives."

He smiled. "In more ways than one." He searched her face to see if she understood the full implications of what she said, but he didn't think so. She wasn't one of them yet.

"Do you have enough land to have a sustainable, profitable operation?"

"I can see your business training paid off. Yes, we think so, but I wouldn't want it to be smaller. Wise Consumer has the neighboring fields, and they've been trying to get me to sell the land to them. Now they're getting attorneys involved. I can't afford many legal fees, and they know it. My parents had refused to sell it, and I have no intention of selling it either. I like running a vineyard, and Luisa likes the marketing-and-promotional side. But I don't like doing the books." He stopped and turned to face Névé directly. "We could use someone to manage the accounting. Would you be interested in a job?"

Névé hadn't expected a job offer, and it caught her by surprise. She wasn't sure what to say.

"You don't have to answer right away, but think about it. We'd love to have you join us. I can put together a proposal for a starting salary."

"I'll think about it, Jeremi. You and Luisa have been so nice to me. I can't thank you enough—and especially what you do for Jona."

"No need to thank me there. The value of his work for the Way is far more than his salary working for the Vine and Branches."

At the office, they stopped in the shade and faced out toward the vines.

"You said that Wise Consumer wanted to buy the land. You didn't say the vineyard. Is it just the land they want, and what would they do with it?"

"Nothing, from what I can tell. They have a large dog kennel, but the fields they own aren't cultivated. This afternoon, I have to meet with my attorney to prepare for my testimony tomorrow in the Blackmon trial, so I'd like to have a pleasant lunch first. Can I interest you in lunch? I know a nice café."

Névé nodded. The picnics were pleasant, but lunch at a café would be a special treat. They went to uptown Bee Cave. She realized that this was the first time she had been in public with him. People they passed had one of two reactions to him. Either they recognized him and smiled, nodding or waving, or they ignored him. Some clearly avoided him, including eye contact.

He led her to a place called the Sojourner Café. Tables against the walls were separated with partitions, and each had an Infi-Scene window. Jeremi chose a table, turned on the window, and selected *Lisbon*. Suddenly, Névé's surroundings were as though she was in an alcove off a steeply inclined street paved with bricks. Buildings were stucco and multicolored. A fuchsia bougainvillea climbed along one wall. Jeremi asked, "Is this scene OK, or would you prefer another one?"

"It's nice, Jeremi. Does it have some special meaning for you?"

He said he'd enjoyed his time in Lisbon, and he talked about his travels abroad and how he came to know what he needed to do when he returned. His excitement about the Way and what they could do was contagious. He tried to pull her more into the conversation, asking her questions about herself, and she knew her answers were not very enlightening. But she would much rather listen to him talk—now that she had him talking—about his experiences and plans. In the course of listening, she realized that she would love to stay here and accept his job offer, but she had something that needed to be done first.

MENSA TRIAL, ROUND FOUR

Rigel insisted on paying for their tickets, claiming a First People discount because he was returning to Lakota land. Claret had never heard of such a deal, but maybe there was no reason why she should have. She acquiesced partly because she couldn't afford three tickets and partly because she'd insisted that the tickets be for an open-ended round trip, thinking they might need an easy out on the spur of a moment. He bought them all one-month open-travel tickets, which Claret thought defeated the reason for the alleged discount, but she didn't argue. At the moment, Rigel was downstairs. He'd gone to the ground floor to use a quiet room so he could Vid-chat with his father. He also needed it for the afternoon Vid-chat on the Cream Team project. Jade was in her room on juror duty. Ember was at school. Because most of her packing was done, Claret decided to turn on the Mensa Blackmon trial.

Sol was in the middle of speaking. "…are returning after an extended recess, requested by both sides to reconsider the case against the defendant and to schedule additional witnesses. Sapphire, what can you tell us about today's schedule?"

"Good morning, Sol. We can expect to hear today from those who were in Real Carrier correspondence with Mensa Blackmon. We don't have complete information on these witnesses. They all appear to be leaders of religious cults operating across the country. The first witness is

Jeremi Duende, and he is well known because of his arrest in August for sedition and his pending trial. Odds are that he will deny any substantive link to Mensa Blackmon. But we heard from murder-scene investigators that Duende's correspondence with Mensa Blackmon spanned the time from the disclosure of the Religion Team's conclusions to Mensa Blackmon's death. Other witnesses are Daniel Goldman, Mohammed Saud, Sari Patel, and Dragon Chen. As I said before, the testimonies of these witnesses were not deemed critical, or the court could have asked for them sooner."

The view for the audience changed from Sapphire to the courtroom.

Sol spoke in his lower, simulated-courtroom tone. "I hate to interrupt, but Jeremi Duende has joined the courtroom by Vid-chat. He is located in the Austin area and runs the Vine and Branches vineyard, although the NAUS Board believes that he runs a great deal more, including a religious cult."

Claret's monitor now showed two camera feeds. One was a close-up of the prosecutor's face, and the second showed a twenty-something man with dark, curly hair and tanned skin. She thought he was attractive in spite of his thin face and large, dark eyes. He leaned toward the camera with an expectant expression.

"Good morning, Mr. Duende. I'm the prosecutor in the Mensa Blackmon trial, as you know, and I will lead off the questions this morning. Let me remind you that you are required to answer truthfully. Failure to do so will result in your arrest and conviction of perjury."

Jeremi nodded. "I understand, Prosecutor."

Claret thought his eyes looked untroubled.

The prosecutor began his questioning. "Investigators of the Mensa Blackmon murder have presented evidence of your having corresponded with Mensa Blackmon before his death. The evidence is Real Carrier letters found at the scene."

Jeremi said nothing. Claret assumed that he was waiting for a question. After a few seconds, the prosecutor continued.

"Do you affirm that you were in correspondence with Mensa Blackmon?"

"Yes."

"Who initiated that correspondence?"

"I did."

"Why?"

"Because I wanted to point out the problems with the conclusions reached by the Exposing the Fallibility of Religion Committee."

"We've read the content of the letters. What gave you the audacity to think that you could change the mind of a brilliant man like Mensa Blackmon?"

"I'm a servant, simply a message bearer. If his mind was changed, it was through the workings of a more persuasive power than I am."

"Mr. Duende, just stick to the facts. Do you believe that you are the one who effected his reconsidering the committee's conclusions?"

"I believe that I was one among others."

"The letters reveal that you gave him the names of the other witnesses who are testifying today. Why did you do that?"

"He needed to look at the whole picture, the bigger picture, and not just the data that the committee had collected. I checked with them beforehand, and they agreed to get involved."

"Unfortunately, we don't have his letters to you. For the record, can you tell the court what happened to those letters?"

"They were destroyed in my downtown Austin office when it flooded."

"And did you receive any letters after the Austin flood?"

"No. Mensa Blackmon was found dead the next day."

"Thank you, Mr. Duende. I have no more questions for this witness."

And neither did the defense attorney.

The studio with the commentators was back in view. Sapphire checked a monitor and explained to viewers that there would be a brief recess.

Sol took the reins. "If I may ask, Sapphire, wasn't there correspondence from others who are unable to testify?"

"Yes, Sol. That is true, although their testimony was not considered vital to the trial."

"Who were those potential witnesses, and why are they unavailable?"

"They're unavailable because they died in the past few months since Mensa Blackmon's death. One was the original Mensa, Mensa Li Fugimoto, who died recently of a heart attack at the age of ninety-nine. The other was Dr. Orion Rising—"

Claret leaned forward and requested volume increase.

"—who was killed in a fall from a subway platform in New York City. Only one letter has come to light showing that they corresponded. Other letters may have been destroyed by Mensa Blackmon for reasons unknown."

"Sapphire, wasn't the last witness you mentioned, Dr. Rising, connected to the woman whom the CBI is looking for and has offered a reward on? Incense Rising, isn't it?"

Claret stood up as if she had received an electrical shock.

"Yes, Sol, you have a good memory. As you know, after his death, she stole his notes and disappeared. The CBI desperately wants her to return the notes and submit to questioning, but it released today that it now believes she may have been tragically killed in yesterday's gas explosion in the New Orleans New French Quarter…"

Claret gasped and the room rocked as though from an earthquake. This was news she hadn't seen and Rigel surely didn't know. She sent him a text to come back up when he could. He didn't respond and was possibly learning the news on the Vid-chat with his father. While the commentator discussion went on, she searched for the *News Feed* and found the story.

News Feed. October 16. Rising Search Called Off. Brought to you by the makers of the WritingWall— inscribing our future. The search for Incense Rising was called off today by the CBI. Director Alfa Zulu stated that undercover CBI agents had a tip from a resident of the New French Quarter in New Orleans that Ms. Rising may have worked at a Real Carrier office, which was near the epicenter of a gas explosion a couple of days ago...

The *News Feed* went on to describe how the hurricane coming onshore had hindered the CBI's ability to get a positive identification. Before she could be arrested, the block where she was last seen was leveled by a blast caused by a leaking natural-gas line, which the CBI also attributed to the storm. There were no survivors in the area and no sign of Incense Rising elsewhere in the New French Quarter, so she was presumed dead and the search was called off. The CBI stated how much it regretted not being able to question Rising.

Claret had no idea how to break this news to Rigel if he hadn't already heard. The voices of the Mensa Blackmon trial were a backdrop to her own thoughts. She turned off the trial to await Rigel's return. She wasn't concentrating on it anyway. Several minutes later, he opened the door, and she knew as soon as she saw his face that he'd heard the news.

A PERSON OF INTEREST

Jeremi came out of his office, looking drained. He, Jona, and Névé sat around the lounge in a blue silence. Jesús jumped into Névé's lap. She rubbed his ears. Luisa came in with some lemonade.

"Well, what did you think?" Jeremi rubbed his temples.

Jona wanted to see Jeremi back to his normal buoyant self. "Short and sweet. I thought it went well."

"I didn't tell them anything that they didn't already know."

"I wonder what their purpose was in even calling you as a witness."

"Who knows? I'd like to have said more, but my attorney made it clear that I should just answer the questions and not elaborate."

Névé had been quiet all morning. No one had asked why, so she didn't say. She did speak now to ask something she had wondered earlier. "Why wasn't your attorney here?"

"He had to appear on another monitor, as he would have been in a courtroom so they could see that he wasn't telling me what to say."

Jona tried again to cheer him up. "Well, at least Blackmon's murder is one thing that you can't be accused of doing."

"No, I suppose that's a bright side."

As the energy ebbed from the group, Luisa said, "I'm sure testifying was no picnic, so why don't we have one out in the vineyard for lunch? I made tomato soup and french bread."

Jeremi smiled. "Luisa's comfort food—and I'm thankful for it."

When everyone agreed but Névé, Jona realized something other than concern for Jeremi's testimony was wrong, and he was the first to probe. "Névé, you've been quiet today. What's up?"

Névé swallowed hard and appeared paler than normal. "I read a new Person of Interest bulletin from the CBI this morning. They're now looking for a young woman caught on camera before the hurricane and in the vicinity of the New French Quarter where the blast occurred. She has blond hair and is accompanied by a large dog." She let the weight of the revelation sink in.

Jona sprang out of his chair. "What the—" He stopped himself before he could let loose with what he had started to say, and he began pacing, his face flushed.

"And that's not the biggest news, which just came up a few minutes ago. The CBI is shutting down all Real Carrier offices immediately. They're claiming overwhelming evidence of national security risk. Several politicians were mailed contaminated samples and have come down with a disease similar to smallpox. The CBI is discouraging travel and public transportation until vaccines can be produced, which will be months."

Jeremi turned to his NetLink, with Luisa right behind him. He located and pulled up the Person of Interest bulletin first.

Before Jeremi could read it, Jona stopped him. "Wait. If they're looking for you, why didn't they just show up here? There are cameras at every train station. If they wanted to know where you are, I'm sure they could find out."

Névé explained that the ones in the New French Quarter were knocked out by the storm, so the CBI probably didn't know that she got on or off a train. It knew only that she was near the Real Carrier office before the storm. With Incense missing—and now the CBI was listing Kit as missing—the CBI knew only that someone by her description had been there before the storm. The CBI claimed that it was trying to account for everyone who might have been killed in the blast.

Jona shook his head. "Probably they want to account for everyone who had contact with Incense Rising and might know something—or have something."

Jeremi projected the bulletin on his WritingWall. It was brief and to the point. The CBI was offering 5,000D for information leading to the identification and whereabouts of a young woman of interest. A camera image of Névé at the bus stop was dark and unclear, probably because of the heavy rain. It was taken during the brief time that the wind had blown her hood back. A large dog stood next to her, but Jesús's head at the neckline of her raincoat was not visible. The wind had blown the lapel up. The bulletin stated that the CBI had accounted for everyone in the New French Quarter near the blast except for three people: a blonde woman on camera with the dog, a woman whom they believed to be Incense Rising, and a man named Kit Larson, who operated the Real Carrier office near the epicenter of the blast. The news item had a quote from a CBI spokesman: "If we had mandatory ID chips for all citizens, this recovery effort would be much easier. The CBI plans to petition the board to make an implanted ID chip a requirement for anyone living within the NAUS borders."

The four of them sat in silence. Jona was the first to speak. "Fortunately, the image of Névé isn't clear, and Jesús isn't visible. If the description had been a blond-haired young woman with a greyhound and a Chihuahua, even the locals in Bee Cave would know who she is."

They all agreed, and then speculation moved on to what they would do when mandatory IDs were implemented. Jeremi suggested that they cross that bridge when they get to it, then added with a smile, "Maybe Texas will secede before that happens anyway."

Névé said that since she had unloaded her news, she was now hungry. She suggested they have Luisa's lunch in the office, where they were sure there were no cameras and microphones, and discuss what she should do. Should she turn herself in, leave, or what?

As they sat around the food, only Névé was eating. The others took occasional bites between long silences, so Névé voiced a concern. "I don't think they could arrest or detain me because I haven't done anything wrong. If we don't have in our possession the Risings' information, then I don't have anything they want. What if we put the copies in a safe place and then I turn myself in?"

Jeremi shook his head. "No way, Névé. You don't want them to have control of you if you can prevent it. They could drum up a charge in order to detain you if they thought you were hiding something. And they have ways of getting information, including drugs, that you don't want to experience. Trust me."

Luisa put her arm around his shoulder. "You never told me they did any of that to you."

"What good would it have done? I'm telling you all now so that Névé doesn't get caught up in something that she has no idea where it could end up."

Jona stopped eating and leaned back in his chair. "I agree. Like Incense told you, she wanted to get Orion's theory out because it needed to get out, but also it made her no longer of value to the CBI. I doubt they'd offer five thousand dólares just to account for everyone after the blast. They want you in case you were given information from Incense. So if we take the option of you turning yourself in off the table, what are we left with? You hunker down inside here, and don't go out in public. Maybe they'll take some time to link the woman in the photo to you, if they ever do."

Luisa pointed out that Névé's cousins would probably identify her when they saw the picture. It looked enough like Névé, and they would recognize María.

Névé spoke between sips of soup. "I already thought about that but hadn't brought it up yet. And they know that I was headed to Austin. With that information, the CBI will begin looking at surveillance cameras in this area and find me."

Jeremi offered up the next option. "You could disguise yourself and leave the area. You've already given a copy of the Orion theory to Blake, although he hasn't been able to post it directly. He told me that he tried yesterday. We'll need the music encryption option, or we can try some other ideas that he had."

Luisa offered to go with her somewhere. "We could travel around, see some sights, or head down toward my parents in Mexico. I think the CBI would have a harder time finding you in a remote area down there."

Névé nodded, thinking about it. "I like that idea. I think I need to do something soon. They won't take long to piece enough together to find me here and then the Rising information."

Jona stood up and paced again. "There's no way I want to let you two leave here to run around the Southwest and Mexico. The next thing we know, some accident will happen to you. If you leave, I'm going with you."

Jeremi said he didn't like any of these options and that they needed to prayerfully consider the choices. Something would become apparent.

Névé thought she knew what the something was. She wasn't going to let Incense down, and she wasn't going to endanger her friends or the dogs. She had wanted an adventure. Now was her chance to have one. She wished that she could consult Jahn, but her cousins would put the CBI on to him as her attorney, and they were well familiar with him already. She would have to go this one alone.

ARRIVAL IN DAKOTA

The first thing that struck Claret as she left the TransPort terminal was that they weren't in Seattle anymore. Her first impression of Dakota was that it was mostly sky. In the parking lot, Rigel had his HelioRunner, and into it they piled the things they carried from the Northwest. As soon as they left the small town—which wasn't much more than the TransPort station, some shops, and a city hall—the second thing that struck Claret was how relaxed Rigel's hands were as he held the steering wheel. He had not put it in auto-drive. He was headed home and in his element.

The HelioRunner began to isolate them within a landscape that Claret had seen in Rigel's paintings posted for sale on the Net. She felt like Alice in *Through the Looking-Glass* as though she'd entered one of the paintings. The chessboard of fields was on a gigantic scale and rolling. Ember had wanted the middle of the front seat, so Claret took the passenger front, and they watched the scenery mostly in silence. They hadn't seen such wide-open spaces since the train trip from Quebec to Seattle.

Jade stayed equally quiet in the back seat. On the train, she had put on dark glasses and slept through much of the trip. The jury had spent late evenings discussing witness testimony, after which Jade would go out for a while, usually to the underground meetings. She had tried to catch up on sleep. But now, she also stared out the car windows, thankful that she had a ticket back to Seattle for whenever she wanted to leave. She was on this trip as a favor to her sister, and she had better not have trouble tying into the Net for the next day of the Mensa Blackmon trial. Something Rigel had said had her intrigued. His uncle had some old paper books in a guest room where she would stay, and she might want to photo them for her friends. She hoped they were something of value and he wasn't just saying that as an enticement. He'd clearly wanted Claret and Ember out here. And Claret didn't think Jade could make it on her own. She was irritated with herself for not staying in Seattle just to show Claret that she could.

Wind buffeted the lightweight vehicle. Rigel pointed out the names of some of the places as they passed. They responded with nods. Ember pointed to a rising column of dust. "What's that?"

Rigel had waited to see if Ember would discover it for himself before he pointed it out. "It's a large dust devil. The wind swirls around into a column and lifts the dust. Then it falls back to the earth, making a giant arch."

Ember craned his neck around to look up as far as he could. "Wow. Can it carry you away?"

"No. It's not a tornado. There are even more serious ones in New Mexico because they have hot air currents and a drier climate, so there's a lot of dust to blow around."

Rigel looked over at Claret and wondered if she thought they'd never make it to the ranch, even though it was only about a twenty-minute drive. He recognized fatigue in her eyes, but her copper hair still shone. A few ringlets had come loose from the ponytail she'd tried to corral them into. He would like to have painted her gaze into the autumn landscape of cattle grazing in pastures or the wind rippling a wheat field. He'd warned her that it was isolated but hoped she'd see the beauty in the giant rolling hills.

Claret's misgivings about the whole trip reached a peak about ten minutes into the drive. Maybe she shouldn't have taken Ember out of school. What if the apartment had to be evacuated on short notice? They still had a lot of things there. What if Ember fell off a horse and seriously hurt himself out here in the middle of nowhere? And what if she fell off the emotional cliff with Rigel that she could feel them standing on the brink of? And how would Jade behave, being here reluctantly at best?

When they pulled up in front of the house, Ember was squirming. "That's a special house. Why is the roof like that?"

"The angles on the house help funnel the wind around it, and the roof can support a lot of snow when we get a big one," Rigel said.

"Oh, wow! I want to stay for a big snow. How big?"

"Taller than you are, sometimes."

"Oh goody," Claret heard Jade mutter.

Ember's mouth formed an *O* as he tried to picture snow that deep. Claret and Jade got out of the car and surveyed the yard while Rigel pulled their cases from the back. Copper and bronze metalwork added color to a garden that showed the signs of late fall. Cadence came onto the front porch. He resembled Rigel, although the father was shorter than his son. Rigel introduced them; they went up the stairs, past four rocking chairs, and into the house.

The large living space, enclosed with stone and glass, was quiet, warm, and inviting after the buffeting cool wind outside. The vista on three sides gave it an open, communing-with-nature feel.

Rigel showed them each to a bedroom. Claret's was Incense's room when she was at home. Some of her belongings were there: one of Rigel's landscape paintings, a large basket of dried herbs, a bow and quiver of arrows hanging on the wall, and a centuries-old First People painting of a hunting party. Her clothes hung in the closet. Rigel had said that he and his dad held out hope that she was still alive. He'd spent a rough day after finding out about the blast, but they couldn't believe that she wouldn't have gotten away if she had smelled gas. Claret thought they were probably grasping at what "might be" in an effort to deal with the pain of what was.

She went to check on Ember and found him sitting in a chair facing the east. His room had the appearance of a guest room. There were no personal items in it. There was, however, an antique oil lamp on the dresser. "Hi, Ember. How's your room? Mine's nice."

"Look outside, Mom. I see *horses*—behind the barn. See them?"

"Yes. Aren't they pretty?" She stroked his hair. "Even though Rigel said he'll teach you to ride, don't pester him about them right away, OK?"

His "OK" came out sounding slow and reluctant.

"Also, don't touch that lamp or anything that looks old, OK again?"

He nodded, and she left him to watch the horses. Rigel was outside standing at the corral at the back of the barn with his dad. He was agreeing with something that Cadence said. She didn't want to intrude, so she sat in a rocking chair on the porch. She buttoned her jacket and shook out her ponytail so that her hair covered her ears. Wind tossed it around like the dust devil they'd seen earlier, so she secured it back into the ponytail. The air was free of exhaust fumes, fried food, and salt water. The latter she would miss, but not the others. The only sounds were ones being caused by the moving air. She closed her eyes and rocked.

Father and son returned to the porch, and Rigel asked Claret if she'd like to take a walk with him.

"Love to."

They headed out toward the corral, where he'd been standing with his father.

"Is your room OK? Do you need anything?"

"It's lovely, Rigel. Thank you for giving me your sister's room."

He nodded and looked as if he was fighting back tears. "Dad says that he doesn't believe she's dead, but he has no proof."

"What can I do to help?"

"When Dad sent me that text to return, he'd received a Real Carrier through a contact. It was probably sent by Incense weeks before the explosion. She said that she had a job and was working on documenting what Uncle Orion had been working on. When she had something, she would be sending it encoded on music for posting on WorldNet." He stopped to consider the situation for a few seconds. Claret could see his jaw muscles moving as he clenched his teeth. "We might actually be able to do this, although we can't know yet if she was able to send something our way before the explosion. I guess all we can do is wait."

"I'd like to think maybe she's in hiding somewhere."

"Yeah. The suspension of Real Carrier is unfortunate. Dad says the First People everywhere are irate about the threat to pass a law that everyone has to have an ID chip."

"So what is it exactly that you'd be posting when it's decoded?"

"Whatever my sister and Uncle Orion were working on. I'm not the physicist in the family, so I'm not even sure. But if Uncle Orion was working on it and he and Incense wanted it out, then that's good enough for me. I'm determined their efforts won't be wasted."

"OK. How can I help?"

He smiled. "Are you sure you want to? This doesn't come without risk."

"Neither does anything else of value, usually."

"You're the communications expert." He pulled her into his arms.

Cadence looked out toward the corral. He hoped that his positive impression of Claret was accurate, because it was clear to him how his son felt about her.

DR. AVARITA BANKS

Avarita was checking the stock market when the last beep sounded, signaling that the group was all on Vid-chat. She checked her short blond hairdo in a mirror that she kept above her Vid-chat screen and made sure that the Wise Consumer tattoo on her forehead was showing. "Good morning, team. I'm Dr. Avarita Banks, and I hope you're stoked with whatever stimulant you use to get your fire lit in the morning, because we are going to roll up our sleeves and get to work making money for Wise Consumer."

The group members reflected her "Good morning" with as much enthusiasm as they could muster.

"The efforts to date to bring the Cream Team into the black have not been exactly successful, so I'm here to launch this team into profitability. Ms. Yen, as you know, was recently promoted. The Uppers were so impressed with how quickly she put together a plan for recovering revenue in the Sino region that they rewarded her handsomely. I imagine she got a big pay raise, too. Wouldn't we all like a pay increase? They're certainly not paying me enough to add this team to my responsibilities, but I don't plan to stay with you long—only long enough to get your costs under control. Milk Products will not tolerate a group that doesn't operate in the black."

Aries's brow wrinkled. "But currently our major costs are associated with small-scale manufacturing and building revenue, both of which are necessary to make us profitable. We won't save ourselves into prosperity. I, too, was brought in to help the team, but miracles don't happen overnight in this business. We're going to have to dig a hole before we can erect a suitable structure."

"And I'm here to help you fill in the hole. And believe me, I can fill a hole."

Aries waded in deeper when she said, "What else do you suggest we do?"

"We are going to implement a three-pronged strategic approach to cutting costs: production, people, and promotion—the three Ps of smart business. I've already drawn up the obvious actions to be taken. At our next meeting, we'll brain jettison additional actions. Regarding production, I spoke to the plant manager, and she will recommend raw material substitutions and alternative shipping methods. Mr. Rising, could you come up with lower-cost designs?"

"Probably."

"Powerful! We need fewer ink colors and more white space."

Rigel needed to make sure that she understood something before they went too far down that path. "The design colors are one of the main selling points, and the ink is a fraction of the total cost."

"But every little bit helps. Plus, it's not just the cost of the ink but the line speed that will be achievable after scale-up."

Rigel rubbed his chin. "Probably, but we'll never earn scale-up if we don't attract advertisers."

"We will never earn scale-up if we don't show profitability."

Aries's frustration was evident in her voice. "You're the doctor. But your strategic approach is exactly what we've been doing, and I don't see how another bloodletting is going to cure this patient. I'm glad we've been leveraged to other businesses so that I still have projects and a contract when this patient has bled to death."

Avarita chose to ignore the last remark. "Thank you for the lead-in to the next issue: people. To address the people costs, you will all be cut to ten percent time on the Cream Team. And I've seen some reference to Project Java. Whatever new business effort that was, it will be cut. No one is to spend time on Java. Got it?"

Claret was the first to answer. "I think I can speak for the team and say, 'No problem.'"

"Perfect! Now, as to promotion, Claret, I want you to cut the size of the ads we've been running and find less expensive sites to run them on—including anywhere adverts are free. Agreed?"

"Possibly."

"Problem?"

"Places. There are limited places where our potential customers might see the ad. Placing it, for example, in the free advert space of *Country Canine* isn't going to reach the right audience. But I'll see what I can find."

"Perfect. We'll discuss further cuts at our next meeting. For now, I have to run and make something called *profit* in my other businesses."

GOING IT ALONE

Névé considered how unhappy Jona would be with her, but this plan was the best for everyone concerned. She had to go rogue as Incense had done, and she needed to do it alone. Not only were the others needed in Austin for now but she also didn't want them taking the risks. Névé had been with Incense for only a couple of days, but she wanted to repay Incense for rescuing her when the hurricane was coming. That act of kindness now connected Névé to this other woman, who was also outside the system. Both of these reasons, or something else she couldn't name, compelled Névé to see the Orion theory published and to risk her life doing so—but not the lives of Jona, Luisa, and Jeremi.

The final planning had taken very little time because she had prepared herself to travel anywhere in North America. Before leaving Michigan, she had loaded maps on her PortAble so she wouldn't need to log in to the WorldNet. The maps showed which few roads were still free and not toll roads. Sometime after midnight, when the others were in bed, she used brown hair coloring and some SunLess tanning lotion, donned a cloak she'd bought the previous day, and walked into El Calderón and then out again with all the other hooded patrons before closing time.

She had had to pay the HelioRunner rental agency extra to make the rental anonymous, something that would certainly be made illegal in the future with the trend toward eliminating anonymous NetLink sites. With the address that Incense had given her of a cousin who could contact her brother in Dakota, she would deliver the information in person.

Like all HelioRunners, hers had the option to be self-driving, but that required connectivity to the WorldNet and global-positioning information. She decided to let it drive itself, even though it was linked to the Net, for the first part of the trip when no one may be trailing her. Then somewhere around Oklahoma, she thought she'd drive it herself so her signal couldn't be tracked. Even though she had driven a car only in simulations when she and Jemma had gotten driver's licenses for the fun of it, she didn't see why she couldn't drive at least part of the trip to Dakota, as long as the sun stayed out to keep the batteries charged. She'd stop at night and charge on the grid.

She had parked the rental car the previous afternoon in a spot a couple of blocks away from El Calderón and now headed toward it. She took her backpack out of the trunk but left her cloak on and got in. Trembling, she turned the auto on and set it for the first destination: Oklahoma City. At some point, when she had been tracked to Austin and discovered missing, the CBI would be checking all transportation out and eventually discover the anonymous rental. But she had enough time to get ahead of the CBI, she reasoned, and hopefully hide her trail. The car pulled smoothly out of the lot and headed toward the highway.

Névé looked at herself in the car's mirror. Besides her slender build and lavender eyes, she looked like a different person, one with dark-brown hair and olive-colored skin. Her hair was long enough now to lie flat, so she had combed it back with setting gel, making her gender less obvious. She closed her eyes for a minute and said a prayer as Marta or Jeremi would have said, praying for a safe and successful trip, but not with the conviction with which they seemed to pray. She realized she still didn't understand how and why they could be so convinced of its effects.

By 3:00 a.m., the HelioRunner was headed north. The hardest part about the whole scheme was leaving the dogs behind.

JEREMI'S HEARING

In the inner office of the Vine and Branches vineyard, Jeremi, Luisa, and Jona sat around the lounge and shared a prayer and a private moment before Jeremi had to leave to appear in court for the hearing to determine whether he would be tried for unlawful activity.

Jona asked if they had seen Névé yet. He hadn't seen her come into the office, and he thought she intended to watch the hearing.

Luisa and Jeremi both shook their heads. Luisa said that Névé's bedroom door was still closed when she had left early, around 7:00 a.m., and she assumed Névé was sleeping in. Névé had gone up to El Calderón yesterday evening for a drink with someone she had met and said she'd be late and not to worry.

Jona was immediately uneasy. "To have a drink with a friend? What friend? She doesn't know anyone yet. Where are the dogs?"

Jeremi noted that they had been in their beds in the living room at the ranch when he left the house at about 7:30 a.m.

Jona relaxed some with a sigh. "OK. She wouldn't go anywhere without them. I'll check in on her in a minute. What did your attorney say yesterday about the possible outcome for today? Anything new?"

"Worst case, assuming they don't manufacture something that I didn't do, I might be charged with sedition through association. Most likely, I'll be rightfully accused of proselytizing. It remains just a hearing to see if

313

they're going to charge me and have a trial. I don't see why it would be worth any effort to go after me unless it's to make an example of me."

Jona thought that Jeremi could be naive and usually expected the best from people. He confided that Névé suspected Wise Consumer might want his land. "She said to me, 'What better way to get it than to put you out of business with legal costs?'"

No one spoke for several seconds.

"Why would a megacorporation like Wise Consumer go after me for a few hundred acres of land?" Jeremi asked. Again, there were a few seconds of silence. Jeremi stood and rolled down his sleeves. "Well, I have a hearing to go to." He stopped as he thought of something else. "Oh, and did we find out what happened to those missing cases of wine?"

Jona and Luisa exchanged glances and shrugged. Jona said he'd look into it while they were at the hearing. While Jeremi and Luisa left for the courtroom, he went looking for Névé.

***

The courtroom was nearly empty, but everyone who entered knew that anyone interested in the outcome would be watching over the Net. And for this hearing, the audience would be large. Luisa sat in the first row of spectators behind Jeremi's chair. The court had just reconvened after a short recess.

The judge entered from the side, and everyone stood. She took the bench and banged her gavel twice. "The next case is the Jeremi Duende hearing to determine if he will be charged with unlawful activity. Prosecutor, what do you present as evidence that Mr. Duende should be charged?"

The prosecutor had remained standing. He was a young man who looked fresh out of law school. He cleared his throat before speaking. "We have presented, Your Honor, copies of the letters that Mr. Duende wrote to Mensa Blackmon and which have entered the public domain as a result of the Mensa Blackmon murder trial. In these letters, Mr. Duende is clearly violating our Religious Rights law number two of the

North American United States, and we ask the court that he be charged with three counts of proselytizing, one for each of the letters."

The judge didn't look up. She banged her gavel and rendered a decision. "I disagree. Those were private letters never intended to be public. Do you have other evidence?"

"Mr. Duende holds weekly meetings where the Bible is read and discussed."

The judge leaned on one elbow and threatened to bang her gavel again. "Is anyone *required* to attend those meetings?"

"No, but it's a public venue, held in an old warehouse."

"That is still not a violation of law two if people willingly participate knowing what the subject matter is. Do you have evidence that Mr. Duende has inflicted his religious convictions or exposed his religious icons on unsuspecting citizens?"

"He runs a bar called El Calderón, which I'm sure you've heard of since you're in the same vicinity. And in it, a sign projects biblical scripture."

The judge nearly smiled. "And that would be what?"

"'For the word is living and active and sharper than any two-edged sword.'"

"Is that a biblical quote?"

"Well, nearly."

"But not exactly?"

"No."

The judge sighed, affecting boredom, and entered something into her NetLink. "What else?"

"His followers run a number of charitable organizations and blatantly display the symbols of the organization, a sword or a footprint or both, around their necks and on their wrists."

"We have no law prohibiting the display of swords or footprints."

The prosecutor opened his mouth to make another protest but must have decided not to. His attention was on his PAL, where he may have been getting instructions from someone not in the room. Addressing the judge, he said, "That is all for now, Your Honor."

She banged her gavel and rendered a decision. "Mr. Duende, you are free to go."

Jeremi sat still for a few seconds, stunned.

The face of the prosecutor as he turned toward Jeremi said not in words but in expression, "You're still in our crosshairs."

Jeremi's attorney stood and extended a hand, congratulating him, but Jeremi didn't feel the relief he should have. The whole thing seemed too easy, and he knew the other side wasn't going to drop its pursuit. "What do you think the prosecutor meant by 'That's all for now'?"

His attorney slapped him on the back and smiled. "Who knows? We'll deal with that when it comes."

Luisa came over and gave Jeremi a hug.

When they were well away from the courthouse and any listening ears, he turned to her. "What did you make of that whole thing? Wasn't it too easy?"

She shook her head slowly. "I have a confession to make."

"And that is?"

Luisa gave him a pat on the shoulder. "You know those cases of missing wine?"

He nodded.

"The judge likes your wine."

***

They arrived back at the Vine and Branches to find Jona upset. He'd found a note from Névé that she would be back in a few days and not to worry. "Don't worry? I can't believe she'd go off without telling me."

"I can." Jeremi motioned toward his office. He took a seat, but Jona and Luisa remained standing.

Luisa tried to calm Jona down. "We'll go after her. I'm sure she'll be fine. She must have her reasons."

Jona stopped pacing to ask Jeremi what he'd meant.

"I feel responsible. We were so busy with our operations and the two court appearances that we didn't consider the predicament facing Névé. She was determined to get out the Rising information, and time and options were running out. We weren't going to be able to mail it, and Blake hadn't yet been successful posting it. The CBI would be here as soon as they had the positive ID from her cousins and a general direction. She'd be on a trail of surveillance cameras from here to New Orleans." Jeremi rubbed the back of his neck. "Let's think about where exactly she's going, and I'll go after her."

Jona paced. "No way. I'll go after her. You may be trailed by the CBI just for being you. I'm nobody now."

Luisa sat down across from Jeremi. "No, I have to go. But where do we think she went?"

For an hour, they discussed where she might have gone and how she might have left. They ruled out walking; it was too slow. Passage on and off trains was too traceable. She had the money to go by air, but then she would have to disclose her identification, so they ruled that out. Jeremi asked if she could drive.

Jona shook his head. "No." Then he thought about it again. "Yes. She and Jemma trained on simulators and got licenses just for something to do when they were sixteen." He stopped his pacing and sat down. "She might have rented a car."

Luisa pointed out that was good and bad news. She was less traceable by the CBI, but then her route was less predictable. She could be driving anywhere.

Jeremi said he thought not. She was on a mission to get the information to someone. The final option had been to encode on music.

Jona held up a finger. "The one contact she had with Incense's family was somewhere in Dakota."

Jeremi and Luisa both asked him if he had the address.

"No."

No one said anything as the situation became clear. She had hundreds of miles of road, and they had no good way of knowing her route because she wouldn't take a predictable one, not wanting to be found. "Somewhere in Dakota" was where she was going, but that was a large target.

THE WORK OF ART

Claret and Rigel drank coffee at the breakfast table in a corner of the kitchen with views to the south and west. Ember was out in the barn with Cadence, and Jade had gone back to her guest room, where she had been reading Orion Rising's books since she arrived. Claret was relieved that the small library had proved to be the attraction that Rigel had predicted.

The sun rose over a clear sky, but a dark line of clouds appeared just above the ridge of hills to the west. Claret wondered what protected the windows from high winds and then noticed grooves along the edges.

Rigel guessed what she was thinking. "We can roll down a windscreen during storms. Sensors on the roof activate the screens if we're not home."

"I see. A lot of people install something similar in the Northwest because of the increasing brutality of the Pineapple Express. Some cover the entire side of the house to shield it from water and wind." She imagined the winds that must rush across these plains.

Rigel displayed on his PortAble an ad from the NAUS president. "Have you seen the recent ad campaign by Sultana?"

"The one with his face in Pacific blue and mint green that incites me to support him in the struggle for peaceful prosperity?"

"That's the one." Rigel ran his fingers through his hair. It shone dark brown, but the morning light revealed a few gray strands. "It's compelling, even if I disagree with the message."

"From what I've read, the ad is intended to work on many levels, especially by stimulating multiple senses. When displayed on an Infi-Scene window, it emits a complex organic smell—both soothing and stimulating. The overt messages are so well put together that a friend of mine claims there must be subliminal messages that are equally effective."

"Listen to the music." He unmuted the volume, and a strain of music filled the kitchen until he muted it again. "Makes you feel a form of reverence for him and his causes, doesn't it?"

"And that's the *work* of a work of art—to move the mind of the viewer, to shift attitudes. This piece does work on the mind. It applies a force and shifts a perception." Claret took a sip of coffee. "I'm reminded of a Walter Benjamin essay called *The Work of Art in the Age of Mechanical Reproduction*, and I wonder what he would think of our age now, more than a hundred years later, and how art is used to manipulate." She met Rigel's gaze. "And as we said, that's what we need to do with Orion's work."

Rigel stared out across the hills. "First People think of a story as being like a path. When you hear a story, you go on a journey, and the experience changes you." He rubbed his forehead. "There's something… familiar…about what we need." He inhaled and then became animated, pulling his hair back in a ponytail with an elastic band. "A ghost dance or spirit dance, as we Sioux call it. That's what we need to go with Incee's music."

"A ghost dance?"

Rigel got up and went over to the centuries-old Lakota painting on the wall, which showed figures in a ring. "I mean a *virtual* ghost dance— a *digital-age* ghost dance. Instead of bringing back the dead, we'll see specters of the future—by having participants simultaneously engage in a virtual experience."

"We could do that, I suppose. They would need a reason to tap in."

"Yes, we would have to somehow draw them in, but if we did, we could transmit information that could then be interpreted in a separate step."

The line of clouds now looked like a half dome closing in slow motion. She got up from the table and joined Rigel in front of the painting. "I suppose if we had enough people connecting in at the same time, we could create what's known as a *virtual hive*. Like bees, it's alive and communicating in real time within an extended landscape, making it impossible to censor. I helped create one on a small, local scale to celebrate an event, but I don't think it's been attempted on a global scale."

"By 'impossible to censor,' you mean that the CBI censors would be overwhelmed and unable to block coded information?"

"Probably. Designed in the right way, we would have a work of art affecting millions of perceivers simultaneously all over the planet. When a video with music is downloaded, the encoded information could be carried with it. Then whoever needs to decode it could be told how to begin extracting information."

Rigel had his hands on his hips. "Antivirus programs won't block it?"

"No. The extra information wouldn't be harmful and wouldn't have the characteristics of a virus. It's just that it's not readable until decoded, and then it reveals a work of larger complexity."

Rigel put their empty coffee cups in the sink. "We'll need a list of scientists to receive the instructions for decoding it."

"How's your dad coming on extracting information from Incense's incomplete message?"

"He's almost done and has copies squirreled away. Let's take a walk and pay him a visit."

Claret put on a denim jacket, and they walked to the barn. The breeze had gained urgency and agency, carrying along dust and leaves on its unknown mission. One of Rigel's kinematic birds waved as he and Claret passed the herb bed. In the barn, Ember brushed one of the ponies, which had his head in a feed bucket. Claret thought that Cadence knew how to entertain kids. His studio was at the back of the barn through double doors that kept out sound, dirt, and odor. Cadence removed his headphones when they came in.

Rigel pulled up a couple of stools, and they sat down across from Cadence. "I think it's time for Claret to hear the score. We're considering ideas on how to get the music out when we have all the information."

Cadence nodded. Claret had found him to be a man of few words, expressing himself through his music. He handed her his headphones, which she put on. Then he touched a couple of points on the tabletop to start the music.

She listened, eyes closed, for three minutes—its entirety. When she opened her eyes, she said, "What a wonderful melody! It's like it goes down a path, taking twists and turns between strains, sometimes doubling back or seeming to. I entered the song and traveled somewhere and then back out."

Cadence nodded. "It's a moving piece of music, aside from the information embedded in it."

Claret stood and paced the room. "You know what it reminds me of? A labyrinth."

Neither man immediately understood the connection. Cadence spoke for both of them. "You lost me. It doesn't confound the listener."

"No, it doesn't. You're thinking of a maze. I'm talking about a labyrinth, a walking path where you enter at a point, meditate to the center, and then follow the path out."

Rigel smiled and mimed shooting a bow and arrow. "You hit it. I think we have a title. Incense didn't give us one."

"'Labyrinth Song'?"

Ember opened the door and stood halfway in. "Mr. Cade, the horses are getting scared of the wind."

ALONE

For the first few hours of the trip north, Névé had allowed the HelioRunner to drive the most direct route. She knew that Jona and the others would not know immediately what happened to her and would not be able to follow. Morning fog had risen into a day overcast and dark. Around noon, the clouds began breaking up. The battery was drained by half, so she stopped at a run-down gas station—an oddity, for most cars ran on solar power—to give the batteries a chance to recharge. She pulled over to the side of the station and considered the situation.

A large, faded-blue sign read, "Exxo_," with an apparent missing last letter. The driver of a pickup truck held together by rust filled it with gasoline and chatted with a grubby-looking man, who Névé figured probably ran the station. Another car pulled off the highway and alongside the other gas pump. Few cars traveled along what used to be a busy route. The station appeared to be the only oasis for gasoline for miles. The level of activity gave her some safety from marauding transients looking for an easy target, so she allowed the solar panels to charge the battery while she slept in the back with the doors locked.

After about an hour in a closed car, the air temperature rose and forced her to get some fresh air. She went into the gas station and used the nastiest toilet she'd ever seen. The whole place smelled like grease and gasoline. A mongrel-looking yellow dog followed her around as if to police any shoplifting.

On the way out, she passed a part of the station that sold antiques. She kept walking but looked around to see if there was anything she could use, although she didn't know of anything she needed. A purple rectangular box caught her eye. It was about the size of a loaf of bread with number scales on the front, dials, and selector switches reading Off/On and AM/FM.

The station attendant came over to her. "Know what that is?"

She shook her head.

"It's an old radio. I'll sell it to you for ten dólares."

She considered the era in which it would have been made and realized that a radio signal received on this device could not be traced. She hadn't turned on the satellite radio in the HelioRunner because she knew the receiving signal was traceable and could be located. She had planned to drive and not use the global positioning from here on. She asked him what kind of programming came over it nowadays and was surprised to learn that antique-radio enthusiasts had taken over some radio bands and old broadcasting equipment and were putting out their own programming, mostly with no commercials. They ran talk shows, political commentary, and music. The attendant seemed quite enthusiastic about what Névé could listen to.

"Does it have batteries that work?" she asked.

"Used to, but they don't make them anymore, and this here's before solar power. But what it's got—even better—is an electrical plug."

Not wanting to use her PAL to pay, she asked, "Can I trade for something?"

"I'd take one of your dog collars."

She had a pink one around her neck and a blue one on her wrist. "No, they're special." Then, in case he thought she meant monetary value, she added, "They have personal value." From her pocket, she pulled one of the coins that Hannah—the Maker seamstress—had given her weeks ago. Névé had suspected they would be useful on the trip, which would take probably two days. She had packed enough food, but she knew there would be incidentals she hadn't anticipated. And she had to get back, too. The farther she got from Austin, the more she realized that Austin was probably where she wanted to be.

The attendant leaned in for a closer look. "Hey, I ain't seen one a them for a while. Sure, I'll trade for it."

"Can I make sure this thing works first?"

"'Course. Let me plug it in right over here. It don't take no time to warm up or nothing." He plugged in a cord that had been in a compartment in the back. His dirty fingers turned the switch to On and began rotating a dial. At first, only faint static came out. He turned up a knob that said Volume. "I gotta get a station. There's a local one round here about ninety." Soon he had a strong signal with a woman reading a news item in a slow, halting voice, not smooth as the New Feed voices.

> Because of the smallpox that continues to spread. Travel is discouraged. People—like us, folks—are being told to cancel public meetings. They're apparently doing just that on the East Coast, where they had most of the contaminated samples turn up. My cousin, who lives near Denver, claims police are beginning to block roads into populated areas and cancel trains and planes. Let's hope this outbreak of whatever it is doesn't make it this far west. But don't be surprised if you get stopped. You probably don't need to be going anywhere anyway.

The announcer paused as though consulting another note or someone nearby, and then her voice continued.

> Except of course the Chamber of Commerce charity fundraiser is this evening at the Prairie Dog Saloon. You do need to get over to that tonight.
>
> In other news...

"I'll take it."

He offered his dirty hand to shake. Against her better judgment, she shook his hand and gave him Hannah's coin.

"You got more of them coins?"

"No. And thanks." She picked up the radio and headed to the HelioRunner before he could ask any more questions. She hadn't seen any cameras in his shop, but that didn't mean there weren't any.

She passed two men who must have just arrived in a truck and an old sedan, which sat out next to the gas pumps, and she caught the end of a conversation.

"…she should be easy to spot. Aren't many skinny albino women running around."

"Ain't likely to be way up here, though."

"CBI says she could be anywhere."

Back in the Runner, she was shaking but didn't want to take time to collect herself. So, she thought, the CBI must have stepped up their efforts to find her if two random rural drivers know that a young albino woman is being sought for questioning. She avoided looking in the direction of the station as she took the car out of auto mode, put it into manual, and then hit the ignition button. Out of the corner of her eye, she knew the station attendant watched. She ignored him and tried to put the car into manual drive, but it wouldn't go. She thought she heard him asking her if she knew how to drive it. If she didn't figure out the problem immediately, she'd have to put it back into automatic to get away from his prying eyes. Her thoughts went back to the simulator. And then she remembered that it wouldn't go into drive without the brake being on, so she put her foot on the brake, and then the car went into gear. When she released the brake, it began moving forward slowly. Her first tap on the accelerator made the wheels throw up gravel. The station attendant shook his head and laughed. Névé managed to move the car forward and back out to the feeder road. With no other cars headed north, she took her time to get up to speed. An hour passed before she remembered to plug in the radio.

The station that it had been turned to no longer came in. She thought maybe they broadcast only at certain times, and then she remembered that the signals came from towers and had a limited reach. Keeping one hand on the steering wheel, she turned the dial as she had seen the station attendant do. She heard static until a man's voice came in clearly.

> ...is reporting that demonstrators, exercising their constitutional rights and protesting the closing of Real Carrier offices, were dispersed today with fire hoses and tear gas. City council members said it was because of the ban on public gatherings until the threat of smallpox —or whatever the disease is—is over.

Névé jumped when an obnoxiously loud beeping came from the radio. She reached over and turned it down, but when the beeping stopped, she had to turn it back up to hear the announcer.

> This is a message from the Emergency Broadcasting System. Weather bulletin. High winds are predicted across the Central Plains and east to the Appalachians. Residents are strongly encouraged to shelter in place.

Névé wondered what she would do if the winds did get too strong to continue driving. The HelioRunner was being rocked by the occasional wind gust, but it was nothing that warranted pulling over.

The buffeting wind continued through Kansas where there were few wind blocks. Even though the weather report was bad and the news discouraged traveling because of the possible smallpox epidemic, Névé convinced herself not to erect mental roadblocks, so she thought about other things, like her time in Austin and New Orleans and her dogs. The only physical roadblock she passed was at an intersection with a highway to Denver. Police had stopped a car and may have been limiting who could proceed. The route north had no such police presence, and in thinking about it, Neve was thankful she was going to Dakota. Travel to low population areas probably hadn't yet been restricted, but the road surveillance gave her more incentive to stop only when she had to.

The next news item made her think of Jeremi and wonder how his testimony had gone.

> According to News Feed, the Trial Entertainment Network today ended the Mensa Blackmon case when the judge said Blackmon's death must have been suicide. He stated that suicide was the only reasonable thing, considering the circumstances and no other suspects.
>
> The news from Seattle in the Northwest Province is that Mount Baker is bulging. Today, scientists said that a bulge has formed on the southern side of Mount Baker. As one resident said, "The mountain looks like it's pregnant." Geo Survey asks for additional funds for an investigation into whether the volcano will erupt. In the meantime, they're telling residents within fifty miles of Mount Baker to consider getting out quick. Residents asked the spokesman whether fifty miles was an extreme distance. The spokesman's reply was that Mount Baker, if it goes, could make Mount Saint Helens look like an amateur. For us here in Kansas, let's hope that when Baker delivers this baby, the winds don't carry it in our direction.
>
> The CBI has stepped up its efforts to locate an eighteen-year-old albino woman, who is sought for questioning in connection with the fugitive Incense Rising. Relatives recognized her from the earlier bulletin and supplied a better picture, which listeners can view on the CBI website. You may want to check it out because the reward is now at fifty thousand dólares.

Névé had been gripping the steering wheel so hard, her fingers were numb. She told herself to stay calm and consider that, fortunately, she doesn't look very similar now to any picture that Leo and Zeta could have provided to the CBI, and a volcanic eruption was one natural disaster that probably wouldn't keep her from making Dakota by late tomorrow.

The road, hours, and plains stretched out before her. A clear afternoon meant that her batteries stayed charged until the sun sank low and began losing its intensity. The wind increased in ferocity, and she was forced to start planning where to stop for the night. As much as she wanted to stay on the road, she also had to have sleep. She wondered if a public place afforded more safety or less safety. She hadn't stopped to go to the bathroom for hours since the gas station stop. When she spotted a hospital, she turned into its parking lot and parked on the leeward side. The lot was well lit and quiet except for an occasional ambulance. No one questioned her when she entered the lobby as if she knew where she was going and found the restroom.

The next morning, the wind had blown itself out and mist rose from the road and fields, pink in the early light. Névé left after the sun came up and the batteries could stay charged. According to the map on her PortAble, she was more than half way. Avoiding other cars and traffic, she made her way back to the nearly deserted highway.

EVER'S GUEST

Claret showed Rigel the *News Feed*. "Baker is possibly going to erupt. I wonder if Jade and I should go move our things to a storage unit somewhere safer."

"Is there anything there that you can't afford to lose or would be upset about losing?"

"Not really. My mother still has a lot of the family memorabilia. Jade and I both have our PortAbles and enough clothes to get by."

"Then I think you should not risk going back until the situation settles down." Rigel noted that the area was still having quakes. The ash from an eruption could be choking, although it would probably be blown toward Dakota, and he assured her they could handle it.

"I hope you don't mind being stuck with us for a while," Claret said.

"I wouldn't want it any other way."

"I don't think Jade will mind. She's so preoccupied with those friends from town she met that I'm not sure she'd come back with me if I left."

Before Rigel could comment, his PAL vibrated with a text message from Ever.

Ever: You won't believe the owl I saw last night. Come to the cedars again to see the nest. 10:00 a.m.

Rigel looked happier than Claret had seen him in days. He punched the air and said he had to meet his cousin Ever. He must have had another message from Incense.

She got up and gave him a hug. "Oh, I hope it's good news, Rigel."

***

A persistent wind from the north and an overcast sky made the morning air chilly and Rigel's horse energetic. Rigel beat Ever to the Valley of the Dancing Cedars and the notch in the cliffs. He settled into a recess that blocked the wind and waited. The last time he had met Ever here, the riverbed had been dry. But today, a stream a couple of meters wide mumbled over the granite rocks toward the east. Rigel would usually have relished the time alone, listening to the wind through the cedars and the water over the streambed, yet he was anxious and distracted about why Ever wanted to see him.

Ever rode up from the west. Some distance away, Rigel could tell that Ever had someone behind him on his horse. A pair of arms wrapped around Ever's waist, and a pair of legs bounced behind his, not held down by the stirrups. Rigel's hopes rose, wondering if he could possibly have Incense with him. But she wouldn't show up here yet, would she? Ever trotted his horse the last few meters, and Rigel was disappointed to confirm what he already suspected. The person with Ever was not Incense, but he had no idea who she was.

Ever stopped a few meters away, let down the young woman riding behind him, and dismounted. "I have someone who wants to see you."

Rigel knew that he had never seen this woman before. She was tall, very thin, and probably wearing one of Ever's suede jackets, for it was too big for her. Her hair was medium brown, and her skin was tanned, but what struck him were her eyes.

She walked over to Rigel and extended her hand. "I'm Névé. Do you know who I am?"

Rigel slowly shook his head. "No." He wondered if she could be a CBI agent.

She nodded and her eyes began watering. She wasn't crying yet but was on the verge. "I was hoping that your sister was able to get a letter to you before the explosion. I was with her a few days prior."

Rigel's guard immediately went up, but so did his hopes. He thought that if she did work for the CBI and was here to get information, she would also be a good actor. At this point, he had nothing to hide. He hadn't received anything so didn't need to lie. "Maybe she did get one out, but I never received it."

She nodded. "It probably would have been held up by the Real Carrier stoppage anyway."

Ever had been stroking his horse, unsure of what to do. Rigel shifted his weight, wondering what she would say next. The wind whistled between the crevasses.

"I have something I need to give you. Something we need to do for Incense." She looked toward Ever and then back to Rigel. "And it's complicated. It may take us a while."

And then Rigel understood why she must be here. Unless this was a trick, she had whatever the CBI wanted, probably the completed work originating with his uncle. Rigel waved to Ever. "Ever, buddy, I'd rather not get you in any deeper than you are now. Maybe you should go while you don't know anything. I'll take her home."

He smiled. "I think I agree." He turned to Névé, maintaining the smile. "You're welcome to come and see me again anytime. I can take you riding, show you Dakota."

Névé nodded and offered him her hand, as though it were a deal. "I can't thank you enough, Ever. Sorry to drop in on you so sudden like I did last night. And, oh, here's your jacket."

"Keep it for now. You can stop by again to return it, and I mean that." He put a hood up against the chill, mounted his horse, and rode off.

As the hoofbeats subsided, Rigel tied his horse to a cedar and motioned to the recess in the rock. "I don't think it'll rain real soon. Let's talk here, where I'm pretty sure we won't be overheard." He took a seat on the rocks and motioned for her to do the same.

Névé squatted opposite where he sat and unraveled her story and the threads connecting her to Incense and to him.

REGINALD
UMBRAGE

Claret and Rigel were so distracted by their surprise guest that they almost forgot about their next project team meeting. Cadence had been working to encode the missing information that Névé brought on the music score from Incense. His work was nearly complete. Névé was asleep on a cot in a den. They all had tried to give up a bedroom to accommodate her, but she insisted on "camping out," as she put it.

Both Rigel and Claret expected the Cream Team project to be canceled. Little progress had been made recently because of reduced resources and lack of interested customers. Claret and Rigel logged into the Vid-chat from separate rooms.

Reginald Umbrage was frowning. "It's about time you all logged in. No wonder this project is behind the timeline and over budget. I run a tight ship. If you're on time, you're *late*. I expect everyone connected by five minutes to meeting time—that's if I decide to renew your contracts." He paused approximately two seconds for effect. "Wise Consumer Foods has many more attractive projects than this one. In fact, this is one of the ugliest projects I've ever seen. I can see why Avarita Banks took a pay cut to sell dog milk." He allowed a couple of seconds to elapse again. "Aries, give me an update."

"Partly because of the actions recommended by Dr. Banks, cash flow improved by ten percent."

"What happened to sales?"

"Sales decreased fifteen percent. Ads placed at political events have been the most successful at garnering customers, but it's not a major election season. Businesses within Wise Consumer have not been as eager to place ads on toilet tissue as we had hoped. We've offered them discounts but have still had few takers. Resource levels have been reduced to five percent of each team member's time."

"Holy Jerzeybell. How did cash flow improve ten percent given a fifteen percent decrease in sales?"

Aries kept an unemotional face. "Dr. Banks's three *P*s of fiscal responsibility."

"Which are?"

"Reducing costs in production, people, and publicity. We worked off inventory, claimed fewer hours than we worked, and delayed payment on some of the advertising."

"Phooey, I'll give you a *P*. Power up! I want an ad that goes out to every computer on the planet that's connected to WorldNet. I want a Mega-Ad campaign like no one's ever seen. I want a monster derecho of an ad campaign. And if that doesn't jump-start the project, then it's dead. How soon can we do that, team?"

Claret hoped that her cheeks didn't appear as flushed as they felt. "We can do one in no time. I suggest a piece of music that will be just right for the ad. Rigel, your artwork is ready, wouldn't you say?"

Rigel nodded, knowing what she was thinking. For the past two days, they had worried over how best to post the music. They had come to the conclusion to send it out to the scientists on Néve's list. He couldn't believe they might actually be able to leverage the Wise Consumer ad. "You bet. But, Reginald, how would it be broadcast to everyone?"

"That's easy. This info is *strictly* Wise Consumer confidential, but we've been working with the NAUS government on just such promotion capability. You've seen the latest Sultana ad? That was its debut."

Claret smiled. "Yes, it was a remarkable ad. We'd love to do something like that for the Cream Team and Wise Consumer."

"Then get me the visuals and music pronto to give to my contacts at headquarters. And power up!"

Claret and Rigel came out of their rooms whooping it up before they remembered that Névé was sleeping in, so then they danced and laughed silently. But Névé heard the celebration and came out to see what was going on.

When they told her, she smiled. "That's great news. What a relief." She sank onto the leather couch. "I feel rested and like I can head back down to Texas. It's where I belong, and you don't need me anymore."

***

Early the next morning, Rigel drove Névé back to her HelioRunner. She had left it in a parking lot in the town where she had sought Ever. The start of her trip several days ago now seemed like weeks ago. She was thankful she had made it without any problems. Now she wanted to make it back in the same way.

Rigel wondered if Névé knew what a risk she had taken. "Névé, you were pretty gutsy to set out on your own from Texas to Dakota. You were lucky you didn't get robbed or worse."

"I think now it wasn't luck. I also think I'll get back OK, too, if I'm careful. I don't plan to stop except to sleep for a while. Thank Claret again for the sandwiches and thermos."

Rigel helped her load the bag of food and drinks in the back seat. "Ever will be disappointed that I'm the one returning his coat, but he'll get over it." Then he gave her a hug. "I can't thank you enough for what you did for Incense and Uncle Orion. Keep in touch? Maybe come back and visit sometime?"

He left her as he met her, nodding with teary eyes.

News Feed, November 11. Wise Consumer Scores with Mega-Ad. WorldNet buzzed today with an innovative ad released by Wise Consumer. Viewers of the ad are taken on a stimulating journey that appeals to all five senses while promoting several of Wise Consumer's stellar new products. The ad went viral within several minutes. An estimated one billion people worldwide experienced the ad nearly simultaneously. Marketers Inc. estimates the ad will take the top honors at this year's Consumer Marketing Awards.

***

Crowd-Source, November 13. News Now! insta-text summary from Crowd-Logs. The Rising Theory. In a bizarre twist of the Wise Consumer Mega-Ad marketing campaign, scientists have extracted a hidden message embedded in the ad. The message describes a unified theory of matter, time, and space—the long-sought-after theory that has evaded scientists back to Albert Einstein, tying together the theory of general relativity with quantum mechanics. Colleagues from around the world who knew Dr. Orion Rising, a professor at a small university on the East Coast, have begun to claim that the theory resembles the incomplete work of Dr. Rising. Crowd-Log entries from some scientists are accusing Wise Consumer of stealing Dr. Rising's work for its own purposes, which have yet to be revealed.

***

Crowd-Source, November 15. insta-text summary. Rising Theory Believed Confirmed. Teams working in India and Switzerland are now claiming to have worked through the alleged unified theory and believe it to be credible. Other scientists are scoffing at the idea that Dr. Orion Rising could have formulated a unified theory, saying that Dr. Rising was not even a Mensa and was merely a professor at a small university.

***

News Feed, **November 16. Wise Consumer: Enabling Worldwide Innovation.** A Wise Consumer spokesperson has confirmed a connection between Dr. Rising and the corporation's team of scientists. A nephew of Dr. Rising's is under contract on an innovative new product, which was featured in the Mega-Ad marketing campaign. At a retreat for the NAUS Board of Directors, Wise Consumer's president, Mensa Bart Yartlesby, described how the corporation continues to contract innovation on a global scale as it has for decades, and he confirmed the connection with Dr. Rising was through a nephew, who provided the music. He explained how the Risings had the seed of an idea but that it took the resources of a corporation like Wise Consumer to launch it for the world to benefit. **This** News Feed **was brought to you by Epic Vacations, for virtual experiences you won't want to miss!**

***

News Feed, **November 18. Global Unrest.** While the scientific community may be divided over what is now being called the Rising theory, leaders of the nine political geographies beyond the borders of the North American United States are not. One of the postulates of the theory is a radical new energy source. Sino-One and the Eurobloc Council have previously accused President Sultana of hoarding resources, and now they claim to know why. They believe he has been attempting to monopolize the resources needed to take advantage of the new technology. The NAUS Board of Directors issued a statement calling the allegations ridiculous and encouraging other nations to cooperate with President Sultana's integrated plan for global peace and prosperity rather than colluding toward hostilities.

News Feed will continue to follow this rapidly changing situation. Recapping the top stories today:

> The number of hattacks reported on infrastructure continues to increase. The NAUS System Board is investigating.

> The bulge on Mount Baker grows. A 6.0 earthquake rocked the area around Puget Sound early this morning, centered somewhere in the San Juan Islands. Geo Survey has hinted that it may recommend the evacuation of the city of Seattle. Residents are asking for contributions to help with evacuations.

> The spread of smallpox in downtown New York City is showing signs of increasing. Yesterday's death toll was 150 victims. The Human Corporation is preparing vaccinations, which will be available within three months at a sliding-cost scale. Sign up for early availability at 1,000D. Projected cost in twelve months is 50D.

This News Feed **has been sponsored by the Human Corporation, makers of Pro-Body, the virus-fighting antibody that is guaranteed to work.**

ZAIN SULTANA

Zain Sultana, president and chief executive officer of the North American United States, lay facedown on a massage table while his robo-partner, RP2, worked on Zain's hamstrings. His doctor sat in the only chair in the room, a stiff metal affair that was making his butt cold through the thin stretch fabric of his pants. "Zain, you saw what happened to Blackmon. I won't continue to prescribe double doses."

"Then I'll find a doctor who will. You know the jam we're in. I need all my faculties running at full throttle." Zain rolled over and lay faceup. "RP, give me the full treatment today. The doctor thinks I'm losing my edge." RP2 started at the calves and worked its way up Zain's thighs. Zain's body also showed the impressive results of drug enhancement.

The doctor waited a few minutes so that he didn't interrupt Zain's massage, and then he continued. "Blackmon's case made clear the dangers of Mensa drugs if not taken as prescribed."

RP2 handed Zain a towel as he swung his legs over the side of the massage table and asked if there was anything else it could do for Zain at that moment. Zain said no and dismissed it.

"Give me the drugs," he said to the doctor.

The doctor reluctantly pulled a bottle from his pocket and removed three pills. Zain chewed them and went over to a treadmill, which he set to a brisk walk.

The doctor was proud of the physical specimen that he'd helped create, but Zain was aging, and the drugs would eventually take their toll. Death had not yet been cured. "Zain, I can enhance the effect of the Mensa drug at normal dose by giving you some uppers. Why don't we try that next time?"

"No. I want the super-Mensa state that Blackmon achieved."

"What he achieved was a state of delusion with suicidal tendencies."

"Blackmon didn't commit suicide." Zain gave the statement a few seconds to sink in. "He wasn't suicidal. He was euphoric with a revolutionary understanding of metaphysics. But he became dangerous. Too dangerous."

"About what?"

"*That* you don't need to know. Just keep the triple dose coming, and you'll keep your job."

As he was leaving, the doctor passed Zain's top advisor, a woman named Libra, coming into the gym.

"Zain, can you stop a minute so we can talk?" she asked.

"No. I need to walk for my health. Doctor's orders. What is it now?"

Libra avoided the metal chair and stood. "Eurasia and the Sino groups are meeting today to decide what to do about the so-called Rising theory. They're calling our recent deals and land acquisitions hoarding and monopolizing. I've consulted our peacekeeping advisors, and they expect a threat of retaliation, possibly even a ban on the exportation of precious metals to the North American United States."

"They don't have the means to put up a resistance. We've been planning for years."

"Many of these confederations still have nuclear weapons. You would be grossly underestimating their anger if you think that they wouldn't resort to using them."

"This isn't twentieth-century barbarism. We also have nukes. Besides, what would they have to gain?"

"A level playing field."

Zain laughed. "We have no reason to fear them." He stepped up his pace. "Holy cow, I feel on top of the world today! We're invincible. You'll see. They'll come begging *us* for resources, and we'll consolidate all ten regions into one. I've spent years ensuring our hegemony."

"Maybe you should lay off the uppers, Zain."

"I'm not on uppers. You non-Mensa people don't understand. You don't see the whole picture as we do. I can visualize just what others are thinking and how they'll act. My powers of prognostication are unprecedented. You'll see."

Libra decided to have a meeting with the doctor. She'd convince him to make some of Zain's pills placebos.

The look Zain gave her seemed familiar, but she couldn't place it.

He continued in a dismissive tone. "Just give me an update when they announce their intentions, and then I'll tell you what they're really going to do and what we're going to do."

Libra turned to leave. She realized then that the look was akin to the one her father would give her when he was being condescending and tolerant of her youthful ignorance.

INTO THE HILLS

Néve was elated to be back at the Vine and Branches vineyard. No longer being a "person of interest" to the CBI helped to make the return trip less stressful, except for the occasional roadblock detour—and the weather. She had driven through a snowstorm, but nothing that seriously stalled her trip. On her arrival, she had to take chastisement from Jona. Jeremi and Luisa simply welcomed her back. Her accomplishing what she had set out to do and traveling alone, in a vehicle she controlled, gave her a confidence and energy that even Jona's disapproval couldn't dampen.

Back in the office, she frequently checked the *News Feed*s to see how the Rising theory would play out. She had pushed a domino that now was causing a cascade around and around an elaborate design. She checked for the third time this morning.

Crowd-Source, November 24. The Rising Theory. Anger has continued to build outside the borders of the North American United States after the release and alleged validation of the Rising theory. The lack of response from NAUS president Sultana to the harsh statement issued from the Eurasian-Sino Coalition has prompted the promise of drastic actions by the Pact.

Texas Secession. Within North America, divisions continue. The Texas District Board voted overwhelmingly this morning to secede from the North American United States, citing philosophical differences. President

Sultana's office has not yet commented, but in previous statements, he made his position clear that Texas would not be allowed to secede, saying, "Texas isn't Key West, and it's going to stay in the country. It can't afford to leave." The newly named Texas Territory governor responded. "We can't afford to stay, considering the NAUS government is now being run by a lunatic."

In response to internal threats to the peace and prosperity of the North American United States, President Sultana has called for a volunteer militia, saying, "Sometimes we have to fight for peace. Citizens of wealth are generously contributing some of their private and corporate militia to maintain the peaceful prosperity that was gained at such a costly price after the Third War. We won't allow a few disgruntled citizens to disturb the liberties of the many."

Névé stopped viewing *News Feed* and turned her attention to the workers who were constructing a windscreen that would roll down over the window and door to the office. Jona had ordered it months ago, fearing harsh weather. Now they weren't sure what it might be called upon to keep out.

Jesús had been sleeping in his bed when his ears perked up. From the vineyard, María trotted up with another dog, a white-and-rust-colored beagle—and by the looks of her, a nursing mother. Her teats were swollen and nearly dragging the ground. Névé let the two dogs into her office so she could examine the beagle. "Who did you turn up here, María? Let's have a look." The dog whined and gave a half-hearted effort to wag her tail. Névé decided the dog needed professional care.

Uptown Bee Cave had a nearby vet, and Névé took the beagle to her as soon as she could get away from the office. The dog had no collar or visible means of identification, so Névé gave her the temporary name of Sanguine because the dog continued to wag her tail when spoken to.

The vet, Dr. Rodriguez, finished the examination and then said, "I'm afraid that there is no ID chip, so we have to conclude there is no owner who cares about her. I'll express this milk to relieve some of her discomfort and give her a shot to stop the milk production."

"But what about her puppies?"

"I don't believe this dog has had puppies. In fact, she doesn't look like she's ever had puppies, but I'd have to do a more thorough examination to confirm it."

"No puppies, but just milk?"

"I know that sounds odd, but that's what it looks like to me. You can take her over to the pound down on the south side of town. Maybe someone will show up to claim her."

"No. I'll tell the pound I have her, but I don't want to leave her there. Maybe I'll keep her." Névé stroked Sanguine while the vet began expressing milk with a breast pump. "Doctor, do you know anything about what Wise Consumer does on the land adjacent to the Vine and Branches?"

"No idea. Why?"

"I was just wondering. She and María came from that direction."

"Well, I think we can be pretty sure they're not raising dogs."

"I'm not so sure. I'm going to keep her at the vineyard, and I may go pay a visit to the property."

"It's restricted, and you won't get in without security clearance. In fact, their security has the right to shoot first and ask questions later." Névé didn't respond. They worked on Sanguine for some time, and the more they worked, the more her tail wagged.

"Thanks, Doc."

"Bring her back in a week, and I'll see that she gets other medication, OK?"

Névé nodded and smiled as she walked the beagle out.

***

Later in the day, Jona came into the office and found Sanguine in a new dog bed. He eyed her and then Névé. "Whose dog?"

"We don't know. I took her to the vet this morning. She doesn't have an ID chip. I told the pound that I have her in case someone shows up missing a beagle."

"And if no one shows?"

"Then I guess I'll keep her."

"Three dogs sounds like a pack."

"Yeah." Névé was paler than usual. "Jona, there's something I've been thinking about this afternoon, and I want to ask you a question. Do you know if we have the same father?"

He looked surprised by the question. "I doubt it. Our mother never seemed to have one partner more than a few months. Why do you want to know?"

"Something I learned in New Orleans might mean that we're not even related."

Jona's surprise turned to concern and puzzlement. "What are you talking about?"

"Kit Larson, the guy who ran the Real Carrier office in New Orleans, suggested that our mother may have been paid by Sugar Queen to have an albino child, and that's why I'm being sued for breach of contract."

"Well, so? We assumed all along that we probably didn't have the same father. It doesn't change how I feel about you and that you're my sister."

"What I got to thinking today is…what if she was just a surrogate mother? Nothing says that she had to be the biological mother. Maybe she was a paid surrogate."

"We could settle this with a DNA kit, but I don't want to because I don't care. It won't change anything for me." He gave her shoulder a squeeze. "I have something that I want to tell you, too. I plan to marry Luisa, if she'll agree."

Névé finally smiled. "I'm not surprised. I'm glad. That's wonderful news!"

"So, see, you'll have a sister, and I know you'll love her even though you're not blood related."

"I love her already. I'm so happy for you, Jona. I didn't understand why people would marry until I stayed with Marta and Jahn." She hesitated, wondering whether to bring up another subject that she needed to talk to him about. "That reminds me—I talked with Jahn today. He said he may want me present in person for a hearing if I can safely come."

Jona thought about the situation for a few seconds. "I'd volunteer to go with you, but Jeremi would much rather go. He'd relish the chance to go with you to Chicago, not that he's any real protection, but I'd feel much better if you went with him as a traveling partner."

"I didn't need one on the way down or to Dakota."

"I don't think you should press your luck."

"Where's your faith?"

"I don't put God to the test. Did you hear that the borders around Texas could be closed?"

ANOTHER CBI VISIT

The air around the ranch took another beating as a silver helicopter descended onto the front driveway. The horses in the corral were whipped into the same tornado of activity. Dust rose, and wind sculptures fell. Cadence and Ember had been eating freshly baked chocolate chip cookies on the front porch, and they protected them from the assault of airborne dirt. Rigel came out on the porch while Claret stayed inside looking out. She called Ember in, who reluctantly came. "You can watch from here," she told him. "They're not here to see you, so let's stay out of the way." Jade had gone to town to an old historical library. Claret thought about her and that she'd be sorry she missed whatever excitement was about to happen. Rigel took the rocker that Ember had vacated and picked up a cookie.

Two dark suits jumped out of the chopper: Juan and Bob again. They came toward the porch. Juan stood on the steps, with one foot on the porch, while Bob sat on the bannister in front of Cade and Rigel.

"Buenos días, *otra vez*, Señors Rising," Juan said.

Cadence took another bite from his cookie and then a drink of milk. "When can we expect the return of my brother?"

Neither man registered surprise. Juan cleared his throat. Bob made a motion of cleaning out an ear. "I must have not heard you correctly, Mr. Rising."

Cadence swallowed a bite of cookie and washed it down with more milk. His throat had gone dry. "We have reason to believe that he's still alive. And you have no reason to hold him now that his unified theory is out."

"And that's what we're here to talk about—how the theory got out. We know that it was embedded in the music that Rigel provided to Wise Consumer."

Rigel waved his cookie at Bob. "We won't deny that. It's not a crime to publish scientific hypotheses. At least, not yet."

"Sí, Señor Rising," said Juan. "But the theory is *problemático* for the NAUS government, no?"

Cadence leaned forward in his rocker. "We just wanted the truth out, gentlemen, because it was my brother and daughter's work. They believed in it enough to risk their lives to publish it. We're not physicists here."

"We want to know if you have anything else to disclose," Bob said. "If so, let's have it."

"No. Nothing."

"La *verdad*, señor," Juan said.

"We're telling the truth."

Bob began groping through his pockets and located cigarettes. "But then you said that last time."

"True. But now the big truth is out. And that's the truth."

Bob lit a cigarette and blew the smoke toward the hills. "We're demanding your silence about how the theory got out. The story you need to remember is that Wise Consumer was an important partner in its ingenious publication. If you can forget everything else that's happened since Dr. Rising's accident, then we'll leave you alone. If you have inconvenient memories, then there are many terminal accidents, viruses, et cetera, that can befall people out here on these plains. Families can end up dead before the nearest neighbor knows what's going on."

"My memory of the past three months is fading so fast that I'm having a hard time remembering what my brother looked like. Suppose you produce him for us."

Bob smiled. "Your brother did die, but we have reason to believe that your daughter may not have."

Cade was the one who smiled now. "Are you sure?"

"Pretty sure. If you hear from her, tell her that we're not going to prosecute and we can help her." Bob stood up, shaking his head. "I hope that we don't meet again."

"Ditto."

The suits climbed into their flying machine and beat a path to the eastern sky.

Cade settled back in his rocker, blinked back tears, and looked relieved. "I wish your mother were here to recite one of those praise psalms," he said to Rigel.

Claret spoke from the doorway. "I can do that."

THE CONCH TRUTH

In the Conch Republic—formerly known as Key West before the island nation seceded—the late-afternoon sun wandered through the open doors of the Conch Republic Pub. Billy, the bartender, cleaned up after a customer and polished the surface of the bar. He poured another scotch for Scotty and asked him for his story of the day.

Scotty came in every day around five o'clock after working on sailboats and spent his dinnertime at the middle of the bar. Billy knew Scotty to be maybe forty, but the sun had dried him like a raisin. He also knew that Scotty claimed a seat in the middle so he could converse with customers on either side, although Midget, a green parrot and a fixture on Scotty's right shoulder after hours, encumbered his view to the right. "I witnessed a good one today. And this story is true."

Midget squawked. "The Conch truth!"

"Haul out your copy of our republic's Conchstitution, and I'll swear on it." Scotty looked to his left and right, nodding that what he was about to say was fact. The only other customer at the bar was a past-middle-aged woman with chemical-red hair and lipstick to match. She sat three seats to the right of Scotty and smoked a cigarette, the most popular drug after alcohol in the Conch Republic. Midget, shifting his weight back and forth, waited for his cues, as he frequently did during Scotty's stories.

The redhead studied Scotty, and Billy noticed her fingernails were also red, as were her eyes. She was seventy if she was a day, and she was becoming a regular. Her name was Deb, and she'd started showing up a couple of weeks ago. He hadn't gotten her history yet, but some of the older immigrants liked to come for the nostalgia of paying in dollars. She pointed at the bird. "Don't that thing ever take a dump down your back?"

Scotty ran his fingers through thin blond hair. "Never, Deb. Midget's civilized. Ain't that the truth, Midget?"

"The Conch truth!"

Billy leaned an elbow on the bar. "So what's the story?"

"This guy shows up to the dock looking for slip thirty-seven, so I point him in the right direction. Well, he stands there looking at this sloop, scratching his head and shifting his weight like Midget, so I mosey down to see what's the problem. He says he's waiting for some woman to show up and asks if there's anything wrong with the sloop in thirty-seven. I said, 'Not that I know of, but the owner's been out of town for weeks. Why do you ask?'"

Billy straightened up and asked a couple who had just walked in what they wanted to drink. They looked like sailors. The woman was tanned and wore sunglasses and boat shoes and had short, dark, windblown hair. The man was tall, lanky, and of African descent. They sat down two seats to Scotty's left and ordered two beers and bottled water.

Billy returned to the middle of the bar and leaned on his elbow for the rest of Scotty's story.

"So he says he saw an ad in *Heard It from the Conch* that this sailboat was for sale for fifty dollars. He calls the number in the ad and talks to some woman, who assures him that the price is fifty dollars. And he says, 'What's wrong with it?' And she says, 'Nothing. Come see for yourself.' So we look at the boat, and it's floating and all and not listing or nothing, when the woman shows up with the registration for sale. He says, 'Ain't you missing some zeros or a *K*? Don't you mean fifty thousand dollars?' I swear again this story's true."

"The Conch truth!"

"So she says, 'No. I got right here in my possession a Net-mail from my husband, who ran off with his secretary to the Virgin Islands—which is totally ironic—and it says to sell his boat and send him the money. So I am.'" Scotty took a drink of his scotch. "The beauty of the situation took a second to soak in. She had a dated Net-mail from him, ordering her to sell the boat. And with them still being married, and with our separation of legal powers from the Big N, she can get away with it. I wouldn't want to cross that babe. We had ourselves a good laugh."

The redhead nodded in agreement and lit another cigarette. "Now that's one smart bitch. I wish I was that smart. Maybe I wouldn't be sitting here drinking my dinner, truth be told."

"The Conch truth!"

"I don't need a damn birdbrain agreeing with me."

Scotty turned to his left and came to a similar conclusion that Billy had: the new arrivals were sailors "You two just in?"

The man answered. "Yes."

"On the *Gilead*?"

"Yeah. How'd you know?"

"Saw it pull in. Nice-looking craft with the black hull and red sails. How long you staying?"

"Awhile. Just rented a slip."

Billy extended his hand rather than ask any questions. "I'm Billy, the owner, and I'm here every day after four." The two shook his hand but didn't offer him their names. Billy continued. "You'll find it real pleasant here. We're not bothered much from up north after the hurricane took the bridge out and the Big N, as we call the NAUS, wouldn't repair it. Gave us our freedom. We like it that way. I miss the income from drivers, but we get enough boaters. Where'd you hail from?"

"Up north."

"Think there'll be a war?"

After a few seconds, the woman cleared her throat and spoke for the first time. "Unfortunately."

"*News Feed* yesterday said if the NAUS doesn't end it quickly, this war might be the one to end all wars. They say they'll go all-out to guarantee their freedoms."

Scotty indicated to Billy that he wanted another refill and then spun a prophecy. "Any fight now'll be to the death. Survival of the fittest and the forgotten. We ain't fit, so let's hope we're forgotten."

Deb blew out a couple of smoke rings. "Nothing here but sailors, parrots, and water."

Scotty winced through a laugh. "Ain't that the truth?"

"The Conch truth!"

After a few seconds of silence, Deb inhaled and added, "Ain't it funny that two First People could come up with a theory that gives us an excuse to kill ourselves off quicker than centuries of their tobacco has, truth be told."

"The Conch truth!" Midget fidgeted on Scotty's shoulder.

"You need a drink?" He held up his glass to the bird, who took a sip.

Deb blew another smoke ring and pointed to his drink. "Hey, ain't that toxic to birds?"

"Probably. It's toxic to us."

The two sailors left. Billy picked up the money and the glasses. The young woman's eyes had started watering. Maybe the smoke bothered her. It took a while for non-Conch folks to adjust. He wiped the bar and asked Scotty and Deb if they wanted another. He then added his two cents' worth to the weighty political discussion. "Oh, I expect any trouble'll pass us by out here the way most things do. And we like it that way, right?"

Jerzeybell Is Back!

News Feed, **December 1. President Mensa Sultana Dedicates Jerzeybell in a Gala Ceremony.** Jerzeybell, the Wise Consumer icon, is back, bigger and better than ever, and just in time to give the North American United States her good luck. President Sultana arrived at the Plaza de Tributo this afternoon and climbed the steps of Jerzeybell's platform before the dedication. He rubbed Jerzeybell's hooves and then gave a brief speech in which he praised Wise Consumer for restoring Jerzeybell. He said, "I feel very lucky to be here today, considering the urgent and serious pressing foreign issues before us. But I didn't want to miss a chance to rub the new Jerzeybell and thank Wise Consumer—a generous, innovative, and profitable corporation."

President Sultana donned a golden robe to protect his suit before being lifted in a cherry picker to a position level to Jerzeybell's head. He made a comment about not wanting to hurt Jerzeybell by busting her in the head with a bottle of champagne, unless she was a Texas longhorn, which drew a laugh from the crowd. But when he opened the bottle, the cork hit Jerzeybell in the snout. President Sultana's only comment was, "Oops!" He then poured the champagne between her ears, for which he received a wild round of applause from the nearly five thousand people gathered for the dedication.

Afterward, the crowd was treated to Wise Consumer's Fresh-Like Loaves and the always-popular Goldfish Sticks. President Sultana had his picture taken in the famous Illusion Fountain, where tourists appear to walk on the water. After waving goodbye, President Sultana left the plaza and went into the Wise Consumer headquarters, where a helicopter took him away from a rooftop heliport. The president is scheduled to give a press conference early tomorrow. Odds are running that to protect peace and prosperity, he will declare war on the Eurasian and Sino Coalition.

The thousands present at the Plaza de Tributo sang and danced into the night.

THE END

ACKNOWLEDGEMENTS

The author would like to thank her editor, Earl Tillinghast, and the readers of drafts of *Incense Rising*: the late Chris Bittler; Linda Cumbie; Emily Hirsch; Lena Ibrahim; Anthony Lehman; Heather Mitchell; James Peacock; Elizabeth Royappa; Alan Smale and Rick Wilbur at World Con; the Glen Workshop with leader Larry Woiwode; the Aspen Summer Words novel editing class with editor Liz Van Hoos and class participants, particularly Dorothea Bonneau; and the Pensacola Writing and Critique Group. And last, but not least, the author would like to thank her husband, Alan, and sons, David and James, for giving her encouragement and the license to write.

GLOSSARY

Term	Pronunciation	Definition
Austin Memorial Lake		Lake that formed after the Austin flood
Baha, Julius	BAH-ha, JOOL-yuhs	President of the megacorporation Wise Consumer
Blackmon	BLAK-muhn	A Mensa who led government investigations, the most recent being Exposing the Fallibility of World Religions
Blazing News!		The latest breaking news.
Bob		CBI agent
Cadence	KAY-dns	First People by heritage, Cadence is Incense and Rigel's father and Orion's brother
Café de Bebidas	Ka-FAY day bay-BEE-dahs	An uptown coffee shop in the town where Névé lives at the opening of the novel
Candi	KAN-dee	A commentator in the Mensa Blackmon murder trial

Carmen Darnelle	KAHR-muhn DAHR-nel	Mensa, partner to Mensa Blackmon, and defendant in the Mensa Blackmon murder trial
CBI		Central Bureau of Intelligence, analogous to the FBI
Claret	KLAR-et	Residing in Seattle, Claret is Ember's mother and Jade's half-sister; red table wine; a deep red
Clarisse	Klar-EES	Incense's neighbor
Cosmo	KOZ-moh	Employee of the Vine and Branches vineyard
Conch Republic	kongk	Key West after it became a nation state
Coral	KOR-uhl	Woman at the train station in Michigan
Cream Team		The second code name for the tissue project
Crowd-Source		A news source that text mines entries on social networking sites and summarizes them into news items
Dólar	DOH-lar	Currency unit of the North American United States; plural, dólares (DOH-lar-ays)
El Calderón	el Kal-der-OHN	A theme bar in downtown Bee Cave
Ember	EM-ber	Claret's seven-year-old son

Eurobloc	YOOR-oh blok	A group of European countries
Ever Runningbrook		Rigel's cousin
First People		Native Americans
Flames		A Chicago underground organization that is considered subversive
Frank		The pseudonym of Incense while she is in New Orleans
Freedom from Religion Law		A law stating that no citizen may erect a structure—physical, organizational, or financial—that promotes a religion
Gilead	GIL-ee-uhd	Kit Larson's black-hulled sailboat
Greenscape University		The university where Orion Rising was a professor
Hannah		A Maker in Illinois, wife of Jesse
Hattack	ha-TAK	A portmanteau of hack + attack used to describe a cyber space attack
Hazel	HAY-zuhl	Train station custodian
HelioRunner	HEE-lee-oh RUHN-er	A solar-powered car
Henry the Eighth		One of Kit Larson's carrier pigeons

Incense	IN-sens	Recently graduated with a PhD in physics, Incense is Cadence's daughter, Rigel's sister, and Orion's niece; aromatic substance burned in religious ceremonies or to create a mood; a pleasant fragrance; to offer incense; to enrage
Infi-Scene Window	IN-fi-seen	A device that looks like a window frame or doorframe and is programmed to simulate views to thousands of places through the use of images, sights, and sounds
Jade	jayd	Residing in Seattle, Jade works as a professional juror and is Claret's half sister
Jahn	Yahn	Attorney, along with Jamz, at the Boanerges Law Firm and Marta's husband
Jamz	jaymz	Jahn's partner in the Boanerges Law Firm
Jemma	JEM-mah	Névé's best friend in Michigan
Jeremi Duende	JER-uh-mee Doo-EN-day	A man accused of subversive activities at the beginning of the novel
Jerzeybell	JUR-zee bel	Located in Chicago's Plaza de Tributo, Jerzeybell was a two-story gold cow and a mascot of Wise Consumer Foods
Jesús	Hay-SOOS	Name given to UD, the Unknown Dog
Jona	JOH-nah	Brother of Névé

Juan	Wahn	CBI agent
Jubal	JOO-buhl	Itinerant that Névé encounters in rural Illinois
Just-Money		A currency exchange based on coins of silver, copper, and gold
La Dama Duende		*The Phantom Lady*, a seventeenth-century Spanish "cloak and dagger" play by Pedro Calderón de la Barca
Kit Larson		Incense's boss, who runs a Real Carrier office in New Orleans
Leo	LEE-oh	Névé's cousin and one of her legal guardians
Luisa	Loo-EE-suh	Jeremi's sister
Lydia	LID-ee-uh	Névé's grandmother
Madam Angeline	MAD-uhm AN-juh-leen	Angeline Violette, self-proclaimed Oracle of the Ancients and friend of Névé's deceased grandmother Lydia
María	Muh-REE-ah	A greyhound adopted by Névé
Marta	MAR-tah	Office manager at the Boanerges Law Firm and Jahn's wife
MeBooks		A social networking site where people can compile an autobiography

Mensa	MEN-suh	In this novel, a person who has an IQ in the top two percent of the population
Merry-Time Marina		New Orleans marina where Kit docks his sailboat, *Gilead*
Milk Products		A long-established, highly successful business unit of Wise Consumer
MyLogs		A social networking site where people can keep a journal
Myvies	MAHY-veez	Self-made movies
NAUS		North American United States, formerly Canada, the US, and Mexico
Nearly Dairy		A division of Wise Consumer that sells dairy-like products
NetLink		A personal computer providing a link to the global communications network, known as WorldNet
Net-mail		Mail over the WorldNet; email
Net-memorial		An online site where people can leave tributes to someone who has died

Névé	Nay-VAY	At the start of this novel, an eighteen-year-old woman living with her guardians in Michigan; the snow that accumulates on a mountain before it is packed into glacial ice
New French Quarter		A rebuilt area of New Orleans that is higher above sea level than the original French Quarter
News Feed		A news source similar to the Associated Press
Noizdead		Sound deadening technology
North American United States		NAUS, a nation comprised of the former Canada, the US, and Mexico
Opti-fiber SunLights	OP-ti FYE-ber	Lighting that utilizes optical fibers to create a feeling of sunlight
Orion Rising	Uh-RAYH-uhn	Professor of physics who has attempted a route to a "theory of everything," which would reconcile small particle physics with the physical laws of large objects
PAL		PersonALink; a device that has the capability of a personal computer but is worn on the wrist
Peace and Prosperity Era		Term given to the time after the War for Peace
Peacekeepers		Volunteer security personnel

Pedestrian Way		Jeremi Duende's organization
Plaza de Tributo	PLAH-zah day trib-YOO-toh	Located in Chicago, the Plaza de Tributo is next to the Wise Consumer headquarters and has as its main attraction Jerzeybell, a Wise Consumer mascot
PortAble		A laptop computer
PPE Capital		A bank
Project Java		The code name for a plan to gain business in Asia
Real Carrier		A service that delivers "real" letters and packages, versus "virtual" mail
Rigel	RYE-juhl	Residing in Dakota, Rigel is Cadence's son, Incense's brother, and Orion's nephew; a star in the constellation of Orion
Romano	Roh-MAHN-oh	Owner of Romano's Used Pets
Romano's Used Pets	Roh-MAHN-ohz	A business that operates a kennel where animals are held before being sold or euthanized
Sapphire	SA-fye-uhr	One of the commentators for the Mensa Blackmon murder trial
Sam West		Owner of Merry-Time Marina

Seven Sisters		Organization of environmentalists; the Pleiades, a star cluster that rises ahead of Orion in the winter sky
Sim-view	SIM-vyoo	A simulated view of a real place
Sino Group		A collective of Asian countries, particularly East Asian
Sirius Milk	SIR-ee-uhs milk	A new product within the Milk Products business unit of Wise Consumer
Sol	sohl	A commentator in the Mensa Blackmon murder trial
Steel		A commentator in the Mensa Blackmon murder trial
Sugar Queen		Manufacturer of sugar products derived from sugar beets; Névé's employer
Sugarstik		A product made of refined sugar by Sugar Queen and used to sweeten drinks
Dr. Tan		The professor whom Orion was on his way to visit when Orion was killed
TEN		Trial Entertainment Network
The Message		An idiomatic English translation of the Bible, completed by Eugene Peterson very early in the twenty-first century

Theory of everything		A scientific theory, yet to be defined, that will explain both quantum theory (an explanation of matter and energy at the subatomic and atomic levels) with general relativity (Einstein's theory that describes matter and gravity on a large scale)
Ticketags		Ground transportation tickets that have a chip for tracking the passenger
Trial by Peers		A televised trial in which the audience is the jury
Tribute Terminal		A sheltered place within a public park where people can compose messages honoring the deceased; messages are displayed on a large screen called a Memorial Board
Unitrek		A passenger train
UD, Unknown Dog		The temporary name given to a homeless Chihuahua
Ursala	UR-sah-lah	Financial manager of the tissue project
Valley of the Dancing Cedars		A deep clef between two hills, located near the Rising ranch in Dakota
Vid-chat		Networking and conferencing tool used over WorldNet connections

Vine and Branches		Vineyard owned by the Duendes
Violet Waters		First People security guard
Virgil	VUR-juhl	Business manager of the tissue project
The War for Peace		A twenty-first-century war fought to ensure global peace
WatchfulDoor		A door that displays a wide-angle view of the scene beyond the door
WeatherNow!		An online source of weather forecasts
Wildfire		First code name for the tissue project
Wise Consumer		A consumer products megacorporation
WritingWall		A high-tech version of a whiteboard or blackboard
You-Foria! Drugs		A company that manufactures a line of products that provides consumers with a feeling of euphoria
Zain Sultana		President of the North American United States, NAUS
Zeta	ZAY-tuh	Névé's cousin and one of her legal guardians
Zing		A social networking site where people post short comments

Made in the USA
Columbia, SC
12 July 2018